CW01426081

PSYCHONAUTIC

By Darren Frey

Dedications

To my grandmother: Thank you for raising me!

To my grandfather: Thank you for teaching me!

To my mother: Thank you for having me!

To my father: Thank you for leaving me!

To my childhood best friend: Thank you for taking up for me!

To my biggest mistake: Thank you for breaking me!

To my uncle: Thank you for hearing me!

And to everyone else who ever inspired me (even you!)

THANK YOU!

For without any of you, my life would not be the same.

I would also like to give a special thanks
to my editor: Louise Sianni
and to my cover designer: Aila Nate

Table of Contents

Chapter One 6

Chapter Two.. 13

Chapter Three.. 19

Chapter Four 29

Chapter Five 42

Chapter Six.. 51

Chapter Seven 56

Chapter Eight 67

Chapter Nine 75

Chapter Ten... 82

Chapter Eleven.. 90

Chapter Twelve 100

Chapter Thirteen.. 108

Chapter Fourteen... 114

Chapter Fifteen.. 126

Chapter Sixteen 136

Chapter Seventeen.. 140

Chapter Eighteen 147

Chapter Nineteen.. 153

Chapter Twenty.. 158

Chapter Twenty-One... 162

Chapter Twenty-Two 170

Chapter Twenty-Three 182

Chapter Twenty-Four.. 194

Chapter Twenty-Five 201

Chapter Twenty-Six 212

Chapter Twenty-Seven.. 223

Chapter Twenty-Eight... 229

Chapter Twenty-Nine.. 238

Chapter Thirty 245

Chapter Thirty-One 256

Chapter Thirty-Two 264

Chapter Thirty-Three 269

Chapter Thirty-Four 281

Chapter Thirty-Five... 289

Chapter Thirty-Six 296

Chapter Thirty-Seven 301

Chapter Thirty-Eight 307

Chapter Thirty-Nine 317

Chapter Forty 330

"Waking up to who you are requires letting go of who you imagine yourself to be."

–Alan Watts

Chapter One

*A*nd that is why I tried to kill myself, the lonely man typed. He slouched in the corner booth, pushing away his laptop while glaring at the half-empty mug beside it. Packed with cream and sugar, the cold mixture had sat so long it thickened to that awful gel no one likes to think about. As bright overhead lighting enhanced the little vision he still had, he eyed the fat round clock hanging nearby on the key-lime-colored wall. *3:44*, it read. *The number forty-four again? … Jesus!*

An aging blond waitress approached the table with a new mug in one hand and a full pot in the other. Knowing the drill, she asked, "Another cup, dear?" Her name tag read *Linda*. Unlike most people Julian had met since boarding a bus over two thousand miles and a year earlier, she was always sweet.

"Yes, please." Julian forced a smile while she poured. After adding more cream and sugar, he took a sip, adjusted the round glasses sliding down his short nose, and returned to his red laptop. Once his soulful, dying eyes had time to focus on the glowing white keys, he placed his fingers and began again.

At the end of 2015, I discovered her betrayal. The cold November night she confessed her sins, I swallowed over fifty Seroquel on top of a twelve-pack. Such a drastic attempt should have killed me three times over, but the next morning I opened my eyes, alive and with a second chance.

Julian took another drink, recalling the countless nights he'd held, and wept alongside, his former love. *"Rub me!" Faith woke me whenever she wanted her back rubbed. "Talk to me!" she'd bark during her regularly scheduled panic attacks. "Turn the water on for me!" The lazy slob even refused to turn the shower on, but like an obedient lapdog, I complied, oblivious to her true intentions for eleven years—a third of my life.*

After she'd withheld sex for the last five years of our relationship, it was a neo-Nazi redneck named Travis who reaped her fruits—not me, the dog. "I don't even like sex," Faith lied all those years. God forbid she told the truth. Admittedly, I was inexperienced when we met, and she never told me what she liked. So, she had me lie there like a corpse, while refusing any position other than grinding me until her fake orgasms seemed believable. Afterwards, my crushed pelvis and I would silently thank a God we'd never believed in that it was over.

Six years of that were followed by the "I don't even like sex" years, until she used the illness from her weight-loss surgery to validate her refusal to fuck me. Once she was thin and healthy, Faith wanted it, but not from me. She was skinny, pretty, and worth the attention of shallow men who were only interested in her holes. So why not indulge?

Julian grunted and took another drink, thinking *it's been over three years and I still can't get her out of my head.* Every time the harlot entered his mind, anger and sorrow followed. He frowned and returned to the bright keys, remembering something Travis once said.

Not only did Faith cheat, she and Travis rubbed salt in my wounds. "Put some bass in your voice, faggot!" Travis taunted. In muscle and intimidation he had me beat, but when it came to wit, "I'm gonna make you suck my peter, faggot," was his best attempt.

Travis was your basic copy-and-paste white supremacist. Like any self-respecting skinhead, he was bald, with elevator-music eyes and the essential mustache and goatee combo. Naturally, he was fresh out of prison and so poorly inked in jailhouse green, his tattoos made the brown finger paintings on public restroom walls look like sacred geometry.

"You want another man to suck your dick, and that makes me *gay?" Despite my fears of confrontation and retaliation, I*

laughed in his face, asking Faith, "You left me for this?!" The irony ...

"He's quite intelligent, actually," Faith assured me. Little green clovers newly tattooed on either side of her face said it all. With her blotchy red cheeks and cartoony fish lips, she resembled a cheap party clown, willing to blow almost anyone in a porta-potty for two-fifty or a Xanax: anything to keep her from mothering our "test-tube baby." Julian snickered, knowing his words ran cold but refusing to care.

Then again, I could see how someone who thought Tom Petty was a racecar driver could find a jailbird—with underlying homoerotic fantasies for the man who'd used his pocket-pussy first—intellectual. Truth be told, I think she was trying to convince herself, not me. Either way, I am sure Aunt Eva and Uncle Adolf would be popular in any backwoods trailer park, considering—. Julian paused, sensing the internal rage building while he cut himself deep with the intangible blade.

His grandfather's voice rang in his ear: *Stop feeling sorry for yourself and be a man!* He wiped a tear from the corner of his eye with the tip of his thumb and brushed away his brown hair. "Get out of your head," he muttered before saving his work and closing the laptop.

The nearby door screeched open, and an older gentleman exited. A cold draft blew the scent of stale coffee and hamburger grease throughout the little diner. Julian shivered and pulled his black leather jacket closer before scanning the other tables. While tapping his foot to the beat, he laughed at the odds of "Mary Jane's Last Dance" by Tom Petty and the Heartbreakers playing softly on the jukebox. The young woman who'd chosen the song was the only other patron there. She sat on the opposite end of the room in a corner booth of her own. Feeling lonely, Julian wanted to say hello, but he was shy.

You are the medicine, brother, and you manifest your reality, the soothing voice of his shaman whispered in his ear. Julian smiled, remembering the love he'd been shown at the *Ayahuasca* retreat the month before, but then sighed recalling the hell it had unearthed.

His grandfather's haggard old voice returned, snarling *Stop feeling sorry for yourself and be a man! Real men don't cry! Real men don't need help! Suck it up!*

An abrupt fit of discomfort from the woman across the diner caught Julian's attention, pulling him out of his head. He observed her long brownish hair and little black dress. Her face was hazy and unclear to his eyes, but he understood the body language. Her shoulders slumped; thin pale legs rattled beneath the table. Once his eyes adjusted, Julian caught a better glimpse. Her cheeks were flushed, and she appeared to be fighting tears as if a war depended on it. *Poor girl,* he thought. The woman glanced in his direction but quickly looked away when she noticed him.

While Julian watched out of empathy, the dismal woman wrote in a small blue book, but eventually she put the book in her black purse and quietly stood. As she approached the door, Julian gained a better view. Her hair shined auburn, not merely brown, and a vanilla scent trailed when she passed. Although it was brief, their eyes met before she left the diner. Her dark, mascara-smeared almond eyes and full red lips melted his heart.

Once Julian returned to his mug, he observed the faded yellow smiley face plastered on the side of it. *Have a nice day* was written in black. His grandfather, Johnny, owned an old shirt with the same yellow face.

The grin was smug, like Johnny's, taunting him without effort. *Have a nice day, stupid!* Johnny's voice echoed again. The face became animated, bobbing its head while laughing at him. *Have a nice day, you stupid, unloved mistake!*

Julian's adrenaline pulsed through him but it only took one flick of the wrist to ease the tension. He cackled as the mug launched off the table like a hockey puck, gliding straight to the floor and crashing loudly. White shards of clay exploded in every direction like a nail bomb. Linda came rushing forward, the sound triggering her motherly instinct. She moved so fast she slid on the wet linoleum.

Hand over her heart, she gasped, "Are you alright?"

"I'm fine," he lied. Inside, he was as shattered as the dull smile and the patronizing hope it represented. *Happiness fades*, he thought, laughing at the broken remains peppered across the floor.

"Sir, excuse me, sir?" Julian opened his eyes and jolted in the booth. Linda stood over him, smiling again. "I would ask if you'd like another cup, but you might want to go home and get some sleep," she said. The old mug still sat next to his closed laptop, half empty and collecting gel.

He rubbed his eyes. "Yeah, I probably should. One of my new classes starts tomorrow night, anyway. Well actually"—he glanced at the wall clock again—"it starts tonight." After laying out a few dollars for the coffee and tip, he zipped his jacket and picked up his laptop.

Linda followed him to the door, asking, "Can you see well enough to get home? I know you can't see good, and I worry about you out there at these hours. East Charleston is a pretty rough section of Vegas as is, but especially this late."

Julian smiled at her concern. "The sidewalk's lit well enough, and I only live a few hundred feet away. I'll be fine." He smiled again before turning to the glass door and heading out in the January pre-dawn cold. He firmly held his laptop against his gut, dragging his feet down the sidewalk as savage wind impaired his breathing.

As he turned right and stepped off the sidewalk towards his apartment, a bicyclist flew past on the curb to his left, followed by a white transit bus on the street. Although the parking lot was black as coal, and his place was at the end of a long walk across it, Julian had grown used to the route. Reaching his building, he held the cold rail tightly and stumbled up two short flights of outdoor stairs to the second floor. There, he stood beneath the porchlight and fumbled through his pocket for the key before unlocking a green wooden door numbered *2277*.

Once inside his studio apartment, no bigger than a hotel room, he turned on the light. To the right of the front door was a window with cheap plastic blinds. Below it lay a lone mattress covered in a red and black comforter with matching pillows, and near that sat a black recliner.

Mounted on the walls of the living area were Julian's flatscreen tv and a small shelf, which housed only a ceramic beer stein once belonging to his father. The stein was antique. An old, well-dressed fellow with a thick gray beard and green coat rode atop a black steed. The man held a short whip and a leer of ill intent, like the one his father had always aimed towards his mother. It was the only physical burden Julian had left of the vile beast. Even that was too much, but he carried it like a burden anyway.

A breakfast nook separated the living and bedroom area from the small kitchen. Adjacent to the kitchen were the closet and bathroom, where Julian changed into more comfortable clothing before climbing into bed. He wore blue plaid pajama pants, gifted to him by Daryl, his only friend back home, not long before he'd moved.

Julian lay in the silent darkness, alone and not feeling much to be grateful for. He wanted to believe in love, life, and purpose, but grew weary of lacking such pursuits that most took for granted. *Why can't I have nice things and be happy? Am I not lovable or fuckable? Am I not meant to be a real father or husband? Why do I even want to bring children into such a world?* He sighed, scowled, and even punched his pillow, unsure what it was he actually coveted.

His time with the shaman and *Ayahuasca* had disclosed a bleak emptiness and a lifetime of denial he could no longer ignore. The dark memories of his past tortured him until his grandfather's heartless lullaby rocked him to sleep. *Stop feeling sorry for yourself and be a man. Stop feeling sorry for yourself and be a man. Stop feeling sorry for yourself and be a man, stupid!*

Chapter Two

After a few hours' sleep and more coffee, Julian took a seat in the second row from the front of a small classroom, near the door. As other students filed in, he checked the clock on the wall—*6:44*—and smirked. He'd discovered synchronicity through numerology after moving to the desert. The patterns now stood out, acting as breadcrumbs. He tipped his head towards the ceiling and closed his eyes. *Thank you.*

The door opened and an older gentleman in khakis and a green cardigan passed Julian's row. He was tall, thin, and aside from a few white hairs, mostly bald. "Hello, hello, everyone," he said in a froggy voice while approaching the instructor's area at the front. He sat a few books on the brown desk and turned to a computer monitor.

The door opened again, and though he faced away, Julian recognized a feminine scent in the breeze that followed. The smell was familiar yet all but mundane. She took the seat behind his. *Déjà vu*, Julian thought as he watched the projector screen slowly descend from an opening in the ceiling.

The old professor cleared his throat and began. "Hello, everyone. I am Professor Scott, and this is Psychology of Dreams. So, if you are in the wrong classroom, that's too bad, because this one will be awesome!" He snickered and some of the students followed. "Before we begin, I am going to call roll." He read from a white printout while scanning the room. "Bonnie Adams? Marco Bentley? Jose Fenton?" Julian listened but was tired, and his mind wandered. He'd arrived early to find his way to class before dusk, and already dreaded walking back to the bus stop in the dark. "Julian Frost?" the professor called, drawing his attention.

"Right here." He raised his hand. As the professor called other names, Julian yawned and shut his eyes.

"Violet Troúton?"

"Here I am," a sweet southern voice chimed from behind. Julian's heart fluttered. He wanted to turn and look but was reluctant to draw attention.

"Did I say your name correctly, 'Tro-U-ten?'" Professor Scott asked.

"Yes sir, you sure did," said Violet.

"That's a lovely name," he added.

"Yeah," Julian gushed in agreeance. *Wait! Did I just say that out loud? Shit!* He blushed and hung his head. *How embarrassing.*

Violet giggled under her breath. "Thank you," she softly said. Her aim was the professor, but Julian also sensed her draw. He exhaled and tried to relax: having looked forward to the class, the last thing he wanted was to humiliate himself.

"So, who can tell me where dreams come from?" Professor Scott asked the class, but no one answered. "Really?" He panned all the young faces. "What are you avoiding?" he teased.

"Visualized thoughts from our subconscious?" asked a young, bookish girl on the opposite end of the room from Julian.

"Well, that's part of it," said the professor. "However, there is no such thing as the 'subconscious.' It's called the collective unconscious." He turned his attention to the entire class, adding, "Also, before I forget, I wanted to say: we will not be discussing lucid dreaming, astral projection, or anything of that sort in here. I offer only a healthy scientific approach."

Although Julian had never been the type to speak up, he raised his hand, and the professor nodded in his direction. "Technically, wouldn't astral projection or inward spiritual experiences be considered science, if dreams themselves are science?"

"What are *you* avoiding?" Professor Scott asked, grinning as a few students giggled.

"Mommy issues," Julian said, letting his sarcasm slip. Most of the class, Violet included, burst into laughter.

Even the professor joined in. "You're gonna be trouble, aren't you?" he teased. "As I'm sure you know, some things are sensitive subjects. With what you're referring to, not much scientific research exists, and for legal purposes, there has to be a line drawn." The professor smiled again before turning back to the whole class to begin his lecture.

Over the next two hours, Julian took notes, often squinting to see the small text on the projector screen. Eventually the clock turned to 8:44, catching his attention again. "Since it's the first night of class, and I am out of slides, we'll stop here," the professor said. "Next week we'll begin learning Jungian archetypes, like the trickster, warrior, and magician. We'll explore how they all relate to dreams. Enjoy your weekend, everyone!"

Julian trembled with anticipation. He'd wanted to turn and look at Violet all evening and finally had the chance. He knew good things come to those who wait, so he waited until the right moment. He reached for his black bookbag on the floor and put away his pen and notebook. Next he swiveled out of the chair and finally saw her, but briefly. Violet's hair was a brownish blur, and she wore white, but Julian only caught a glimpse as she walked out the door.

He exited the classroom and followed not far behind, down a long hall towards the stairway at the end. Under better lighting, her hair glowed, appearing auburn and reaching the small of her back. She was short, thin, and wore a hand-crocheted white shawl.

Julian began down the first set of stairs, which led to the front door of the building. Intensely focused on Violet, he missed the step in front of him and shot forward, down the stairs and out of control. He danced a jig, trying to regain his footing, but failed miserably and flew straight into her soft embrace. After he caught his breath, Julian looked into her eyes. *Oh, my God! It's her!* He knew those eyes.

"Are you alright?" Violet asked. Her full red lips and dark almond orbs melted his heart for the second time.

How is this possible?! The sad young woman from the café and Violet were the same. "I—I—I'm fine." His heart pounded with joyous anxiety as he stood speechless and awestruck.

"You should be more careful. It's Friday the thirteenth, after all." She winked.

"Damn, y—you're right," he stuttered. He'd forgotten about the date but chuckled at the odds. "Thank you, Violet, I—"

"It's no problem—Julian, right?" Their eyes remained locked the entire time as Julian admired hers, a beautiful shade of dark brown.

"Yeah," was all he could say. On the inside, he giggled and kicked like a court jester gone wild in an opium den, but on the outside, he imagined himself a deer caught in headlights.

She gave no indication of remembering the previous encounter, but it was irrelevant. Her cat-like reflexes made him feel like a love-struck puppy dog. "Well, Julian, be careful out there." Her smile entranced the timid man. "Do you drive?" she asked.

"No, I—I take the bus." He sighed, remembering the long walk ahead.

"Can you see outside? There isn't much lighting." Her face drooped with concern.

"I don't know. I have never walked out of here at night, but I'm sure I'll make it." He tried to appear confident, smiling and squaring his shoulders, but Violet laughed.

"You live over on East Charleston, right?"

"Yeah." *She remembered me!* "I only have to take one bus to get home, luckily." He grinned again, unable to believe the synchronicity. He'd seen the number 44 three times throughout the day, guiding him, and now he knew why. *Is this fate? Did I manifest this?*

"Well, have a safe trip home, and a lovely weekend," Violet said.

"You too, and thanks again!" His grin stretched the distance, and his thoughts bubbled into an observation of how perfect and beautiful the moment was. As the two walked toward the door, he rambled on, not wanting it to end. "I am legally blind and have an eye condition, Retinitis Pigmentosa, and sometimes I—"

"It's fine. I understand." Other than the moment of concern, her smile had remained since their eyes met. "You just need to be careful," she repeated. As they headed outside, she turned towards the parking lot before looking over her shoulder, saying, "I'll see you next Friday." She threw up her hand and wiggled her fingers. Julian waved back and headed in the opposite direction, inching down the dark sidewalk towards the bus stop.

The entire parking lot was dark, and he took his time, taking baby steps and relying mostly on passing headlights to lead his way. It was over a quarter mile to the intersection, but the heavy bag hanging from his broad shoulders was good exercise. Once Julian made it to the bus stop, he retrieved his phone and checked the transit app. *4 minutes away*, it read. A small crowd waited on the narrow curb as the cold wind thrashed relentlessly. He had started zipping his jacket when someone on a bicycle came speeding by.

"'Scuse me," the cyclist casually announced just as he passed. Another commuter quickly stepped back, colliding with Julian and knocking him off balance. He tripped on the edge of the curb, and the weight of his bookbag pulled him down into the street. A second later, the tires of an oncoming car horrendously screamed like a queen, stopping less than a foot from his head. The bright headlights shone directly in his eyes and the vehicle's horn blasted his ears clean.

He quickly stood, staring past the headlights, vibrant purple hood, and white racing stripes of a roaring classic Firebird. The small auburn driver came into focus and their eyes locked again. "Violet?" Julian's tailbone throbbed, but he ignored it, making his way to the passenger door, where she had stretched across the seat to roll down the window.

"You just keep falling for me, don't you?" She giggled sweetly and shook her head.

He smirked. "How the hell does this keep happening?"

"Fate, maybe?" She batted her eyes. "I don't believe in coincidence. Get in!"

"Y—you don't have to give me a ride home," he stuttered.

"You've almost got yourself killed twice since class ended. I can't just let you go off on your own and keep a clear conscience." She placed her black-polished fingertips on the door handle. "Come on," she insisted. "Clearly the universe wants it."

Her voice. Her scent. That face. The universe. There it was, a burst of cosmic adrenaline, ready to destroy him if he made the wrong decision. *She is right,* he thought. *This is fate. Go with her, you idiot!*

"I … umm. Are you sure?"

"What're you avoiding?" She winked.

"Okay," he yielded. "I'll go." Violet smiled as he opened the door and slid inside. As he sat his bag on the floorboard, she hit the gas. The engine ripped, roared, and thundered like the gods as the Bird took flight into the cold Mojave night.

Chapter Three

A n air freshener shaped like two cherries hung from the rearview mirror. But rather than cherries, the Firebird's interior, like Violet, smelled of vanilla. Julian breathed slowly, trying to relax. *Calm down*, he told himself. *Don't fuck this up!*

"So, how did you fall in the street?" Violet asked.

"That guy on the bike," he sighed. "Some jerk knocked me over when he rode by. It was an accident, but they didn't even apologize."

"People are assholes," she said while merging southbound onto the freeway. "Are you alright, though? It looked like you landed pretty hard."

"I'm used to it," he groused. "Why are you getting on the freeway? Are you taking me home, or …?" Unsure what to expect, Julian's mind wandered. *Shut up and be a man, stupid!* his grandfather's voice snarled in his ears. The thought of him at such a moment was infuriating. *Fuck off, miserable old prick!*

"Are you alright?!" Violet asked again.

"Yeah, why?"

"What? Oh, nothing," she stammered. "Do you want to go home? Call it intuition, but you seem like someone who could use a friend. I don't know about you, but I could sure use one and it would be nice to do something fun tonight."

"Like what?"

"Something proactive and hands-on, you know?"

"We could shoot some pool or something." *Pool? Really?*

She giggled and said, "We can play a game of pool. That sounds lovely, but it's been a while for me, and you might kick my ass if you're any good."

"I haven't played since I was little, living in Virginia."

"You're from Virginia?!" she asked. "You don't have the accent."

"Well, I'm originally from Saint Louis," he said, watching the colorful bright lights of the strip creeping by on the left, illuminating the surrounding darkness. "My mother was from Virginia. When I was nine, my father died, and we moved to the Appalachian Mountains. That's where I grew up."

"It sounds like you're pretty well traveled," she said.

He blushed. "Well, I've been to twenty-nine states and Washington D.C., so far," he admitted. "I've seen a lot of the country. I would love to see more and travel abroad at least once before I die."

"Wow! That's quite an accomplishment," she admired. "You're still young and have plenty of time left to see whatever you'd like."

"Yeah, well, you're younger than I am," he said, unsure how else to respond.

She laughed, asking, "How old do you think I am?"

"I'd say early twenties."

Her laughter continued until she cleared her throat and mumbled, "I am twenty-seven."

"Really?! You don't look that old," he said. "You're passing the twenty-seven club."

"The twenty-seven club? What's that?"

"A lot of famous rock stars died at twenty-seven—Jim Morrison, Jimi Hendrix, Janis Joplin ... the list goes on."

"Ooh. Hendrix is my favorite guitarist ever, and I absolutely adore Janis!"

"So did my grandma," he said.

"I followed her ever since she first started."

Wait, what?! "Since she started?" Julian looked in her direction, unable to see anything more than occasional glimpses of her silhouette. "She died before either of us were born."

"Oh, I—I meant ever since I started listening to that kind of music," she mumbled again. "I've liked her ever since I got into rock and roll." The ride grew awkwardly silent for a moment until she changed the subject. "So, how old are you?"

"Thirty-seven."

"Seriously?! You sure don't look it. You have a babyface, dear."

He laughed and said, "Everyone tells me I look like I'm in my early twenties."

"You do, and your voice is so soft for your age, but I like it."

Again, Julian blushed. "Where are you from?" he asked.

"Well, I came here from New York, but I grew up in Savannah, Georgia."

That explains her accent, he thought. "I've been through Georgia a few times but never got to stop and explore."

"It's alright, but New York is more exciting," she said.

"I went to New York a few times with my ex."

"How'd you like it?"

"It was very crowded, that's for sure, but I had some great experiences. I saw Manhattan from the top of a double-decker bus. I also visited some cool museums and even saw the Statue of Liberty."

"New York's a popular city, for sure, but it wasn't always so crowded. At one time, the streets were mostly dead at night."

"How long ago was that?" He looked her way again. "I thought New York was always busy."

"Oh, I—I heard stories from a lot of older people I met when I was younger."

The ride grew silent again, and Julian nervously twiddled his thumbs until he cleared his throat and said, "If you don't mind me asking, why were you so upset at the diner this morning?"

"Oh, that," she sighed. "Let's just say someone hurt me, someone who I thought was my friend. If you don't mind, I would prefer to just leave it at that."

"I understand." *I hope I didn't offend her.* As they exited the freeway, he asked, "Do you know anywhere we can go? I haven't seen much of the city yet." Julian's dying eyes were full of amazement, looking from left to right at all the flashing neon colors ahead.

"Yeah," she said. "I need to park first, but there's an arcade with pool tables close by." She turned onto Las Vegas Boulevard and there they were, in the thick of it on a Friday night. Julian had visited the strip once or twice after dark but had been either on the bus or the sidewalk, never getting such a spectacular view. He dropped his jaw, his excitement something only a childhood Christmas morning could match. Ahead, the Eiffel Tower glowed in gold on the left, and the Statue of Liberty stood tall on the right.

"Holy shit!" he gasped. He observed everyone on the sidewalks ignoring the cold for a good time, and smirked. "It's funny. Even in the dead of winter, the strip's still packed like this."

"People are crazy about this place, no matter the weather," she said, concentrating on the congested traffic. As they passed a flashing sign, bright shades of red and white lit the inside of the car. Julian caught a good look at Violet and her natural smile. *She is so beautiful.*

The Firebird approached a white high rise on the right, where they turned off the strip towards a parking garage. "So, what brought you out here?" Julian asked.

"I wanted something new," she said. "When I saw the psychology class, I knew I had to take it." Violet found a parking space and asked, "What about you? What's a skinny thing like you doing out here by yourself?"

How does she know I am alone? "I also wanted something new. In Virginia, I got sick of sitting there every day on the same couch my mother died on, trying to get my family to include me. I wanted to have a little fun before I go blind," he said, lowering his head in shame. "My condition is degenerative and getting worse with age."

Amidst his self-loathing, Julian felt he'd said too much, but to his surprise, Violet appeared sympathetic. "That's awful," she said. "If you don't mind me asking, how did your mother die?"

"She drank herself to death," he said. "Well, it was cirrhosis of the liver, brought on by a lifetime of alcohol abuse and hepatitis C. She got it in the nineties when she was with her abusive drug addict boyfriend, Bill."

"And you kept the couch she died on?!" Violet's tone changed, implying intrigue and possibly disgust.

"Her second husband, Hank, slept on it until he almost died the same way she did. He went into a nursing home, and once it was just me, my grandpa started charging rent, and I couldn't afford a new one—or anything besides groceries and my bills."

"He charged you rent to live in your mother's house?!" Her eyes bugged out. "Wasn't he charging Hank rent?"

"No," he sighed. "I paid him five hundred dollars a month. Twice, the greedy prick asked me for six hundred. I saved that son of a bitch Hank's life, and that was the thanks I got."

"Saved his life?"

"Hank was also an alcoholic, and an idiot! He ate a fish sandwich after it sat out for two days in the hot August heat and got too sick to keep drinking. He slept for three days until DTs set in. He would have died if I hadn't called an ambulance. I also called his mother, Dolly. She showed up at the house before the EMTs, but she was more worried about giving me grief than his health. Normally a mother would say, 'Thank you for saving my son's life,' but not her. The crusty old hag got in my face and screamed, 'You don't care about him! You only want this house for yourself!'"

"Some mother," Violet grumbled.

"Somehow, Hank was brain damaged from it. At the time, nobody knew he would go into a nursing home. Hank was an asshole, but I didn't want him to die. It had nothing to do with getting rid of him."

Violet grunted, appearing to share Julian's disgust. She asked, "How were you supporting yourself?"

"I get a disability check because of my eyes." He blushed in embarrassment. "It's a rural area, without public transportation, or anything for a blind person to do."

"How were you able to afford to move out here, if you were broke?"

"My grandpa gave me half the money back, but I feel like it was just to get rid of me," he said. "To him, it was a joke. Before I left, he mocked me. He said, 'Don't forget me when you make your first million.' After I moved, he sold the double-wide as a rent-to-own, and the guy who bought it only pays him four hundred a month. Do you know how it feels to know a stranger is paying less to live in my mother's house than her own son was?" He wanted to cry but had no tears.

"That's awful," Violet commiserated. "At least your grandfather helped you move." She spoke softly and looked on with empathetic eyes, as if unsure what else to say.

"I suppose," he mumbled. "But it's not right. It shouldn't cost more to live in my mother's house, in some redneck shithole, than in Las Vegas." He rolled his eyes and slumped his shoulders. "I figured if I was going to pay that much, I might as well go somewhere less depressing."

"You were hurt really bad, weren't you?" Violet asked, turning the key and pulling it from the ignition. She placed her hand on Julian's shoulder as their eyes met. She stared through him as if witnessing his entire life story. Her red lips briefly quivered before curling to a heartfelt smile and quelling his creeping sorrow.

"I have," he muttered. "How'd you guess?"

"You're not that hard to read," she said and gently pulled her hand away.

As the touching moment faded, Julian noticed the barrage of exquisite cars and trucks lining the lot in all shapes and sizes. Bright fluorescent lights showcased posh modern marvels in shades of apple green, turquoise blue, and ember orange. Classic muscle cars flared red as lust, white as virtue, and black as death. His eyes twinkled at such a sight. "Where are we?"

"This is the Vegas Parliament." Violet extended her hands, glorifying the scene. "My father owns a big share here, and it's where I stay when I'm in town." She opened her door as Julian reached for his bookbag. "You can leave that here if you want. I'll drive you home later," she said. He nodded and sat the bag in his seat after opening the door and stepping out to the filthy concrete. The garage smelled of gas and exhaust fumes. Although they were out of the wind, the air was just as cold here. He zipped his jacket and joined Violet behind the car.

"So, where to?" he asked, staring at the oil-stained ground and watching his steamy white breath scatter with each exhale.

"Come on," she said. They walked alongside one another, out of the garage and onto the sidewalk. When Julian stumbled in the dark, she took his hand and wrapped her cold fingers around his. He blushed again. Once they reached Vegas Blvd, he could see much better. "The arcade's about a block away if you'd still like to shoot a game of pool," she said.

"I'm fine with whatever you'd like to do."

"We'll see what happens. The night is young, and we have options." Her cheeks glowed as she pulled him into the arcade. Being a Friday night, the arcade was packed full of kids and teens. The entire storefront was open, and the windy chill of the Vegas Valley spread throughout. Violet only wore the white shawl and a thin blue dress beneath, Julian noticed.

"Aren't you cold?" he asked, unzipping his heavy black leather jacket to offer her.

"I'm fine," she said. "I don't get cold." As he re-zipped his jacket, they found an empty pool table and a couple of cues mounted on the wall nearby. "Not to be rude, but can you see good enough to play?" she asked.

He laughed and said, "I don't know, but I guess we can find out." He smiled and reached for one of the cues, but it slipped from his fingers and loudly crashed with an echo on the cement floor. They both laughed at the perfect irony.

"You're funny," she giggled and smiled. "I like that." With radish red cheeks, Julian picked up the cue and replaced it with another from the rack. Violet selected hers and put a handful of quarters in the coin slot on the side of the table. The balls released and rolled to the opening.

"I'll rack, and you break?" Julian peered up from the table, his round glasses sliding off his nose. Violet nodded in approval as he placed the balls inside the plastic triangle atop the green felt. The actions took him back. "My dad used to let me rack the balls when we'd play, before he died." He carefully centered the triangle and pulled it away. "You ready?" he asked, taking a small cube of blue chalk from the side of the table. He backed away and chalked the end of his cue.

Violet nodded and stepped up to the front of the table, positioning herself accordingly. She gently pulled her right arm back, then forward, focusing on her target. She pulled back once more like it was a bowstring, and then she fired, blasting the chalk-stained cue ball into the head of the pyramid. Her shot had quite the force behind it. "Nice!" Julian grinned, admiring her strength and accuracy.

"Not bad, huh?" She smiled as the balls scattered. Two stripes went in a corner pocket. "I'm stripes and you're solids," she said before taking a second shot and missing. "Your turn!"

Julian stepped up to the table and cleared his throat. He leaned in, focused his aim, and took the shot. To his surprise, he sank the orange five ball. "Good job!" Violet cheered.

"Thanks," he said. He took his next shot, focusing on the seven ball, but missed.

"Aww! Almost," she playfully teased. They both laughed as she took her shot, sinking the eleven, then the fifteen.

"Damn, you're kicking my ass," Julian said, amused and even turned on.

"You said your father used to shoot pool?" she asked.

"Yeah, he played at a lot of bars with his baseball buddies."

"Baseball buddies?"

"Yeah, Saint Louis is baseball country, and back in the eighties, when the Cardinals were on top of the world, one of his hobbies was playing in the local minor league."

"Was he any good?"

"He was okay, but nothing special. He could've spent more time with me and my mom." He paused as if struck with a realization. *Why am I telling her all of this? Is this what I always do? No wonder women don't like me.* Johnny's voice was quick to intervene, shouting: *stop feeling sorry for yourself and be a man!*

"What happened to your father?" Violet asked.

"I honestly don't know," he said, and she tipped her head. "He died in jail, but …" He paused again and sighed. "It's a long story."

"I understand," she said. "Don't worry about it." It was like she knew what to say. She placed her hand on his shoulder again, admiring his jacket for the first time.

"Nice coat, by the way. I love the skulls." Julian looked down at the black jacket with gray reflective skulls embroidered in the leather, wrapping across the chest, arms, and back.

"Thanks," he said. Violet nodded and turned her attention back to the game. She took her next shot but came up short. It was Julian's turn, and he also missed. He grimaced. *Come on. Why can't I be cool and impressive for once?*

"Not to be rude, but are you bored?" she asked. The way her lips scrunched, and her eyes wandered, she appeared to be up to something. Julian laughed at such an adorable sight, forgetting his frustration.

"Why? Did you want to do something else?"

She smiled and said, "Come on. I want to show you something on the north end of the strip."

"Okay, but I didn't bring enough cash for a strip bus pass, though. I only brought enough for a regular pass. So, unless you're going to drive, I—"

"Don't worry about it," she interrupted. "I have unused passes for the strip bus." She pointed at her purse and took his hand. "Come on," she repeated. "You've gotta see this before you die."

Chapter Four

Once swiping their passes, Julian and Violet boarded a crowded bus that stunk of fresh cannabis. Once they found two empty seats near the back, Julian offered Violet the one by the window. As he squirmed, trying to get comfortable, Violet asked, "Are you alright?"

"Yeah, I'm just sore from what happened with that idiot earlier," he grumbled.

"I have a feeling most of the people here are inconsiderate assholes," she said.

"I know what you mean. I have only let two people in my apartment since I've been here. I wanted to make some friends, but one of them stole my camera. The other stole a twenty dollar bill. I didn't notice until it was too late. After that, I gave up."

"That's terrible."

"It's nothing new," he said. "People have stolen things from me for years. Because of my vision, they've always gotten away with it. If I confront them they threaten me."

"They sound awful. It sucks that people have taken advantage of you, but at least now you know to keep your guard up."

"Now, people just steal my time," he said. "I met a woman online a few months ago. We talked for a week. One night, she invited me to have a drink with her at a bar across the city. I spent over two hours on two buses to get there, and after only five minutes, she ditched me."

Violet rolled her eyes. "What a bitch," she said.

"Vegas is too heartless for me. On television, they make it sound so glamorous and exciting, but they don't tell you about all the crime, murder, child sex trafficking, or the police refusing to do anything about it," he said.

"Yeah," Violet breathed. "If they did that, nobody would come here. 'Sin City' is not just a gimmick, and 'What happens in Vegas stays in Vegas' is a saying for a reason. This place is a modern Sodom and Gomorrah."

"I honestly didn't know what I was getting myself into when I came out here. Now that I've gotten to know Las Vegas, I loathe it."

"So, why are you here?"

"I told you, I wanted to enjoy myself before I went blind."

"I don't buy that. You can have fun anywhere, but for someone with an eye condition like yours, you shouldn't be here by yourself. It's not safe for you here. So why did you choose Las Vegas when you could have gone anywhere?"

Julian chuckled. "It's silly, but my intuition brought me here. Just over three years ago, my ex-girlfriend, Faith, cheated on me and got pregnant. When she told me what happened, I tried to kill myself, but luckily, I survived. After that, I knew I had to get away. I'd never thought about Vegas before then, but a voice told me to take what little money I had, get on a bus, and come anyway. So, I did."

"What did you do when you got here?"

"I spent two months at a hostel on the strip."

"What was that like?"

"It was fun, but I couldn't afford to go out and do anything. If I had seen this place for what it was, I probably wouldn't have come back. At the hostel, I met a lot of people from all over the world. Most of them were nice to me, but eventually, I went back home to face reality. After I moved in with Hank, though, I immediately wanted to come back. Last year, I finally gave up on life in Virginia. After my grandpa offered me thirty-five-hundred dollars, I boarded another bus and here I am."

"Wow! That's impressive. I admire your courage, but your grandfather should be ashamed of himself for making you feel unwanted."

"Yeah," he sighed. "It wasn't just him. There's more you don't know about, but—"

"It doesn't matter. It sounds like he threw you away. I have only known you a few hours, but I see you, even if he could not. You are a good person, and especially with your disability, you deserved better."

"It's funny." He smirked. "My mom always told me, when my grandma died, the family would turn against us. I never believed her. 'She's just drunk and talking out her ass,' I'd say, but she was right. My problems never mattered to them. Everything they ever told me was lies to compensate for their lack of a heart or spine." Julian lowered his head and sighed again. "My mom died on December twentieth, two-thousand-thirteen, only two days before her fifty-third birthday, and just six months after COPD killed my grandma. When they died, I was so angry. I've carried so much resentment and guilt towards them and myself ever since," he confessed.

"Approaching Caesar's Palace," an automated male voice announced over the bus speakers as the transit slowly came to a halt. A small crowd exited through the back door and others entered through the front.

"I feel like my grandpa never forgave my mom for marrying my dad," Julian continued. "A few years after he died, she got with Bill. My dad only beat my mom, but Bill beat us both," he muttered. "My grandpa knew what was happening in that house and did nothing to help us. My mom made her own choices, but I was a child. I feel like he vicariously punished me for her mistakes."

Violet placed her hand on Julian's knee and changed the subject. "What did you say your eye condition was called?"

"Retinitis Pigmentosa, or RP for short," he said. "It's hereditary and incurable."

"What does it do to you, if you don't mind me asking?"

"I have progressive tunnel vision. My peripherals are closing inward."

"So, you can't see things from the sides?"

"I can, but not far," he said, locking eyes with hers. "I see your eyes and the bridge of your nose. The rest of your nose, cheeks and forehead are a blur. I can't even see your mouth or hair."

"Wow! I had no idea," she gasped. "Is tunnel vision the only thing it causes?"

"No, it also affects my balance, scanning, and focus. Like a digital camera screen, sometimes I have to stare at things for a moment to see them. I also have night and color blindness. I have difficulty telling certain shades of pink and orange, and green and blue apart."

"And you moved out here all by yourself?!" She slowly shook her head from side to side in disbelief. "You know, even if they are impaired, your eyes are beautiful. Blue is my favorite color, after purple, I mean."

"Thanks," he said, blushing again. "I wish I could see as good as I used to. At one time, I could drive, but now I'm usually too nervous to even walk anywhere. I mostly stay to myself and work on my book. I love to write and—"

"Approaching Sahara and the Stratosphere," the automated voice announced.

"That's us," she said. "Come on." After Julian stood, Violet took her purse and slid out of the rubbery blue row of seats. They made their way towards the door as the bus came to a stop at the curbside. When the automatic doors opened, they stepped out to the sidewalk. Violet pointed up, saying, "Check that out."

Julian followed her finger with his eyes. Across the street, three massive white concrete pillars swept upward, combining to form a tall tower that stretched over a thousand feet high. At the top, a dark, cylindrical structure, surrounded in red and white lights, overlooked the city. Julian's jaw dropped as he observed from the outskirts of the tower's toenails. "Wow!" he gasped.

"Come on," she said. "We're going to the top." Violet offered Julian her hand, asking, "Can you see?"

"I think I've got it, but I'll let you know if I fall behind," he said, thinking, *she is so sweet.* Her mindfulness was touching, and though they'd just met, he felt loved—not in a lustful sense, but a real connection.

They crossed the street and entered through the casino, where the midnight crowd was thick. Even with endless rows of flashing slot machines, the casino was dark and carried a stench of cigarettes. After wading through the sea of greed, they reached a long escalator. They passed several storefronts after taking it to the next floor.

"This place looks like a shopping mall," said Julian.

"Most of the casinos look like this," Violet said as they neared a counter at a set of elevators. "Let me do the talking up here. They are weird about who they let go up," she added. A short, chubby woman with thick glasses and long brown hair stood behind the counter. She wore a black vest with a gold oval name tag reading *Starla.*

She smiled and said, "Hi, how may I help you?"

"We'd like to go up to the lounge, on one-o-seven, please," Violet said, returning a smile.

"Yes, ma'am. Just step through the turnstile, and when the attendant comes back down, tell him where you want to go," she said.

"Thank you!" said Violet. She and Julian passed through the shiny metal turnstile and waited. "You're in for a treat," she said.

When the elevator arrived, they were greeted by a tall, slender man with smooth, dark skin, also wearing a black vest and gold oval name tag. His read *Larry*. "One-o-eight, please," Violet said. Once the elevator reached the top floor, they entered a stuffy, dim hallway.

"I saw what you did there," Julian chuckled.

"You have to be a guest to come to the roof unless you buy a ticket for one of the rides. Otherwise, the bar on the floor below is as high as we're allowed to go."

"You naughty devil, you," Julian playfully teased.

"Yeah, I'm not going to pay those prices for the rides," she added.

"What rides?"

"Come on, I'll show you." She took his hand and they walked down the hallway to a short set of white stairs. At the top, clear glass doors led outside to the observation deck, where the wind was much heavier from a thousand feet above the strip. Aside from a few mounted lights, Julian could not see much at first. Violet helped him up to the rail, where he saw everything. Below stretched a grand web of light, expanding in all directions for miles, surrounded by vacant darkness. He stood in awe.

"It's beautiful, isn't it?" she asked.

"It is," he replied, observing the lavish grid. "My mother once told me it was on her bucket list to fly over Las Vegas at night. She never did, but last month, I saw it from above for us both when I flew back from San Francisco. It was pretty, but nothing like this!" He closed his eyes and took in a deep breath of cold air.

"Do you have family in California, or were you visiting friends?"

"Neither," he said. "Well, now I can call them friends, but I didn't know them beforehand." Violet looked intrigued. "I went to an *Ayahuasca* retreat."

She raised an eyebrow, asking, "What's *Ayahuasca*?"

34

"It's a psychedelic drink, brewed with *chacruna* leaves and the *ayahuasca* vine from the Amazon jungle. It contains dimethyltryptamine and a female plant spirit."

"And you drank that?! Why?"

"Because I was so desperate to find the source of my pain and learn how to fix it. But by doing so, it unleashed all these repressed emotions from my past. Now they are coming back to haunt me by opening my eyes to certain truths my ego never let me see before. Now that I can feel the pain properly, I am learning how to let these emotions go."

"You know, after you mentioned the Amazon, I believe I've actually heard of *Ayahuasca* from a few people I know from South America."

"It's a very powerful medicine that exposes the subconscious mind."

"Interesting," she mused. "But don't you mean the 'collective unconscious?'" She flicked her tongue, sticking it out very briefly, and giggled, mocking Professor Scott's remark from class. After she and Julian shared a laugh, Violet cleared her throat and asked, "So, how's all this working for you, with accepting and letting go, I mean?"

Julian lowered his head. "Sometimes, I don't know."

"You just said you're learning to let go. What changed in the last few seconds?"

"Nothing's changed, it's just, saying it out loud made me realize—perhaps I'm fooling myself. Sometimes I feel like I can move mountains, until something small and inconvenient happens. Then I want to give up and let the mountain barrel over me so I can die and find peace. Overall, I feel hopeless." He lowered his head.

"I hope you don't take offense, but I call bullshit," she said.

"What do you mean?"

"The way you speak about your family and how they hurt you, it sounds like you are aware of what you need to heal. That is a huge step, but you are way too hard on yourself. You have all this shit built up inside you, but you are taking steps to resolve it. Be proud of yourself. Deep shadow work takes time."

"I know, but I'm tired of all the dark thoughts and memories piling on top of one another. A part of me wishes I never touched *Ayahuasca*. I know it's helping me uncover my post-trauma, but not with letting it go. Sometimes I feel like ignorance truly is bliss."

"Are you really so lost and hurt that you'd rather go through life unaware of what torments you than brave the storm and move to calmer waters?" She placed her hand over his, resting upon the cold steel rail. "You carry the weight of the world on your shoulders but still have the willpower to carry on. You are so uncertain, yet bold and optimistic. Why do you think that is?"

"I don't know."

"I've learned enough tonight to know you are a lot like me. You're lonely and just need an open-minded friend you can talk to. I hope this doesn't sound weird, but I feel like I have known you a lot longer than just tonight."

She sees right through me, but how? "Some people try to understand, but it's often patronizing," he admitted. "I feel like I'm going to spend the rest of my life alone, and it's not fair."

"You're not alone right now, are you?" She playfully nudged him with her elbow.

"No, but you know what I mean."

"You just want someone to love and complete you, don't you?"

"Yeah."

"That's where you're making a mistake. The only person who should complete you is you. Learn how to love yourself." She offered a reassuring smile.

"I get it, but I—"

"You want a companion, right? We all do, but we should never look to others to complete us. People can bring out the best and the worst in us, but only you can love yourself the way you want to be loved."

Julian stared off into the distance, allowing her powerful words to resonate. "I'm going blind," he said. "I wake up every morning terrified of what may come. Then when the day is over, I climb into bed and fall asleep with the anxiety of knowing how bland and lonely it will be all over again. I've tried reaching out to my grandpa and others in the family, but no one cares. None of them have any empathy or compassion for me."

"I don't want to sound like a bitch," she began. "But I want to tell you something." Julian's eyes met hers again. "It's not their job to care. You said your family hurt you, right? That is on them. You did everything you could. Do you think they lose sleep over it?" She was blunt and to the point, but Julian was not offended. He respected her direct approach. "This is your life to live, not theirs."

"You know, you sound like the most logical and realistic person I've talked to in a long time. Nobody appreciates honesty or realism. I feel like humanity is a parody of itself."

"Truth is truth, but lies can be anything, and the truth is people lie," she said. "Nobody wants to believe in truth because reality scares them. Although it might sound absurd to a deep thinker like you, they aren't strong enough to survive in the real world. So, they create their truth through false delusions and if it hurts others, so be it. You're right, humanity is a joke. Society has changed so much since I was a little girl, and I mourn what they once were."

"'They?'" Julian asked. "You're part of the human race, too," he snickered.

"'We,' I mean," she corrected herself. "I also want to love and be loved, but it's like you said: no one appreciates the truth. Fantasies are easy, but to see the big picture and tackle it head-on requires so much more than most people are capable of."

Nearby laughter drew their attention to a small group of teenagers standing under one of the lights. They were waiting in line for a white swing set. One by one, the teens took a seat and strapped themselves in. "Watch what happens," Violet said.

The seats lifted high, and the mechanism slowly spun in a circular motion. The dangling seats picked up speed and swayed off the side of the tower. The only thing separating the teens from the ground below was over a thousand feet of open air. Julian watched the kids spinning round and around, much braver than he would be. "They've got some balls," he chuckled.

"They also have a cart up here, like a rollercoaster. It slides right off the side, only stopping at the edge, leaving you feeling like you're gonna fall," she said.

"Fuck that!" Julian exclaimed, and they both laughed. "I'm too chicken to dangle that high up," he said. "I have a fear of falling, I guess." Violet playfully giggled as they watched a few others ride the swing. Then they took a slow walk around the observation deck, observing the city lights from all angles.

"I bet the daytime view of the Sierra Nevadas is just as amazing," said Julian.

"I wouldn't know," Violet mumbled. "I've never seen it."

Finally, they headed back to the elevator and ground below. Most of the shops were closed, but the casino was still full of gamblers. It had been a wonderful night, and Julian was happy. A smile remained glued to his face as they left the casino and walked down the sidewalk to the closest bus stop.

They did not have to wait long before an empty transit arrived. Each took their own row of seats near the back so they could have more room. Violet sat in the row behind Julian; he sat with his back against the window.

"So, what'd you think?" she asked. "Wasn't it beautiful up there?"

"It was great! Thank you for taking me," he said.

"You're welcome. Thank you for a nice evening. I needed it." When the mood grew silent, Violet asked, "So, what are you majoring in at school?"

"Creative writing," he said. "I'm taking two writing classes back to back on Mondays and Wednesdays."

"I should've guessed," she giggled. "I remember you said earlier you like to write. Becoming an author sounds like a dream worth having."

"I wouldn't call it a dream, but it's all I have left, and I'd be a liar if I said I wouldn't want the money and opportunities that came with writing a bestseller."

"You have a good story to tell. Most people never get the chance to pursue their dreams, and even if you wouldn't call it that, you still have all the time in the world to pursue it. 'Shoot for the stars,' they say."

"Thanks! I'm not used to encouragement," he said before yawning and rubbing his heavy eyes.

"It's good to let others encourage you, but don't hang on peoples' every word," she said. "While it's not always intentional, people will only hurt you when you rely on them for everything. We have our own two legs to stand on, and so do they."

"You're really wise, you know that?"

"I'm just me," she blushed. "I know how it feels to be where you're at. It's hard, but as the cliché implies, it does get better—but you have to believe in yourself. Then, you will raise your vibration and manifest reality in your favor."

Who the hell is this woman? Julian was so turned on he wanted to kiss her but refrained. With no one getting on or off the bus, the ride back to Violet's stop was quick. On their stroll back to the parking garage, she held Julian's hand, walking slowly by his side until they reached her Firebird. She turned the heat up and waited for the car to get warm before pulling out and driving away.

"Did you have fun tonight, like you were hoping for?" Julian asked.

"I did, thanks to you," she said. "Last night, I lost a dear friend. Well, at least I thought we were friends," she added under her breath. "After I told her something about myself, she said we couldn't be friends anymore."

"I'm so sorry," he said, patting her thigh. It was an empathetic reaction but he quickly pulled away, thinking he'd broken certain boundaries by touching her there. "Sorry," he repeated.

"It's fine, dear," she said. "I don't blame her. People are people, and not everyone vibes well together. It took me a while to open up to her. Now, I know why."

"Why?"

"It doesn't matter anymore," she said. "What about you? Did you have fun?"

"I did. It feels good to talk. I mean, I talk to my friend, Daryl, from back home, but even he doesn't get me anymore. We lost touch with each other for several years and we just started reconnecting before I came out here. Now, I freak him out with some of the things I say. With you, I feel like I can be open and honest."

"Of course you can," she said. "You know, I was honestly a little worried about what you'd think, getting in a car and going on an adventure with a stranger, but sometimes taking chances can change everything. Considering how we kept meeting, I guess it was meant to be."

"Where've you been all my life?" Julian gasped, unsure where the words had come from. *Oh my God! Did I just say that out loud? You idiot! You fucking idiot!* He blushed. "Umm … I mean, hi."

"Hi," she chuckled. "I've been around, waiting for the stars to align, I suppose."

Julian was so embarrassed he remained silent most of the way home. Once they passed the diner where they'd first noticed each other, he pointed out where to go. Violet passed all the buildings leading to his and parked in front of the stairway.

"Would you like to come in?" he asked.

"I don't know. It's late, and I should probably get back."

"Are you sure? You showed me something beautiful tonight, and I feel like I made a true friend. The least I could do is show you my apartment. I don't have swings or rides, but it gets me through the day and night."

"Oh, alright then, if you insist," she chuckled and flicked her tongue. "Let's check it out!"

Chapter Five

Julian slipped off his black sneakers and put away his jacket and bookbag. "Can I—I get you something to drink?" he asked.

"No thanks, I'm fine," Violet said, quietly standing at the door. Her demeanor had changed. She seemed nervous and more reserved. Julian sat on the edge of his mattress, motioning to his recliner for her to sit. Like a cautious doe, Violet slowly approached.

"Are you alright?" His heart raced and stomach churned. *Great, she saw my shitty apartment and now, I guess it's over.* Knowing the body language well, he already expected the worst.

"I'm fine. I'm not used to being in other peoples' homes, is all." She looked around the room, scanning his meager walls. "I like your tapestry," she added, staring at a colorful tie-dyed cloth with a black tree, hanging above his bed.

"Thanks. I bet you don't know anyone who sleeps under a tree, do you?"

She giggled. "No, I can't say I do."

As the moment grew silent, they locked eyes again. Julian had wanted to kiss her all night, and he was tired of resisting the temptation. Only sitting a foot from each other, he leaned forward, closed his eyes, and offered his quivering lips. Violet awkwardly backed away, whispering "I can't."

Julian's heart sank, and he became swept with dread. "Why not?"

"It's complicated." She lowered her head, appearing regretful. "You wouldn't understand."

"I am complicated, myself. What's wrong? You can talk to me."

"You are sweet, and I see your intentions. It's just that I'm not exactly a dating or hookup kind of person."

"I wasn't trying to hook up with you. Tonight, I felt something real."

"I understand. I also had a great time, and I also felt something, but can't we just be friends?" Her brown almond eyes grew bigger and brighter, as did her cheeks when she looked up and smiled.

"Okay." *But why does it always have to be this way for me and so easy for others?*

"We can still go out at night after class and have fun together, right? I'd like that."

"Me too," he said. Violet leaned closer and wrapped her arms around his shoulders. Her body was cold to the touch, but a warm, benevolent energy flowed between them. Julian shut his eyes and softly exhaled, feeling comfortable in her embrace.

"I should probably get going. I'm getting sleepy, but we—" Violet gasped, jerking her head from Julian's shoulder and releasing her grip. He opened his eyes and watched fear wash over her face. Violet stared in horror beyond Julian, fixated on the window. He looked over his shoulder and saw the early morning blue shining through the cracks of the blinds.

She lunged to her feet. "Where's your bathroom?!"

"It's back there, through the closet." He pointed towards the door. "Are you alright?"

"Are there any windows back there?!"

"No, why?" Without answering, Violet bolted towards the bathroom. First, she slammed the closet door, and then the bathroom door. *What the hell?!* "Violet?! Are you okay?!" He approached the first closed door.

"I'm alright! I—I'm just using the b—bathroom," she stuttered.

"Okay then, just let me know if you need anything." He returned to the living room and sat on the recliner. *What the hell just happened?* He turned on the television to give her privacy. Twenty minutes passed and she hadn't come out. *What the fuck is she doing in there, shooting drugs or something?* "Are you alright in there?!" She didn't answer. He approached the door again and knocked. "Violet? ... Hey!" Hearing nothing, Julian took a deep breath and placed his hand on the knob.

"Wait a minute!" Violet beseeched. "Don't come in here!"

"What are you doing in there? You're not shooting drugs, are you?"

"Seriously?! No! I—I'm sick and just need to sit here a while."

"Sick? Is there anything I can do?" He opened the first door and took a few steps towards the sink, between the closet and second door.

"Don't come in here, Julian, please!"

"Why not? I want to help you."

"If you want to help me, just back away. I'm sorry, but I can't tell you what's wrong."

"What?! But this is my apartment!"

"I know, but I need you to back off, please! Just let me stay in here until it gets dark tonight."

"Tonight?! You're going to stay in there all day?!" *I have met some batshit crazy people out here, but Jesus Christ!* He laughed ironically, trying not to lose his cool. *Why does this shit always happen to me?* "You can't just stay in there all day!"

"I can and I will! I like you, Julian, but if I come out of the dark, I will die, and I'm not going to die, not today. If you try to force me out, I—I will hurt or kill you if I have to." Her voice was full of cracks and shame but deadly serious. "And I don't want to do either."

"Excuse me?!" His jaw dropped. "Is that a threat?! Because I will call Vegas Metro on your ass if that's how you want to play!" As Julian's heart bludgeoned from the pit of his stomach, he took a breath and tried to collect himself. "Look, I—I don't want to call the cops, but you're scaring me, and I—I'll be damned if I'm going to let anyone push me around and threaten me!"

"I told you, I don't expect you to understand, but I can explain everything if you just give me a chance."

"But I have to let you just sit in there all day?! That doesn't make sense."

"When has life ever made sense to you, Julian? What part of what your grandpa or your mother did makes sense?"

"You don't know what they did to me!"

"I know your mother abandoned you. She left you with your grandparents and ran away to Myrtle Beach with Bill, claiming it was to keep you safe, but she really did it for him. I know for three years you didn't know where she was or if she was even alive. After Bill stabbed her on the beach, he almost killed her, didn't he?"

Julian gasped. *I never told her that.* "H—how do you know?"

"I …" She sighed. "I can read your thoughts."

"Bullshit!" He took a step back from the door, ready to run for his phone in the living room.

"There's things about me you wouldn't understand."

"No shit, Sherlock! If you can read minds, wh—what am I thinking right now?"

"You're scared and confused."

"Really?! A goddamn child could've figured that out! … Seriously! What am I thinking?!" She said nothing. "I knew it!" He snarled and flung his hands outward in a fit. "All you women are the same! You, my mother, and Faith, who fucked—"

"Her brother, Travis?" Julian lost his breath and stumbled back a step. She said, "I am not full of shit. You loved her with all your heart, and she betrayed you."

"H—how do you know all this?" he repeated, but Violet said nothing. "Answer me! How did you know about that?!" Panic struck, ripping away at Julian's fragile psyche. *How is this happening? How is it even possible?!*

"It's possible because I hear everything you think. I know you originally came back to Las Vegas to be isolated from anyone you care about, intending to try and kill yourself again, right?"

The truth hurt when it stared Julian in the face. Overcome with shame, and too shocked to speak, he listened. "I read you all night, even in class and at the diner. I heard your thoughts as you wrote them on your computer. I couldn't help it. They were so vivid. So many times, I wanted to comfort you and say, 'It's okay,' but the last thing I wanted was to scare or hurt you," she cried. "There are things about me I can't explain right now, I just can't."

As Julian listened, the blast beats in his head, heart, and lungs slowly eased. He regained his breath but remained cautious. *What now?* He cleared his throat. "I—I didn't know you at the beginning of the night, but I went with you because I followed my heart. I came back here wanting to die, until I discovered Ayahuasca. After it revealed the source of my trauma, I convinced myself to push on and trust my intuition. I took a big chance last night, and I don't think anything happens by accident." Julian placed his palm against the closed white door, pleading, "I feel like the least you could do is tell me why you locked yourself in my bathroom. Y—you said you want to be my friend. So be my friend and talk to me."

"I can't go in the sunlight," she said. "Out of context, it sounds crazy, but it's true."

"So, you threatened to kill me if I opened the door?"

"You don't understand. Sunlight will kill me."

"That doesn't make sense. How could sunlight kill you?"

"I told you, I can't explain it, not like this. I don't want to frighten you any worse than I have, and I don't want you to think I'm crazy, because I am not. Please, just let me stay in here today and I swear I will show and tell you everything tonight."

"I—I want to believe you, but how—"

"Please, Julian," she cried. "Just leave me be for now, and I will swear something to you." She sniffled and snorted. "If you'll trust me and let me stay in here today, I swear I will change your life, and you will be happy."

"What the hell are you talking about? I—I am so confused."

"I know you are, and I am so sorry that I frightened you. Just give me a chance and tonight I will show you everything, but you have to trust me."

"Are you just going to sit in there all day?"

"I'd like to curl up in your bathtub and go to sleep."

Julian paced the floor, confused, tired, and not thinking clearly. Finally, he broke down and said, "Alright, Violet. You can sleep in there. and I'll tell you when it gets dark." A part of him still wanted to call the cops and tell them a crazy lady was holed up in his bathroom, unwilling to come out, but his soft heart and passive-aggressiveness gave in. He wanted to trust her and see where the rabbit hole went. *Trust. Why care anymore? For all I know, I am already dead. If I die, at least the pain dies too.*

"Don't think like that!" Violet insisted. "I am not going to hurt you if you keep your word. I don't ever want to hurt you, but I don't want to die either."

Julian rolled his eyes at her absurd claims, but she knew so much, and his intrigue won. "Okay, Violet, I will let you sleep."

"Thank you so much, Julian!" Although she sobbed, her voice had grown cheerful. "I swear, I will keep my word."

"Alright then," he grumbled. "I'll be out here if you need me." Julian was still shaken, but deep down he trusted his intuition. He walked back into the living room, listening to Violet thumping in the bathtub, trying to get comfortable. *Is this even real?*

His mind scrambled as he took a seat, eyeballing his black smartphone, wondering what would happen if he called the cops. In one scenario, the police would drag her out in cuffs, kicking and screaming without incident. In the less pleasant outcome, the cops would be hacked to pieces by a knife-wielding psychopath, spattering the walls in pig blood. The horrendous death rattles would alert Julian's neighbor, Gus. He'd run in to find the femme fatale atop Julian's carcass, digging his eyes out of his skull like melon balls, laughing like a hyena as she did it, then moving on to Gus, leaving no witnesses.

Julian snapped out of it and picked up the phone, but did not call the police. Instead, he sent a text message to the only person he could: Daryl. *Are you busy? I need some advice*, he typed, poking *send* before setting the phone down and listening for movements in the bathroom. He heard nothing until his phone rang. Daryl's name appeared on the screen as Julian answered. "H—hello?"

"What're ya doin'?" a deep voice with a strong Appalachian twang asked.

"Hey," Julian gulped. "Wh—what's goin' on?" He'd hoped Daryl would just text. Knowing Violet could hear, he walked outside barefoot on the cold balcony.

"What kind of advice d'ya need, bub?"

"I got myself in a situation. I met a girl last night, and we had so much fun together—"

"Is she hot, bub?!"

"She's gorgeous, but that's not—"

"So, what do you need advice about, where to put it?" Daryl cackled like a crow.

"No, smartass," Julian grumbled. "When the sun started coming up, she freaked out and locked herself in my bathroom."

"Damn, bub, are you that bad in the sack?" Again, he laughed.

"This is serious, Daryl! She told me the sunlight would kill her, and if I tried to come in there before dark or call the cops, she'd kill me!"

"Whoa, hold on! Is she still in your bathroom?"

"Yeah, but there's something else." He paused for a moment, knowing how insane it would sound. "She told me she could read minds."

"Read minds?! She sounds like a whack-job."

"That's what I thought, but she knew things I never told her."

"Like what?"

"She knew about Faith cheating on me with her brother, and things my mom did."

"How'd she know that? Ya had to of told her, Julian. You know people can't read minds."

"Don't you think I thought about that? I know it sounds crazy, but she had no other way of knowing."

"Julian, you're my brother, and I love you, but you need to settle down."

"What are you talking about?"

"Those drugs ya took, they're turning you crazy."

"What drugs, the Ayahuasca?"

"Yeah."

"Goddamn it, Daryl. That's not even what this is about. I—"

"Let me finish," he interrupted. "I think you're imagining things."

"This has nothing to do with that. I just had the greatest night of my life before all this. It's not in my head. She's in my psychology class, for fuck sake!"

"Alright, so, there's a girl in your bathroom, and she says sunlight will kill her, right?"

"That's what she said."

"What the hell is she, a vampire, or somethin'?" Daryl laughed and Julian followed.

"Very funny, asshole."

"Well, I don't know what to tell ya. Maybe she's got a weird skin condition or something. If ya think she's a threat, call the cops and have them run her off."

"She swore that if I trusted her, she'd change my life."

"What the hell does that mean?"

"I don't know, but she seems to have money. She has a nice Firebird and stays in a high rise on the strip. It's weird, but I trust her."

"Maybe she's gonna sweep ya away somewhere and make an honest man out of ya. Then, you two can take drugs together."

"Would you shut the fuck up about that? This is serious!"

"Hey, don't cuss me! I'll kick your ass, bub."

"Listen, I'm sorry, but this is freaking me out. I am tired, and haven't slept but two hours in the last two and a half days. Now, I'm afraid to shut my eyes while she's here."

"I told ya all I know. If it were me, I'd call the cops."

Julian sighed. "I can't explain it, but I don't think she's a threat to me."

"Then why'd ya text me asking for advice? I just got home from work late last night after spending nine hours on the road. I only have a few days with my old lady and the girls before I have to go back. I love ya, bub, and I'm not trying to be an asshole, but wha'd'ya want me to say?"

"Honestly, I don't know. I guess I was scared and confused."

"You're the one who's always tellin' people to trust their gut. So, put up or shut up, son."

"Yeah," Julian muttered.

"I do worry about ya, all the way out there by yourself. I know you're lonely and just want to find a girlfriend or whatever, but you need to be careful. Las Vegas ain't Gunnar, ya know."

"I know. Unlike Gunnar, Vegas has things to do, and the women don't all look like they're related."

"Did you just call everybody here inbred?"

"Not everybody," he said, and they shared a laugh.

"Well bub, I reckon I'm gonna jump off here and relax. I ain't been home in two weeks, and I'm tired. Just be careful. If ya need me, ya know you can call or text any time."

"Thanks, brother. Sometimes I don't think I'd be alive if it weren't for you."

"'Everything happens for a reason.' You told me that once. Have a good one, bub, and don't forget to wear a condom." Daryl laughed again. "Anyway, I'll holler at ya later. Bye, bub."

"Bye, asshole." Julian snickered as he pressed the *end call* icon. He opened the door and walked back inside, listening for movement in the bathroom but hearing nothing. He checked the clock on his phone before putting it on the charger. *6:44* it read: exactly twelve hours after Violet sat behind him in class. He lay down and removed his glasses, setting them on the arm of his recliner. Despite everything, Julian grinned, sure he'd done the right thing. He yawned again and shut his restless, burning eyes, with nothing to feel sorry for, unlike before. His final thoughts were of his grandfather and what he would say to him. *I AM a man, stupid!*

Chapter Six

S ometime after dark, Julian opened his eyes. *Is Violet still here?* He put on his glasses and reached for his phone, but it was not where he'd left it. *What the hell?!* He ran his hands across the dark carpet, searching for the charger cable before following it to a vacant end.

He grunted and wobbled to the light switch, flicking it up, but nothing happened. "Goddamn it!" He growled and stomped towards the bathroom, calling her name. "Violet?!" He opened the first door and tried the light switch for the sink, but nothing. He cleared his throat and knocked on the second door. "Violet? Are you still in there? It—it's dark now, and I'm coming in."

Julian took a deep breath and placed his hand on the knob. He twisted and pushed. "Violet?" He flipped on the light, and the overhead bulb lit the room, but she was not there. "Are you fucking kidding me?!" He clenched his fists.

After returning to the pitch black living room, he felt around the floor for his phone again, but it was not there. He opened the front door and saw that her car was also gone. "Fuck!" he yelled at the top of his lungs while furiously pacing the cold wooden deck and punching the metal rail. The door next to his squeaked open. A short, bald old man in a white wife-beater stuck his head out, appearing shaken and confused.

"What the hell are you doing, Julian?!"

"Someone stole my phone and fucked up my lights while I was asleep!"

"Someone took your phone?!" The man tipped his head. "Why would they do that?"

"Because people are pieces of shit, Gus, that's why!"

"Hey, calm down. You might've just lost it. Would you like to use mine to call yours?"

Yeah, I've lost it, alright. "Sure," he grunted in disgust. Gus disappeared behind his door and returned a moment later with a small gray flip phone, handing it to Julian. He dialed his number, and it rang.

"Hello," a female answered.

"Where the fuck do you get off, taking my phone?!" Julian shouted.

Violet laughed. "Where the fuck do you get off, telling someone what I told you? I trusted you!"

"Wh—what do you want from me?!" Julian's heart fluttered and he grew nauseous. "I was scared, and I thought—"

"I trusted you with my secret! No wonder your ex fucked her brother. You must be terrible if you would drive someone to fuck their own family. Or did you just not have much down there to offer her?"

"Wh—why are you doing this?!" Julian felt the tears coming as his anger gave way to sorrow.

"Why did you survive that night? Why didn't you just lie there and die, the pathetic, miserable, blind pile you are?" She laughed as Julian cried.

"I—I want my phone back!" he sobbed.

"I—I—I want my phone back!" Violet mocked and laughed.

"What's wrong with you?! I really liked you, Violet. Why do people like you have to exist?! Why can't I meet someone who'll just accept me?!"

As Julian dropped to his knees and cried, Violet kept laughing. Gus heard everything, and even he joined in, adding, "What a whiney little faggot!"

Julian let the phone fall from his hand, still hearing Violet laughing on the other end. *Why did I survive? I just want to die!* He curled up in a ball, covering his ears and closing his eyes as he imagined everyone who'd ever hurt him hovering over him and laughing, like Gus and Violet, while he just wanted the torture to stop.

"Julian?" Violet's voice calmly echoed. "Hey you!" She spoke again, soft and sweet. Julian opened his eyes and nearly jumped off his mattress, holding his chest, breathing heavily, and covered in a thin layer of sweat. Violet sat on the recliner, wide-eyed and smiling at him. "Hey you," she whispered. "Did you have a bad dream?"

"Yeah," he gasped. "You could say that." He rubbed his eyes and looked towards the window, observing only darkness through the cracks. The fluorescent light in the kitchen shone dimly and he saw his phone and glasses where he'd left them. "What time is it?" he asked while putting on his round specs.

"It's almost seven, I think."

With so many questions on his mind, Julian sighed in relief, thanking God it was only a nightmare. He cleared his throat and asked, "What was all that about earlier?"

"Last night I saw something in you I never have with anyone else. I was having so much fun, I lost track of time. That never happens to me. I never meant to scare you, but unfortunately, with my kind, scaring people is inevitable."

"But you threatened to kill me. I mean, I thought I was good to you."

"You were amazing, I promise."

"Then why did you threaten me?"

"Because exposure to sunlight would literally kill me, and I got scared. I didn't know how else to keep you from persisting."

"But don't you realize how crazy that sounds? The sun can't just kill you."

"It'll kill me and others like me."

"Others?" Julian raised an eyebrow.

"Yes, there are others like me. There's not as many as there used to be, but there are others who have the same gifts I do."

"What gifts?"

"If I just said it, you would think I was insane."

"You already proved that you can read my mind. That's insane enough, but you were invading my privacy. What's to stop you from knowing everything I do?"

"You're right. Technically, I did, and I could, but I can't help it. I was attracted to your vibrations and energy. I can't really explain it, but I've felt it before. Your pain and sadness broke my heart. I admit, I let my mind wander through yours, and before class was over, I wanted to know everything about you, but I wanted to find out by you telling me." Her confession was chilling, but her honesty was the opposite.

Julian's curiosity piqued. "Did you already know who I was when you sat behind me?"

"Yes."

He smiled as he stood, stretched, and yawned. "So, you said you wanted to show me something and change my life. What did you mean?"

"I'll show you." She winked and smiled as if she had a secret and was bursting at the seams to share it. "Come to New York with me, tonight, and you'll see."

"Tonight?! I can't afford to—"

"It won't cost you anything, I promise."

"Violet, I'd love to, but I got class Monday afternoon."

"We'll be back Monday morning."

"How are we going to get there—fly?"

"Yes."

"But plane tickets are expensive. I'm not going to make you buy me one, especially if we're only going to be there a couple of days."

"We're not taking a plane, but don't worry about that."

"You mean, we're taking a helicopter?!"

Violet cupped her hands over her mouth, laughing. "You're just too adorable." Julian blushed. "Come with me," she said, taking his hand in hers. "I think you'll like what you see."

"What are we going to do in New York?"

"We're going clubbing."

"Clubbing?" he said. "We're in Las Vegas, and you want to fly all the way to New York so we can go clubbing?"

"It's not just any club. It's my father's club and my home, Leviticus."

"The club is called Leviticus?"

"Yes, Leviticus, the home of the forsaken."

"Interesting. Is it a goth club or something?"

"You could say that," she chortled. "It's a place where the unwanted are wanted, and dreams become reality. So, will you come with me?" She batted her brown almond eyes and playfully nagged. "You'll have the time of your life, I promise."

Finally, he gave in. "Can I take a shower first?"

"Of course you can!"

"I wanted to tell you something first." He took a deep breath, remembering the events of the horrific nightmare. "Y—you might already know this, but when you were in the bathroom earlier, I talked to my friend, Daryl, and told him what happened."

"I heard."

His heart skipped a beat. "I—I was scared, and I—"

"It's okay." She gently tightened her grip on his hand. "I told you, I usually don't go into people's homes nor lose track of time so easily. I was also scared, and I am so sorry. You had every right to reach out to your friend."

"You're not mad?"

"Of course not. You did nothing wrong." She smiled and released his hand. "Now, go take a shower and gather an extra change of clothes if you'd like. Then we'll go."

"If you want, you can watch TV while I'm in there. I'll be right back." Julian gathered some clothes and showered. After he finished, he dried off in front of the steamed bathroom mirror, watching his thin gut nervously pump with each breath. He put on blue jeans and a buttoned, black polyester shirt with red thorns trimming the short sleeves and tail before grabbing an extra change of clothes.

He opened the bathroom door to find Violet sitting in silence. She smiled and examined him head to toe, squeezing her narrow nostrils and sniffing twice. "You look so handsome, and you smell great!"

Julian blushed and said, "Thanks." He took his keys and unplugged his phone from the charger, slipping them into his pocket before replacing the schoolbooks in his bag with the extra clothes and a spare phone charger. Finally, he put on his leather jacket and sneakers. "I'm ready whenever you are," he said.

"Alright then, let's go." Julian took a deep breath and followed Violet out the door, unsure what may come next, but ready to embrace it regardless.

Chapter Seven

As Violet's Firebird soared down the freeway, Julian sat quietly, pondering many questions until he finally cleared his throat and broke the silence. "How'd you learn to read minds?"

"Let's just say something happened to me one night, a long time ago."

"B—but what—"

"Just wait. I know that's a tall order, but as I said at your apartment, you won't believe me unless I show you."

"I understand, but you're leaving me in the dark, and I'm a little nervous."

"I know, but don't be afraid. I swear I am not going to hurt you, and it will all make sense soon. Let things happen little by little. You of all people should know: the ego can only handle so much at once. Besides, 'actions speak louder than words,' they say."

Julian chuckled. "That's what I tell my grandpa whenever he pretends like he did nothing wrong. His actions proved more than his words ever could."

"He sounds like a narcissist and a bully," she said.

"Sometimes I feel like I brought it on myself."

"How so?"

"The last few years of my grandma's life, she was frequently in and out of the hospital with COPD. The closer her death came, the more she was admitted, because of her breathing problems. Just like they hated my father, my family also despised Faith. They saw her for who she was, a user and master manipulator, I'll give 'em that, but I was lonely and blinded by infatuation. I didn't care what anyone else thought. Faith was my first relationship, and for a time, it was good; until she showed her true colors as an emotionally— and sometimes physically—abusive control freak."

"So, they didn't like her. That wasn't your fault. Why blame yourself for wanting to be happy?"

"Faith and I wanted children. For the first few years, we tried, but nothing happened. It turned out she had polycystic ovaries and needed to take medicine to ovulate. Once she could get pregnant, Faith decided she didn't want my child anymore because my RP could be passed on, since it's hereditary."

"What?!" Violet gasped. "Seriously? Is she really that dense to have kids with her brother and think they wouldn't be more fucked up than a child with your eye condition?"

"Well, Travis is actually her half brother. They have the same mother, but different fathers."

"Tow-may-tow, tow-motto," she quipped. "It doesn't matter. One is just as bad as the other."

"Yeah … I'm ashamed of myself for being so stupid. Even before Travis came along, Faith got her wish. She manipulated her grandma into getting her a loan to get the fertility treatments and buy donor sperm. Once she had everything she needed, Faith had her first child, Michael. Even though he wasn't mine, I signed the birth certificate because I still wanted to be his dad."

"You're a father?!"

"I was, and I genuinely tried. I got up with him every morning. Faith was always too strung out on Xanax from the day before to get out of bed and help me. I loved the little guy, and he loved me. His first word was 'Dada.' For two years, I treated him like gold and never cared that he wasn't mine."

"So, what happened?"

"In early two-thousand-thirteen, Faith took Michael and left me alone in the house her dad was letting us live in. She moved in with her ninety-year-old grandma. Faith had gastric bypass surgery a few months earlier, and it made her sick. She said I couldn't take care of them both, even though that's what I was doing all along. Sometimes she took Michael and me to the park so I could spend time with him, but she wouldn't even get out of the car."

"Around the time my mother died, Travis got out of prison after serving seven years for God knows what. He and Faith lost touch as children, and when they reunited as adults, it was all over for me. They found each other on social media, and she started ditching me to spend time with him. She'd flake on me when I needed to go to the doctor, grocery store, or anywhere else for that matter. Sometimes they'd call and taunt me on the phone with Michael right there, hearing everything they said."

"Some mother," Violet added.

"This went on for two years, and no one I turned to cared. Despite their relationship as siblings, I knew something wasn't right. They showed up at my door one day, and Travis told me I had a month to get out. Faith was with him, but she wouldn't even look at me. 'It's no wonder your father killed himself, faggot,' Travis mocked and laughed at me. 'If you were my son, I would've done the same.' Faith told him all my secrets like they were a joke to her." A tear rolled down Julian's cheek, and he wiped it away.

"Did you leave after that?"

"Yes. I moved in with Hank for the summer of fifteen, but just before my thirty-fourth birthday, things got worse. Hank and I never got along. Between his hateful, drunken resentment, and everything else, I also started drinking heavily for a while. One night, I was drunk and got on the internet, asking Faith's older sister, Carol, if Michael was okay. She told me to forget about him and move on. I became enraged and verbally ripped her apart with every dark insult I could muster. After the fact, she took me to court for internet harassment, and I had to serve fifteen days in jail."

"Oh my God! Are you serious?"

"Yeah, and to beat it all, Carol told me because she's a Christian, she forgave me—but she took me to court anyway." He snickered at the irony. "Luckily, jail wasn't that bad. The other inmates knew I didn't belong there and even took my poor eyesight into account."

"Well, that's good."

"The day I got out, Faith called me. She broke down and cried, saying 'You don't know what I've been through this summer.' She said Travis and one of their cousins got drunk and high one night, stole an ATV, and vandalized a church. Then Travis wrecked the ATV into a parked car. Faith told me the cousin who was involved named her as a third suspect to lighten his sentence. She said she needed a lawyer and was desperate."

"And let me guess," Violet grumbled. "You went back to her?"

"I did. I was weak, soft, and stupid, just like my grandpa raised me to be, but I felt bad for her. So I used the opportunity as an attempt to save the family I spent eleven years building, but it was all a lie. Faith never needed a lawyer. She had me giving her my entire disability check every month for legal counsel, but it was for Travis. I was suspicious of the two all along and I finally questioned the nature of their relationship. 'That's sick! I would never fuck my brother,' she said at first. She acknowledged it was disgusting and wrong, but she could no longer hide her baby bump. One day, she finally started opening up to me about it. She said, 'There was this one time, I accidentally sucked his dick.'"

"What the fuck?!" Violet laughed so hard she swerved on the highway and nearly choked on a lack of air.

"Yeah. 'Accidentally?' I asked. 'What'd you do, trip and fall on it, and say, 'Well, since I'm already down here, I might as well suck it?'"

"That's sick," Violet said.

"Eventually she admitted everything. Apparently, her weight-loss surgery resolved her polycystic ovaries, and she got pregnant. That's when I tried to kill myself. I wrote 'No love' on the wall above my head with a magic marker, intending her to find me that way. But when I woke up, I knew it wasn't my time, and I left for good. You should have seen how Faith cried when I told her where I was going. She was devastated."

"Sadly, I never got to see Michael when Faith conned me into coming back. Nobody in her family knew I was there. To this day, Michael calls Travis 'Dad.' Since he was only two the last time he saw me, I imagine he doesn't even know I exist."

"That is so sad," Violet said and gently rubbed Julian's shoulder. "I have tried wrapping my mind around it since I was a child, but I don't know how anyone could bring themselves to have sex with their family. It's tragic!"

"What's tragic is Faith still doesn't take care of him. Her aunt is Michael's legal guardian now. The whole family harassed me until I gave up my parental rights. They wouldn't let me see him after I left, but they wanted my money anyway. I had to pay child support he never got, until Faith was finally busted for welfare fraud six months ago. After she and Travis had their second child together, and to keep the paternity of their first one a secret, Faith claimed I was the father. Travis got out of jail, but he went back again, and

Faith was too lazy to get a job and support their little mutants on her own. If social services knew her children were products of incest, who knows what they would do? So, I was forced to take a DNA test and prove I wasn't the father. It was humiliating and hurtful, but she eventually got caught after I spoke to the right people."

"Good!" Violet exclaimed. "That fucking cunt deserves whatever she gets for what she did to you." After clearing her throat and softening her tone, she said, "I'm sorry, I know language like that isn't very ladylike of me, but I grew up a tomboy on a plantation. I may be a Georgia peach, but I cuss like a sailor and call it like I see it."

"It's fine." Julian turned his attention to the bright strip in the distance while noting the heavy traffic on the opposite side of the freeway, thinking *she's a cunt, alright. So why can't I forget about her?*

"Do you still love her?"

"What?! I ... umm ..."

"Yeah, you still love her." Violet gently patted his knee. "I understand. You were together eleven years, and as sick and twisted as she is, we cannot help who we love."

"I know. I love the idea of ... of who I *thought* she was in the beginning, but not who she became. I often ask myself how I ever loved her. We were never right for each other, but we were stubborn—and I was so scared to be alone, I put myself through hell for codependency."

"You were just lost, lonely, and so desperate to have someone in your life, you'd go dumpster diving to feel something, good or bad. What she did wasn't your fault."

"No, but it was my fault I put her before my family," he said, fixating on the long strip of bright lights in the distance.

"How?"

"My mom and grandma always wanted to meet Michael. By the time he was born, I couldn't drive anymore. We lived in Central Virginia, four hours from Gunnar. Before Michael was born, Faith took me to see my family at Christmas and other occasions, but they never visited me. She said if they wanted to see him bad enough, they could've made the drive for once."

"But why was Faith so hellbent? I get that she was probably frustrated, but why keep two grandmothers from seeing their grandchild?"

"My mom was a careless drunk, and she had hepatitis C. She was always falling, getting cut, and hurting herself. She even gave it to Hank. She claimed she got it from a blood transfusion after Bill stabbed her, but it was probably from something drug related."

"So, Faith didn't want to take a chance on infecting the baby? I can understand that, but what did your grandmother do?"

"Nothing. My mom even had to go to the hospital at UVA in Charlottesville every few months because she was so sick. Whether before Michael's birth or after, they never bothered to stop and see me, or any of us. They drove through Staley, where we lived, every time, and if they wanted to see him, they would've put in the effort. They knew I couldn't drive and had no control of the situation."

"They never got to meet Michael, did they?" Violet asked while stomping the gas pedal and speeding up to pass a few slower cars on the freeway.

"No, they didn't." He lowered his head again and swallowed a lump. "Then, when my grandma died, no one even told me. In her final months, I knew she was getting sicker, but I didn't know how sick. No one told me anything, just that she was in the hospital. Sometimes I wasn't even sure if they were telling me the truth or not. Then came the day it happened. It was a Friday in June or July. I can't even remember which month anymore. I just got out of my group therapy session that Faith insisted I took. She let me listen to a voicemail message my aunt, Bobbi-Jo, left on her phone—because I wasn't allowed to have one of my own."

"What did she say?"

"She said, 'Julian, your grandma wanted me to call and tell you she loves you and forgives you.' Bobbi-Jo's voice was a little sad, but I didn't realize it was because my grandma just died within the hour. She didn't tell me that part."

"Why would she do that?"

"Because somebody didn't want me there. It might've been because they knew Faith would be the only way I could get there, and my grandma hated her. I mean, it was my grandpa who gave

Faith's phone number to Bobbi-Jo. I can't even recall a single conversation or interaction I ever had with my aunt, unless I spoke first, or somebody told her to tell me something. But there she was, rubbing it in my face. That was the only reason she called."

"Is Bobbi-Jo your mother's sister?"

"Sister-in-law. She's my uncle Clint Senior's third wife."

"Either way, she shouldn't have done that. You loved your grandmother, didn't you?"

"Yeah. She went along with everything my grandpa said, but she loved me and practically raised me. She treated me better than anyone in the family did. My grandpa and uncle ridiculed her for showing me such empathy and tenderness. 'You're too easy on him.' 'Stop babying him,' they'd say. She was more like my real mother. Then I met Faith, and everything changed." As Julian sulked, Violet's tender touch briefly caressed the side of his hand, offering some comfort.

"You said Bobbi-Jo said your grandmother forgave you. What did she forgive you for?"

"Although I wasn't sure the extent of her health, I knew she didn't have long left. I could have been there, but what could I have done? I called the hospital the day before she died and spoke with a nurse who told me my grandma couldn't talk. I asked the nurse to tell her I love her, I was sorry for not being there, and for all that went wrong after Michael was born."

"So, she called to tell you your grandmother loved and forgave you, after she passed, and didn't even tell you she was dead?"

"Yeah."

"How do you know she was already dead when she called you?"

"My grandpa slipped and told me a few months ago. I last saw my aunt and uncle at his house on Thanksgiving two years ago. After my grandma died, none of them would talk to me. I even apologized for anything I might have done to offend them. Bobbi-Jo and Clint Senior told me they had no problem with me, but Clint Junior—my idiot jock cousin—would 'kick my ass' if he ever saw me again. Even my grandpa told me it was big of me to apologize to them, even though he knew what they did. Now they know I know the truth, and they still won't talk to me."

"So, because of your aunt, you didn't get to say goodbye to your grandma at all?"

"No. Since I didn't know, Faith and I took Michael to the beach in South Carolina that Sunday. Later that night, when we finally made it to the hotel, I texted my grandpa and asked him how she was doing. He told me she died on Friday, and her funeral was the next morning if I wanted to come."

"No one bothered telling you at all that weekend?"

"No, not until we just got to the beach and put a very cranky one-and-a-half year old to bed and were able to rest ourselves. We were on the road all day and exhausted."

"Wow … just wow." Violet's voice broke and like Julian, she sounded as if she could cry.

"I remember bursting into tears and telling Faith, 'My grandma's dead.' She asked me if I wanted to go to the funeral, which we probably could have just made if we woke the baby, packed all our shit, reloaded the car, and drove all night, assuming Faith didn't pass out at the wheel and kill us all."

"What'd you say?"

"'No.' I said no because of the hassle. I was angry and hurt they could do that to me. I also knew Faith would do something, anything to mess it up for me. She always did. No matter what I tried to do, she'd always have an excuse; pretending she was sick, faking a panic attack—anything to get her way. There was no point in arguing with her. She'd only gaslight me if I did." Feeling the guilt wash over his entire body, tears instantly poured down Julian's face and he sobbed. "Rather than even try, I said no. Then, I faced the consequences."

"What consequences?"

"My mother thought I turned against the family. She was already dying from cirrhosis of the liver, and the decades of alcohol abuse ruined her memory and all sense of herself. The last two times I spoke with my mom on the phone, she and Hank threatened to kill me if they ever saw me again. She died two months later, on December twentieth, Michael's second birthday, and only two days shy of her fifty-third birthday. No one ever told her the truth. After everything she did to me, she died hating me, never knowing why I wasn't there."

"Did you go to her funeral?"

"No. Faith laid a guilt trip on me about missing Christmas with her and Michael. Besides, after all she said and did to me over the years, I didn't want to."

"I can understand that. Do you feel guilty for not saying yes to Faith, about your grandmother?"

"I do now," he muttered. "It wasn't my grandma's fault, and I feel like I let my anger towards them outweigh my love for her."

Violet placed her hand on Julian's thigh. "It's not your fault. Do you hear me? You tried to do what you thought was best, and you cannot blame yourself for what any of them did to you. One day they will face judgment."

"Yeah," he groaned. "That's what I've said all along. I am a cliché Libra and believe in justice. They deserve their karma."

"In the end, everyone pays a karmic debt, good and bad," she said.

"After my *Ayahuasca* experiences, I confronted my grandpa with everything he did, and he hasn't been the same towards me since. He knows what he did, and how it made me feel, but he doesn't care. He shuts down and gaslights me as if it's all in my head. If anyone deserves their karmic debt, it's him and my aunt."

"So, do you miss Virginia?" Violet asked, changing the subject.

"I miss Daryl. He was the only real friend I had. I mean, the Appalachian Mountains are beautiful, but otherwise, the only other fond memories I have are of spending time at one of my other aunt and uncle's mini-mansion. I loved that house and spent a lot of time there when I was little, before they left it behind and moved to Richmond. Otherwise, I hated it there."

"At least you had that, somewhere fun to explore, and a friendship that's lasted so long. That's rare, especially nowadays."

"Yeah, I don't know what I would've done without Daryl. He was like a big brother and we were usually always together, especially when my mom was with Bill. Not long after my mom abandoned me, and I moved in with my grandparents, Daryl's parents got divorced. He moved with his dad to Kentucky, and we lost touch."

"He was there for you exactly when you needed him to be. The universe gives us what we need when we need it. That's why you survived your suicide attempt. It wasn't your time, and the universe had to break you to fix you."

"Yeah, that's how I got here and found the *Ayahuasca*, and you," he said, sensing Violet's eyes on him.

"You're a survivor and an inspiration! I know you're writing a book about your life. Think of what it could do for others who went through the things you did. It could give them hope."

"That's something else I took from the *Ayahuasca*, using my experiences to write my book for my own healing, and to help others."

"What if someone were ready to end it all, but they read your book and decided life was worth living?"

"It would be nice, but I'd just be scared no one would read it."

"Go for it anyway. What're you avoiding?" Violet giggled as she merged off the freeway.

"Mommy issues," Julian said and they both laughed.

"You lack confidence in yourself. After everything you've been through, it's understandable, but you are a total rock star, and you don't even see it."

"I wish," he chuckled. "That was my dream when I was younger, to stand on stage, larger than life, with everyone worshipping me."

"I know."

"Yeah, I guess you would," he teased.

"Dreams come true for those who deserve it, trust me."

As they passed beneath a stream of bright red lights, Julian caught his first peak of Violet since leaving the apartment. Her narrow, curved chin and pointy little nose were those of a princess, in his eyes. *I could stare at you forever*. Violet placed her palm over her lips and blushed.

She turned onto the strip, with the Vegas Parliament close enough for Julian to see it. "I thought we were going to the airport," he said.

"I never said that."

"But aren't we flying to New York?"

"Yes."

"So, what are we doing here?"

"You'll see." She pulled into the garage, claiming the same parking space as the night before. Julian took his bookbag from the floorboard and opened the door. "Follow me," Violet said. He walked alongside her until they came to a silver double-door elevator and she pressed the only button.

"Do we have to go to your room first?" he asked.

"No, we're going to the roof."

"Oh shit!" His eyes bugged out. "You have a helicopter on the roof?! Who the hell are you?!" Violet laughed as the elevator dinged and the doors opened. They entered and she hit the button for the roof.

As the doors closed, and the elevator ascended, she said, "You're about to find out."

Chapter Eight

T he shiny elevator doors opened, giving way to a clear amethyst sky. Julian shivered in the wind, adjusting his glasses and panning the nightscape. To his left, the distant tip of the Eiffel Tower peaked over the rooftop. Aside from a faint, centered white circle, and the small enclosure housing the elevator shaft, the roof was vacant. "I thought we were flying. Where's the helicopter?" he asked.

"We are, but I never said we were taking a helicopter," Violet replied.

Julian looked left to right, shrugging his shoulders, fluttering with anxiety. "What are we doing here? You didn't bring me up here to throw me off, did you?"

"What?! No! Stop being so paranoid."

"Then what's going on?"

She removed her white shawl and balled it up. "Can I put this in your bag?"

"Y—yeah, s—sure," he stuttered. She unzipped the bookbag hanging from Julian's shoulders while he asked, "How are we going to get there?"

"I told you before, I have abilities," she mumbled, stuffing the shawl inside the bag.

"Yeah?" Julian watched Violet's silhouette tucking her long hair into the back of her dress.

"Listen," she exhaled. "Don't freak out, but I'm going to do something, but before I do, I want you to relax, okay?"

Julian's stomach churned and he took a few steps back, ready for anything. "Wh—what are you going to do?"

"Don't be mad, but I've wanted to do this for a while, and frankly …" She turned towards the nearby ledge, grinning. "I just can't resist." She charged full blast towards the edge of the roof.

"Violet?!" Julian shouted as he watched her swan dive off the side of the Vegas Parliament. "What the fuck!!!" He hobbled towards the edge, but before he could take more than three steps, Violet soared above the ledge, laughing like a child and hovering in midair with the bottom of her dress flapping in the wind. There were no strings, smoke, or mirrors holding her up, and it was not an illusion.

"How's this for a rooftop ride?!" she giggled. Julian stumbled and fell backward, landing on the same sore spot as the night before.

"H—how?!" he gasped. *Is this real? Am I dead? Is she God?*

Violet landed at his feet and helped him up. "I told you: I had to show you instead of just telling you."

"Wh—what the h—hell are you?!" Julian shouted. "Y—you scared the fuck out of me!"

Violet smirked. "I'm sorry, I shouldn't have done that, but the Aries in me couldn't resist."

"You crazy bitch!" he shouted, but instantly regretted it. "You—you could've just shown me another way!" He placed a hand over his rapidly beating heart, trying to catch his breath.

"I know, but you're fun to fuck with. Besides, you need to toughen up some." She winked and poked his nose. "So, shall we?" She extended her hand to the sky.

"What?! You—you mean fly?!" His gut rumbled louder, and Violet giggled while slowly nodding her head. "I—I don't know about that."

"Why not? You said you flew to California last month."

"Yeah, in a fucking airplane!"

"If you hold on to me, it's just as safe, and much faster, I might add."

"Am I supposed to ride piggyback?" Julian's body trembled. "I—I mean, won't I weigh you down?"

"I'm stronger than I look."

"What are you?!"

Violet sighed. "That's what I'm taking you to New York for. That is what I want to show you."

"Why me, though?"

"Because you are wonderful, and the trust you gave me today moved mountains. I also promised you the time of your life and answers, and you deserve them both."

"But why?"

"Why ask so many questions? Why not just follow the rabbit?"

"How long will it take us to get there?"

"Thirty minutes, maybe."

"What?! Only thirty minutes?! How fast do you fly?"

"Fast enough." She grinned. "You'll need to keep your eyes shut and put your glasses in your pocket or bag unless you want to lose them."

"This ... whoa!" Julian tried to find the words. "It—it's just all—"

"Weird? I know, but it's okay to feel the way you do." She took his hand. "All I'm asking is for you to trust me again."

"Okay. I—I will."

"Breathe through your nose," she said. "Also, you can rest your head on my shoulders, but keep your eyes closed and don't accidentally fall asleep. If you need me to stop, squeeze me with your knees, alright?"

"O—okay," he said, uncertain.

"You need to be alert and hold on tight," she insisted. "We'll be moving so fast that if you fall, my odds of finding and catching you are slim to none." As she released his hand, Julian trembled harder. "I know it sounds scary, but if you just hold onto me, you'll be fine."

"That's reassuring." He nervously chuckled, minding his cautious heart pounding beneath his ribcage.

She nodded and spun around. Julian took a step towards her and placed his arms around her skinny shoulders. At 5'9", he nearly towered over her. Violet stood roughly 5'4", the same height as both his mother and Faith. "Don't forget your glasses." Julian removed his round specs and placed them in his jacket pocket. "Are you ready?" she asked

He took a deep breath and mumbled, "I—I guess."

"Okay, here we go." Julian's feet imperceptibly lifted from the surface, then they slowly rose high above the strip. He wanted to look down but was too scared.

"Alright," she said over her shoulder. "We are going to go fast now. We should be there in thirty minutes. Just stay calm, close your eyes, and breathe normally through your nose."

"Okay," he muttered. *Dear God, please let me survive this.*

Like lightning, they were gone in a flash. All became cold and empty. A loud cracking sound, like breaking glass, grew to high pitch squeals. They broke barriers beyond sound, and although he never looked, Julian saw it all with his third eye. He was discovering the impossible, and like an onion, reality and his ego were peeling away in layers. *What's real? What's not? What is she? What am I?* As if no time had passed, they came to a stop. A newfound warmth overtook Julian's body, soothing what he'd endured. Then they gently touched solid ground and he opened his eyes.

After catching his breath, he turned his head away and vomited. "You're okay," Violet assured, placing her hand on his back. "It's normal." Julian heaved another time or two before catching his breath and clearing his throat. The taste of bile gave way to a familiar scent on the breeze, one he could never forget. The garlicky aroma of pizza and Chinese food combined and filled his nostrils. For a moment, he forgot everything, losing himself in a happier occasion from his past. Under other circumstances, he would have enjoyed it more, but now his gut scowled.

"Welcome to New York!" Violet said.

Julian observed his dark surroundings. "This is so fucking crazy!"

"Pretty cool, huh?" Violet giggled.

"None of this is logical! Something happened to me when I took the *Ayahuasca*, d—didn't it?" He wobbled and lost his balance, but Violet caught and stabilized him. "Everything's changed, and I—I don't even know what's real."

"You're okay, Julian. Just breathe. In through your nose"— Violet inhaled through her nose to demonstrate—"and out through your mouth." She slowly exhaled through her puckered lips, and Julian did the same. "You're waking up," she said. "You're letting go of what no longer serves you and what your ego refused to believe."

"So, how was it, Hell Belle?" the bartender asked. Her freckled, rosy cheeks lifted as she grinned. "How was college?"

"Not even a hello first, Anna?" she asked, speaking with a Scottish accent.

"Excuse me, love. Perhaps I shoulda kissed your arse first?" Anna teased and the women shared a laugh.

"It was fun," Violet said, glancing at Julian on her left.

Anna smiled. "Who's your new friend?"

"This is Julian. We met in class."

Anna nodded at Julian. "'Ello, I'm Anna."

"It's nice to meet you," Julian returned her smile.

"Is anyone in the kitchen yet?" Violet asked.

"Eric's back there. Why, you hungry, Julian?"

"Yeah," he said.

"Alright then, love. Let me get you a menu." She walked to the end of the bar and returned with a laminated white menu.

"Thank you," he said.

"Mmhmm," Anna nodded.

"Can you see it?" Violet leaned forward to assist him as he squinted his eyes, trying to focus on the small print.

"How much is a cheeseburger with everything on it?"

"I told you not to worry about it, Jul, I got it," she said.

"Are you sure?"

"Yes, I'm sure. It's my treat."

Anna nodded and asked, "Would you like anything else, love … a drink perhaps?"

"Can I get a sweet tea?"

"Alright then. Let ne tell Eric, and I'll get it right out."

"Thank you," he said before turning to Violet. "What about you? Aren't you hungry?"

"Yeah, but I got my own thing in my apartment. I also need to take a shower."

"Do you want me to bring my food with me, or …?"

"No, you can stay down here and eat. I just wanted to get you squared away first. Is that alright? I won't be gone long."

"Nobody will bother me, will they?"

"No, but if anyone asks, tell them you're my friend. Anna will be right here. Just don't wander off or anything. Do you want me to take your jacket and backpack up to my room with me?"

"Okay." He unstrapped the bag from his shoulders and removed his jacket.

"Okay," Violet repeated. "You eat, then we can go upstairs, and I'll introduce you to my father."

He nodded and cleared his throat. "Listen, I don't know what the hell is happening, and this might sound crazy, but there's something I wanted to ask you. Am I dead?"

Violet laughed. "What do you mean, 'dead'?"

"Sometimes I feel like the night I tried to kill myself, I succeeded."

"Why would you think that?"

"Because it should only take fifteen of those pills to kill someone, and I took over fifty. When I was in my second night with *Ayahuasca*, I had this vision—and a feeling—that I am trapped in hell, and it's up to me to work my way out."

"Wow! That's deep, but no. You're not dead. I told you before, you survived because it wasn't your time. As for all this, you're just being slowly let in on a secret you never knew was possible." As Julian tipped his head in confusion, Violet winked and patted his thigh. "Now, I'm gonna go upstairs for a few, but I'll be back shortly. Then, I would love to hear more about your *Ayahuasca* experience, and I'm sure Dad would too."

"Yeah, sure," he said. Violet smiled and nodded as Anna approached with Julian's burger and tea.

"Hey, Anna, Julian is visually impaired, and since we're about to open, could you keep an eye on him 'til I get back?"

"Yeah, no worries," she replied, setting Julian's drink and plate down in front of him. He licked his lips at the sight of the thick cheeseburger with all the trimmings, surrounded by a hot batch of fries. "Enjoy, love!" Julian smiled and nodded in thanks.

"I'll be back, Jul," Violet said, headed towards the open doors.

Julian picked up the big, juicy burger and took a bite, smiling and thinking, *goddamn, that's good!*

Chapter Nine

The clock struck eleven and the doorway to the night's redemption opened to the public. Julian sat at the glowing bar, having finished his delicious meal. He watched the trendy, goth-clad patrons filling the room in eager anticipation of being part of something different. Loud heavy metal blared over the house speakers while Anna became busy nearby, tending the long line of customers looking for a bite or dose of liquid courage. As Julian waited for Violet to return, he wondered, *what if she doesn't come back and I end up stuck here?* It had been roughly thirty minutes since she'd left, but like a puppy with separation anxiety, it felt like an eternity.

A bald man with a dark mustache and goatee took a seat on the stool to Julian's right, where Violet had sat before. He wore a tacky blue suit and tie. Julian took one look at the guy and immediately thought of Faith's brother, Travis, of the same dead-eyed expression, and his heart instantly sank.

The man stared at Julian, making him even more uncomfortable. He tried to avoid eye contact, but then the man spoke in an unrecognizable accent. "Have I seen you here before?"

"No, sorry. This is my first time." Julian smiled, trying to be polite, but the man maintained the same blank stare. Julian fidgeted in the stool, growing nervous and impatient, wanting to tell the man to stop staring, but instead tolerating it.

"Are you sure?" the man persisted.

"It wasn't me," Julian replied. "I don't even live in New York."

"Where do you live?" he asked, speaking in a low raspy volume, barely above the loud music.

"Las Vegas."

"Ah, Sin City," he dead-panned. "You must know Violet." The man rolled his eyes.

Julian's ears perked, hearing the name. *He knows Violet. How bad can he be?* "Yeah, she's my friend."

"Apparently, she's everybody's friend lately."

What the hell is that supposed to mean? "She's been really nice to me."

"I bet," he groused. "What's your name?"

Julian's internal alarm sounded off. Something did not feel right about the guy. He hesitated, then asked, "What's yours?"

"I asked you first."

"I'm Julian, a—and you are …?"

"Bern!" Anna shouted from the end of the bar. "Leave the lad alone. He's here with Violet, and I think you're creeping him out."

"Sorry, my love. I just wanted to meet the guy." He offered an exaggerated grin. "Any friend of Hell Belle's is a friend of mine."

"Don't mind Bernard, Julian," Anna interjected. "My husband's got a way of catching people off guard. He didn't mean no harm."

"Yes, Julian, I apologize," said Bernard.

Julian could not deny the unsettling, overcast vibes, but he said, "It's alright," swallowing his pride and forcing a smile. "It's nice to meet you."

"Likewise," Bernard said, extending his right hand. Julian reached out with his, and they shook. Bernard's grip was firm. "Have you known her long?"

"We met last night in a class we're taking together."

Bernard chuckled. "You two just met yesterday, and she's already brought you to New York?!" His eyes widened. "She's usually more careful about who she lets in her life, but lately …" He slowly shook his head, producing a ticking sound with his tongue against the roof of his mouth. "For her to bring you here so fast, especially after her other friend two nights ago—I don't know what's gotten into her."

"What do you mean?" Julian asked.

"Surely, you know what she's capable of, right?"

"Yeah."

"So, Julian," Bernard said slowly. "How do you think the world would react if they knew vampires existed?"

"Wait, what?!" he gasped. *Did he just say 'vampires?'*

"I said, how do you think the world would react if they knew about us?!" Bernard raised his voice, appearing to mistake Julian's confusion for not being heard over the music.

Violet can read my thoughts, fly, and she is afraid of the sun. Is she a vampire? Are they all vampires? If so, how is this possible?

"'Cause it is," Anna shouted from the other end of the bar and winked.

"What's that, my love?!" Bernard looked in her direction and shouted.

"Ah, nothing. I was just trying to remember a song I heard earlier," she said, flashing a half-grin.

What the hell is going on here?!

"Wait!" Violet suddenly appeared from behind, placing her hands atop Julian's shoulders. "What's going on?" She took the stool on Julian's left.

"Hey! There you are." Julian exhaled in relief.

"Here I am!" She giggled as Julian caught a whiff of her fresh, clean vanilla scent. Her hair was neatly brushed back, and she wore a white sundress with green vines and purple flowers printed all over.

"You look nice," he said, fixating on a silver ankh pendant dangling from a chain around her neck. "I love your necklace," he added.

"Thank you." She beamed. "So, what did I just walk into?" Violet looked at Bernard, Anna, and back at Julian.

Bernard said, "I was just telling your new friend, Julian, that you're usually more careful about who you associate with."

"Yep," Violet said shortly.

"I figured he must be pretty special if you just met him yesterday and already revealed yourself to him." Bernard grunted, panning between her and Julian, maintaining the same dead expression. "Didn't you just bring that Chloe girl in here a few nights ago?"

"Yes, and yes." She smiled before shifting her gaze to Julian. "You want to—"

"Because as I was telling young Julian here," Bernard interrupted. "It would be terrible if the public caught wind of vampires among them. You know what'll happen."

"What the hell are you trying to do, Bern?" Violet rolled her eyes in disgust. "What is this?"

"Nothing, I—"

"No!" she snarled. "You know what you're doing. You know I've had so much trouble making friends, and after Chloe, yeah, I needed to go out and enjoy myself." She took a breath and placed her hand over Julian's, resting on the glowing bar. "Fate brought us together," she said, patting his hand and grinning in Bernard's face. "Fuck me for wanting a life outside of this building, right?"

Bernard smirked. "I know the last thing we need is to expose ourselves to outsiders, and you should know it too."

"Why don't you let my father be the judge of that?"

"Am I—I not supposed to be here?" Julian asked.

"You're fine, Jul. Bernard just likes to think he knows what's best here, and sometimes he tries to make decisions that aren't his to make."

"Oi!" Anna barked from the end of the bar. "How 'bout we make the decision to calm the fuck down, eh? There're other people in here!"

Bernard nodded and said, "Very well then, my love. I have business across town, anyway." He stood and extended his hand once again to Julian. "It was nice to meet you," he said. They shook hands again, but this time, Bernard's grip was much tighter. He squeezed so hard it nearly prompted a facial reaction in Julian.

He forced a smile, saying "Likewise." *Cocksucker!* Violet chuckled. *I know you can hear me, but can Bernard?* She gently dragged her index finger along his thigh, writing "*NO.*"

"Alright then," said Bernard. "Enjoy your evening." He nodded to Anna before shrugging his nose at Violet and disappearing into the thickening crowd.

"Sorry about him," said Violet. "It's a long story. He's always got a stick up his ass about something. Just ignore him." She looked at Julian's empty plate, adding, "If you're finished eating, you want to come upstairs and meet my father?"

"Yeah, I'd like that."

"Alright, then. Take my hand and follow me." They stood and Violet led Julian through the large crowd of patrons either dancing to the music or conversing.

"Is a band playing tonight?" Julian asked, noticing all the overhead lights shining on the empty stage.

"A little later," she said. They exited the chapel and made their way back to the red hallway where people of all ages lined up against the walls, waiting for their turn to give blood.

Julian gasped—it all made sense. *Sunlight, mind reading, flying, and blood. … vampires do exist!* The revelation nearly swept him off his feet.

"Yeah, we do," Violet whispered in his ear as they squeezed through the crowd. "I just didn't want you to find out that way."

"Wh—why didn't you tell me?"

She leaned close again, whispering, "Let's wait 'til we get upstairs. Someone might hear us." They pushed past the clubgoers and entered the musty old stairwell again, climbing the steps to the fourth floor.

Violet retrieved another key and unlocked a black metal door. On the other side waited another hallway. Dingy green walls and three overhead light fixtures lay ahead. The hall was roughly twenty feet long, with two white doors centered on each side, and a black door at the opposite end.

"Are one of these rooms yours?" Julian asked, observing the shiny numbers on the doors as they passed. *40 … 41 … 42 … 43.*

"That's my apartment—number forty-three," she said. "We're going to my father's, though." She pointed at the black door on the end with two silver fours centered near the top.

"No way," Julian gasped. There it was: *44.*

"What is it?"

"You mean you don't know?"

She raised an eyebrow. "Know what?"

"The number forty-four."

"What about it?"

"In numerology, the number forty-four acts as a breadcrumb, a confirmation from the universe that you're following the right path."

"Really? I've never followed numerology, but that's interesting. Do you see the number often?"

"Yeah, I've seen it several times since the diner, but until now it was always on clocks."

"Wow! Are you serious?" Her eyes twinkled.

"Yeah. It all started after the *Ayahuasca*. I believe I tapped into a certain energy or frequency. First, I saw eleven-eleven on clocks and elsewhere. Later, I started seeing other numbers, like twenty-two, but the most common is forty-four."

"You're exactly where you need to be, Jul."

"I love that by the way: 'Jul.'" He blushed. "No one's ever called me that before."

"I know," she said. "If you think I'm gonna call you Muffin or something silly like that filthy inbreeder did, you got the wrong gal." They both laughed.

"So, Jul's a pet name?"

"No, it's a nickname. Faith treated you like a pet. Do you want me to buy you a leash and collar? Or how about a little food and water bowl?" She teasingly flicked her tongue.

"Very funny." He smirked, cleared his throat, and scratched the back of his head. "Before we meet your father, I wanted to ask you something." He and Violet locked eyes. "You drink blood, right?"

"I do."

"And you get it from the patrons here, right?"

"Yes."

He took a deep breath and asked, "Have you ever killed anyone?"

"Do you really want to know? How would you feel if I gave you the answer you don't want to hear?"

Julian grew nauseous. He shut his eyes and contemplated his next question. "Are you going to kill me?"

"No, I'm not."

"Why did you bring me here?"

She placed her hand on his chest. "When I came to Las Vegas, it was because my life was unfulfilling here. I was lonely and looking for something new. Like you were led out west by your intuition, so was I. It was fate that we met, and I knew it from the start, but when you're a vampire, you can only be open with certain people. I was so terrified to tell you about myself, and truth be told, I still am."

"Why?"

"Because you've had such a fucked up and traumatizing life, you get scared, anxious, and worked up so easily. This has all been so much for you to take in, and you are handling it so well, but now that I've gotten to know you, I'm afraid of scaring you away. I don't want that."

"What do you want?"

"I want to show you not everyone is terrible, and I wanted to do something special so you could see your potential for yourself."

Julian tipped his head in confusion. "What are you going to do?" he asked.

"It's a surprise."

"I like surprises, but I—"

"That'll come later," she interrupted. "Right now, I want you to meet my father." Julian swallowed a lump as Violet turned the knob and pushed the door open. She looked over her shoulder and said, "Follow me."

Chapter Ten

Julian followed Violet through the doorway of apartment forty-four. Upon entry, he sensed a warm, inviting presence. He panned the bright room that had shaggy white carpet, burgundy walls, but not a window in sight. On the opposite side of the room, a white Victorian sofa stretched roughly seven feet. A shallow hallway stood at the left end, and on the right sat an elegant brass chair, cushioned in red velvet, resembling a medieval throne. In the adjacent corner was a square glass coffee table.

Hanging on the wall above the sofa was an old painting of Paris at night, with the Eiffel Tower the focal point. The sky was a dying shade of turquoise, and the only light in the eerie scene came from a pale full moon in the backdrop. "That's beautiful, isn't it?" Violet asked.

"Yes, it is," Julian replied. "Your father has great taste."

"Why thank you!" said a male's voice from out of Julian's view. "It brings me pleasure when others appreciate the fine art of another time." Julian turned his attention towards the hallway, fixating on a tall, thin, and pasty figure wearing an all black suit and tie. His milky blond strands flowed long, and aside from a few loose hairs, it was all tied neatly behind his head.

"I—I try to find beauty in everything," Julian stuttered.

The man smiled. "It is a rare gift, I'm afraid, especially for those damaged like yourself." His voice was deep, but he spoke smoothly, just above a whisper. Julian tipped his head, peering at Violet as the lanky man stepped closer. Expecting someone who appeared older, Julian gasped when he saw his youthful face more clearly.

The man boasted high cheekbones, thin pink lips, and a long, narrow jawline. "My apologies," he said, extending his hand. "Where are my manners? I am Xavier Van Abarrow." As they greeted one another, Julian took note of Xavier's pleasantly tender grip.

"It's nice to meet you, sir. I'm Jul—"

"Julian Frost," Xavier interrupted. "I know." Again, Julian's eyes shifted towards Violet. Xavier smiled. "Oh, she told me nothing." He asked Violet, "How are you, my sweet?"

"You know me, Dad. I am simply divine."

"That you are, my child. I trust your psychology class went well?"

"I think so," she squeaked. Grinning ear to ear, she added, "As you can see, I made a friend."

Xavier made eye contact with Julian. "You must have questions."

"Actually, I'm still trying to process everything." Julian was in such awe of the vampire's presence his heart nearly beat out of his chest. "I've seen the impossible become possible, and while I do have questions, they are mostly about my sanity."

Xavier chuckled. "You are confused and terrified, yet humble and far braver than you think." He placed a well-groomed hand upon Julian's timid shoulder. A delicate vitality in the exchange soothed the blind man's heart. "So long, you've held dormant powers within; such fire, passion, and most of all"—he leaned close and whispered—"wrath." Xavier removed his hand and backed away as Julian quivered with chills.

"You longed for a father figure to love and teach you to be a man. Instead, you were scarred—chastised for carrying traumas beyond your control. Your family shunned your cries for decades, but that torment shaped you into who you are today."

"I …" Julian tried to speak, but the sudden revelation was too much. Steady tears fell from his eyes and blurred his vision as Xavier's blunt words cut deep, devouring his withered ego and giving way to an unresolved painful truth he needed to face.

"Are you okay, Jul?" Violet asked to which Julian slowly nodded. She took his hand and whispered, "You are so strong" in his ear.

"Your entire life, you pulled on a bowstring, lying in wait and building momentum as the tragedies of time sharpened the arrowhead. One day you will let go and tell your story. If I may be so bold, the notion frightens me," Xavier said.

Julian wiped his face, cleared his throat, and sniffled. "Wha—what do you mean?"

"Everything happens for a reason. Coincidence does not exist, only synchronicity and the law of attraction. All actions have consequences. 'We reap what we sow,' as they say." Xavier paused to offer a knowing nod and smile. "Look how different the world appears since your suicide attempt. Notice the fear and ego you released just since meeting my sweet daughter. Some would go mad witnessing someone fly, or read their mind, but not you. You trusted her because you trusted your intuition. You have a gift like few other humans in the modern world."

Unsure of what to make of the vampire's words, or how to respond, Julian settled on "It's hard for me to trust anyone."

"Because you put trust in the wrong people. You were so desperate for love and affection from others, you never learned to love or trust yourself first," the vampire said. "Unfortunately, it took many years of pain and heartache to break the cycle and discover the source of your pain. It was a difficult experience, but experience is the only schoolmaster worth having."

"Speaking of experience," Violet interjected, "I wanted to do something special for Julian. I told him I would change his life, or something to that effect."

"How sweet." Xavier smiled. "You've a heart of gold, my dear." He kissed the back of Violet's hand before turning back to Julian. "Tell me, do you have a dream?"

Julian thought for a moment, then asked, "Wouldn't you already know?"

Xavier smirked at that. "I do. However, I am asking if you do."

"I don't know … win the lottery and live like a king forever?" He chuckled, but Xavier only stared. Julian's face straightened and he said, "I guess I don't know."

"Don't worry, Jul. We'll take care of you." Violet giggled, playfully nudging him with her elbow.

"Wh—what do you mea—"

"You know, Dad," she quickly changed the subject. "Julian has taken *Ayahuasca*."

Xavier's eyes twinkled. "Do tell …" He stroked his chin, appearing intrigued.

"I took it twice. It brought the source of my pain to the surface, and overall, it showed me how to heal myself."

"And how may that be?" Xavier asked.

"To write a book about my life. It didn't occur to me until afterwards, but it became clear nonetheless."

"What was the experience itself like? What did you see?" Xavier asked.

Julian took a deep breath before clearing his throat. "On the first night, I was so nervous," he slowly began. "Beforehand, I spoke my intentions in prayer. I asked for the ability to let go of the past, to learn how to love myself, and to reveal my life purpose. And then … not long after I drank, I blacked out. Wherever the medicine took me, I entered a big room with party streamers and balloons. Everything was gold, purple, and green, like Mardi Gras. I didn't see faces but I felt welcomed by the spirits. It was like a homecoming party."

"I believe that was your ancestors," said Xavier.

"When the party began, I was in a room similar to where the ceremony was taking place. It was dark and only lit by candles."

"I thought *Ayahuasca* ceremonies took place outdoors," Xavier remarked.

"It was the middle of December and very cold outside. The shaman held the ceremony inside a cabin one of their friends owned," he said as Xavier nodded. "Not long after I was surrounded by these spirits, I was alone. The room became something more like a dark, ancient temple made of stone. I was lying face down on the floor, crying like a heartbroken child. It was then … the entire room, surrounding darkness, and even the ground disappeared. I was in a cloudy blue sky with a golden bright sun shining behind an angel." Julian smiled, remembering the loving embrace. "She looked like a biblical cliché, dressed in white, with flowing blond hair, and smiling at me. She cradled me in her arms and said, 'I am so sorry, Julian. I am so sorry I hurt you.' She comforted my inner child and just kept saying, 'I am sorry. Please forgive me.' Then, I awoke to find the shaman, Michele, holding me in her arms, whispering, 'You are safe now. You were only a frightened child who needed love.' Later I learned—while I was unconscious, I reached up for her, like a baby would for their mother."

Violet placed her hand on Julian's arm and asked, "What if that angel was your mother, trying to make amends for what she did to you?"

Julian quivered at the idea. "I thought about that, but my mom had brown hair. The angel's hair was blond, and it was not her face."

"In the astral realm, earthly appearances do not always matter," said Xavier. "She apologized and asked for your forgiveness. Violet is correct, it may have been your mother reaching out to you the only way she could."

As another revelation hit Julian, new tears formed, and he grew dizzy. He started to sit in the fancy chair but stopped himself. "Is it okay if I sit?" he sobbed.

"Please do." Xavier bowed and extended his hand.

"Thank you, sir," Julian softly whimpered.

"Please, call me Xavier. My employees call me 'sir.'"

Julian nodded and took a seat as he snorted and wiped his face with his shirt. A moment of silence passed while he collected himself and allowed reality to set in. He cleared his throat and said, "I'm okay."

Xavier took a seat on the sofa, and Violet followed. Moving on, the blond vampire asked, "What happened the second night?"

"It was more intense," Julian said in a low voice. He cringed, thinking about the foul taste of the medicine.

"Did it make you sick?" Xavier asked. "They say it makes you violently ill before anything happens."

"I vomited a little, but it was mostly dry heaves. A few others were throwing up so hard I thought they were dying a time or two. There's a certain diet you are supposed to follow a few months beforehand to prepare for it, and I don't think they took it as seriously as I did."

"With the sickness aside, you could have taken it the third night, but something scared you, did it not?"

"The second night didn't go well. Unlike the first night, where it was calm, I panicked from the start. A few minutes after I drank, several white ghostly figures started flying around me while I was still conscious. They scared me, and it triggered a panic attack. Luckily, Michele worked me through it, asking me to close my eyes and take deep breaths. Seconds later, I blacked out."

Violet leaned forward, placing her elbows atop her knees, asking, "What happened after that?"

"I found myself on a dark, empty street. Everything was colorless and grainy, like an old movie. I lay dying on the cold asphalt while many unfamiliar faces crowded my body and stared. Despite my pleas, no one helped me. Then, my grandpa appeared—naked, frail, approaching death, and quivering in fear." Julian shrugged, recalling the horror in Johnny's callous eyes.

"How did you feel?" Xavier asked.

"Scared. Even after all he's done, I was scared of losing him. After that epiphany, he vanished, and my dad's face appeared. He smiled, as if he was happy to see me at death's door. Like my grandpa, he said nothing. Instead, he also disappeared, along with the other faces. I thought I was alone, but that's when I heard my grandma Gin's voice in my ear."

"What did she say?" Xavier asked.

"She said, 'It's okay to let go, Julian. No one will hold it against you, and everyone will understand.' I don't know what she meant by that."

"Perhaps she was telling you to let go of the guilt you have carried since her death," Xavier suggested.

"I suppose you're right," Julian murmured. "At first, I thought I was dead, and my grandma was there to help me cross over. Just as I was prepared to accept my fate, a firm, invisible grip took my hand. Another voice, deep and masculine, said, 'I am here to help you.' I was lifted back to the bright, blue sky, like the night before, and was met by the angel again. She said nothing but held me while I cried in her arms."

"Wow!" Violet burst out.

"I finally opened my eyes and lay awake the rest of the night, shivering and scared shitless. The next morning, it took a pediatric chiropractor—from Saint Louis of all places—holding and comforting me for hours, assuring me I was alive, before I calmed down. After that, I wanted no part in the third ceremony."

Xavier appeared taken aback. He cleared his throat and asked, "What did you learn from all this?"

"Aside from losing all denial about how my family feels about me, and wanting to write my book, I took away an understanding that when I die, I will be welcomed with love. I will become one with the infinite again. Everything I take from this life: experiences, imagery, pain, pleasure, and so on, is to invoke ideas. I will use these ideas to create my heaven and build upon it, like a lucid dream. Although I didn't see these things, I just knew them."

"That's a very interesting theory," Xavier said. "Who is to say you are not creating such a heaven now? 'You are the medicine, brother, and you manifest your reality.' Is that not what your shaman, Michele said?"

Julian trembled, hearing the words. He said, "There's a flip side to that."

"Oh?" Xavier raised an eyebrow.

"If I am manifesting reality, who's to say anyone or anything outside my perception of reality even exists? What if neither of you are real?" He panned between the two vampires. "What if I'm not even real? Sometimes I wonder if I am nothing more than a digit of text in a computer, pulsating through a fiber-optic cable."

"It is a paradox," Xavier chuckled. "I believe we are all individually conscious, but who can truly know? Some say we are figments of God's imagination. I think the point of the game is we are not supposed to know. Therefore we use faith as a crutch."

Julian tipped his head. "What do you have faith in? I mean, aren't vampires dead?"

"We believe in free will, just like humans. Vampires can believe whatever they wish. As for this fictional theory that we are dead—" He laughed. "If I were dead, how could we have this conversation?"

"That's a good point. I guess I have a lot to learn about vampires."

"Do we scare you, Julian?" Xavier asked.

He gulped. "Honestly … a little, but if I were in danger, would I have made it this far?"

"Truth be told, if we were going to kill you, nothing we told you would matter. However, we do not kill people." Julian exhaled in relief. "Despite what fictional stories may say, not all vampires are savages. Besides, my sweet daughter likes you, as do I." Both Xavier and Violet smiled. "Believe me, Julian. I have lived in this city for two hundred years and have known many people. I do not say that lightly. So please take my generosity in stride."

Two hundred years?! Julian was stunned. "I—I won't," he stuttered. Then he looked at Violet and said, "Last night you told me you are twenty-seven. How old are you really?"

She lowered her head, muttering, "I was twenty-seven when I was given the gift. That was in nineteen-forty-four." She smiled like she knew what saying the number would mean to him.

Julian laughed at the odds. "You're one hundred and two years old?"

"I will be, in April."

He smiled, saying, "You're beautiful for your age," and she immediately blushed. "How'd it happen?" he asked.

"Another time, perhaps," Xavier said, checking a round, golden pocket watch clasped to one of the buttons on his jacket. "It's time to go downstairs and 'get the party started,' as the kids say."

Everyone stood and Violet took Julian's hand. She winked and said, "Come on, Jul. Let's go have some fun!"

Chapter Eleven

B y the time Julian, Violet, and Xavier made their way to the chapel, the club was packed, with an active dance floor, crowded tables, and a long line at the bar. The vibrant lights shining from behind the stained-glass windows digitally bathed the patrons in brilliant shades of red and gold. Violet held Julian's hand as they wiggled through the sea of people dancing, conversing, or otherwise not paying attention.

"So, who's playing tonight, anyone I've heard of?" Julian asked.

"Just the house band, but they are great," Violet replied.

Xavier leaned close, softly resting his thin, icy fingers on Julian's forearm, asking, "Would you care to accompany me to meet them?"

The vampire's touch sent chills down Julian's spine, and he shivered and nodded. Violet released his hand, saying, "You need to help him, Dad. He's legally blind and can't see good."

"I know," Xavier replied. "Do not fret, I will take good care of him. Be a dear and have a seat at our table."

"Have fun, Jul. You'll do great." Violet winked before disappearing into the crowd.

Julian tipped his head, wondering, *what the hell is that supposed to mean?* Xavier gently gripped his upper bicep and led him to a closed black door at the left of the stage. With a nod of mutual recognition to a black-clad bouncer, he opened it and Julian followed him inside a dimly lit hallway. They passed the stage entrance on the right and entered a plain, white-walled room on the left. A minibar, an old couch, and four men drinking around a folding table occupied the small dressing room.

"Hey! There he is!" one of the men joyfully shouted as he stood. He was tanned and muscular, with long, dark frizzy hair. He wore matching black leather pants and an open vest, his jacked torso exposed. The other three men raised their glasses in the air and bowed their heads.

"Good evening, gentlemen," Xavier said. "I want to introduce a friend of mine and Violet's." He put his arm around

Julian's neck and presented him to the band. "This is Julian Frost." The men greeted him with the same bowed heads and tipped glasses. Xavier pointed to the man in leather and said, "Julian, this is Peter, the lead guitarist and singer of my house band, the Black Casket Affair."

"It's nice to meet you," Julian said.

Peter smiled. His eyes were bloodshot, and he stunk of booze. "Likewise, brother!" he slurred.

Xavier took a step forward, saying, "I have a request."

"Anything, boss," replied a man with a full dark beard.

"That's Anders, the bassist," Xavier told Julian before turning back to the others. "After you finish your first song, I would like to make an announcement."

A middle-aged man with a beer belly hanging out of his black shirt asked, "Is everything alright, sir?"

"Everything is fine, Jack." He told Julian, "That is Jack, the rhythm guitarist." Xavier cleared his throat and announced, "Tonight, we are going to make Julian a rock star."

"What?!" Julian gasped.

"I said, we are going to make you a rock star," he repeated.

"What?! I mean, why?!"

"Because my daughter made you a promise. What kind of a father would I be to deny her such a request?" Julian tried to speak, but nothing came out. Xavier looked into his eyes and said, "You did a good thing for her, and I trust she already told you this, but you deserve it."

"Are—are y—you serious?" Julian stuttered. "Wha—what do you want me to sing?"

"You are a writer, yes? Sing one of yours."

The fourth bandmate spoke up. "Yeah, man, just give us an idea for a beat and a key, and we'll tear the roof off this place!" Appearing younger than the others, he had lightly tanned skin, a brown buzzcut, and his white tank top revealed two arms fully sleeved in tattoos of snakes, skulls, and women's faces. "I'm Bishop, the drummer, by the way," he said.

"Hmm …" Julian closed his eyes and thought for a moment before remembering a poem he once wrote and set to a simple chord progression. "Alright, I think I got one," he said.

Bishop smiled and asked, "Can you hum it for us?"

Julian hummed a slow, simple melody. "It's three verses. The first and third are the same."

"Alright, brother! We got you," said Peter.

As Julian's thoughts raced, he grew nervous. His heart pounded and his adrenaline pumped like gasoline. "I don't drink much anymore, but if I'm gonna do this, can I please have one?"

"Of course, brother!" Peter staggered to the minibar on the opposite side of the room, stocked with a small collection of liquor bottles and empty glasses. "What's your poison? We got whiskey … rum … tequila … vodka …" Julian cringed. Vodka was his mother's drink of choice until the day she died, and he'd always had a mental block against it.

"How about tequila?"

"Ah! I like the way you think, Joey!" He poured half a glass and handed it to Julian. "I'd offer you a chaser, but we don't do that here," he snickered.

Julian grinned. "It's fine," he said. "And my name is Julian but thank you." He turned up the glass and practically chugged the nearly three shots. "Thanks, I needed that!"

"One more thing, gentlemen," Xavier added. "Julian is visually impaired—he cannot see well. So, if he requires assistance on stage, please try to help him." All four men nodded.

Oh my God … this is crazy! Julian was both ecstatic and frightful but also feeling something he never thought he would again: alive. He looked at the empty glass and asked, "Could I get one more, please? … Maybe a little extra this time?" He smirked, already feeling the warm and fuzzy effects of the first drink.

Peter filled the glass to the top. "Sip on this one, brother." He checked his wristwatch and turned to his bandmates. "Alright boys, it's about that time!" The others proudly stood from their chairs and filed towards the door, primed and ready to hit the stage. The energy became electric as the drunken front man howled, then screeched, "Let's do this!" One by one, the four musicians exited the room, and moments later were met by a sudden eruption from the eager audience in the chapel.

"Come, Julian," Xavier said, motioning him forward. "We can wait at the side of the stage until they finish their first song." Julian took a sip from the glass and followed Xavier out of the dressing room and across the hallway into a dark backstage area.

The band's equipment was ready on stage and red spotlights blared from above. At least a thousand people were jammed inside the chapel, roaring in content as the men approached their instruments. Peter took his guitar from its stand and unnaturally growled into the microphone. "Good evening, lovely devils! We are the Black Casket Affair, and you are all here because you're filthy sinners!" The crowd ate it up, screaming in approval.

First came a drumbeat, followed by the bass, rhythm guitar, and finally Peter's drowning riffs and vocals. Julian swayed side to side while mindful of his beverage.

Once the song ended, he silently prepped himself. *You can do this! Be a man!* Xavier took his free hand and led him up a few steps to the stage, then indicated that he should wait there at stage right. His heart blasted as he looked at all the smiling faces of excited people below. He scanned the tables along the stone walls at the back of the chapel, looking for Violet, but could not spot her.

Peter stepped away from the microphone as Xavier approached. The earsplitting crowd instantly fell silent for their hero. He smiled down on everyone. "How are you doing tonight, my lovely sinners?!" A sudden boom from the onlookers rocked the chapel in answer. "Thank you, thank you. ... I just wanted to come up and quickly say a few words if I may, because we have a special treat for you."

Xavier extended his right hand and motioned Julian forward. Holding the half-empty glass, he slowly made his way to center stage. "We have somebody who came all the way from Las Vegas to be here tonight," Xavier continued. "He wants to sing you a song because he loves you as much as I do!" Again, the crowd went wild as Julian grinned, goosebumps covering him head to toe. The moment was surreal; he pinched himself to make sure it was not a dream.

"They say this man is a wordsmith, with a silver tongue and a beautiful voice." As Xavier praised, Julian blushed. "And by the way, ladies, he is single." Chuckling, Xavier cupped a hand to the side of his mouth like he had a secret to tell. "And from what I hear, he is great in the sack." He winked to the crowd, and Julian's jaw dropped. An endless number of beautiful women near the stage, the type he would never expect a first glance from, were already flashing him *fuck me* eyes.

As he stood motionless, a shriek echoed from the rear of the chapel, pinging him back to reality. He adjusted his glasses and squinted before he finally spotted her. Violet sat behind a round table in the back-right corner. He could not see her face, but she was waving her arms. *You can do this*, he reassured himself.

"Ladies and gentlemen, show some New York love for Julian Frost!" As Xavier stepped away from the mic stand, most of the crowd cheered. The band started with a slow, bluesy tune. Julian stepped up to the mic, swaying to the rhythm, still holding his drink. He took another gulp and visualized the lyrics. After a deep breath, he shut his eyes and began.

"Mystic woman … Do your dance.
Mystic woman … Put me in your trance.
You're a mystic woman in a mystic world …
… Words can't tell you what you mean to me.
So, come on mystic woman, and get mystic with me …"

Julian's voice was soft and melodic. Most of the female patrons cheered and gushed as he finished the first verse. He took another drink and noticed Violet staring in his direction, dancing in her seat with her arms high above her head. He winked at her and swallowed the last of his tequila. A stagehand appeared from nowhere to take the empty glass. With both hands free, Julian pulled the microphone from its stand, becoming more flexible and open with his movements. He danced around the stage like a wild man— brave, smiling, and losing himself in the music before the second verse began.

"Mystic woman … Tell me your thoughts.
Mystic woman … Show me your soul.
You're a mystic woman in a mystic world.
… And words can't tell you what you mean to me.

So, come on mystic woman, and get mystic with me."

As Julian reached the ending of the verse, Bishop beat out an epic drum fill that led into a ripping guitar solo from Peter. Julian continued dancing around the stage, entranced by the moment and fueled by more confidence than he'd ever had.

For the final verse, Julian repeated the first, still dancing and wooing the female audience members, all fixated on him. In the end, he bowed to the applause. "Thanks, y'all," he bantered into the microphone while receiving the most approval he ever had from strangers.

He placed the microphone back on its stand as Xavier motioned him to the side of the stage, where he told Julian: "That was wonderful."

"Thanks! I've never felt anything like that before in my life!"

Xavier smiled and patted him on the back. "They loved you! Now, why not join in and dance with them?" Before Julian could answer, Xavier leaned closer and whispered, "You can have any of them you want," in his ear.

"Wha—what?!" Julian did a double take.

"The mademoiselles … if you want to lie with any of them, I have a feeling it would be quite easy to."

Julian's heart skipped a beat. "What?!" he repeated, frozen in shock.

"What part of that do you not understand?"

"B—but what about Violet?"

"What about her?"

"I—I really like her and—"

"And she likes you, but don't abstain because of a crush."

"A crush?" Julian snorted, feeling insulted.

"Yes, a crush," he repeated. "You know little about my daughter. You currently look upon her with lust, not love. It is understandable. However, she has experienced numerous emotions as of late which are queer to her. Be patient and love yourself for now. You must learn self-love before you can properly love anyone else, especially my sweet Violet."

Before he could respond, Xavier took Julian's hand and placed a bronze key in his palm. "Take one, two, or however many you prefer to room twenty-two on the second floor. Do as you will."

Julian remained awestruck and unsure how to react. "Wow! I, uh … but what if—"

"Dad!" a man called out, appearing from behind and cutting Julian off. "We have a situation!" Julian's vision was blurred, but he fixated on the young man's concerned gaze. He wore a buttoned red shirt. His hair was dark and short, and his eyebrows were thick.

"What is it, Eric?" Xavier asked.

"There's some guy, Christopher something, and he's trying to get inside. He's out there screaming you killed his daughter!" Eric's eyes were wide with panic.

"Show me where he is," Xavier said. His calm tone and stance had changed. He peered over his shoulder at Julian and said, "Go play. I have a club to run," before turning and following Eric through the crowd.

What the fuck?! Julian's curiosity got the better of him. Though slow and dizzy, he managed to follow close behind. Ahead, he watched the men approach the exit to the chapel then halt at the doorway. Julian staggered closer and adjusted his eyes. He saw a man with golden brown curls stopping just above his ears, and he seemed to be in a fit: furiously scowling, yelling, and throwing his arms around. Because of the music, Julian was unable to hear, but he noted the scene had drawn Violet's attention as well. She stood near the men.

With concern, Julian watched her watching them. He took a few steps forward until the man's angry face became clearer, showing him to be in his late thirties to early forties. Julian looked at Violet again, and this time she noticed him approaching. She placed her palm up and mouthed, "Stop." He obeyed, freezing where he stood before turning his attention back to the man yelling at Xavier.

He wore a bulky brown overcoat over a large, fit frame. Despite the man's aggressive demeanor, Xavier never moved. When the band finished their song and paused to tune a guitar, Julian, and everyone else in the chapel, heard everything. "I know what you are!" The man's teeth clenched, and he growled like a tiger. "I know what all of you are, and so help me God, I'm going to prove it!" The man's deep, belligerent voice was hoarse and raspy.

"Get him out of here, Eric," Xavier calmly said.

Eric took a step forward and reached towards the man. "Don't you fucking touch me!" He violently swung Eric's hand away. "I'll be back!" he snarled. "Mark my words! I will be back tomorrow, and I'll bring my friends! You goddamn demons are going to pay for what you did to her! I swear it!" The man turned and stormed out of Julian's view. Eric followed him into the lobby, chasing him away. "I'll be back!" the man echoed from afar.

"And I'll thr-r-r-ow you out again!" Xavier shouted back, obnoxiously rolling his "R," and swinging his arm at his side in a circular pitch towards the front door. Some of the clubgoers laughed, and everyone clapped. He turned to the onlookers and said, "Don't mind him. Some let their imaginations run wild." He panned across the room, extending his arms, saying, "Please, enjoy yourselves, my loves!"

The band began their next song as Xavier turned towards Violet and the table where she'd returned. Julian watched as he took a seat beside her. Despite the limited lighting and his inebriated bad eyesight, Julian saw Violet clearly. A specific purple aura glowed from her fair skin, pleasantly illuminating the forefront of his peripherals and taking priority in his uncertain world. Her calm stare whispered sweet lullabies in his ears, soothing his rattled soul to near nonchalance.

A gentle tap struck Julian's back, and the moment faded. He turned and saw two wide-eyed young women in black lipstick standing side by side, smiling. "You're Julian, right?" the one on the left asked. She was thin, with short, spiked blond hair, and taller than the other. She wore a matching black tube-top and pants, along with a studded leather collar.

"Yeah," he said, scanning her friend on the right, standing roughly 5'6", with long dark hair and curvy hips. She wore a tight, black spaghetti-strap top, barely covering her large breasts.

"I'm Carmen," said the brunette.

"And I'm Sarah," said the blond.

"Hi," Julian nodded.

"You were great up there!" Sarah added. "Has anyone ever told you how cute you are?" Julian blushed. Before he could answer, each of the women took one of his hands.

"Come dance with us," Carmen insisted. They led him into the thick of the dancefloor where all the black-clad goths stomped their combat boots and shook their asses, having the time of their lives.

The band was playing a cover of The Velvet Underground's seductive classic, "Venus in Furs," and though Julian knew his dance moves were silly, he refused to care. Like he had on stage, he lost himself in the music. With Carmen at his front, and Sarah firmly pressed against his back, Julian was the meat of the sandwich. Sarah reached around and gripped Carmen's hips. The young women danced in alignment as the brunette spun around, slowly twerking her round bottom against Julian's crotch. He moved with the women to the beat, quickly becoming aroused. Carmen turned back to face him, pressing herself against his pounding chest. He smirked, ignoring his anxiety as the ladies kissed one another over his right shoulder. Carmen provocatively glared at him through her left eye. She wanted him; they both did. Julian knew it. The kisses moved to his neck, then his ear. Their wet, warm tongues intertwined like mating snakes, with his lobe a helpless little mouse.

Julian swallowed a lump before sliding his hands behind Carmen's back. As they danced and played, he grew brave, moving south and gripping her rear end. As he pulled her even closer, she purred in his ear and her nipples hardened against his chest through each of their shirts. From behind, Sarah placed her hand beneath Julian's crotch, brushing his semi-erect penis. As she moved further with the same hand, Sarah rubbed her fingertips against Carmen's groin in a circular motion, tickling Julian as she did.

Sarah playfully bit Julian's earlobe and whispered, "Is there somewhere we can go?" Her warm breath against his neck invoked chills.

"Upstairs," Julian moaned. Carmen slowly backed away and grinned, taking his left hand while Sarah took his right, headed towards the exit. The trio approached Xavier's table, where he and Violet watched them pass. Julian's guilty eyes locked with Violet's. She appeared to force a smile—even offering a thumbs up while a questionably somber gleam in her precious almond eyes remained apparent. He looked at Xavier, whose pleasant smile was more genuine. He bowed his head and raised a cone-shaped glass full of a dark red substance, toasting Julian and wishing him good fortune.

As tempting as they were, Julian instantly wanted to trade both women for Violet, but he thought she'd given him everything she possibly could. The night was her gift to him. *But why me,* he asked himself once again. *Stop feeling sorry for yourself and be a man!*

Julian found himself staggering up the steep and narrow stairs again. As if seeing and maneuvering wasn't hard enough, the ladies clung to him tightly, kissing his neck and each other's painted black lips. Upon reaching the second floor, Sarah opened the door. On the other side, a replica of the fourth floor hallway housed five more doors. The last on the left was marked *22,* in silver numbers. Julian quivered, using an unsteady hand to remove the key from his pocket, attempting to unlock the door until Carmen intervened. She took the key and twisted the knob, and the women entered the room first.

With Violet burrowed deep in Julian's mind, he faced the open doorway, drawing a deep breath, and wondering, *is this really what I want? What am I doing?* Before he could take another breath or further question his intent, the ladies collectively reached outward from the cool darkness of the room for his shirt collar, forcefully yanking him inside, and slamming the white door shut behind them.

Chapter Twelve

Julian slept through the night and into Sunday afternoon before waking to cold, dark silence. The ladies were long gone, but their scent remained in the air. His first thought was not of them or Violet, but Xavier's accuser. *You goddamn demons are going to pay for what you did to her!* He shuddered and slid his hand across the silky bedsheet, disoriented and unsure of where he'd left his glasses and clothes. A thick blanket fell to the floor when he stood. Blindly reaching for the wall, his fingertips connected and slid along the cool plaster. Eventually, he found a switch near the door. The bright light was like fire to his delicate gels, and he squinted to scan the surroundings. His glasses sat on an end table beside the king-sized bed, with his clothes piled on the floor below.

Julian put on his specs and got dressed. Though his shirt was ripped and missing several buttons, he wore it anyway. After opening the door, he gave the room a final look and grinned, satisfied with his decision. *Now what am I supposed to do?* Unsure where to go, he entered the stairwell and climbed to the fourth floor. He tried to open the hallway door, but it was locked.

Well, shit, He considered knocking, but the last thing he wanted was to wake anyone, especially vampires. *Vampires.* He chuckled, questioning such an anomaly. *What the fuck is going on?* Unsure where to go, he turned back towards the stairs when the sound of another door opening came from behind the locked door. Julian listened as the door closed and echoing footsteps approached. He turned to face the door again as the steps grew louder until evidently reaching the other side.

The door opened, and Violet poked her head through, her emotionless face instantly lighting up and laughing when she saw him. "Damn, boy! They did a number on you, huh?" She cupped her hand over her mouth and blushed while still laughing.

"I—I wasn't sure if you'd be awake yet," he said, gazing upon his flower and instantly forgetting about the night before.

"Dad and I were already awake. He is visiting with a friend in his apartment."

Julian nodded. "How did you know I was out here?"

"We heard you coming up the stairs, and at the door."

"You heard me from all the way in there?" He motioned past Violet, towards the door at the end of the hall, number *44*.

"There's a lot of things we can do, but yes," she said while opening the door all the way, allowing Julian to pass through. "Like last night, my father knew what to say to you. The way he made you face some of your fears and doubts," she said, walking alongside him.

"What about it?"

"You can never heal unless you feel." She took his hand in hers. "Because of his words, along with all the work you have done on yourself as of late, those emotions came out of you. My father triggered some of them, and you reacted accordingly."

"Your father is very intimidating, but he seems like a good man. That other guy scared me though, the one who came in the club, saying Xavier killed his daughter."

"That's a lie!" Violet fumed. "We don't kill people. My father is a visionary. He believes vampires and humans can coexist, even if we do live in secret. There was a time we had to kill to survive, but now we only kill in defense."

"But he knew about you. He knows you are vampires."

"He called us demons, actually." She smirked. "But you're right, he seems to know who we are."

"So what now?"

"Right now, you should probably change your shirt." She giggled as Julian examined his ripped shirt and blushed.

"About that … I—I—"

"You did nothing wrong, Jul."

"But I feel guilty," he said as the pair stopped in front of Violet's apartment.

"Why feel guilty? You should feel like a million bucks," she said, opening her door. "I certainly do, now."

"Because I came here with you, and I know you said you just want to be friends, but what if I wanted more?"

Violet looked over her shoulder and sighed. "Julian, you're great, amazing, actually, and the fact that you're still standing after everything you've endured is nothing short of a miracle, but—"

"But what?"

"You're a human and I'm a vampire."

"What if I don't want to be human anymore? What if I wanted to be like you?"

"I'd say you would be doing it out of lust, or perhaps spite."

"Why does anybody do it?"

"Not all of us had a choice," she said before disappearing into her dark apartment while Julian waited in the doorway. A moment later, she returned with his bookbag, and handed it to him.

"What do you mean?" he asked, unzipping the bag and retrieving his spare shirt.

"Some of us would've died if it didn't happen."

"Is that why you did it?" he asked, replacing the torn black shirt with the new one.

"I don't want to talk about it right now," she mumbled. He gave her the bag and she disappeared again before returning to the doorway.

"Why did you bring me here? Be honest."

"I already told you. I wanted to repay you for showing me a good time Friday night, and trusting me at your apartment."

"I don't believe that."

"What do you want me to say?"

"Look at you and look at me. You have everything. I am going blind, emotionally ruined, and constantly torn."

"You're better than you realize, but you are wrong. I don't have everything."

"What makes you think I can't or don't want to be a vampire, like you?"

"Because you never knew vampires existed until last night, and now you suddenly want to be one—not for you, but for me. Have you even once asked yourself, 'Why would I want to be a vampire?' since you learned the truth about me?" Julian said nothing. "Think about it." Violet closed her door and faced Xavier's. "Take your time and really think it over." She opened number *44*, and Julian followed.

"Check!" An old man's voice declared from out of view. Violet took Julian's hand and led him across the room to the short hall. A thick scent of cigarette smoke filled the air as they entered an open doorway on the left. Like the living room, the walls were burgundy, and the floor had the same shaggy white carpet. On the opposite side of the room, a painting of a skinny young child hung from the wall. Long blond locks wept like a willow tree, and she wore a blue dress. The wide-eyed little girl's grin stretched across the bottom half of her face, exposing several missing baby teeth. In her tiny hands, she held a whittled brown knight-in-armor figurine.

In the center of the room was a small round table with a chessboard atop and game pieces arranged accordingly. Xavier sat on the right, hair down, black shirt untucked, and sleeves rolled to his elbows. On the left, an elderly man in a black clergy uniform and white collar concentrated on the game. He had salt and pepper hair, a thin, wrinkled face, and two-thirds of a hand-rolled cigarette hanging from between his lips.

"Not yet, old man." Xavier chuckled, using one of his white knights to claim the priest's black bishop, threatening his king. Xavier peered away from the table and his eyes widened in surprise. "Oh, Julian! Good afternoon."

"Good afternoon," Julian replied.

"I trust you had a good night?"

"You could say that."

Xavier nodded before pointing at his opponent, saying, "This is Father William Grant."

The priest looked up from the board and said, "It's nice to meet you." He flicked his cigarette against a small green ashtray resting on his side of the table.

"It's nice to meet you too," Julian replied.

"Father Grant is an old friend of ours," Xavier said.

"Yeah," the priest grunted, making his next move. "Xavier's really stuck it out for me throughout the years." The weary old man spoke slowly from his throat, with a rough voice like he'd been a smoker for most his life.

"The string goes both ways, my friend," Xavier remarked.

Father Grant took a drag from his cigarette, turning back to Xavier, "So, this man, he thinks you killed his daughter?"

"Yes," the vampire replied, taking one of the priest's pawns.

"I saw on the news this morning—another body was found last night, a little boy," said the priest. Xavier sighed and closed his eyes while slowly shaking his head. "Listen, old friend," Father Grant continued. "I know there are things you won't tell me, nor do I want to know, but in the name of the Lord, just tell me this. Do you know who's doing it?"

"I do not," Xavier said. "That makes six now. There are rumors that the bodies were all viciously attacked, and I fear it could be a vampire."

"One of yours?"

"No. The other covens, even the kingdoms ... L'abisme, Taltosia, and Raz Ahrim know this is my territory. They know hunting is forbidden in New York. It would not be wise to break the truce. We have enough blood for all who live here, or come seeking my sanctuary, and there is no need to kill anyone."

"Xavier, your people are vampires, and killing is in their nature. Not all of them share the same compassion for life as you do. One of them is bound to act out," said the priest.

"But we are not like that!"

"You're not, but only you can account for you. How loyal can someone damned to immortality, with a thirst for blood, really be? Remember, there was a time even you had to kill for your food." Feeling like a fly on the wall, Julian shivered hearing such revelations from the priest.

"I know that," Xavier muttered. "I have changed since then. After I left Paris and came to America, I saw the world in a new light. I found myself living like the humans I used to hunt, and I remembered what it was like to be one of them again." He used his rook to take the priest's queen. "The others are here because they follow my example, and between us, I do not think whoever is killing these people is doing it for food."

"The whole purpose of my being here now, and doing what I do, is to show others, like Violet and Eric, we can thrive. Vampires can live in plain sight. We do not have to kill anyone to enjoy the forbidden fruits only we can harvest. The world is changing, and if our kind is to survive, we must change as well."

"But look at what you're doing, Xavier. You've been here ever since you were banished from Paris, and with this club ..." The old man paused to catch his breath and take another drag from his cigarette. "It was only a matter of time before someone caught on."

"Yes, you have been telling me this since the sixties, when you took your vows. What have I been telling you ever since?"

"To let you worry about it," the priest grumbled.

"To let me worry about it," Xavier repeated.

"But someone found you and called you out in front of everyone. You can't just sweep that under the rug."

"They thought he was mad," Xavier said.

"The point is, he knows what you are, or at the very least, he thinks he does," the priest said, making his final move. "Doesn't that scare you?"

"It does," Xavier admitted. "That part worries me indeed, but again, William. ..." He looked into the old man's eyes. "Let me handle it." He turned his attention back to the game and used his queen to trap Father Grant's king. Defenseless, and with no choice but to lose, the priest accepted defeat. "That is checkmate, old man," Xavier announced with a subtle smile.

"Gah! You caught me on one of my bad days." The priest rubbed his cigarette butt in the ashtray and slowly stood from his seat. "Good game ... older man," he teased. "I gotta get going anyway. I'm having some new pews delivered."

"Thanks for coming by," Xavier said. "Any time you want to chat or have another rematch, you know where to find me."

"You're on!" The priest pointed his index fingers in Xavier's direction and grinned before waddling towards the door.

"Hey, William," Xavier called after him. Father Grant turned back to face him. "Eric is down in the office. On your way out, could you tell him to gather the others at my table? Tell him I am calling a meeting and will be down shortly."

"Yeah, I can do that," he said. "How is he, by the way?"

"Eric?" Xavier's face straightened. "He's fine, but why ask me, rather than him? He misses you."

"I know," the priest sighed. "It's just strange and awkward, even after all these years."

"Do what you will. He does love and miss you. I am sure it would mean a lot if you talked to him."

"Alrighty then," said the priest. "Just be careful with this guy. Something seems off, and the last thing you want is to get caught." Father Grant turned back to the door, passing Julian and Violet, nodding at both.

"It was nice seeing you, William. Take care," said Violet.

"You too, dear," he replied before exiting the room and leaving the apartment.

Xavier turned to glare at Violet. "I told you to leave Julian in your room."

"I know, but I think our secrets are safe with him. Besides, Julian wants to join us."

Xavier chuckled before turning an eye to the blind man. "Is that so?"

"I …" Julian hesitated, unsure how to respond.

"You only discovered vampires last night, and now you want to sell us your soul?" he cackled. "Tell me something, how are you enjoying yourself so far?"

"I … I—I'm enjoying it," Julian managed.

"I imagine you think I had something to do with those ladies last night, yes?" Violet grunted at her father's question.

"Well, y—yeah … you told them to—"

"I said you were single and good in bed. You did the rest. Like a lantern, you glow, and have a unique quality. It is true, I put the idea in the air, but I forced nothing. Because of my words, your confidence thrived. Call it a placebo effect, but that is how you attracted those women. You have power, not as a vampire, but a human."

"See?!" Violet tugged on Julian's hand. "I told you, you are a goddamn rock star, and don't even see it."

"You want to be a vampire because you believe that is what it will take to achieve your dreams, but last night when I asked, your dreams were a mystery to you. Take time to ponder, I insist." Xavier stood from the table. "If you want to be a vampire, come with us downstairs. I called a meeting because I asked a favor from Violet's brother, Eric, last night. We have much to discuss about the disturbance."

"You want him to come with us?" Violet asked. "I trust him, but last night, Bern got a little pissy about me bringing him here."

"After you brought Chloe in here, can you blame him? With this murderer on the loose, Bernard is nervous. But unlike Chloe, I like Julian. You trust him, and I trust you. Let me worry about Bernard. If he has anything to say, he can say it to me." Xavier faced Julian and asked, "Are you okay with this?" He gulped and bobbed his head, saying nothing. "Very well." Xavier extended his hand towards the door. "Come, children."

Chapter Thirteen

At the bottom of the stairs, Julian held Violet's hand, following Xavier through the dark hallway that had glowed red the night before. Upon entering the chapel, Xavier stopped and said, "Julian, stay quiet and say nothing unless you are spoken to, understand?"

"I do," Julian said. His heart raced with uncertainty. Ahead, Anna, Bernard, Eric, and Bishop, the drummer from the Black Casket Affair, were gathered at Xavier's corner booth. The rubbery red cushions squeaked as Xavier scooted inward first. Violet followed, and Julian sat on the end.

Bernard yawned and rubbed his eyes. "Why the hell did you wake us up for?" he asked. Before anyone could answer, he pointed at Julian, demanding, "And why the fuck is he here?!"

"I invited him because Violet and I trust him," Xavier said. "His presence is not the issue. That little hiccup from last night is."

"The only hiccup I see is the human!"

"Do you have a problem, Bernard?" Xavier asked.

"You're goddamn right I do!" He slammed his fist on the table. "This is all getting out of hand! Between these killings, and Hell Belle exposing us to random outsiders, it's going to get us caught or worse!" Bernard seethed and his cheeks rapidly pumped in anger. "First, she brought that fucking cunt in here, and now someone else." He looked at Violet. "If he also decides he doesn't like us, are you going to kill him too?!"

Just as Julian's breaths grew heavier with anxiety, Xavier held up his hand, silencing the bald vampire. "I understand your concern, but—"

"No, you don't understand! If you did, you wouldn't be so goddamn careless and let him in here with us. Anna told me what happened last night, about that curly-haired asshole coming in here. What's next?!"

"If you do not feel safe here, Bernard, you and Anna would both be welcomed back home at L'abisme," Xavier said.

"I ain't going nowhere, love," Anna replied. "Leviticus is my home, and I ain't scared." Bernard shrugged his nose and rolled his eyes.

"Thank you, Anna. I appreciate your loyalty. You would all be safe in Paris, and you are free to leave if you wish," Xavier said, making eye contact with each person at the table. "When I opened this club, I had a dream for vampires to live in a changing world. Unsuspecting humans obliviously donate blood, so they can dance, eat, and drink while we survive. For two hundred years, I have called New York City my home. Even before Leviticus, I never had problems here, and I shan't now."

"We are only here because you were excommunicated from L'abisme, or else you'd still be living it up in Paris and fucking anything that moved," Bernard said, briefly glancing at his wife.

Xavier sighed and slowly shook his head. "I was kicked out, not excommunicated. I am here because I chose not to return. Like me, you and the others are here of your own free will, Bernard. After I came to America, I gave up my deviant lifestyle because even if I look like a boy, I grew up."

"I bet you never told the human why you got kicked out, did you?" Bernard asked.

"No, because it's no one's business but my own."

"You fucked the king's daughters!" Between antagonizing remarks, Bernard glared in Julian's direction.

Xavier chuckled and said, "To be fair, I only fucked them once."

"Yeah, all three of them at once!" Bernard added, quickly glaring towards his wife again. "Before Caanis kicked you out, he cut off that little cock of yours. You're lucky he didn't make you eat it!"

Anna elbowed Bernard. "Are ya finished, Bern?"

"I'm just saying, imagine being the poor bloke who'd have to chisel that gravestone. 'Here lies Xavier. He ate his own cock, and he died,' is what it would say."

Xavier's eyes shut tight in annoyance, but he grinned and asked, "Are you trying to humiliate me in front of our new friend, Bernard? Because if you want to bring up the past, compare cocks, and talk about eating them, why not tell Julian about those years your mouth rested on your maker's, you subservient chalice of gilded piss and menses?" Everyone else at the table erupted in laughter except Julian, who covered his mouth to keep from doing the same.

Bernard's cheeks fumed red, and he snarled, "You mother—"

"Whoa there!" Eric extended his hands to symbolize a barrier. "Calm down, guys. There's no reason to fight. Let's relax and handle this with a simple conversation, please."

"I'm sorry," Xavier said. "I should have refrained from such pettiness."

Bernard took a breath and sighed. "I'm sorry too, everybody. I'm just worried."

"Well, we might all have a reason to be," Eric added.

"What did you find out?" Xavier asked.

"The guy last night, his name is Christopher Cauldwell. I ran a full report on him."

"And?" Xavier's ears perked.

"This guy is the real deal—he and his brother, Kevin. They are both highly decorated Navy Seals, true grit, walking tall kind of guys."

"Great," Violet sighed. "I guess that's what he meant when he said he would bring his friends tonight."

"So, this guy conveniently shows up the same night the human does?" Bernard snapped again.

"Cauldwell was here because of his daughter, not Julian," Eric said. "So, unless you have something useful to say, shut the fuck up already, Bern." Bernard sat back in the booth, rolling his eyes and brooding.

"Who was his daughter?" Xavier asked.

"Her name was Catherine Cauldwell, a nineteen-year-old college student at NYU, and the third victim of whoever's doing this."

"Is it really another vampire?" Anna asked.

"The details were vague, but apparently the victims were all mutilated and drained of blood," said Eric.

"If it were a vampire, wouldn't there be fang marks?" Julian blurted without thinking. Everyone laughed, including Violet and Xavier. "What's so funny?" he asked.

"We don't have fangs." Eric smiled.

"Who the hell would be numpty enough to do this in New York of all places?" Anna asked.

"Clearly, someone with no regard for the truce," said Eric.

"What if the queen's prophecy is coming true?!" Anna exclaimed. "What if this is what starts the wa—"

"Not to interrupt irrelevant bullshit about rogue vampires and so-called 'prophecies,'" Bernard interrupted. "But we have other things to worry about right now. What the hell are we going to do if that asshole comes back tonight?" He looked at everyone, even Julian.

"We have to kill him," Bishop said. "We can take his corpse up to the Arctic Circle and drop it in the ocean. No one will ever know."

"We're not killing him." Xavier insisted. "He knows about us, and probably told others. The first to get blamed for his disappearance will be us."

"So, what's the plan?" Bishop asked. "I—I don't like this at all, and if another vampire is killing people, we have to—"

Xavier placed his palm up to Bishop's mouth, silencing him. "If he comes back, let him in," he calmly said. "I will talk to him."

"I don't think that's a good idea," Violet said.

"Why not?"

"Last night, Cauldwell didn't seem like he was interested in talking. If he comes back, we should stop him in the lobby and go from there. Bishop is right, and if Eric's information is correct, we need to handle this now. If killing him, or anyone else involved is what it takes, so be it." Xavier frowned but said nothing.

"That's all fine and dandy, Hell Belle, but another question we need to ask ourselves is how Cauldwell found out about us to begin with," Eric said.

"He's a Navy Seal. Perhaps he has access to information and connections," Bishop suggested.

"Maybe, but I don't buy it," Violet said. "That seems too convenient."

"Listen," Xavier said. "I want all of you here tonight." He individually made eye contact with everyone again.

With a million questions blocked by the confusion running through his mind, Julian disobeyed Xavier again, asking, "What about me? What should I do?"

Violet smiled and said, "Don't worry, Jul. You just sit there and look pretty. We'll handle it."

"But should I be worried?"

"No, you'll be fine, I promise."

"Bu—but what if—"

"What're you avoiding?" She took his hand and repeated, "Let us handle it."

"Yeah, Julian, listen to Hell Belle. She's not gonna let anything happen to you," Anna said. "She likes you far too much." Both Violet and Julian blushed.

"Does anybody have any questions?" Xavier asked, looking around the table.

Julian had wondered for a while, but he finally gained the courage to ask, "Why do they call you Hell Belle, Violet?"

"Oh … it was a nickname I got from a phase I went through," she said.

"A 'phase'?" Eric snickered. "You call that … a 'phase,' sis?"

"Yeah, doofus, I do." She glowered.

Eric shook his head, mumbling, "Whatever floats your boat, I guess," under his breath. Violet stuck her tongue out and shook her head back at Eric, mocking him.

"Very well, children. Go back to what you were doing. There is still plenty of time to rest before we open," Xavier said. "Bernard, I need you here, at the door tonight. You too, Eric. Come get me if Cauldwell returns."

"I will," said Eric.

"Until then, could you do a little more digging and see what else you can find out?" Xavier added.

"You got it. I'll get on that now," he said. Xavier nodded. "Oh, and Dad. I don't know what you told William, but thank you."

Xavier warmly smiled and said, "You're welcome, son." He panned the other faces at the table, concluding with "Enjoy your evening, everyone."

Julian watched everybody exit the booth on the opposite end while retrieving his phone from his jeans pocket. The clock read *4:44*. He shivered when he saw what the battery power read: also *44%*.

"Do you mind if I go lie down for a while, Jul?" Violet asked.

"I don't mind."

She smiled, took his hand, and said, "Come on."

Chapter Fourteen

"Hey there, sleepyhead." Violet's soft voice blew like a cool breeze on a warm summer day. Julian slowly cracked open his eyelids, finding her smiling over him.

"What time is it?" he groaned, wiggling his cold toes against a fluffy brown sofa.

"It's almost ten," she said. "The club will be opening soon." Julian reached for his glasses, which sat in front of him on a wooden coffee table. He took a deep breath through his nose, catching Violet's fresh vanilla scent. She wore a little black dress like she'd had on at the café, and her hair was neatly brushed.

Beneath a bright light, Julian caught a good look at her apartment, with bare white walls and fuzzy gray carpet. Aside from her sofa and coffee table, the only other furniture was a black leather chair to Julian's right, against the wall. After scanning his surroundings, he yawned and asked, "When are we going back to Vegas?"

"It'll be around four-thirty here, but a little closer to two when we get there. Is that okay?"

"That's so trippy," he giggled.

"What is?"

"All of this. I feel like it's an elaborate dream."

Violet laughed, saying, "I assure you, it's not a dream." She playfully poked the tip of his nose. "Want to go downstairs now?"

"Sure. Just let me take my phone off the charger and get my jacket. I'm cold."

"I'll get them for you," she said, retrieving his items.

"Thanks." He slid the phone into his pocket and put on his jacket. At the front door, he slipped on his black sneakers.

"Let's go," she said. Julian followed Violet out the door and watched her lock it from the outside. After reaching the stairwell, they descended.

"All these stairs are a real pain in the ass," Julian quipped.

"It's good for you," she said. "You only gotta climb them one more time later, when we go back to Vegas."

"Hardy fucking har!" he teased.

"But … but … I'm just a-playin'." Her sweet southern drawl flourished as she teased back.

Julian's heart swelled. "Your accent is so adorable," he said.

"Thank you."

At the bottom, they passed through the red hallway and entered the chapel. "'Ey, guys!" Anna greeted them from the bar. She wore an olive-green tank top, with her red hair pulled back in a braided ponytail.

Violet threw her hand up, asking, "Was Bern any less bitchy when he woke up?" as she and Julian each took a seat at the glowing purple stools.

"Eh, who knows? He was still asleep when I woke up. I reckon he'll be down soon."

"Has Dad been down here yet?"

"Nah, I haven't seen him since earlier." She looked at Julian and asked, "You hungry, love?"

"I'm starving, actually."

"I saw you stumble out of here with those ladies last night. I bet after all that, you could eat a horse, eh?" She and Violet laughed while Julian blushed.

"A fat steak would be nice," he said. "Do you have steak?"

"Yeah, we got steak," Anna said. "How you want it cooked?"

"Medium rare, please."

"Alright then. Let me see who's on the grill, and we'll get it ready for you." Anna disappeared through a set of swinging silver doors, returning a moment later. "Want something to drink?"

"Can I get a beer?"

She collected a glass and filled it at the tap before handing it to Julian. "Your steak'll be out soon," she said.

"So, how'd you enjoy the weekend?" Violet asked.

He abruptly laughed with a mouthful of beer, nearly choking. After swallowing it, he said, "Well, it wasn't what I expected, but aside from that Cauldwell guy last night, I've enjoyed myself."

"Don't worry about him."

"Will I ever get to come back here with you?"

"Do you want to come back?"

"Yes."

"I'd really like that too," she blushed.

"I am curious about something. Earlier, that whole thing with Bernard talking about Xavier getting castrated, was that true?"

"Yes. He's lucky that's all that happened. That and getting being sent away, I should say."

"Why was he spared?"

"Because Caanis, the king of L'abisme, is his maker. To kill him would have symbolically been the same as killing his own child, adoptive or not."

"Bernard said it was because he slept with Caanis's daughters. I couldn't imagine Xavier being so …"

"Slutty?" She snickered. "From the stories I've heard, he used to be much different than he is now."

"I could see how losing your dick would change that," he said, immediately regretting the bad joke. "I'm sorry. I shouldn't have said that."

"Don't worry about it, Jul. Even he laughs about it sometimes, when people aren't using it as an insult."

"I am only relying on fiction, but wouldn't it grow back? I mean, don't vampires regenerate after they are wounded?"

"You're right. You are relying way too much on fiction, but it's okay. Burns, cuts, and broken bones heal fast, and if we lose our hair, it also grows back. Losing limbs and parts is permanent. Skin quickly grows around the wound, but we cannot regrow bones or appendages that are completely lost. So, when my father got cut, he lost it forever."

Julian took a drink and asked, "What about my eyes?"

"Your eyes?"

"Since I haven't completely lost my vision, could becoming a vampire cure me?"

"It's possible. I'm sure my father could tell you more. After his banishment, he traveled the world, researching all he could about who we are and what we can and cannot do. That's why he came to New York. If it wasn't for that, I …" She hesitated before closing her eyes and muttering, "I would not be here."

"What do you mea—" The kitchen doors swung open, interrupting Julian. Anna approached with his plate in one hand and a rolled napkin with silverware in the other.

She smiled and sat it all down in front of him. "Enjoy," she said.

"Eat up, Jul. I'm going to go grab my own dinner, and I'll be back shortly," Violet said. She patted his thigh and stood.

"Okay, I'll just be here," he mumbled with his mouth already full. She headed towards the lobby. Julian took a few more sips of his beer while practically inhaling the juicy ribeye. The food was excellent, but he could not shake a strange sense of dread, thinking, *I have no part in this, and if something happens, what am I supposed to do?*

"If he comes back, he'll open a can of worms on himself that we'll take care of," Anna said from the other end of the bar. "You worry far too much, love." Her freckled, pale cheeks raised with a grin as she approached, saying, "He doesn't even know who you are."

"I wish everyone would stop reading my thoughts," Julian grumbled. "It makes me uncomfortable."

"Look, I'm sorry, but I can't help it. Your thoughts speak like words from your mouth, and I hear them as such. None of us are deliberately trying to pry or invade your privacy. Do you think I like hearing hundreds of men and women in here, thinking about their perversions? If my husband heard some o' the things men think when I serve them drinks, he would've murdered them in plain sight."

"How come you, Violet, and Xavier can read minds, but not Bernard?"

"Bern was made by someone else. When a vampire makes another, they pass on certain powers," she explained. "Xavier and I were made by Caanis, in Paris. Bern was made by another."

"Can he fly?"

"Yeah, and he's the fastest here, but not all vampires can fly either. Those are your cave dwellers. They mostly live in L'abisme—the largest of the kingdoms, below Paris, deep in the catacombs. Traditionally, they live with other vampires who can fly and hunt for them. All the vamps who hunt and fly travel hundreds of miles or more, so no one traces it back to their homes. Well, all except the Ahrims, that is."

"The Ahrims?"

"Raz Ahrim is in Egypt. They don't care if they hunt local or not."

"Could a vampire from one of the kingdoms be killing people here?"

"If it's a vampire, it's possible," she said. "The thing is, all three kingdoms, and even the few small covens know we're here. They know the consequences if our discovery came out in the open. That would be a disaster."

"I could imagine."

"No, love, you don't understand. We've lived in the shadows since the dawn of life. We've only been exposed once, but we got lucky then. In these modern times, our discovery would mean a war unlike we've ever seen, and the end of humanity. We all know it's coming. It was prophesized centuries ago by Dajhri, the queen of Taltosia."

"Wha—what do you mean?"

"L'abisme's the most empathetic of the three kingdoms. Some of them even try to follow Xavier's examples, but not the other two. All Taltosians hunt, but they, nor the hunters from L'abisma, don't let their victims suffer. The Ahrims are another story. They're savage, sadistic, and inhumane. When they kill, they torture their victims. Some are even known to cut off limbs and sever spines while their prey is still alive."

Julian shuddered. "Why would they do that?"

"It's fun for them. There was once a time when all vamps were monstrous, but as the world changed, most vamps changed with it. The Ahrims refused to leave the old ways behind. Raz Ahrim is where it all began."

"You mean, where vampirism began?"

"In the bible, they were called the Land of Nod."

"Whoa! Wait a minute! In the bible, the people Cain encountered after he was banished were vampires?!"

"Yes. The first vampires were the cursed children of Adam and his first wife, Lilith."

"Wasn't Eve Adam's wife?"

"Eve was his second wife. Like Adam, Lilith was created from the Earth, and they were equals. After Lilith gave Adam many children, she developed free will and broke her submissive chains. Adam refused her, so he prayed to God for a woman he could control. As the story goes, Lilith, along with the children she conceived with Adam, were cast out. The bible won't tell you that part, but haven't you ever wondered where all those people came from?"

"Why would God do that to his own creation?"

"Because he's cruel. They say God created man in 'His' image, after all. God is a narcissist who sided with Adam. That's why Eve was created from his rib and served him like a dog until her final breath. Naturally, Lilith was scorned, and 'hell hath no fury.' It's unclear how she and her children received the dark gift, but some of the ancients say it was through the blessings of demons who lived long before the universe was created."

"I don't know what to say, or believe for that matter, but that's deep," Julian said before finishing his beer, attempting to process Anna's story.

"Most vamps fear the Ahrims. They're not just the eldest kingdom, they're also the strongest and hungriest for power. They consider themselves gods and haven't even made a vampire in thousands of years. Their king, the Raja Kahíji even cut out his own tongue and forced the others to follow suit, and now they refuse to communicate with anyone outside their kingdom. Despite their snobbish self-entitlement, they always respected the truce that exists within the three kingdoms. However, if the world discovered our existence, a war would ensue like none other. It's not certain, but the Ahrims would be the most likely to start such a war. Then, humans would hunt and kill anyone they believe to be among us. Vampires would kill in troves, even each other."

"Why would vampires kill their own kind?"

"Because the war would mark the end of days. We would have to kill humans to keep them from killing us, and without the worry of hiding, vamps like the Ahrims would rise and fight for supremacy while they had the chance. There was a time many other kingdoms existed, but after thousands of years, there are only three left, and a handful of small covens like this one. All the other kingdoms fell or were conquered. There's not as many of us as there used to be, and now our species is endangered, and at its most vulnerable." Julian could not believe what he heard. He grew lightheaded and nauseous. "Are you alright?" Anna asked.

"You—you're telling me the end of the world is that close?!" he asked, shivering in panic.

"It's always been that close. You just never knew until now."

Julian's thoughts shifted to Cauldwell again. *I know what you are,* echoed in his ears. His vision grew fuzzy and distorted. *Goddamn demons!* The room spun and his booming heart drowned out any other sound. "I—I can't breathe!" he shouted, frantically huffing.

"Okay, just calm down … relax," she said. "You're having a panic attack." Anna reached across the bar and placed her palms on his shoulders. "Breathe with me, love, breathe. …" She slowly drew air through her nose and out of her mouth. Julian followed her instructions but thought he was going to faint.

"What's wrong?!" Violet's voice rang in Julian's ears from behind. She appeared by his side, asking, "What is it, Jul?!" Her eyes ping-ponged between him and Anna.

Anna said, "He's having a panic attack."

"Why?! What happened?"

"I told him about Lilith, the kingdoms, the war, and what'll happen if we got caught."

"What?!" Violet balled her fists and clenched her teeth. "Why the fuck would you do that?! … The fuck's the matter with you?!"

"Oi! Don't talk to me like that! I was just answering his bloody questions! What's it matter? I reckon he's gonna join us anyway, eh?"

"No, Anna! He hasn't decided, and neither has Dad. Even if he had, you don't throw something like that on someone! You should know better!" Violet put her left arm around Julian's neck and pressed her cheek against his, whispering, "Just relax, okay?" in his ear, before shrugging her nose at Anna.

"Fuck you, Hell Belle!" Anna spat. "We're all living on the day-to-day since this killer's been leaving bodies around the city. You brought that damn girl in here, and we saw how that went. Then, you brought Julian in here." She pointed her finger in Violet's face. "You're the one who exposed him to all this, and for what? Because you're lonely, want a companion, and think he's the 'man of your dreams?!' You're reckless, so don't flash your cunt at me, because I didn't do a bloody thing but talk to him!" She rolled her eyes in disgust as the first wave of patrons started piling inside the chapel. "Now, if you'll excuse me, I got a bar to run." She wrinkled her crooked nose at Violet before stomping away to the other end of the bar.

Violet turned back to Julian. "Are you okay?"

Catching his breath, Julian looked into her eyes and asked, "What did you drag me into, and what did she mean by 'companion'?"

"It's exactly how it sounds. I wanted a friend or someone I could eventually open up to, and who might accept me for what I am."

"And your friend, Chloe—when she didn't accept you, you killed her, didn't you?" Violet sighed and lowered her head. "I'll take that as a yes," he muttered.

Tears began pouring from Violet's eyes. "What do you want from me?" she sobbed.

"Excuse me?!" Julian pushed her hand away. "What the hell do you want from me? Why did you get me involved in this, and not even tell me how close we all are to the end of the world?!" He waited for an answer, but she said nothing. He slammed his fist against the bar. "Why?!"

"How was I supposed to explain something like that to you? You started in the dark, and I knew opening up to you would take time. After everything Friday, I knew meeting you was fate. I knew I had to bring you here." She snorted and rubbed away the tears.

"I am so sorry if I deceived or hurt you, but you're not the only one who's had a terrible, lonely life. I have too." Her lips quivered and her brown almond eyes were smeared with runny mascara, just like the first time Julian saw her up close. Even shocked and frightened, he could not resist her face. It was perfect, and he could not help but melt in her arms. "Do you want me to take you back to Vegas now?" she asked.

"Can you?" he sighed. "I—I'm sorry, I am overwhelmed, and need to think. Is that okay?"

She lowered her head and mumbled, "I understand." Julian was shattered by her sorrow, and instantly overcome by guilt. "Come on," she said, standing from the purple barstool.

Julian followed and she took his hand, leading him into the packed lobby. Eric and Bernard stood at the main entrance checking IDs, collecting cash, or directing clubgoers to the blood labs.

Xavier emerged from the crowded red hall, wearing a black suit and welcoming grin as he laid eyes on his daughter and their newest friend. "Good evening, children," he said.

"Dad, I'm going to take Julian back to Las Vegas now," Violet said.

Xavier's smile faded. "Why now?" he asked, panning between the two.

"Anna told him some shit a little too soon, and it scared him."

"What do you mean, 'scared,' Julian?" he asked.

"When Violet brought me here, she didn't tell me what's about to happen."

"And what is about to happen?"

"She said there's going to be a war if you get caught."

"It's always been that way," Xavier said.

"The point is, it's all been a lot to take in."

"I understand," Xavier said. "It is a lot to digest, but you have handled it well."

"That's what I told him," said Violet. "I kinda felt like I revealed too much too soon. It's my fault."

"Everything happens for a reason, my sweet," Xavier replied. "So, Julian, once you return to Las Vegas, are you going to tell anyone what happened here?"

"I won't say anything incriminating or that would raise questions, if that's what you mean."

Xavier's smile returned. "I believe you. Will we see you back here again?"

Julian swallowed a lump and said, "I'd like to, but I need some time to process everything."

Xavier nodded. "I understand." He told Violet, "Take some bags of blood with you from the freezer, if you're—"

"Where the fuck is he?"

The loud disruption had come from the doorway. Julian's heart sank and his panic returned at hearing the belligerent voice again. "I said, where the fuck is he?!" The voice grew louder as the crowd parted to either side of the lobby, and the big man with golden curls and brown overcoat emerged. He was not alone. Behind him, two other men followed close. One was dressed in camouflage fatigues and matching cap with a smug grin plastered across his face. The other, with short, golden hair, the same color as Cauldwell's, was draped in a long black trench coat. The man in black raised a sawed-off shotgun, sending horrified patrons running for their lives. As they screamed and clogged the exit, the loud music from the chapel left everyone inside it oblivious to the scene unfolding nearby.

"Hey!" Eric shouted, approaching the man with the gun. "Get the fuck out of here with that thing!" The man smirked and shoved the barrel in Eric's face. "Whoa there, buddy," he gasped, raising his hands in compliance. "Just take it easy, alright?"

Christopher Cauldwell lifted his hand to the gunman, motioning to wait. He panned the room until he locked on Xavier. "You!" he roared. "You killed my daughter!"

"I didn't kill anyone, sir," Xavier calmly said. "I swear—"

"Shut up!" the militant growled. "My baby girl was mutilated, killed, and even decapitated by a vampire! You are a vampire, a demon who shouldn't even exist, and you expect me to believe you had nothing to do with it?!" Cauldwell took a few steps closer as Julian grew short of breath.

"I don't know what you're tal—" Xavier attempted, but he was hushed by Cauldwell's raised index finger.

The militant looked over his shoulder to the man in black. "Brother, if this thing says another word before I give him permission, blow his boy's brains out in front of him." The man smirked again, cocking the shotgun and pressing the barrel against Eric's temple.

"As for you," Cauldwell said, turning back to Xavier. "I want your head on a silver platter, but even more than that"—he paused for a moment, appearing to wipe away a tear—"I just want my little girl back. She was my life, and you took her from me."

"Listen, sir." Xavier cleared his throat and slowly lifted his hands in front of him. "I am not your enemy, and I am not saying someone didn't do something horrible, but we are—" Cauldwell turned back to the gunman and nodded. Without warning, a shot was fired.

"Eric!" Violet screamed.

In a flash, Eric disappeared. The bottlenecked patrons surrounding the doorway were hastily knocked aside by an unseen force. Finally alerted, the crowd inside the chapel raged in horror, frantically rushing out in all directions, unsure where the shot had come from. Bernard vanished as if erased from existence. Before Julian could react, Xavier yanked him away in one hand, and Violet in the other.

"My glasses!" Julian was pulled away so fast, his round specs flew from his face and he was unable to catch them. The trio shot through the red hall and straight up the stairwell in a matter of seconds, stopping at the door leading to the roof.

"We must get out of here!" Xavier shouted as he pushed open the door.

Julian became frantic. "My glasses! I lost my glasses!" Another gunshot echoed from downstairs, followed by screams of the innocent crowd trying to escape. Seconds later, more shots followed. Bullets hit the upper parts of the stairwell. "They're fucking shooting at us!" Julian cried.

"Come on!" Xavier motioned him to follow.

"What about Eric and the others?!"

"They know where to go!" Violet shrieked. "They won't hurt the other people! … Come on!"

Julian was frozen in fear. "But we—we—we can't just leave—"

"They're coming!" Xavier shouted, "Come on!" He grabbed Julian by the arm, forcefully pulling him through the doorway as footsteps rushed from below, growing louder by the second.

"Follow me to Vegas, Dad!" Violet howled. She turned to Julian. "Ride with him," she said. "Remember to shut your eyes and hold on tight!"

Julian quickly wrapped his arms around Xavier's shoulders, watching Violet blast into the frigid darkness. "Hold on, son!" Xavier said, shooting from the roof with Julian on his back, trailing his daughter and parting the night sky.

Chapter Fifteen

He had obeyed Violet's commands when riding on her back to New York, but with Xavier, Julian grew brave. He opened his eyes. As deafening crackles rattled his eardrums, he perceived darkness with occasional white tracers of light. The high velocity was so intense, he could only withstand seconds of such mesmerizing physics before his eyes became too itchy to remain open.

After the initial excitement wore thin, Julian reflected on the men who had eagerly opened fire into the crowd. Despite everything, he understood Cauldwell's grief. Though clearly psychotic, he had lost his daughter, and had showed far more compassion for her than his grandfather, Johnny ever did for his own. On the other hand, they shot at Eric, and casually, at that. That Julian could not forgive.

Once they landed on the Vegas Parliament's roof, Violet shouted, "What the fuck?! … What the fuck are we going to do?!"

"Calm down," Xavier said. "We must talk to Charlie. Come on!" He pushed the round button at the side of the shiny elevator doors.

"I can't see anything," Julian said, stumbling in the dark. Still visibly shaken, Violet took his hand.

"Do you have a spare pair of eyeglasses at home, Julian?" Xavier asked.

"Yeah, but right now, I can't see shit. … Who is Charlie?"

"He owns the Las Vegas Parliament," Xavier said.

"Is he a vampire?"

"No, but he's a trusted friend who can help us." The elevator dinged and the doors opened. They stepped inside, and Xavier pushed the number 2 button.

"What the hell are we going to do, Dad?" Violet repeated. "They'll find us here!"

"We have some time. For all we know, they got arrested. Besides, Eric got away, and you know your brother. He will keep both eyes and ears open."

"But still … They could've gotten away!"

"Perhaps, but the police will still be looking for them, and they have no idea where we went."

"Wait a minute!" Julian exclaimed. "Along with my glasses, my bookbag is still there!"

"Nobody should find it," Violet said. "It's locked in my apartment, and the fourth floor is always locked. The cops consider those residential apartments and unrelated to the club itself. So, nothing should be bothered upstairs."

"The police are the least of my concern. When it is safe, we must go back and purge anything incriminating," Xavier said. "Julian, was there anything in your bag that might give you away if someone were to find it?"

"Just my ripped shirt from last night, another pair of pants, and boxers, but I took everything else out."

"Good. What about you, Violet?"

"All my school and Vegas shit are in my car, down in the garage."

The elevator stopped on the fifth floor, and the doors opened. An older man and woman entered. "Going down?" the man asked. He was short and round, with white hair, and he wore a red Hawaiian shirt beneath a denim jacket.

"Yeah," Violet muttered. The remainder of the ride was awkwardly silent as the old lady smiled at the three. She had curly gray hair sticking out from the open top of a blue sun visor.

Though his vision was more impaired than usual, Julian noticed his reflection on the shiny door. His hair was cowlicked and stuck straight up. Violet's looked like a wild thorn bush, and most of Xavier's pale strands hung loosely from the rest of his thinned ponytail. *Jesus Christ, we look like shit!* Violet cupped her hands over her mouth and giggled. Xavier joined her and Julian followed.

The elevator reached the casino floor and the doors slid open. First the couple waddled out, then the others. "Follow me," Xavier said. Violet held Julian's hand as they passed row after row of flashing red, white, and blue slot machines.

After passing a few crowded table games, they approached a short hallway, stretching nearly six feet. The walls were painted gold, and a single wooden door was closed at the end, with a sign reading *Employees Only*. Xavier placed his hand on the shiny brass knob and twisted, but the door was locked. He knocked four times in a specific pattern, suggesting a secret code.

A few seconds later, the door clicked and opened. An older, well-groomed gentleman emerged, with wrinkled olive skin and a thick head of short dark hair. He wore a gray suit and tie. After a look of surprise, a slow grin formed on his rounded face. "Well, well. What are you doing here, Mister Van Abarrow?!" The man's voice was rough, but he spoke in a friendly tone.

"I need your help, Charlie," Xavier said.

Charlie's smile quickly faded. "Of course. Come in," he said, standing aside for everyone to enter the small, cluttered office. "So, what can I do for you?" He took a seat behind a brown desk with a computer set-up on top.

"I've got a problem, back in New York," Xavier said. "Not even an hour ago, someone opened fire in my club."

"What?!" Charlie's eyes bugged out. "Did anyone get shot?"

"I don't think so, but could you look it up on your computer and see if you can find anything out?" Xavier asked. Charlie nodded and quickly began typing on the keyboard.

"Since it just happened, there won't be anything on there yet," Violet said.

"Wait! Here it is!" Charlie said. "It looks like someone posted a video on social media nine minutes ago."

"Let me see it," Xavier said.

Charlie spun the computer monitor around so everyone could see, and he pressed play. The video appeared to be from a cellphone. While Julian could not make out many of the details, he squinted, seeing enough to get the gist. A large crowd of people stood on the sidewalk, outside the club. Two police cars were visible with blue lights flashing. First, an officer led out the man in camouflage. Both his hands were cuffed behind his back. The camera followed their walk from the door to the cruiser in the foreground. After the officer put the man in the backseat and shut the door, the crowd erupted in cheers. The cruiser drove away.

"We're bringing the third one out now!" a voice announced from out of view. The camera shakily moved back to the front door of the club where a cuffed Christopher Cauldwell was being led to the other white cruiser. The crowd cheered louder as the ringleader passed, with random insults hurled from the timid patrons.

"Rot in hell, cock-smoker!"

"Don't drop the soap!"

One of the officers directed their attention to the crowd, yelling, "Everyone, shut up! No one got hurt and we got all three of them. Let us handle it!"

The cheers continued as the officers pushed Cauldwell forward. "You don't know what you're doing!" he snarled. "Let me go after the real threat!"

"You are the threat, Goldilocks," someone shouted from the crowd.

"Mark my words! I am going to kill all those goddamn vampires! I swear it!" Cauldwell said as the laughing officers forcefully shoved him into the cruiser, slamming the door in his face. The car sped away and the satisfied crowd cheered louder.

One of New York's finest turned to the mob. "The show's over! Go home," he said, turning his attention to the camera. "And turn that shit off!"

The video ended and Violet gasped. "He said 'vampires!'"

"He did, and everybody laughed at him," Xavier said. "However, we are not out of the woods yet. My guess is the shooter will be in jail longer than the others. I will try reaching out to Eric, but we need to move after the day comes and goes."

"Navy Seals opening fire in a New York City nightclub and screaming about vampires will probably make the national news," Julian said. "Especially with that video, it'll be viral by morning."

"He's right, people will talk," Charlie said. "What can I do to help?"

"We need money and somewhere new to lay low. Leviticus is unsafe right now," Xavier said.

"How much money do you need?" Charlie asked.

"I don't know, Charlie, but something tells me this is far from over." Xavier sighed, resting his hand over his face, appearing disappointed and deep in thought.

"What should I do?" Julian mumbled.

Violet asked, "What do you want to do?"

"Give him a ride home, Violet," Xavier said, turning to Julian. "You are not one of us. You are impaired and cannot defend yourself as we can. The last thing I want is for you to get hurt or killed because of this."

"But what am I supposed to do if they come to Vegas and all hell breaks loose?"

"It won't."

"You don't know that, Dad," Violet interjected, placing a hand on Xavier's forearm. "I don't want to leave Julian alone."

Again, Xavier sighed. "What do you want to do, Julian?"

"I'm scared, but at the same time, I've never felt so alive, if that makes sense." He winked at Violet. "Everything happens for a reason, right?"

"Okay," she said. "So, now what, Dad?"

Charlie raised his hand again, seemingly afraid to speak out of turn. "Look, I can give you a few hundred thousand dollars, but—"

"How about you buy my shares?" Xavier interrupted.

"B—buy your sh—shares?!" Charlie stuttered. "B—b—but that's seventeen million dollars!" Xavier flashed Charlie a stern glare. "I—I guess I c—could do that, b—but—"

"Excellent!" Xavier's eyes shimmered.

"But where will we go, Dad? We can't stay here," Violet said.

"I don't know yet, my dear, but it has to be somewhere big enough for all of us at any given time, at least until we can figure out something else."

"Yeah, true, but …" Violet stopped dead in her tracks. "Wait a minute."

"What is it?" Xavier asked, raising an eyebrow.

"Julian, didn't you tell me your aunt and uncle have a really big house they abandoned in Virginia?"

"Yeah, but they're not going to just let us live in it. Besides, it's right behind my grandpa's house, and I don't think—"

"If it's big enough to suit our needs, I could buy it from them," Xavier interrupted. "You said they abandoned it?" he asked, stroking his chin.

"Yeah, they've tried to sell it, but nobody has ever wanted to buy it."

"May I ask why they left?"

"They have two daughters. Once my cousins grew up and moved away, the house was too big for just the two of them. They moved to Richmond about twenty-five years ago. With the hefty price tag, the house has been on the market ever since."

"So, it has not been maintained in all these years?" Xavier asked.

"It has, actually. There's a smaller house next door, where another aunt and uncle of mine once lived, but they also left the area after my great grandma Heiti died. The people who live there now get paid by my uncle George to look after the place in case they ever sell it."

Xavier nodded. "How much money are they asking for it?"

"I don't know, but it's got to be at least a million, if not more."

"Does it have a sizable attic or a basement without windows or openings for daylight?"

"It has a huge basement with four guest bedrooms, a bathroom, living room, and even a small kitchen. It's underground, without windows, and the only way in is from inside the house. It's like an apartment, and everyone I met at the club could fit comfortably. There are three more bedrooms, a library, a game room, and another bathroom upstairs. All the windows could be boarded up if needed."

"It sounds very nice," he said.

"It is. It sits high on a hillside, overlooking several houses below it, including my grandpa's house and my mom's old house."

"If I may," Charlie interjected. "If this man knows who you are, the last thing you should do is buy a house. I mean, if he found you before, he'll find you again."

"He's right," Violet said. Xavier rolled his eyes in frustration.

"And odds are, if he knows you, he might know Violet too," Charlie added.

"Fuck!" Violet exclaimed, placing her hands on her hips.

"Does he know *him*?" Charlie pointed to Julian.

"No," Xavier replied. "He sang a song with the band last night, but that was before Cauldwell came in."

"Most of the people there probably don't even remember my name," Julian added.

"Well, there you go," Charlie said.

"People are going to know I don't have that kind of money, and eventually somebody will start putting things together," said Julian.

A sly grin slowly stretched along the length of Xavier's long jaws. Violet took notice, also smiling. "What?" she asked.

"I have an idea," he said. Both Violet and Julian tipped their heads. "This is Las Vegas, right? And we're in a casino … right?" His eyes locked with Julian's.

"Yeah?" Violet's smile became a wide grin as Julian's eyes bounced back and forth between her and Xavier.

"Julian, pick a number between one and ten," Xavier said. "What?!"

"I said, pick a number between one and ten."

"I—I don't know," he said before closing his eyes and thinking. "Seven?"

Xavier took a step forward, placing his hands on each of Julian's shoulders, saying, "Congratulations, Julian Frost. On behalf of the Las Vegas Parliament, I would like to be the first to congratulate you on your seven-million-dollar jackpot win!"

"What?!!!" Julian shrieked, instantly seeing stars. "What?! … What?!" he repeated in a loop. "What?!"

"You just won a seven-million-dollar jackpot!" Violet cheered.

"I—I—I … but tha—that's your money," Julian struggled.

"I have ten million, and you now have seven. I'm giving it to you," Xavier said.

"F—for what? To buy the house for you?"

"It would be yours, but yes. We need somewhere to stay until this is over."

"How long?" Julian asked.

"A year, two, perhaps. Would you be okay with that?"

"What would I have to do?"

"You need only put up a front that you got lucky in Vegas," he said. "Unfortunately, you would have to quit school, but imagine returning home to get the last laugh. The house would be yours, and you may use this money to fill it with luxuries."

As the fantasy became reality, Julian grew dizzy. He stumbled, placing a hand over his heart, and struggling for air. "I—I can't breathe," he gasped.

Violet came to his aid, placing her arms around him as Xavier and Charlie looked on. "He's having a panic attack," Violet said.

"Here, come sit," Charlie stood from his black office chair and Violet guided Julian to sit.

"Take off your jacket," she said, helping him pull his arms from the sleeves. "Breathe, sweetie," she whispered in a soothing tone. "Breathe." She turned to Charlie and asked, "Could you get him some water, please?" Charlie nodded and reached inside a small refrigerator next to his desk, retrieving a clear plastic bottle for Julian.

"Thanks," he panted, attempting to catch his breath. His hands tremored as he broke the seal, unscrewed the lid, and took a drink. Using his shirttail, he wiped cold sweat from his face.

Watching him closely while his body relaxed, Violet asked, "Are you alright?"

"Yeah," he mumbled before taking another drink. "I'm okay."

"Listen, Julian, this is very important," Xavier began. "Violet's going to take you back to your apartment. I want you to pack everything you can carry that is important to you and get rid of the rest. You will have to leave behind your bigger items."

"I understand. It's just stuff, and I didn't have much to begin with."

"In the morning, when your aunt and uncle have woken, I want you to call and give them the news. Tell them you won the money at a slot machine, and you will pay them cash."

Julian sighed. "I'll have to call my grandpa to get their phone number. I haven't talked to him in a few weeks and trying to convince him I'm not lying will be difficult. He never believes anything I say, especially if I told him something like that, but I will try." He took another drink and laughed. "This is all just … wow!"

As the vampires giggled at Julian's excitement, Charlie raised his hand again, saying, "Xavier, if you'll follow me, we can square away the deal, and I'll get your money."

"Very well," Xavier said. "Julian, would it be satisfactory if I gave your share to you tomorrow night?"

"That's fine," he said, sipping the water a few more times before Violet helped him to his feet.

Xavier approached and took Julian by the hand. He shivered at the vampire's icy touch. "You may not be one of us, but I will always watch over you as if you were. We will be your family and love you for the beautiful soul you are." His words melted Julian's heart. The corners of his naked eyes moistened as Xavier tightly embraced him in his arms. It was the most pleasant and meaningful hug Julian ever felt. Despite his whirlwind of emotions over the weekend, he knew love took the forefront.

Letting go, Xavier asked Violet, "Do you have your keys?" Violet smacked her hands against her sides. A jingle rang from a small pocket in her dress, and she winked. "Alright then," Xavier said. "Take him home and come back immediately."

"Come on, Jul." Violet took his hand and led him to the door.

Before they left, Xavier said, "Remember, Julian, do not tell anyone about anything else. You may tell your family you won the money, but nothing to raise suspicion."

"You mean more suspicious than winning seven million dollars?" he snickered.

"This is Las Vegas. It is not suspicious, only luck," he said with a priceless grin.

"I don't know what to say, other than thank you, Xavier." The two bowed their heads to one another. Then Julian left the office with Violet by his side, heading back through the casino, down the elevator to the garage, and to the purple Firebird. After letting the car run for a minute with the heat turned up, they hit Las Vegas Boulevard, due north.

The entire ride, Julian was silent, with so many thoughts, none of them lasting long. "Be ready to go by dusk," Violet said after parking in front of his building. "I'll be here not long afterward." Julian opened the passenger door and stepped out. "Do you have your keys?" she asked. He tapped his pockets like she did before, and his keychain also jingled. "Okay," she said. "Just checking."

Julian grinned, staring at her blurry shape in the darkness. "I … umm …" He swallowed a lump and sighed. "Be careful going back, and have a goodnight, Violet."

"You too, Julian," she softly replied. He shut the car door and turned towards the steps. Firmly gripping the cold handrails, he carefully climbed the stairs while Violet waited for him to reach the top. As he unlocked the door, he listened to the car backing out of the parking spot, turning to look just as she drove away. He puckered his lips and blew her a kiss, hand extended below his chin. "I love you."

Chapter Sixteen

Julian lay awake the remainder of the night, far too anxious to sleep. When the desert sun finally rose, so did he. After showering and retrieving his spare glasses, he brewed a pot of coffee and paced his apartment, unsure what to tell his grandfather. Once it was ready, Julian sipped his coffee, staring at his phone.

Be brave, he told himself. *You are a man!* Finally, Julian picked up the phone and dialed Johnny's number. He set the volume to speakerphone and placed the device next to him on the arm of his recliner.

"Hello …" Johnny answered. His voice was deep, haggard, and raspy.

"Hey, Grandpa," Julian began.

"Hey!" Johnny grunted in surprise. "What are you doing?"

"I …" Julian paused and cleared his throat. "I have some good news."

"What?"

"Last night, I won the jackpot at a casino."

"You did?!" His tone changed and he chuckled under his breath.

"Yeah, I did, and it's a lot."

"How much?"

Julian's heart roared, but he closed his eyes, took a deep breath, and said, "Seven million dollars."

Johnny laughed before barking, "Bullshit!" in a snotty tone.

"I know it sounds crazy, but I—"

"Bullshit!" he repeated, still laughing.

"I don't care if you believe me. That's not why I called."

"You're right, I don't believe you, but what do you want?" The laughter ended, and his voice faded to careless annoyance.

"What's Aunt Scarlet and Uncle George's phone number?"

"Why? Don't you be bothering them, now! You hear me?"

"I don't want to bother them. I want to buy their house."

"Julian, you can't afford that place."

"I can now," he gloated.

"Bullshit!"

"Then what do you have to worry about? Let me make an ass of myself. Either way, what's it to you?"

"Julian, they're asking over a million dollars for that place. It's too big for just you, anyway."

"Yeah, well, let me worry about that."

"I guess …" he chuckled. "You got a pen?"

"I do," he said, then added the number to his phone's contact list as Johnny read it off to him. "Thanks, Grandpa," he said.

"So, you're moving back home, huh?"

"Yeah, I am."

"Why?! I didn't think you ever wanted to come back. Why not just go somewhere else if you want to move?"

"Because I want to come home. It's too hectic and unfamiliar here. Besides, I miss Daryl, and this place no longer serves me."

"I knew you wouldn't last long out there. I knew as soon as I sold your mom's house, you'd want to come back."

"Why do you have so little faith in me? What did I do to you that was so bad?" he asked, rolling his eyes.

"Julian, we're not going to start this shit again, and if that's why you really called me, I'm hanging up now."

"I called you to get Scarlet and George's number."

"Well, you got it. Go on and call them, but you and I know damn well: you didn't win shit!"

"We do, huh?" Julian cackled. "I'll show you."

"Goodbye, Julian." Johnny hung up.

"Joke's on you," Julian mumbled. He was annoyed but refused to let it ruin his mood. After taking another drink of coffee, he dialed Scarlet and George's number.

An older female voice answered on the third ring. "Hello?"

"Hi, Scarlet?" Julian asked.

"Yes," she politely replied.

"Hey, it's Julian. How are you doing?"

"Hi, Julian! I'm well. How are you?"

Julian smiled, appreciating his aunt's more pleasant tone. "I am great, actually. I got your number from my grandpa, and I was calling because I won some money out here in Vegas, and—"

"Wow, really?! That's amazing! How much did you win?"

"It was a lot. That's why I called. I wanted to buy your and George's house in Gunnar."

"You do?! Isn't it too big for just you?"

"Well, it's not just me that'd be moving."

"Ah … you finally found you a good woman, huh?" she giggled.

"Something like that."

"Well, I'll have to talk to George, but we're asking a lot for it."

"Yeah, that's what Grandpa said. He said you're asking over a million."

"Well, we listed it at one-point-two, but we haven't had an offer on it in so long. … Let me call and talk to George and see what he says. He's down at the office right now, but if you can afford it, I'll see if he'd be willing to sell it to you for an even million, since you're family, and so we can finally sell it."

Family. Julian replayed his aunt's word in his head as a tear ran down his cheek. "Wow! Really?!"

"Yeah," she said. "We didn't think we would ever get rid of it, honestly. This number you called me from, can I call you back at it in a few minutes?"

"Yes, you can."

"Okay then, Julian. I will call George and then call you back."

"Alright, Scarlet. I'll talk to you soon!"

"Okay, bye-bye," she said. The call ended and Julian finished his coffee. Ten minutes later, Scarlet called back. She gave him her and George's address and agreed to meet the following night, assuring him she could have the appropriate legal documents drawn up by then. "Yeah, I'll fly into Richmond and catch a cab," Julian said.

After hearing the good news, he spent the rest of the day packing the few possessions he refused to leave behind. He filled a tall black suitcase and a green hiker's backpack with his clothes, personal hygiene items, and his father's beer stein. He collected everything else and put it all in trash bags. Knowing anything of value would be taken by the homeless, Julian made several trips to the dumpster until his apartment was bare. He even gave his flatscreen television, microwave, and recliner to his neighbor, Gus.

As everything fell into place, evening approached. When the sun began to set, Julian packed the last item he wanted to take, his red laptop.

What the fuck am I doing? What if she doesn't even come? What if I just gave away my shit, missed my writing class, and embarrassed myself with my family for nothing? There it was, the crippling anxiety and the questions he'd never bothered asking himself. He shut his eyes and remembered to breathe, just like Violet would say. *She'll come*, he assured himself. Sure enough, her Firebird landed at 6:44 on the dot, and there came a knock at his door. When Julian answered, he was greeted by the angel herself, with a smile so serene not even God could fathom such beauty.

Violet took Julian's hand, posing a question of her own, "Are you ready. Jul?"

Chapter Seventeen

Julian was nauseous with anxiety, spending most of the ride back to the Parliament in silence. Once comfortable enough to speak without the fear of vomiting, he told Violet what Scarlet had said. "So, are we staying in Vegas tonight, since we aren't supposed to go to Richmond until tomorrow?" he asked.

"After dark, Dad flew back to New York," she said. "He has your money, and he wanted us to come after I picked you up."

"Was going back alone a good idea?"

"Dad never talked to Eric or the others, but he spoke to William. The police were all over the club last night, and they interviewed several witnesses."

"What did they find out?"

"That a couple of guys, led by a belligerent psychopath, came in with a gun and started shooting. Luckily no one was shot. From what I understand, Cauldwell gave the police Dad's name, but that won't mean much to them. A few of the patrons told the police Eric got away, but everything happened so fast, none of them actually saw what happened."

"How does Father Grant know all this?"

"Eric has sources, and William said he came to see him this morning before daybreak. He told Dad Eric would meet us at the club. Since Cauldwell and his men are behind bars, it should be safe for the time being."

"What about the others? Where are they at?"

"Bern and Anna are hiding in the city somewhere, but Eric doesn't know where. No one's heard from Bishop, so I don't know where he is."

"I hope he's okay."

"I'm sure he's fine," she said while exiting the freeway. "We're vampires, and we know how to take care of ourselves when things get hairy."

"And the cops are treating Cauldwell like he's insane?"

"Yeah, but they have also been looking for Dad, since he owns the club. So, he went on ahead to talk to them before we all meet up."

"Why would he do that?!"

"Because the police think Cauldwell lost his mind. If Dad cooperates, it will get them off his back, and buy everyone some time to figure out what they're going to do." Once Violet reached the Parliament and parked in the garage, she glanced at Julian's bags in the backseat, next to her own, asking, "Is that everything?"

"Yeah."

"You can wear your backpack, but even with my strength, I don't know if I'd trust myself flying that far while carrying you with you on my back, plus me carrying your suitcase."

Julian shrugged his shoulders, asking, "What do you want me to do?"

"Could you make do without it for a few weeks?"

"What do you mean?"

"Once we get settled in Virginia, Charlie's going to have Dad's money and my car delivered."

"Can you trust him?"

"Yes. He's an honest man, but he's also scared of my dad. The funny part is, Dad would never harm Charlie, unless he gave him a reason." She winked, adding, "But Charlie doesn't know that."

"I guess that's why he was so quick to buy Xavier out last night, right?" Violet nodded. "Alright," he agreed. "I can leave it."

"If something happens, I'll fly back here and get your suitcase myself."

As Julian stood in the elevator, headed towards the roof, his gut churned, knowing what lay ahead. "I don't think I'll ever get used to this part. Flying, I mean."

"It'll get easier," she said as the doors opened.

"Well, that's reassuring," he nervously chuckled. Violet flicked her tongue at him.

Julian removed his spare glasses and placed them in his jacket pocket as Violet led him to the center of the empty helipad. "Are you ready?" she asked.

"As ready as I can be, I guess," he mumbled. Violet turned her back, and Julian wrapped his arms around her.

"Remember, hold on tight, and if you need me to stop, just squeeze me with your legs," she said. Like before, she slowly ascended into the cold, windy sky, high above the Las Vegas strip. "Alright, Jul, here we go!"

Julian closed his eyes and rested his chin on her shoulder. She blasted off like a thunderbolt into the night. Along the way, Julian occasionally opened his sleep-deprived eyes, refusing to chance zoning out or dozing off. Eventually, the pair landed on the familiar rooftop in New York. Julian retrieved the glasses he'd brought with him, and Violet unlocked the stairwell door. She helped him to the top of the stairs, where he took hold of the rail and followed Violet to her apartment on the fourth floor. Once inside, he reclaimed his bookbag and stuffed the contents in his green backpack.

Violet gathered some clothes and small odds and ends. She pointed at Julian's empty bookbag, asking, "Are you going to use that?"

"No, but you can."

She put her belongings in the bag, saying, "Dad and Eric are probably in the chapel … and I'm hungry. Let's go find them."

Downstairs, Violet took Julian's hand and led him through the quiet, dark hall and lobby, where the front doors were tied shut with chains and a padlock. "Could you look around the floor and see if you can find my other glasses?" Julian asked.

Violet nodded and he watched her search the floor, finding nothing. "In all the commotion, they were probably kicked off somewhere. I am so sorry," she said. Julian grumbled and rolled his eyes while Violet examined a large hole in the wall left behind by the first shotgun blast. "Those fucking monsters!" she seethed in disgust, placing her tiny left hand over her face. As she wept, Julian took her free hand and cupped both of his around it. She pulled her other hand away from her gloomy, wet face and slowly looked into his eyes. Like always, her somber brown almonds melted his empathetic heart.

"Sometimes people snap and become unhinged," he said. "They had no right, but what would you do if someone killed your child?"

Violet sighed. "I know death. I also know loss. I have loved, lost, and I have killed." Julian knew she was a killer, but the verbal confession sent chills throughout his body. To his surprise, he was otherwise emotionally indifferent. "I have taken people from their families, and families from their people," she continued. "We all have. It's what we do, so we can survive as such selfish and privileged creatures."

Julian thought deeply about such privileges, but he also knew the consequences of his choice. He took a deep breath, and out it came. "I want to be like you, a vampire. I want the world to be my playground, too." Her eyes instantly lost their gloom and twinkled so brightly they could have sparked a fire. "But I don't want to take innocent lives to sustain my own," he added.

Violet firmly squeezed his hands and said, "We have a good thing going for us—getting our food, but there are no guarantees we always will. You're still holding on to your moral fiber. It's understandable, but you have also questioned reality almost every day of your life. Even as a child, and with all you have experienced, a part of you already knows reality is a game we manifest as we go. If you felt threatened by any of this, you wouldn't be here."

"I told your father something similar about reality, and whether or not anything truly exists. Do you remember? 'It's a paradox,' he said, and I agree."

"I remember," she said. "Maybe it does, and maybe it doesn't, but isn't that the nature of purpose and faith?" Julian slowly bobbed his head as his heart fluttered, taken aback by her existential view.

All grew silent as they lost themselves in each other's eyes, joining hands again. Standing so close, Violet's warm breath tickled Julian's neck with each exhale. It was always about waiting for the right moment: that perfect, present moment. Julian took another deep breath and made it count. He shut his eyes, slowly inching his lips forward. His left eye peaked open. In the dim light, he observed both his immortal's eyes, sealed shut. Her inviting, pillowed lips were parted slightly, eagerly awaiting his. He advanced until their flesh lightly grazed.

"No!" A deep, horrendous wail shattered the entirety of the club, obliterating the moment and practically scaring Julian out of his shoes.

"What the fuck was that?!".

"It came from the chapel!" Violet called out, sprinting towards the entrance. Julian ran too, nearly barreling her over when she came to a sudden halt. "My God!" Her shrill cry rang grotesque and macabre to his ears.

Julian looked where she looked, but his vision was obscured. As his eyes adjusted, he followed a spattered red trail along the hardwood floor until two shiny black shoes and a pair of black slacks came into focus. Tucked inside the pants was a matching black shirt, covering a torso that lay belly up. Two inanimate hands hung from the long sleeves. At the neck, the head was missing. Only a gory red stump remained, surrounded by more blood.

"Who—who is that?!" Julian cringed, immediately looking away and gagging.

"Da—Daddy?!" Violet whimpered like a frightened child.

"I ... I—I do not understand," spoke Xavier, out of view. Julian's eyes followed the direction of the voice to the blond vampire, who knelt beside the body.

"Violet ... who—who is that?" Julian asked again.

"It's Eric," she cried. "They killed him!" Her face imploded with a mixture of anger and grief. "Who the fuck did this?!" She wailed and paced in circles with her cheeks puffed, arms extended, and her fists balled like she was ready to unleash the wrath of God upon a lowly snowflake.

"You know who," Xavier replied.

"Something's not right," she said. "After last night, it wouldn't make sense to just come in here and do this!"

Xavier sighed, saying, "Obviously there are more than three of them," as he rubbed his eyes, trying to stop the tears.

"Where's his head?!" Julian asked with alarm.

"They must've taken it," Xavier said. "Cauldwell said his daughter's head was also taken. This was meant to send me a message."

"How did this even happen?!" Violet asked. "Last night, they couldn't even catch him!"

"Well, they caught him somehow!" Julian said.

Violet looked at Xavier and asked, "Could they still be here?"

"I do not think so. If they were, we would already know."

Violet dropped to her knees beside her father, screaming, "What the hell are we supposed to do now?! My brother is dead!"

Xavier stood and helped Violet to her feet. "We have to get out of here," he said. "Julian, did you speak with your aunt and uncle?"

"Yeah, they're going to sell it to me," he murmured.

"Okay, your seven million dollars is in that suitcase over there." Xavier pointed towards the dark, glass bar where the biggest suitcase Julian had ever seen rested. It was at least five by four foot, plain black, with a long metal handle on one end and wheels on the other. "I want you to take it and buy the house."

"Aren't you coming with us?" Violet asked.

"I must take care of something first."

"What do you mean?" she asked.

"I need to figure things out. If the two of you are with me, neither of you are safe," he said. "And Eric deserves a proper burial."

"We need to kill them all for what they did to my brother!" Violet howled. Xavier approached her and embraced her in his arms, calming her erratic behavior. After she took a few breaths and cleared her throat, she pulled away and said, "If it wasn't for that son of a bitch coming in here, and thinking we had something to do with his daughter, my brother would still be alive, and this place would be filling up right now, not chained and padlocked!"

"What do you mean, 'chained and padlocked'?" Xavier asked.

"The front door has a chain around the handles with a big padlock on it. You didn't do that?" she asked.

"No, I did not. When did you two get here?"

"Just a few minutes ago. First, we went to my room so I could get some things. I figured you and Eric were down here. When did you get here?"

"Just now. I went to the precinct to clear things up. Then I walked here and came in through the back kitchen entrance."

"What happened at the police station?" she asked.

"I pressed charges against all three of them. I have no intentions of appearing in court, so, without me there, Cauldwell and his friend will be set free in a month. As for the shooter, Kevin Cauldwell—the brother—I do not know what will happen to him."

"So we have a month before they will be out looking for us?" Violet asked.

"That will give the two of you enough time to set the house up to your liking, blend in, and get cozy."

"We're supposed to meet his aunt and uncle tomorrow night, in Richmond."

"After that, go to the house, get settled, and I'll find you when the time is right," he said.

"But what about Eric's killer? They are still out there," said Violet. She took another look at the corpse and her tears returned. "I'm scared, Dad."

"Me too, my sweet child." He pulled her close again and slowly caressed the back of his fingers down her cheek, wiping away her tears. "Bernard and Anna are safe. I am sure Bishop is too. But fret not, I will take care of it." He kissed her forehead and muttered, "I love you, Violet," forcing a smile for his daughter amidst such a bleak moment.

"I love you too, Daddy," she said, tears flowing like wine.

Xavier came to Julian, whispering, "Though she overpowers you, a delicate flower lies beneath. Please, be good to her."

"I will give her my all, I swear."

Xavier tried to smile again, but he only nodded before shaking Julian's trembling right hand. He turned back towards Violet and said, "Go to the freezer vault in the kitchen and take as many bags of blood you can carry. Find somewhere safe and dark until you go to Virginia. Please be careful." Xavier gave Violet a final hug before saying, "Now, go, my children." After Julian followed Violet to retrieve several pint-sized IV bags of blood from the locked freezer, she took his hand and obeyed her father's orders, leaving Xavier and what remained of her brother behind.

Chapter Eighteen

Julian and Violet took a cab through the Lincoln Tunnel to New Jersey. They arrived at a tall brick building, which overlooked the Big Apple from across the Hudson. A small white sign hung loosely above a clear glass door, reading *City-Side Hotel.* "This is a safe place," Violet said. She and Julian took their luggage from the trunk and walked side by side into a small lobby with a sliding glass window. "I'll do the talking," she said. Julian nodded, silent, queasy, and in shock since leaving the club, unable to remove the grisly image of Eric's mutilated corpse from his mind.

Violet tapped a small silver bell next to the window, and an older, bald gentleman with dark liver spots appeared. He slid open the window. "Yes?"

"Hello, I'd like to get a room for tonight and tomorrow night, please," Violet somberly said.

"Right, then," said the man. "That'll be one hundred and forty-four dollars." Violet handed over a fifty and a hundred-dollar bill from her purse.

"Keep the change," she said.

The man smiled and handed her a brass key. "You're in room eleven," he said.

"Thank you," she replied, handing the key to Julian. "Hold this for me, please," she said, taking the handle of the large suitcase with the money in one hand while leading Julian to their room at the end of a dingy white hallway with the other. Inside, Violet used sheets and blankets to block any shred of light from getting past the motel's curtains in the morning. "That ought to do it."

"Are you sure it will keep the sunlight out?" Julian asked.

She sternly glared, saying "As long as you don't take it down, it will."

He looked at the neon red numbers on the generic alarm clock that sat atop a wooden end table next to the queen sized bed. *2:22*, they read. Although still traumatized, Julian curled up on his side of the bed and yawned. "If you're tired, get some sleep, Jul,"

Violet said, sitting on the other side of the bed, facing away from him.

Offering sympathy, he gently rubbed his hand down her back. "Are you okay?" he asked.

"No, but I guess I'll have to be," she mumbled, placing both hands over her face and crying. Julian pulled her closer and wrapped his arms around her from behind. She laid her moist cheek against his shoulder.

"I—I don't know what to say, but everything will be alright, I promise," he softly whispered.

"He was my brother," Violet sobbed. "We both received our gifts around the same time. You would have loved him. Eric was always so sweet to me—e—e." As Violet's voice crumbled, she wept harder, rolling over, and burying her wet face in Julian's chest.

"Shh … I got you," he whispered, gently rocking her. "It's okay. It's—"

Thump. Thump. Thump.

"What the hell?" Violet pulled away. A loud, consistent banging drew their attention to the wall behind the bed, vibrating with each muffled echo from the next room over.

Thump! Thump! Thump!

The banging grew louder and faster, followed by the sounds of a female moaning in pleasure. Despite the somber mood, Julian and Violet giggled, knowing what was going on. "Oh no! John! Not there! Don't put it there, John!" the woman squealed. Julian watched Violet's jaw drop, laughing and clearly getting a kick out of it.

He thought fast, wanting to keep Violet's mood uplifted. "Give 'er hell, John!" Julian shouted. Violet's cheeks exploded in laughter. "Lay the fire to it, John!" he continued.

"Shh!" Violet quickly covered his mouth with her palm as the laughter continued. The banging and moaning stopped, but Julian's gesture had the desired effect. "You're crazy! You know that?" Violet said while still laughing and trying to contain herself.

"I know." Julian smiled before taking his glasses off. After setting them on the end table, he stretched his tired legs and wiggled his toes. With Violet's tears gone for the time being, he asked, "Are you alright?"

"I will be," she said. "Thank you for making me laugh."

"You're welcome," he replied.

Violet yawned, also stretching out on her left side, facing Julian with her elbow against the mattress and her cheek resting against her palm. "Tell me more about Gunnar and this house," she said.

"Gunnar's just a little coal mining town in southwest Virginia. I hated it there. When I left, I swore I would never go back."

"I know how you feel. I never wanted to go back to Savannah, but I did, one more time after I moved to New York."

"How did it go?"

"Not so well …So, this house—is it just big, or is it also unique and nice?"

"Both. The living room has a massive stone fireplace, and the floor is smooth granite."

"Damn! It sounds lovely."

"They also had a long dining room table, like you'd expect the cliché mansion to have," he said as Violet smiled. "I'm excited to show you but nervous about being close to my grandpa again."

"To hell with him. If he was worth the effort, he would've defended you, or at the very least, made Bobbi-Jo tell you about your grandmother's passing. People like that are terrible and feel nothing but their own pride."

"You're right. I just wish I could accept it," he said, yawning again and rubbing his heavy eyes, fighting sleep.

"Get some rest, Jul. I'll be joining you shortly."

"Okay," he mumbled with his eyes already shut. "Goodnight, Violet."

"Goodnight, Julian," she whispered.

***

Several hours later, Julian awoke, opening his eyes and jolting forward. He drowned in sweat, heaving so deep he was nearly hyperventilating. Once remembering where he was, he caught his breath and placed a hand over his racing heart. After panning the cool, dark room, he lay back and shut his eyes, assuring himself: *It's okay. You're alright. Everything is fine*, just like he'd assured

Violet, fast asleep beside him. As her vanilla scent filled the air, Julian focused on the steady rhythm of her breathing.

He tried to clear his mind and go back to sleep, but he saw only Eric's remains and Christopher Cauldwell's golden curls and brown overcoat standing above it. With a sinister grin, the psycho-militant looked in Julian's direction, piercing a hole through his heart with his eyes. "I know what you are, Julian!" he snarled. "Goddamn demon!"

Gasping for air, Julian opened his eyes. The lights were on, and Violet sat in a blue padded chair at a small table in the corner of the room. He caught his breath and shook off the unsettling feeling of watching her sucking red liquid from a clear tube connected to a plastic IV bag, as if it were a juice pouch. Although he'd never seen her feed before, Julian watched, unphased and indifferent. When she noticed him watching, she pulled the small tube away from her crimson lips, licking away the excess. "Hi," she muttered.

"Good morning." He shivered, yawned, and pulled the cover away, asking, "What time is it?" as he stood and stretched his arms above his head.

"It's almost seven PM," she replied. "What time are we supposed to meet your aunt and uncle?"

"I told them we'd be there by eight. Scarlet said she was going to make us dinner."

"I can't eat regular food," she said. "The only thing vampires can safely consume is blood and water. Anything else will rupture our stomachs and kill us."

"We'll improvise," he said, observing the now empty IV bag on the table. "I don't know how much blood you have or how it works, but even though it was frozen, it won't stay good for long, will it?"

"No, it won't. I'll need to put it somewhere cold as soon as I can. I don't have much, but I should be fine for a few weeks. I know you've got to be hungry, though. When we get to their house, be sure to fill your belly."

"You're a nurturer, aren't you?"

"I'd like to think so. You deserve to be loved."

"You make me feel loved," he said while putting on his glasses. For the first time since finding Eric, Violet smiled with sincerity.

Julian walked to her side of the bed, taking her hand in his while peering deep into her hopeful almonds. "I love you," he said. A tear formed in the corner of her eye as they silently lost themselves in the other's gaze for what seemed like an eternity. It was not the right time to kiss her, but the moment was much more than that.

"I …" Violet began, but her flood gates burst and she broke into tears again.

"Come here," Julian whispered, pulling her close and wrapping his arms around her sunken shoulders. She laid her cheek against his chest and he lightly rubbed the back of her head while holding her tight. Her vibrant energy pulsated from her body to his, and the embrace lasted long after they let go. He could still feel her touching him, even when she was not.

She snorted, wiped her tragic eyes, and asked, "Are you ready to go?"

"Yeah," he said before putting on his sneakers and jacket.

"We can launch from the roof. We have to use the fire escape to get up there." Violet walked to the window, removing the makeshift shades and sliding the glass open. "If I carry the suitcase with the money, and your smaller bag, do you think you can make it up there with your green bag?"

"Is there a rail to hold onto?"

"Yes, and I will be right there if you need me."

Julian approached the window, asking, "How many floors is it?"

"Eight," she said.

He sighed but agreed, strapping the green bag to his back and watching Violet hang the smaller black bookbag on hers. "Alright, let's go," she said.

Slowly they made their way to the roof. Out of breath, Julian huffed, puffed, and asked, "Are—are you … are you going to be okay with me on your back while you carry that suitcase?"

"We don't have nearly as far to go this time. I'll fly slower, but it should only take a few minutes to get there," she said. Julian nodded and put away his glasses. Only moments after becoming airborne, they landed. Julian opened his eyes as Violet announced, "We're here, Jul. We're in Virginia. Welcome home."

Chapter Nineteen

As he and Violet stood beneath a dark overpass, Julian put on his glasses and scanned the area. Bright yellow streetlights shone in the distance; overhead, traffic rumbled down I-95. "Whoa!" Julian gasped. "You weren't lying. We got here fast!"

Violet giggled and said, "Get their address, and we'll find a taxi."

Julian took a few breaths to collect himself before retrieving his phone and finding the address. "Okay, I got it." Violet took his hand and slowly led him down a dark sidewalk towards the lights. A block away, they reached a busy intersection and waited for a passing cab until Violet threw up her hand and caught the driver's attention.

On their way to Scarlet and George's house, Julian straightened his hair, wondering what he would say. "I'm nervous, Violet. I haven't seen them in years, and they probably think the same of me as the others. I hope it goes well."

Violet took his hand and their fingers interlocked. "It will be fine, Jul, I promise," she whispered in his ear.

Once they arrived at a little white house on a suburban cul-de-sac, Violet paid the driver and they collected their bags. After the cabbie drove away, Violet opened the suitcase with the money and removed several thick, paper-clasped bundles, placing them inside the black bookbag. Julian caught a glimpse of all the cash and nearly salivated at the sight.

After Violet collected the million, she closed the suitcase and zipped the bag. She took Julian's hand, leading him up the short, paved driveway with a green car and silver SUV parked at the top. As the pair followed the porchlight, a short, thin woman opened the front door and greeted them. "Hey, stranger!" she said. Julian smiled politely, taken aback by how much his aunt aged since he last saw her. What was once short and dark red hair had turned gray. Her face was wrinkled, and she wore thick, brown-framed glasses and a plain green sweater. As Julian made it to the door, Scarlet reached out and hugged him. "How are you?" she asked.

"I've been good, Aunt Scarlet. How about you?"

"Oh, we've been doin' alright." She looked at Violet, smiled, and said, "Hello there, I'm Scarlet."

Violet smiled back, saying, "Hi. I'm Violet, Julian's ..." She paused for a second. "Friend," she nervously chuckled.

"It's nice to meet you, Violet. That's a beautiful name," she added. Violet blushed as Scarlet took a few steps back through the doorway and stood aside. "Well, come on in, you two," she said. Julian motioned Violet to go first. She walked on and lightly bowed her head to Scarlet as she entered the small home.

"So, Julian, you hit it big in Vegas, huh?" Scarlet asked as he scanned the living room with tan carpet, white walls covered in various family photos, and the scent of broiling meat in the air.

"Yeah," he said, grinning at Violet. "Do you want us to take off our shoes, or ...?" Julian asked, looking at his feet.

"Nah, you're fine. Come, have a seat." Bright light showered the room, but it took Julian time to focus and learn the layout. Violet helped him to the nearby cream sofa, and they took a seat. "It'll be a few minutes before dinner is ready, but we're making hamburgers," Scarlet said. "Is that okay?"

"Sounds great," Julian said, remembering a few nights earlier when he'd eaten the burger at the club. Violet sighed, placing her palms over her cheeks and eyes, trying not to cry.

I am so sorry, he thought. It was Eric who'd made the burger, and Julian had forgotten all about it, never thanking him for it. *I wish I could have gotten to know him.* Violet pulled her hands away from her face and took Julian's left hand, pulsating her sadness through the exchange. Julian sensed the emotion, along with gratitude and empathy.

"Actually, the burgers are ready now," an older man's voice announced from another room. He stuck his head out from the doorway and smiled. "Hello, Julian," he said. George's hair was dark and short. He had sunken cheeks and a wrinkled forehead.

"Hey, George. How've you been?" Julian asked.

"Doing well and working hard," he laughed. "You and your girlfriend come on in and grab a seat at the table."

Violet nudged Julian with her elbow. He thought fast, cleared his throat and said, "Violet can't eat anything. Sh—she's sick, and her doctor has her on a strict water and vitamin diet for right now."

"Oh, dear. That's too bad, Violet. Is everything alright?" Scarlet asked with a look of concern.

Violet smirked. "Yeah, I've just been a little deficient lately, and I am doing a cleanse of sorts. I hope I haven't offended you," she politely added. "The food smells great."

"Well, you're more than welcome to come sit at the table with us," Scarlet said, motioning for them to follow her into the small dining room with a square wooden table and four chairs.

"So, you want to buy the old house, Julian?" George, sitting opposite Julian, asked while stacking slices of tomato and onion on top of his burger.

"Yeah," Julian said. "I always loved that house. Since I hit it big, I wanted to buy it."

"Well, we're glad the place meant so much to you, Julian. We always loved having you there," said George.

As Julian made two burgers and helped himself to some home fries from a clear glass bowl, Scarlet said, "My sister would be so proud of you if she were still here, Julian."

He sighed, knowing the subject of his grandmother would come up eventually. "I … umm. About my grandma, there's a reason I wasn't at her funeral," he said as his heart boomed faster and chills stabbed his nerves like icicles. "I—"

"It's okay," Scarlet interrupted. Sitting to Julian's right, she reached across the table and placed her frail, wrinkled hand over his. "You don't have to explain," she said. "We don't know what happened, but I know you were in a bad spot. At the funeral, Bobbi-Jo was telling anyone who would listen that you and that girl you were with was at the beach, and you refused to come. As close as you and Gin were, I knew something wasn't right."

"What?! We left for the beach on Sunday because nobody told me anything. Bobbi-Jo left a message on Faith's phone but never told me Grandma died." Julian grunted, shook his head, and quickly finished his first burger, trying to forget Bobbi-Jo's obnoxious face.

"Your grandpa or somebody should have told you," said George. "Someone could've come to Staley and got you. Hell, if we knew, we would have picked you up on our way through."

"Well, not everyone shares your empathy," said Julian. "I made mistakes too, but you're right. Bobbi-Jo rubbed it in my face by calling me at all. I don't know why they did it." Julian lowered his head. From his left, Violet took his other hand.

"It's over with now, and there's nothing anyone can do," Scarlet said.

"She's right, Julian," said George. "It's a hard pill to swallow, but you need to put it behind you, understand? People do terrible things. Sometimes it's just for the hell of it."

"They're both right," Violet added.

Scarlet smiled and said, "I like her, Julian. I think this one might be a keeper."

Violet blushed and said, "Thanks. I'm tryin' to straighten him out."

As the subject concluded, everyone finished their food. Julian even scarfed down a third burger and second helping of fries while Violet enjoyed a glass of ice water. Everyone talked a little more before Julian handed over the money and signed the deed. George gave him the keys to the house, and Scarlet hugged them both, saying, "Bye, Julian, I hope you enjoy the house like George and I once did."

Julian strapped his green bag to his back and shook George's hand while Scarlet told Violet "It was very nice to meet you." She walked them to the door and waved goodbye as Violet led Julian down the dark driveway with one hand and pulled the big, black suitcase with the other.

"See," Violet said. "Not everyone in your family feels the same about you. They are both nice people." She briefly laid her head against Julian's shoulder as they walked. Once they were out of sight, she found a dark place to blast off towards Gunnar. "Could you show me a map on your phone, so I can see where to go?" she asked.

Julian retrieved his phone, entered the info, and showed it to Violet. "Here you go," he said, showing her the screen.

"Okay. It'll be five minutes at the most." Julian quivered and his gut rumbled at the idea. "After this, you won't have to fly anymore for a while, unless you just want to," she teased.

"I need a vacation," he grumbled before putting away his glasses and stretching his arms around Violet's shoulders.

"I'll be quick, I promise," Violet said before shooting high into the clouds. Julian instantly became nauseous as his full belly churned with the high velocity. He took shallow breaths to avoid vomiting until he couldn't take it anymore. With the sides of his knees, he squeezed against Violet's thighs. "Are you alright?!" she shouted before slowly coming to a halt, hovering in midair.

"I ... I think ... I think I'm gonna—" Before he could say it, Julian's dinner spewed from his mouth and both nostrils like a ruptured dam. He tried to hang his head to Violet's side and avoid a mess, but as he did, the heavy green bag on his back shifted weight to the side, and Violet squirmed to get a better grip on the heavy suitcase.

"Shit! ... Shit! ... Shit!" Julian panicked as the wet vomit became a slick lube, and he slid off Violet's back.

"Julian!"

Chapter Twenty

This is it. This is how I die. Julian closed his eyes and accepted his fate, plummeting and instinctively kicking and waving his arms wildly. As certain death approached, his body tensed, bracing for impact. Expecting to see his life flash before him, he experienced only darkness and cold air.

"Gotcha!" Mere feet from the ground, Violet snatched his hand. Seconds later, they landed on a dark, gravel road, surrounded by trees. "Oh my God!" Violet huffed and puffed. "Are you okay?!"

Julian's heart bludgeoned so fast, he thought it would attack him at any moment. "I ..." he gasped before vomiting again. His head hung over, and his hair blew in the cold, mountain wind, tickling his cheeks. Violet stood by his side, gently rubbing his back while he finished. "Wh—what the fuck?!" he croaked, trying to catch his breath.

"You almost died! That's 'what the fuck!'"

"I—I—I am sorry, Violet," he gasped. "Are you alright?"

"I need to wash my hair, but I'm fine," she said. "What about you? Are you okay? I am so sorry I didn't catch you."

His heart ran with the bulls, and his adrenaline was on high alert, but he said, "I think so."

"I told you, you need to hold on tight." She panned the wooded area around them. "Where are we?"

Julian put on his glasses and took his phone from his pocket, finding their location on the GPS. "I know where we are," he said. "We're only about twenty minutes from the house. Route four-sixty is just down this road a little way."

Violet took the handle of the suitcase and said, "Let's walk a while and see what happens. Flying wouldn't be a good idea right now because I don't want you to get sick again. Here, let me carry your backpack." She pulled the green bag from his back and strapped it on over top of the smaller black bag on her back.

Holding Julian's hand, she led him down the crunchy gravel road towards the main highway. Along the way, Julian took deep breaths through his nose, catching the familiar woodsy scent of Appalachian Mountain air. Once reaching the four-lane, they walked alongside the metal guardrail. "So, this is where you grew up?" Violet asked, breaking the awkward silence.

"Unfortunately," he mumbled.

"Well, I know you don't like it here, but we'll make it work," she said. "I grew up in mucky Georgia, and I wouldn't ever want to go back there, but this place seems quiet and peaceful."

"I've left this area a few times, trying to escape it, but I always left for someone else, and never myself. When I moved to Vegas, I did it for me, and learned independence and got used to relying on myself."

"And look where it got you."

"Yeah, millions of dollars, and covered in barf," he chuckled.

"It's not that bad," she laughed. "It's mostly just on your shirt and there's a little in my hair, but that's it."

"I just almost died." He snorted in disbelief.

"If I hadn't stopped when I did, you would've, but luckily, I caught you," she said. They continued over a mile down the highway, holding hands while cars, trucks, and the occasional motorcycle passed with their headlights illuminating the way. "How far do you think you can walk?" Violet asked.

"I'm not sure, but honestly, I'm exhausted."

"Alright, if you want, we'll stop at the next road we find, going up one of these mountains, and I'll fly us the rest of the way. I'll go slower, so you don't get sick again."

"That's fine."

"So, you said the house has a big basement, right?" she asked, attempting small talk.

"Yeah, it does."

"Do you know if they left anything behind when they moved? I noticed they didn't have much in Richmond."

"Scarlet told me on the phone they left some things behind, but I'm not sure what. I haven't been in there since Thanksgiving, nineteen-ninety-two. My mom went up there drunk. She embarrassed everyone and I never went back."

"Alcohol will do that. I am sure she meant well, but she was likely damaged after your father died."

"You're right. He messed her up badly. She drank since her teens, but the abuse made it worse. I spent so long trying to get her to stop, but it was like beating a dead horse."

"My father also drank. I know what it's like. Because of alcohol, he did a bad thing to me once," she mumbled with a hint of sadness in her voice.

Julian looked in her direction, asking, "What do you me—"

"Look out!" Before Julian knew what was happening, Violet yanked him several feet from the road as a car came speeding by, nearly sideswiping them both.

The car never stopped. Instead, the driver honked their horn, and a male voice shouted, "Get the fuck off the road, y'all!" from their window as they passed.

"Fuck you!" Violet barked back. She turned to Julian and asked, "Are you alright?"

"Yeah," he said. "Welcome to southwest Virginia."

"Goddamn assholes," Violet mumbled, guiding Julian back to the curbside. "We need to get off this road," she said. "I think I see a dirt road up ahead. Is your stomach okay now?"

"Yeah, and we're not very far away," he said. Once they reached the dark, dirt road, Violet helped Julian away from the view of the highway. He showed her on his phone where to go, and after strapping the green bag to his back again, Violet took flight, slower than before. Seconds later, they landed.

To Julian's right, a brick garage with a closed white door was illuminated beneath a dull orange streetlight. Thirty feet beyond the single-car garage stood a massive brown brick house. "Holy hell!" Violet gasped in awe at the two-story structure. "This is it, right?"

"It is," he said, also looking on in amazement. Behind them, the driveway stretched nearly two hundred feet to the hollow's mountain backroad with naked trees growing wild on each side. Ahead, the pavement ran beneath and beyond a carport that had two thick brick pillars holding up its left side, with the right side attached to the house. Violet took Julian's hand, guiding him down the driveway towards a bright porch light above the side door, which led to the kitchen. Along their left, a steep and brushy hillside tumbled down over a hundred feet, with Johnny's house at the bottom.

Julian retrieved the ring of keys from his pocket once they reached the white kitchen door, which had one large, clear glass oval window centered on it. Unsure which key fit, he tried them all until finding the right one. After he finally unlocked the door, he took a deep breath and turned the knob. The cool, lifeless scent of an old, unused house filled Julian's nostrils while his priceless grin said it all. As the reality slowly set in, he turned to Violet and said, "Honey … we are home!"

Chapter Twenty-One

Inside, a small area separated the door from the kitchen. Julian slid his hand across the wall, searching through the darkness for a light switch. Luckily, his aunt and uncle had never had the power shut off and had said he could take some time to get it transferred into his name. "Here, let me help you," Violet said, finding it instantly and flipping it on. An overhead light illuminated the small room housing a washer and dryer. Ahead lay a closed, brown wooden door with a diamond-shaped glass window, and behind it, the kitchen awaited its new owner.

Violet opened the door and turned on that light. Julian followed, watching her fixate on the matching chrome stove, refrigerator, and sink. "Ooh! That reminds me." She opened Julian's black bookbag and pulled a plastic shopping bag from the bottom. Inside were several IV bags of blood. "They're still cold!" she said, placing them inside the freezer.

Then Violet saw the dark dining room through the kitchen. Specifically, she appeared drawn to the table; only its polished wood edge reflected light from the kitchen, while the remainder hid in the shadows. Violet glided towards the dining room and turned on the light. "Wow! It's huge!" she gushed. Four elegant wooden chairs sat on either side, with one at each end. The overhead light fixture, surrounded by a white shade, dangled above the center of the table, exposing a thin film of dust along the top.

"It's cold in here." Julian shivered, remembering his shirt was still damp.

"Do you know where the thermostat's at?" Violet asked.

"I'm not sure."

"Come on," she said. "Let's go find it!" She took Julian's hand, leading him back to the kitchen, across the terracotta floor. Opposite the appliances was the entrance to the living room.

Violet walked ahead in the dark, finding the light switch on the other side of the wall. "Oh my God!" She appeared to have died and gone to heaven as she stood on the cold granite floor.

To their left began the wood-paneled wall, with two large white curtained windows and a front door to the driveway. A large, light-gray stone hearth fireplace stood over twenty feet away, on the far end of the room. The stonework stretched the entire wall, reaching the high ceiling above. The firepit was carved deep and wide into the center, and the tall hearth took up over a third of the wall, with a wooden mantle above it. Just to the left of the hearth, an antique grandfather clock stood tall and proud, with black Roman numerals and its shiny brass workings dangling behind a clear glass door.

"This room is beautiful!" Violet marveled, trotting like a giddy schoolgirl over to the fireplace and taking a seat on the two-foot-high hearth. "Goddamn! They put a lot of money into this place, didn't they!" she asked.

"I'd say," Julian chuckled, observing the old furniture. A brown sofa with floral cushions was centered in front of the hearth, with an oval wooden coffee table between it and the firepit. To the right of the hearth, in the corner, stood a golden brown door with a shiny brass knob. "That goes to George's old office," Julian said.

"What does your uncle do?"

"He was a trust fund baby, and his family has an investment club. They own all sorts of things and do nothing but reap the rewards."

"That's pretty smart, actually," she said.

"Yeah, if only all of us could be so lucky," he laughed, forgetting his own recent luck. Violet placed her hands on her hips and playfully scowled at him. "Oh, yeah, right. Sorry," he mumbled, flustered with embarrassment. "Honestly, it just hasn't sunken in yet."

"It's fine, but you apologize too much." She smirked and playfully flicked her tongue. "You don't have to worry about luck. It's been on your side for a while now."

He nodded. "Yeah, you're right."

"Hey! There it is!" she said, hopping to her feet and pointing to a small white box with a silver dial on the wall. She twisted the knob to the right and air began gushing from the vents. "How's seventy-seven, for now?"

"We'll see," he said.

The thermostat was mounted to the right of the office door, on the adjacent wall. To the right of that was another wooden door, leading to the downstairs bathroom. Further along the wall was a third door. "That one goes to the basement," said Julian.

"I'll check that out later," Violet said.

Just to the right of the door, two wide, warm brown wooden steps stood at the base of a fancy staircase. Curving, they stretched nearly six feet in length at the bottom. A matching polished wood banister curled at the end and followed along the beautiful craftsmanship of the remaining steps, tapering along the way to the second floor. Another light switch was mounted at the base, and Julian flicked it on. He held the rail and began to ascend while Violet followed closely behind. A thinner banister was attached to the wall on the left, and the landing ahead was spacious enough to function as a room.

"This is weird," said Julian, stopping near the top and staring at the left corner of the wall a few feet ahead.

"What is it?" Violet asked.

He pointed ahead. "In that corner used to be a TV where I played video games with their daughters, Deidra and Hayley." He turned right, stepping aside for Violet to enter the open room, which had white walls and a baby blue carpet. A window was opposite the staircase, with another on the other end of the room, roughly fifteen feet away. He slowly panned the game room. At the other end, sat an old memory. "Whoa!"

"What?" Violet asked.

He slowly approached a small metal folding table, surrounded by metal chairs with padded brown seats. "This is where we used to play board games with Scarlet. They used to have a whole bunch of them over here on the—"

Julian lost his breath and his jaw dropped when he saw the portion of the wall with white cubby shelves filled nearly to the ceiling with various games and toys, just like he remembered from his long lost childhood. He swallowed the lump in his throat when he realized everything was exactly how he remembered. Numerous stacks of boxes in many sizes and colors stood before him.

"They just left all this here?!" Violet asked, showing equal amazement.

"I guess they didn't have anywhere else to put it all," he said. After admiring the cache for a moment, they moved on. Turning right, they entered a dark hallway leading to the rest of the second floor. Violet flipped on another light switch, revealing another hall on the left, a dark green door ahead, and a closed brown door on the right. "That was Hayley's room," he said.

Violet pointed at the green door, asking, "What about that one?"

"It goes outside to the balcony."

"Ooh! A balcony?!" She started towards it.

"Yeah, it's what's above the carport," he said. She opened the door and Julian followed her outside into the cold again.

The covered balcony, which had been screened in, was roughly ten square feet and stood high above the driveway, overlooking the entire hillside. Route 460 was nearly a quarter mile away at the bottom.

Although street and porch lights shone from various points along the hill, all else was dark. "You know," Julian began. "I bet this would be a great spot to watch the fireworks on the fourth of July." He pointed towards the right of the hill. "Every year, people over there shoot off tons of them."

Violet hung her head and sighed. "I love fireworks, and I bet they would be lovely from up here, but I wish I could see this view like you'll get to in the daylight."

Julian sympathized, taking her hands in his. He said, "I wish I could see what you do in the darkness," staring in her direction, catching a glimpse of her silhouette from the light coming from the open door.

"But you see things I don't," she muttered. "You see life and I see death. I said goodbye to such beauty long ago. After decades of unsuccessfully searching, I came to accept what I wanted didn't exist and my dreams only ever deceived me. I thought I would spend the rest of my life alone in the darkness, and after everything. ..." She paused as their foreheads met.

Julian brushed her hair aside, whispering, "There's beauty everywhere: light, dark, and everything in between." He closed his eyes and said, "Life is what you make of it."

"Death is no different," Violet muttered. Julian could no longer take it. A voice inside his head screamed, *this is the moment.* He readied his lips, but before making contact, Violet backed away and began to cry.

"I—I'm sorry." He opened his eyes and took a step back.

"It's okay," she sobbed. "I'm just sad, and I can't do this right now. I want to, but not like this, not in vain."

"I understand," he said as Violet snorted, cleared her throat, and wiped away the tears. "You want to see the rest of the house?" he asked.

She cleared her throat and said, "I'd like that." They went back inside and shut the door, turning towards the longer stretch of hallway on their right. Julian pointed out the rooms to her. On the left side were two doors. "The first one is the upstairs bathroom. The other one is the master bedroom." Centered at the end of the hall was another door. "That was Deidra's room."

A lone door was centered on the right side of the hall. "This was George's library," he said before opening the door and turning on the light. The musty old smell of books filled his nostrils as he gazed upon the collection. "It's just like I remembered."

All four walls were lined with dark brown shelves, jam packed with books. Violet's eyes widened as she slowly walked through the room. "This is amazing," she said.

"You like it, huh?" Julian grinned.

"I do! Dad would too." Violet slowly patrolled the shelves, looking up and down at all the books. "Most of these appear to be about law and business, but it makes sense, I suppose."

"Yeah, I doubt you'll find anything fun like Bukowski or Hunter S. Thompson in here, but you might come across something interesting."

She turned back towards Julian and asked, "Do you read much?"

"Not anymore."

"Because of your eyes?"

"Yeah, pretty much," he sighed. "I used to read, but even large print is too small for me unless it's on my phone or laptop, where I can adjust the size." Violet took another look around the room before returning to the door.

"Let's go check out the basement!" she said, perking up and taking Julian's hand. Downstairs, Violet opened the basement door. Another set of stairs led down. She flipped on the light and descended, with Julian following behind her. "Hold on to the rail when you come down," she said.

A stale, unpleasant odor was in the air at the bottom. "It stinks down here," he said.

"Yeah. It'll be alright though. It just needs a woman's touch." They were facing another hallway, with two closed doors on each side and a larger space at the end.

"These are all extra bedrooms. There's a small kitchen, bathroom, and living room at the end, there," Julian said, pointing down the hall.

She opened all the doors to let the rooms air out before searching the rest of the area for openings to the outside. "And you're sure sunlight won't get through anywhere down here?"

"I'm sure. This is all underground, and everything is sealed tight. She nodded, smiled, and yawned while stretching her slender arms high above her head.

"I am tired and I'm sure you are too," she said. "I also need a shower and so do you."

Julian laughed. "You're right, I do need a shower, but I'm too excited to sleep."

"I know you are, but we have all the time in the world. This is your house now." Violet turned back towards the steps and said, "I'm going to get my things and take a shower. Then I'll decide which one of these rooms I want to pick. I thought I saw a hammock in one of them. I'd like to use it, if that's okay."

"Of course, it's okay, silly." Julian smiled. "You're the reason I am here. This whole place is just as much yours as it is mine."

"You're so sweet," she said as they headed back up the stairs. She collected the suitcase and black bookbag and yawned again. "Alright, I'm going to go shower and lie down. You'll see me again when it gets dark, tomorrow, but if you need me before then, be sure to shut the basement door behind you before opening any of those other doors."

"I will. And Violet, thank you for all of this. I … I love you."

She smiled and silently looked into his eyes for a moment before saying, "Have sweet dreams and a good night, Julian."

"You too," he said, watching her turn away towards the basement.

Julian took his green bag up to the master bedroom, picked a clean change of clothes, and showered. Once he finished, he stood naked, staring at himself in the steamy mirror, thinking, *I cannot believe this is happening.* It was then that heartbreaking wails came from the metal vent on the tiled floor. From the basement two floors below, Violet cried.

"Eric," she moaned in agony. "My sweet Eric."

Julian wanted to go down there and ease her pain but knew there was nothing he could do for her mourning. … *And who am I, compared to someone she had such a strong bond with for God knows how long?* Julian listened as her cries went on for several minutes until they abruptly ended. *My poor flower.*

After he was dry and dressed, Julian walked back down to the living room. Although he had his own bedroom, it was too quiet upstairs and he wanted to be closer to Violet. He stretched out on the dusty old sofa and shut his eyes. He lay there for hours, listening for more sounds from the basement, but heard nothing. Finally, he looked at his phone, which read *7:44*.

With the sun slowly rising over the surrounding mountaintops, he put on his glasses and stumbled through the dark, in search of the stairs. He found them by tripping over the bottom step and falling to his knees. "Fuck!" he grunted under his breath, trying not to make too much noise.

He stood and climbed, paying great mind to the banister. Ignoring the light switch, he followed the short wall around the large landing to the hallway and green door.

He opened the door and was met by an icy gust. He slowly walked barefoot along the frigid balcony towards the screen, while the surroundings became visible in the blue, early morning light. As he looked straight down, his grandfather's much smaller house came into focus. Because of the angle, only the gray shingled roof was visible. To the right of Johnny's house was his great-grandmother Heiti's old place. The single-story house was nearly a century old, with chipped white clapboard siding and a gray cinderblock base. Gin's mother, Heiti, had died in the early nineties, and although Julian had few memories of her, she had always been kind to him.

After taking in a deep breath of fresh mountain air, Julian watched the bright yellow sun cautiously peeking over the mountains like a shy toddler. He smirked, looking down on all the other little houses with a sense of accomplishment. For so long he'd wanted to be king of the hill, standing above the others, looking down on a family of peasants who never thought he was worth a damn. His life goal had been to give them all the middle finger, saying "I won." If those words could even begin to validate such a rare twist of fate, indeed he had.

Julian looked further down the hill, towards the highway and his mother's old cream-colored double-wide. He closed his eyes for a moment, recalling all the blood, sweat, and tears he spilled there while learning how alone he truly was. Then he opened them and smiled, no longer feeling forgotten or alone. He was blessed, knowing if it were not for such tragic lessons of abuse, neglect, and abandonment, he would not be where he was.

A small cemetery with a few visible headstones caught his eye. It stood atop a short cliff behind his mother's old trailer. Julian had spent many days there as a child, hiding from his mother's boyfriend, Bill, when he had nowhere else to go or anyone to protect him. The difficult memories of all the times he'd sat in the tall grass at the grave of someone else long forgotten by the family brought tears to his eyes.

With the sweet taste of victory in his mouth, Julian wiped away the tears. Still fixated on the graveyard, he whispered, "I did it, baby uncle. I won."

Chapter Twenty-Two

*D*ing ... Dong ... Ding ... Dong ... Ding ... Ding ... The mighty old grandfather clock loudly chimed, announcing the third quarter of an hour. With moments of joy tattered by unsettling thoughts of how he'd gotten there, Julian slowly settled into his new life. He tried being positive and optimistic for them both but could not ignore the wilting sorrow in his flower's eyes regarding Eric's death. "I have something for you," he said, blushing as bright embers crackled in the fireplace.

Violet approached from the kitchen, wearing a purple dress and her white shawl. "I hope you didn't forget and buy me a box of chocolates," she teased.

"No, it's nothing like that, but I didn't know what to get someone who can have anything she wants. So, I found and made you something," he said, holding freshly picked daisies in one hand and a homemade card in the other.

"Well, just so you know, I've never really celebrated Valentine's Day before, but for you I made an exception." Violet's red lips curled upward to a thoughtful and heartfelt smile, and her brown almond eyes sparkled in the fire's reflection. After she'd moped and mourned for weeks, her smile was a breath of fresh air. "When Charlie delivered my car, Dad's money, and that big safe to keep it in, I also got my things back, along with something I wanted to give you," she said.

"Really?! What is it?"

"You first," she said, still smiling, looking down at his hands.

"Here." He handed her the flowers. "I wanted you to have these." She took the daisies and held them to her nose, blushing all along.

"Oh my," she lightly giggled. "Thanks, Jul!"

"I also made you this." He handed her a folded piece of notebook paper. On the front was a poorly drawn heart, with *Happy Valentine's Day, Violet!* written in sloppy handwriting.

"Aww!" She opened it and read aloud: "Dear Violet, this has been one of the toughest, yet best months of my life, and I am so grateful to have spent it with you! I love you. Forever yours, Julian."

Again she blushed, and they hugged. "Do you want your present now?" she asked, picking up a small white box from beneath the coffee table.

"Sure," he said, smiling curiously.

"Close your eyes and hold out your hand."

Julian shut his eyes and opened his hand with his palm facing up. "It's not something gross, is it?" he teased.

"No," she laughed. "It's nothing gross, I promise." She placed a smooth round object, with some weight to it, in his hand. "Okay, you can look now."

He opened his eyes to see a shiny black ball. He spun it around in his hand until finding a white circle with a black *8* printed in the middle. "An eight-ball?"

"Remember the game of pool we played the night we met?"

"Yeah."

"I swiped this from the table before we left. I wanted to keep it to remember you by, in case I never saw you again, but now I want you to have it." Julian got cold chills. The gesture was so sweet, he felt like he could cry. "Happy Valentine's Day, Julian."

"Happy Valentine's Day, Violet," he repeated, looking back at the sentimental gift. "And thank you. I love it!" He focused on his father's beer stein on the fireplace mantle. "I know where I want to put it." He placed the ball on the mantle, symmetrical to the stein, with the *8* facing forward.

After sitting back down, he used a little black remote control to unmute his massive new ninety-six-inch television, mounted on the rough stone wall above the mantle. "Let's see what's on TV," he said. Violet scooted to the opposite end of the sofa, curling her bare feet up to her side, getting comfortable.

The TV was set to channel thirteen, showing the eleven o'clock national news. Julian was about to change the channel when the reporter said, "Up next, we have footage from earlier today of ex-Navy Seals Christopher Cauldwell and Rick Smith, two of the three men responsible for a New York City nightclub shooting last month, as they were released from police custody this morning."

"The hell?!" Violet exclaimed as she sat forward.

The two men stood on a sidewalk across the street from the camera. Christopher Cauldwell's golden blond hair blew in the wind, a dirty mess, and both men had visible bags under their eyes. Rick Smith, the man who'd worn camouflage at the club, pointed out the camera to Cauldwell and glared at the person holding it with ill intent.

"Hey! Hey you! Get the [censored] out of here!" Smith snarled, making an exaggerated swatting motion towards the camera.

"No, wait," Cauldwell said. "Bring yourself over here, kid!" His raspy hiss prompted the cameraperson to cross the empty street. "Yeah! Come over here," the militant instructed.

"Ye—yes, sir?" came a young man's voice.

"I hear I'm a celebrity now," Cauldwell said. "So, I want everyone to hear this loud and clear, you understand?" His animal eyes shifted from the cameraman to the camera itself. "I want everybody to know, vampires are real!" Violet gasped, sinking into the sofa and breathing rapidly.

"Are you alright?" Julian asked.

"Shh!" She placed her hand on his knee and listened.

"I don't give a [censored] if you think I'm crazy. Do your research and ask yourself why so many god[censored] people are dying in such sickening ways! Ask yourself why the leader, Xavier Van Abarrow, ran a nightclub in New York City! Ask yourself, why his daughter, Vi—" The footage abruptly ended, cutting back to the male newscaster in a blue suit.

"Okay, I've just been told by my producers that we needed to cut the footage," he said.

"Oh my God!" Violet squeaked in shock.

"It's okay," said Julian. "Xavier will take care of it, right?"

"I—I don't know," she sobbed. "Cauldwell knows my name! If they didn't turn it off, he would have said my name on television!" She placed her hands over her eyes and cried, "I just want my dad to come back!"

"And, of course," the newsman continued, "Last month, the Navy released a statement detailing the men's dishonorable discharge and the Navy's disassociation with Cauldwell, Smith, and gunman Kevin Cauldwell. In late December, Christopher Cauldwell's daughter, Catherine, was one victim in a string of bizarre murders that have plagued New York City over the past three months. Sources say Cauldwell and his men attacked the club, reportedly believing the owner was a 'vampire.' When an onlooker's cell phone video of the trio's arrests went viral, this story made national headlines."

Violet looked at Julian and said, "I feel like I should be out there doing something, or at least looking for my father, instead of just sitting here."

"I promised him I would take care of you."

"I can take care of myself!" she retorted. "I just wish I knew where he was."

"I'm sure he's fine," Julian said, placing his hand on her curved back, attempting to comfort her. "He's staying away on purpose, so he won't attract any attention here. I mean, wasn't that the point of coming here anyway?"

"I know, but—"

"But nothing. Xavier trusts you, and he wanted you to stay here with me."

"You're right," she sighed. "You're very observant for a blind guy, you know?" She briefly chuckled and wiped away the tears.

"In a related story out of New York tonight," the newsman continued, "An eighty-one-year-old Catholic priest, Father William Grant, a beloved staple of the Greenwich Village area, has passed away."

"What?!!" Violet screamed as a headshot of the smiling old priest flashed across the screen. "No! … No! … Why?! Why him?!" She immediately broke down again, leaning forward with her elbows pressed against her thighs.

"Police say foul play was involved but have yet to release any further information at this time," the reporter concluded.

"Why?!" Violet wailed as she tipped onto her side, collapsing into Julian and crying her heart out. He wrapped both his arms around her and lowered his head to hers.

"Shh …" He softly whispered in her ear, "It's okay. I've got you. It's okay … everything will be okay." Finally, she sat up and leaned back into the sofa, rubbing her eyes and smearing her mascara like so many times before.

"They killed him! William was such a sweet and gentle man," she whimpered. "He had nothing to do with this, and they killed him!"

"Why would they do this? I thought they were after Xavier," Julian said.

"Because William might as well had been one of us! I knew him since he was only seven years old and still had his whole life ahead of him," she cried. "It was in nineteen-forty-four, that I met him, Eric, and my father."

"When you became a vampire?" Julian asked, and Violet nodded. "How did it happen?"

"I'd spent my entire life working on my parents' orange and peach plantation. I always wanted more, but while my two older brothers had all the love and support of my father, he never saw me worth much more than a stupid girl with stupid dreams. To him, I was nothing more than an extra farmhand," she said.

"Both of my brothers went to college, but I never got good grades in school. I refused to get handed off and married like the few friends I had, who were falling into the routine of squeezing out babies and living their lives as subservient sex dolls. So, my father put me to work and never cared about my dreams or ambitions, only my brothers' and his own."

"What were your dreams?"

"Back then, my dream was to be an actress. I wanted to see myself on the big theater screens, knowing all those people watching movies were there because of me, a big Hollywood starlet," she said, chuckling at her own words.

"So, what happened?"

"I worked on the plantation until my twenty-seventh birthday, but from the time I was nineteen, I'd been taking local acting classes. I performed in several plays around Savannah, and everyone loved me, even my acting coach. He said I had the perfect look, a catchy name that could take me places, and talent just as good as the women who put asses in all those theater seats. Throughout those years, I saved as much money as I could. Then, on my birthday, April eleventh, I boarded a bus, bound for New York City and my new future."

"Were you scared?" Julian asked, remembering how nervous he'd been when he moved to Las Vegas.

"At first, I was terrified. I felt like I was going to puke the entire way there."

"What did you do when you got there?"

"I quickly found a job at a small diner, like the one where we first met. It was convenient for me because it was only a few blocks from my apartment. Then once I got settled, I found a new acting coach and even made a few friends at the diner."

"I bet they loved you, didn't they?" Julian asked.

"My co-workers at the diner did, but my acting coach, and the women I took classes with, not so much," she scowled. "They were rude, and unlike my peers back home, the younger, prettier actresses all had cut-throat attitudes. Even my coach ridiculed me, saying 'You're too old for the business!' 'Nobody wants to pay money to see a dumb tomboy farmgirl!'"

"That's terrible," Julian grunted. "But at least there's a silver lining." Violet tipped her head. "While you are sitting here, seventy-five-years later, as beautiful now as you were then, most of them are worm shit, or so old and ugly they make worm shit look good."

"That's a lovely thought," she laughed, blushing.

"So, what did you do?"

"I felt humiliated and knew I would never get anywhere working with those people. I left the school but stayed on at the diner. Luckily, I adapted to big city life quickly, and the last thing I wanted to do was go back to Georgia, especially as a failure. My father already thought I was a fuck up and going back would've only stroked his ego."

"Your dad sounds a lot like my grandpa."

"He was a narcissist and loved rubbing my mistakes in my face to compensate for his own failures," she said.

"You know, even though they were different, it sounds like our paths were similar," he said.

"Yeah, that was one of the first things I noticed when you told me about your family. We have more in common than you think."

"So, what did you do after you quit acting classes?"

"I wasn't sure what I wanted to do or where I'd go next. I lived in the city another four months before the night I was left alone at the diner until closing. There were usually two of us working the late shift, but the girl who was supposed to work with me that night never showed up."

"Were you scared to be there alone?"

"Not at first, I wasn't. Until the last hour, the shop had a lot of people in it, but then, there were two, and finally, just one." With her tears gone, Violet cleared her throat and sighed. "He sat at a small, round table, dressed in black, and with the palest blond hair I ever saw on a man."

"Xavier?" Julian asked.

"Yes," she said. "It started raining hard outside an hour before he came in. With everyone else wanting coffee, he never stood out until the crowd thinned. When I asked him what he wanted, he said, 'Water.' I laughed and teased him a little about it. 'Isn't there enough of that outside?' I asked, but his serious eyes pierced a hole right through me. He said, 'I prefer clean water.'" Violet snickered in her attempt to mock Xavier's voice.

"Then what happened?"

"I got a little freaked out. It wasn't his words or black suit, but those eyes. His whole face gave me chills, but those eyes, cheekbones, and let me tell you," she smirked and closed her eyes. "He had a jawline for days." She opened her eyes before moving on. "But then, he started speaking nonsense, or at least I thought it was nonsense."

"What do you mean?"

"He said he had a dream about me. Then, he told me it was his eight-hundredth birthday, and he knew he was supposed to be there but didn't know why."

"His eight-hundredth birthday?" Julian asked. "He was born in eleven-forty-four?" For a moment, he froze after the number presented itself again. Violet nodded and Julian asked, "What did you say?"

"Well, I feel weird admitting this now, but despite his odd words, haunting features, and youthful appearance, I thought he was kinda cute. I don't know what made me sit at his table with him, but since no one else was there, I did." Violet closed her eyes again, appearing deep in thought. "In no time at all, he told me my entire life story, even things I never told anyone. Some of the things I locked away in the shadows as a child, he saw. I never knew until that moment the true power of words and what they can do to a sleeping mind."

"What did he say to you?"

Violet opened her eyes and took Julian's hand. "He said he was a vampire, and the purpose I searched for in life was something he could give me. Naturally, I got scared. He flashed that smooth grin of his and assured me he wasn't there to hurt me, but I didn't know that."

"He said, 'You have a purpose, and you will change the world.' Then he said, 'I want to take you away from this life of uncertainty and give you absolute divinity.' I had no clue what that even meant, but I took it as a threat."

"What'd you do?"

"New York back then wasn't nearly as hectic as it is now, or as dangerous as it was in the seventies and eighties, but for those rare occasions, we kept a wooden baseball bat behind the counter. I darted for it and held it high above my head, ready to knock a home run."

"What did Xavier do?"

"He laughed, and it angered me. I remember what I said, word for word. 'I might be small and a lady, mister, but I am from the south, and I will fuck you up if I have to!'"

Julian laughed. "I'm sorry, but …" He covered his mouth, trying to contain himself, but his eyes nearly crossed he was laughing so hard.

"Yeah, yeah." Violet snickered, rolling her eyes. "It's funny now, but when it happened, I was scared." She straightened her face and said, "I was dead serious, too. He knew I was, and that's when he laid a crisp twenty-dollar bill on the table. I damn near lost it when he did. 'Water's free,' I told him, trembling like a virgin in a whorehouse, I'm sure. 'Keep it,' he told me. 'That will take care of your rent.' I asked him why he wanted to scare me and then give me so much money, but he left the diner, saying nothing. After that, I broke down on the floor, crying so hard it physically hurt. At the time, I couldn't begin to process what happened. My ego cracked, and somehow, I knew there was more to the universe than I had allowed myself to believe."

"What did you do after that?" Julian asked.

"Once I gathered my composure and closed up for the night, I began my short walk home, carrying my purple umbrella. Even though the rain slacked off, I kept it close in case he came back."

"You were going to fight off a vampire with an umbrella?" Julian asked, trying not to laugh again.

"Would you shut up?" Violet flicked her tongue and nudged his shoulder with the back of her hand. "I was nervous. After my breakdown, I felt like a weight had been lifted off my shoulders, but I didn't know what to expect. At one point, just on the opposite side of the road from my apartment, I swore I heard footsteps. 'Who's there?!' I shouted, knowing I was only scaring myself. Once I was convinced that no one was following me, I turned to cross the street, but I didn't even look. Before I knew it, the most god-awful pain hit me hard, and I went flying into the side of my apartment building."

"Oh no!" Julian gasped.

"I lay on my back, a crumpled mess. All I could smell or taste was blood. I tried to move but was too weak. My breaths grew shallow and burned like fire. The vehicle never stopped, and the streets were empty. 'This is it for me,' I told myself. As my life faded away, I prayed for heaven."

A few more shiny tears formed in the corners of Violet's eyes, and she wiped them away with her fingers. "That's when I heard his voice again," she continued. "'I knew there was a reason I followed you,' he said. I couldn't see him, but I sensed his presence standing over me. At first, I thought he came to finish me off, but it was nothing like that. He picked my broken body up from the sidewalk, and though I faded in and out of consciousness, it was like

I flew through the air. He held me tight, and all I could think about were the superheroes in my brothers' comic books."

"Now you are one of those superheroes," Julian said. "You're something beyond this world."

"Maybe," she said. "But when he took me from that dirty, wet sidewalk, I was dying. He kept shaking me and screaming my name. 'Violet! Don't you die on me, child! You've got a purpose to fulfill,' is what he kept shouting until my body finally gave out and I died."

"But he brought you back," Julian said.

"He did," she nodded. "When I regained consciousness, his wrist was against my mouth, and his blood dripped down my throat. 'Drink, Violet. You must drink,' he said. The taste was awful, but the more I drank, the more life I felt coming back into my body. Finally, he pulled away and allowed me to rest."

"I must've lain there for two or three days before I felt like moving a muscle," she said. "I heard all sorts of strange voices, and sometimes I couldn't decipher if they were real or inside my head. Finally, the day came I found the strength to open my eyes. 'Eric! Hey, Eric. She's awake!' A startled little boy with short dark hair was staring at me like he saw a ghost, then he ran away somewhere. 'I'll get Xavier,' an older voice echoed in my ear. After that, I fell asleep again. My body was so weak, and it had taken all the strength I had to open my eyes and see the younger boy's little childish face."

"Then, a few hours later, I think, I awoke again. 'My sweet Violet, you are getting stronger, but you must feed,' Dad said before he placed a cup to my lips and fed me more blood. It was so hard to get it down my throat without gagging. The little boy came back, asking, 'Is she the new vampire, Eric, the one you and Xavier were talking about?' Eric shooed him away. 'Go find Mom, William, and tell her to read you a Baby-Bible story,' he said."

"'He's getting big and starting to look just like you,' I heard my father say. Then, Eric said, 'I think he looks more like our dad.'"

"Were Eric and Father Grant brothers?" Julian asked.

"They were," Violet said. "At the time, Eric was not yet a vampire. It wasn't until later he chose the gift."

"Why did he choose to become a vampire?"

"I … I don't know."

"You couldn't read his mind?"

"No, I couldn't read minds for a while, and even once I discovered the ability, for so long, I couldn't choose whose mind I read. It all just came to me at random, like with you. I never could read other vampires' minds, and by the time I learned how to control it, he was like me. We came into a lot of our powers together, and there was a time we were very close, but he rarely let anyone in on his personal life." Violet sighed and grew silent before she cried again.

Nearly ten minutes passed in silence. After Violet's tears ended, Julian asked, "Do you like it here?"

"Why do you ask?"

"You've been so sad since we got here, and I know it's because of Eric and Xavier, but do you like it here, in the mountains, and with me?"

At first, she said nothing, but then she confessed, "I honestly don't know."

"I know you're used to city life and being around a lot of people. The only time you go out now is when you hunt, and—"

"When I hunt?" She sat up, cleared her throat, and glared. "Is that what you think? You think I go hunting?"

"Well, you ran out of blood a few weeks ago. Ever since, you go out every other night for several hours and never come back with IV bags, so—"

"So, you assume I'm going out and killing for it?"

"I don't know," Julian said, minding his nervous heart, pounding heavier than it had in weeks.

"Just because I don't bring blood back with me, it doesn't mean I can't get it without killing. Haven't you paid attention to anything my father and I told you about how we live?"

"I—I have, but I—"

"You assumed, right?"

"Violet, what are you doing?!" he whined, feeling trapped and unsure how to respond. "I'm sorry, but what do you want from me? I still don't know what to think about any of this. Until last month, I didn't even know vampires existed. I … I'm sorry."

Violet took a breath and a moment to calm down. "I'm sorry, too, Jul," she said. "I didn't mean to snap at you. I'm just … I don't know." Her shoulders sank, and she lowered her head.

"You're sad. You lost people that were close to you, and your father is missing. You have every right to be upset, but I want you to know I have nothing but good intentions and love in my heart for you, I promise."

"I know you do. I just wish I knew what to do."

"Follow your heart and do what you feel is right. That's all I want." He yawned, adding, "Well, maybe some sleep, too."

"Go get some rest, Jul."

Not long after he made sure Violet would be okay, Julian said goodnight and headed towards the stairs, leaving his delicate flower sitting quietly by the fire. "And Jul," she said as he began up the bottom steps.

"Yes?" he asked, turning to face her.

"Thank you."

Chapter Twenty-Three

"Julian!" Violet groaned. "Hey, Julian! Someone's at the door!" Her sleepy voice echoed through the vent on the floor. Julian's eyes popped open, and he was instantly blinded by the sun shining through his bedroom window.

Knock … Knock … Knock!

The sound came from the kitchen. Julian grabbed his glasses from the nearby nightstand and quickly made his way down the hall, through the game room, and down the steps.

Knock … Knock … Knock!

"Hang on! I'm coming!" His vision was blurred, but he knew the layout well enough to make it to the kitchen fast, opening the first door and unlocking the second.

He twisted the knob and opened the door to a large, hazy figure. "What're you doing, bub, sleepin'?"

Julian's vision was still blurred, but he smiled at the burly bear of a man, surrounded by sunlight. Before he could even focus on the big man smiling back, he shouted "Daryl! How've you been, brother?"

"I told you I'd come by the first chance I got," Daryl said as his face became clear. He was tall, standing 6'3", with short brown hair, a beard, and a broad bald spot atop his head. He was tanned and built rock solid, with the look of a man who'd spent his entire life doing hard work. He even wore an old white t-shirt with *Peachy Keene Mining Corp.* written across the chest in faded black letters.

"Well, I'm glad you finally got to come check out my palace," Julian chuckled, moving aside to let his old friend in.

"Whose Firebird is that there in the driveway?" Daryl pointed at the purple car. "That is badass!"

"That's Violet's."

"Violet, huh? Who's Violet?"

"She—she's my girlfriend."

"I don't reckon?! You got some money, and now you're gettin' some honey, ain't you, bub?" Daryl cackled, playfully elbowing Julian's chest.

"Funny," he chuckled. After entering the kitchen, Julian extended his arms to his best friend, and they shared a hug.

"So, where is she, bub, your lady friend?" Daryl asked, panning the kitchen and dining room area. "Nice table, by the way," he added.

"Thanks. I … umm. She's sleeping," Julian said, motioning Daryl into the living room.

"Whoa!" Daryl's jaw dropped when he saw the fireplace and giant television. "Damn, bub! This place is nice!" Julian lightly cringed at Daryl's loud volume but still appreciated the compliment. "This was Scarlet and George's house, right?" he asked.

"Yeah, it was."

"How much did this place cost?" he asked before saying, "Wait, how much did you actually win?"

"Seven million," he said.

Daryl jumped, nearly knocking himself off his feet. "What the?! … Seven million dollars?! I—"

"Shh!" Julian placed his left index finger over his puckered lips.

"Oh, sorry," Daryl sarcastically whispered. "That's crazy!"

"I know, right?" Julian grinned.

"How much did this place set you back?"

"An even million."

"Wow! And it's just you living here?"

"Violet lives here too."

"Really? Aren't you worried she's taking advantage of you?"

"No, I'm not. Violet has her own money. I met her in Vegas."

"Ah … and she came out here with you when you hit it big, huh?"

"No, it's not like that."

"Alright, if you say so, bub. If you care about her, that's all that matters anyway, right?"

"Yeah, you're right."

"I mean it, Julian. You deserve a good woman. I'm not talkin' 'bout some crazy bitch you met on the strip or somewhere, that'll lock herself in your bathroom," he said as Julian's heart skipped a beat. "I'm talking about a woman who'll treat you right, you know?"

"Yeah, well … there is actually an explanation for that."

"For what?"

"Well, it turns out you were right. Violet has a skin condition and just got out of the hospital the day before from a sunburn." Julian hated lying to his friend, but he had no choice. "That's why she was scared to come out of my bathroom."

"She was in the hospital for a sunburn?" Daryl raised an eyebrow.

"Yeah."

"Damn … is she an albino or something?"

"No, she's just … she has a rare condition, and the sun hurts her."

"So, is that her, Violet, I mean? Is she the one you texted me about?"

"Yeah."

"She was with you before you won, too, wasn't she?" he asked, favorably smiling.

"Yeah, she was."

"So, I'd ask if you could gimme a tour, but since Violet is upstairs sleeping, maybe another time?"

Not wanting to take the time to explain why she was in the basement, Julian said, "Yeah, we were up late last night."

"I bet," Daryl giggled. "My old lady and the girls went shopping in Bluefield, and they won't be home until later this evening sometime."

"How long are you home for?"

Daryl rolled his eyes in the back of his head, thinking. "Today's Saturday, right?" Julian nodded. "Yeah, I go back to Georgia on Monday."

"That's a hell of a drive, especially as much as you do it," Julian said.

"Bub, you're tellin' me. I hate it. I wish my old lady could move down there with me, especially since the girls are both mostly grown and getting old enough to take care of themselves now."

"That's why you got to enjoy the little moments, so they can add up to big ones."

"That's true," Daryl nodded. "Hey! You want to come over to the house with me for a bit before my girls come home?"

"Umm … I … yeah, sure. Why not?" His thoughts immediately went to Violet, wondering if she was still awake and hearing what they were saying. "Can you bring me back before it gets dark?" he asked.

"Yeah, I'll bring you back before then." Julian was already dressed, only needing to put on his jacket and shoes. He still wanted to let Violet know he was leaving but did not want to draw any suspicion towards the basement.

Thinking *I'll be back before dark, Violet*, he shrugged and said, "Alright, let's go."

"Wait," Daryl paused. "Ain't you going to tell your lady friend where you're going?"

"Nah, she'll be fine," he said.

"Alright then." Daryl followed Julian out the kitchen door to his green pickup truck, parked behind Violet's bird.

Julian climbed into the high passenger seat, and Daryl backed down the driveway until coming to a spot he could turn around. They pulled out of the driveway and rode down the hollow's single-lane mountain road. Julian watched the side of his grandfather's honey-colored house approach on the right. A red pickup truck sat in the driveway behind the converted double-wide.

"Have you been to see your grandpa since you've been back?" Daryl asked.

Julian sighed. "Not yet."

"Why not?"

"I just haven't gotten around to it." They rode past Julian's mother's old double-wide on the left. The sight of it made his gut churn and teeth clench. "Man, I hated it there. Getting out of that house and moving to Vegas saved my life," he said as Daryl reached the mouth of the hollow and turned right onto the highway. After following the Levisa River on their left for a half mile, Daryl turned onto a two-lane bridge that passed over the river. Halfway across, the signs at a railroad crossing on the other end of the bridge flashed red and a bell rang, signaling the oncoming train.

"Oh shit, hang on, bub!" Daryl hollered, hitting the gas harder and shooting towards the track like a cannonball. Just before the orange and white striped bar lowered, the green club-cab passed through to the other side.

They rode down a straight patch with houses and trailers to their left as the coal train passed on the right. At the end of the long bottom, Daryl's gravel driveway began, leading up a short, steep hill to a white single-wide trailer at the top. To the right of the trailer sat an open garage housing two blue four-wheelers and a big black Harley.

"Damn, bro," said Julian, observing his surroundings. "You're set up nice, aren't you?"

"Yeah, I can't complain," Daryl said.

To the right of the garage, a big white pontoon boat with a roof sat atop a blue metal trailer-pull. "Whoa! When'd you get that?"

"Last summer," Daryl said.

"It's really nice."

"Yeah, I only got to take it out on the lake twice. The first time, me and my oldest daughter's boyfriend went fishing and rode it around to see how fast it'd go. The other, me and the old lady took it out. We did a little fishing and went swimming."

"I've always wanted to go out on one of those," Julian said.

"Well, I tell you what, bub, this summer after it warms up, we're all going to take it out to Flanigan Dam, and you'll have to come with us."

"Alright." Julian got out of the truck, following Daryl to his front porch and through the door. "Man, I haven't been in here in so long," he said, slowly panning the living room and the kitchen on the left.

"Yeah, I'd say the last time you were here was right after Daddy had the trailer put here, back in ninety-seven, wasn't it?"

"Yeah, probably."

Daryl headed towards the kitchen, saying, "Grab a seat, bub. You want something to drink? We got sweet tea."

"Yeah, sure." Julian sat on a navy-blue recliner near the front door. A moment later, Daryl returned with Julian's tea. "Thanks."

Daryl nodded, taking a seat on a black recliner across the room. "You know, I like this place, and it was nice of Daddy to give it to me after he moved, but I miss the old house," he said.

Julian took a drink. "I'm sure you do. We both had a lot of good times back then."

"Yeah, we got into all sorts of crazy shit before the old house burnt down, huh?" Daryl smiled before grabbing his television remote. "Well, let's see what's on TV," he said, flipping through the channels. "That reminds me. Did you see all that shit on the news last month about those Navy Seals shooting up that nightclub in New York?"

Julian's heart instantly sank, and nausea filled his gut. "I … umm … no, what happened?" he instinctively asked.

"Three Navy Seals went into a club and started shooting at the owner, claiming the guy was a vampire," Daryl said, chuckling at the absurdity. "Can you believe that shit?" As his palms began to sweat, Julian grew sickly and panic-stricken, finding it difficult to catch his breath. "Are you alright?" Daryl asked.

"Yeah, I—I'm fine," Julian muttered, closing his eyes and taking a few calming breaths.

"In the guy's defense, someone killed his daughter."

"Really?" Julian asked, playing dumb.

"Yeah. There's a serial killer loose in New York right now, and one of their victims was the daughter of one of the Navy guys. It's sad that he'd get so torn up over it he'd blame something silly like vampires."

"People mourn differently," said Julian. "If he's a Seal, I'm sure he's seen all kinds of fucked up shit as is."

"Yeah, I guess you're right." Dropping the subject, Daryl put down the remote, settling on an old action movie from the '80s. He looked at Julian and said, "I bet you got all sorts of stuff in mind to buy for your house over there, don't you?"

"Umm …" Julian fumbled for a moment. "I haven't really thought about it, honestly."

"Why not? You're richer than hell now. Enjoy that shit!"

"Would it make sense if I said I'd feel guilty about spending it?"

"Why would you feel guilty? It's your money."

"Yeah, but the way I acquired it, I … well, let's just say, it was given to me, rather than actually won."

"What do you mean?"

"It's hard to explain, but I feel like going nuts with it wouldn't be wise."

"I still don't follow, but it's your money. Do what you want with it."

Julian sighed. "It's complicated."

"That's kinda always been your thing, though, hasn't it? Being complicated."

"What's that supposed to mean?" he asked, taking another drink of tea.

"You've always had weird ways of doing things, like how you disappeared and reappeared a year later. I didn't want you to go. After all those years we were apart, and then when you and Faith broke up, we started getting close again. Then, you left for Las Vegas."

"What'd you want from me, Daryl? I was alone in that house, and the negative energy was too much for me to handle. I couldn't walk through the kitchen without always thinking about what Bill did to me, or without visualizing my blood all over the floor. I couldn't even go in the bathroom without still seeing Bill's druggy friends staring at me like they used to when he made me shower with the door and curtain open."

"Yeah," Daryl lowered his head. "I remember. I never understood why he did that or why your mommy let him."

"He wanted to humiliate me. My mom was always too high and scared to do anything, and I was too weak, and like her, also scared."

"Let me tell you something, bub. Now, you know I've always shot straight with you, whether you like what I had to say or not, right? You can't see good, and you were never a fighter, or at least the physical kind, but you are not weak. You're the most resilient and intelligent person I know. After everything you had to deal with growing up, you came out on the other side beating the odds. Statistically, you should be a psychopath, but you were always better than that."

"Thanks," he said. "It was just painful to be there, you know? The memories hurt, and since the *Ayahuasca*, I've started revisiting all these repressed emotions again so I can learn how to put them behind me. When I was a child, I had no choice. My grandpa could have done something, but he just let it happen. I'm grateful he and Grandma took me in after Mom abandoned me, but I feel so cheated. What Bill and my father did wasn't my fault, but I feel like they all held it against me anyway."

"Speaking of your grandparents, do you know why I quit coming around when you were living with them?"

"I always wondered, but why?"

"There were so many times I'd come see you after I moved to Kentucky with Daddy and got my driver's license. I would even bring girls with me sometimes because I knew you were alone and everyone at school was always mean to you. After Miranda and Clint Junior got popular in high school, they turned their backs on you, and I know you didn't have a social life. I wanted you to feel like a normal teenage boy, but every time I came, they told me you weren't home. Even when I came at night, your bedroom light would be on, but they lied to me anyway."

"What?!" Julian nearly choked on his drink. "Are you serious?"

"I thought you didn't want me coming around anymore, and that's why I quit making the effort."

"I never wanted that," Julian muttered, nearly weeping. "While Clint Junior and Miranda were out living it up with the popular kids, my grandparents kept me sheltered those three years Mom was gone. After you moved, I thought you made new friends and forgot about me."

"After everything we've been through, growing up together, how could I forget about my brother?"

"Why would they do that?!"

"Do you remember that time Daddy walked in on you getting out of the shower, and he saw all them bruises on your back?"

"Yeah."

"Daddy went out and got in his truck without sayin' a word and drove over to your mommy's house. He was ready to beat Bill to death, but that scrawny little mullet-headed bastard was too scared to come outside. I wonder if your grandparents held something against us for trying to help you. I mean, Mommy and Daddy were always good to you, and your grandpa might've held that against us, since he wouldn't ever do anything. Your grandma was a good woman, but compared to your grandpa, there was nothin' she could do."

"Maybe," Julian said. "Men who beat women and children are scared of men who don't. I always knew Bill feared your dad. My grandpa was scared of Bill, so what's that say about him? It makes me wonder how he ever talked my grandma into having three kids with him."

"Three? Don't you mean two?"

"I never told you?" Julian asked. "They had a third child named James, but he died before I was born. He's buried in the graveyard behind Mom's house."

"Really? I never knew," Daryl said.

"I only know because Mom told me once when she was drunk. If she hadn't, I would've never known he was there. Nobody else in the family ever mentioned him or went to visit him, but I did. When we were kids, and I had nowhere else to go and hide, that's where I'd go."

"I'm sure she told you for a reason," Daryl said, finding something new to watch on television and lightening the mood.

As the day progressed, Julian relaxed, finding comfort in visiting his old friend. Eventually, he looked at the clock on the wall, reading 4:34. "The girls should all be home soon," Daryl said. "We're having hotdogs for supper tonight. It ain't much, but you ought to stay and eat with us."

"I would, but I should probably get back before it gets dark," Julian said.

"Well, I can help you with getting to the truck and back inside your house, if that's what you're worried about."

"No, it's not that. I just wanted to get back before Violet wakes up."

"Well, how late does she sleep?! She should already be up. Besides, she ain't your mommy, and if you want to have dinner with your old friend, you should."

"Eh … alright then, I'll stay," Julian said.

"Good, 'cause I'm makin' the hotdogs. In fact, I should probably get started on them. You want some more tea?" Daryl asked, preparing to go to the kitchen.

"Yeah, sure," Julian said, handing his empty glass over.

Later, Daryl's wife, Tara, and their teen daughters, Lily and Kayla, returned home. Each had at least two shopping bags in their hands. "Hey honey," Tara greeted Daryl. As she passed Julian, she politely smiled and nodded. Tara was short and thin, with dark brown hair that hung just below her shoulders.

"Hey babe, how was your day?" Daryl asked.

"Tiring," she said. "I'm ready to eat something and go to bed." From his seat, Julian watched Daryl at the stove, cooking the hotdogs and chili while Tara sat at a small dining table.

"I went over and saw Julian this morning, and then we came back over here," Daryl said. "I told him he could have supper with us. Then, I'm gonna take him back home."

"Alright," Tara said.

Daryl's daughters came out of their bedrooms, sharing a laugh. "Hey, Lily," Daryl said, catching his oldest daughter's attention. "I bet you don't remember him, do you?" he asked, pointing at Julian.

She stared at him, appearing confused. "No, I can't say I do."

"That's Julian. You were only about three or four the last time you saw him."

"That's probably why I don't remember him, Dad," she snickered. Like their mother and father, both girls had dark brown hair. Like their mother only, both were short and thin.

Daryl giggled, and once he finished cooking dinner, said: "Let's eat!" Everyone had their fill of chilidogs and potato chips. After their food settled, Daryl was ready to give Julian a ride home. The clock read *6:38*, and it was completely dark outside. "Are you ready, bub?" Daryl asked.

"Yeah, let's go," said Julian, patting his full belly and putting on his leather jacket. On his way out, he held onto Daryl's elbow while maneuvering across the porch and through the driveway. Once they made it to the truck, Daryl backed out of his spot and glided down to the long, paved bottom below.

"You know, I meant what I said, bub. This summer you'll have to go to the lake with us, you and Violet, if she's still living with you. We'll have fun like we did when we were kids."

"I'd like that," Julian said.

After the short drive, Daryl turned left onto Julian's road. While passing Johnny's house, he said, "You really should walk down and see your grandpa."

"I will, eventually, but not until I feel comfortable," Julian said.

"Does he even know you're back?"

"I've been home almost a month, so I'm sure he knows. I just haven't talked to him yet."

"You should. You'll feel better, I guarantee it."

Daryl turned onto Julian's long driveway. After they drove past the garage, Julian gasped. A cold sense of dread crept upon him when he saw Violet's car was nowhere in sight. "What the hell?" he muttered under his breath.

"Well, it looks like your lady went out somewhere," Daryl said, stopping at the carport with the kitchen door a few feet away. The overhead light was on, and Julian could see the kitchen light shining through the door.

His heart tremored and his mind raced, wondering where Violet went. "I think I got it from here," he said.

"You sure, bub?"

"Yeah, it's just right here."

"Alrighty then. Have a goodnight, and don't wear yourself out with your girlfriend!" Daryl giggled, and Julian snickered sarcastically on the surface while sweating bullets within.

"I'll try." He slid out of the truck. "Goodnight, Daryl. Thanks for having me over, and thanks for dinner."

"You're welcome, bub. I'll holler at you next time I'm home."

"Alright," Julian said. He shut the truck door, took a deep breath, and entered the house as Daryl drove away.

"Violet?!" he called, looking around the kitchen. Nothing appeared out of place. He went into the living room, where the lights were on, but the television was not. "Violet?!" he called again, praying she would answer. She did not. Julian opened the basement door, shouting, "Violet?! Are you down here?!" Again, nothing. He turned back to the living room in sheer panic as something white on the coffee table caught his eye. *What the hell is that?*

He approached the table, where a single sheet of notebook paper sat with writing visible on it. His heart sank as he picked it up, thinking, *oh God!* After drawing a deep breath and clearing his throat, Julian adjusted his glasses and read.

Dear Julian,
    I am sorry but I cannot do this...

Chapter Twenty-Four

Julian had barely slept since Violet left him. When he did, he woke each morning, nauseated and wanting the day to end. Somewhere deep within himself, between gloom and self-medicated despair, he dreamt a hope she would return, refusing to accept the creeping reality she might not. From somewhere far away, Julian watched himself slipping back into the gap again, the same gap he moved to Las Vegas to escape. He had not shaved since she left and he'd rarely even bathed. He had neither the strength or the willpower to do anything but sulk.

He framed Violet's letter and placed it atop the mantle near the eight-ball, to serve as a prickling reminder of something sweet that had been dangled before him and plucked away yet again. *How dare you think you deserve anything more than a world of shit and hypocritical mockery!* The "Dear John" letter was difficult to look at, but it was from her, along with the eight-ball, and he refused to part with either.

As Julian backed away from the mantle, his father's ceramic beer stein caught his attention. He rolled his eyes and sneered at the dark memento, wondering, *why the hell is that damn thing so important to me?* Arthur, his father, had been an abusive monster, among other things, though Arthur's parents called Julian and his mother, Marcie, liars. "Our perfect son could never harm a fly," they'd say. Marcie was far from a saint, but Arthur was the Goddamn Devil in Julian's eyes. Having carried the stein everywhere he went for nearly thirty years, he grimly admitted it was time for some of the old ways to die. With little effort, Julian took the stein and violently slammed it against the rough stonework on the wall. The cup shattered into several pieces, and he smirked at the sight and at the idea of how little he cared.

After taking a seat on the old brown sofa, Julian reached for the TV remote, flipping through the channels before quickly losing interest and turning it off. He stood and paced the living room, thinking, *maybe I should go see him.* He was starting to feel guilty about not visiting Johnny. It had been a few weeks since he'd even gone outside, and if nothing else, the fresh air and exercise would do him good.

Giving in, he slipped on his black sneakers and walked out the living room door. The fresh spring weather was neither cool nor warm, but the sky was overcast, and the trees were growing leaves. He followed the other side of the driveway, passing under the carport and walking down the steep hill towards his once-favorite aunt and uncle's smaller two-story yellow house at the bottom of the driveway.

When Julian was young, he'd spent a lot of time in his Aunt Edith and Uncle Dean's house. Dean played country music, and although he never went anywhere with it, he had a music room on the bottom floor. Dean played an acoustic guitar, and Julian often banged on a tambourine to the beats. He missed them and wanted to catch up, but after his grandmother's funeral, Johnny refused to give him their phone number, saying, "They don't want to give it out."

Julian rolled his eyes and shifted his thoughts to the time Bill beat him so badly that evidence of gashes and bruises were left all over his face, giving Johnny no choice but to react. Bill had nearly beaten Julian to death that time. He even broke Marcie's arm in a rare instance of her trying to protect her son. When Gin took her to the emergency room, Johnny took photographs of Julian's battered young mug. At the time, Dean and Edith had already moved away, but happened to be visiting Gin and Johnny. The pictures were taken in front of them, and Julian felt it was only to keep up appearances and nothing more. Of all the times Bill brutalized Julian and his mother, Johnny finally had real evidence and could have had him arrested. As he proved, though, that would defeat the purpose of basking in the opposite of doing the right thing.

Julian continued down a narrow gravel road. To his left was the brushy hillside below his house, eventually clearing out to a smooth, grassy knoll. On his right, beyond Dean and Edith's old front yard, another road and row of houses were divided by a small creek running down the mountain, separating one side of the hill from the other. Ahead was his great grandma Heiti's old white house, where the gravel road veered to the right and crossed a small wooden bridge above the creek. Julian turned left and walked through the grass toward Johnny's honey-colored, converted double-wide. He approached a small embankment that led, like a ramp, down to the driveway and den door. Julian had never knocked on that door in his life, but after swallowing a lump, he did.

"Come on in!" Johnny's haggard old voice announced from the other side of the white door with a large, centered window. Julian twisted the knob and walked inside.

"Hi, Grandpa."

Johnny sat in his gray recliner, facing his television. "Hey, Julian," he grumbled. "I was wondering when you were going to walk down here."

Julian kicked his shoes off at the door and walked to the other side of the den to a sofa on Johnny's left. "Well, I've been busy, being rich and all. You know how it is. Wait ... never mind," he said, snickering at his smartass remark.

"So, you really won, huh?" Johnny chuckled as light reflected off the top of his shiny, bald head.

"Yeah, I told you I did."

"Well, I guess you were right. Have you decided what you want to do with the rest of it?" Johnny asked, refusing to look Julian in the eye.

"Not really. I had a girlfriend of sorts, who—"

"A girlfriend? Did you meet her in Las Vegas?"

"Yeah, I did, but—"

A slow, obnoxious grin formed across Johnny's face, and he laughed, cutting Julian off again. "I'm sure you'd have lots of girlfriends if they knew how much money you had. I bet that's how you found that one, ain't it?"

"No, it's not. I met her before I won the money."

"Yeah, buddy, I bet you did."

Julian's eyes widened and he dug his unkempt fingernails into his sweaty palms. "Are you saying I couldn't get a girlfriend without the money?" he asked.

"Well, no, but before the money, you could only attract someone like Faith."

"Violet is nothing like Faith," he said, feeling insulted. "We met at school, before the money. It's because of her, I got it to begin with."

"Okay, then," Johnny grumbled. "Is she still up there with you?"

"No, she left."

Johnny grinned even wider, asking, "Where'd she go?"

"It's not really any of your concern, Grandpa, but she left me."

Johnny laughed and his grin stretched its widest yet. "She got tired of you already, huh?"

Julian glared. "It's complicated," he said. "I love her, but we both have our own problems."

"Oh God …" Johnny grunted. "You best not start feeling sorry for yourself again or be bringing up a bunch of shit from the past, because I don't want to hear it."

"I'm not trying to do anything other than have a conversation with you," he said. "Sometimes I ask myself, 'Why do I even try?'"

"Try to do what?"

"To find my own answers, convince myself that you care about my emotions and wellbeing, or why I can't just let go of people and things that no longer serve me," he said while Johnny stared at the old western on his television, appearing to not even listen. Julian sighed again and said, "I came down here because I thought we could have a heart to heart." Even though Johnny refused to face him, Julian never looked away. "When I went to California and took *Ayahuasca*, all these underlying emotions that I hid away for so long resurfaced. My inner child is wounded, and I need to heal it."

"But you're not a child anymore, Julian. You're thirty-four years old."

"I'm thirty-seven, actually, but that's not the point. I was hurt so deeply as a child. Since I was unable to defend myself back then, and nobody else was willing to do anything, all the trauma and emotions were repressed. Lately, they're coming back out, forcing me to deal with them so I can let it all go and move on."

"Well, what do you want me to say? Hide them again, so they won't bother you," Johnny said.

"What?!" Julian's teeth clenched. "Are you serious? … Fucking seriously?! God damn you for saying that to me!" Julian wanted to cry, but he fought it off.

"If you're just going to cuss me, get the hell out of here!" Johnny growled. "That shit you took did something to you, and you're crazier than hell now! You're damn crazy, you hear me?! You are crazy, and you need help! All that shit happened in the past, and I don't even know why you would bring it up now, all these years later. There's no reason why you can't get over it. Do you think I sit and dwell over things? I don't, because I am a man, and there's no reason why you can't be one, too, if you would just grow up."

"Not everyone is wired that way, and I thank God I am not wired like you. You call yourself a man? What kind of man would just sit here and let their daughter and disabled grandson get the hell knocked out of them and do nothing? I thought all you backwoods hicks were supposed to snap so easily over shit like that. I mean, Daryl's dad was ready to beat Bill to death because he saw some bruises on me, while you did nothing!" Julian stopped for a breath, huffing and puffing while his entire body shook.

"You don't know what the hell you're talking about, Julian. Things happened differently than you remember!"

"Excuse me?! Differently than I remember? When I was six, I watched my dad drag Mom down the street by her hair, holding it from inside his truck window. He could have killed her. I remember it like it was yesterday, do you? Do you remember all the times I ran away from the house, and came up here, crying and begging you to not make me go back? … I sure as hell do! You did nothing but sit here and watch television or go to your Lion's Club meetings every Wednesday night, driving right past us, and going off to pretend like you gave two shits or a good goddamn about the blind, but didn't give a fuck about your own impaired grandson. All you cared about was what others thought of you!"

Johnny finally made eye contact, saying, "Your mother brought it all on herself."

"My mother made many mistakes, but I was an innocent child. So, stop gaslighting me. Be a real man and take some responsibility!"

"I don't even know what that means or what you're talking about, but don't you think I have enough on my mind without your bullshit? Your grandma and I were married fifty-three years, and I have sat here ever since she died, hurting, and dealing with that. All you care about are your problems, and the last thing I need is you coming in here and throwing all your bullshit in my face. I had nothing to do with it!"

Julian laughed. "You are right about that, Grandpa. You had absolutely nothing to do with helping us. But you know what's funny? Grandma died six years ago, and despite your previous contradiction, you're still sitting here, upset about it. Well, she died in the past, right? Why is it okay for you to hurt or dwell but not me? What makes you so goddamn superior?! … Huh?!!"

Johnny's eyes burned with the fury of hell. He gritted his dentures and growled, "Shut up!"

"You are unbelievable! I mean, do you know what Daryl told me? He said the reason he quit coming around me all those years ago, when he moved to Kentucky, was because you kept telling him I wasn't ever home, when I was. Why would you do that to me? He tried to help me be social and make friends. You never let me do a damn thing! Clint Junior was failing the sixth grade because Bobbi-Jo was always giving him alcohol, and that stuck-up beachball, Miranda was free to do whatever she wanted with her friends, but God forbid I ever got to go out and feel normal, right? I never drank or used drugs back then like Bobbi-Jo's dead junky son did, but I guess that's why I wasn't good enough, right? God forbid I don't fit the traditional redneck stereotype."

"Bah! … Shut up!" Johnny repeated. "Daryl's a liar, and full of shit!"

"Don't!" Julian seethed, pointing his index finger at Johnny. "Just don't."

"You need to leave."

"Fine," Julian grunted. "I tried, but this was a bad idea." He stomped towards the door and slipped his shoes back on. Before opening the door, he looked over his shoulder at Johnny and said, "There's something I want to show you before I leave," while reaching inside his right blue jeans pocket.

"What?" Johnny asked, turning his head towards the door and giving Julian his attention.

"Do you remember before I left, when you were charging me rent, and kept saying I made as much money as you do, and you don't know why I was always broke?" Johnny said nothing. Julian pulled his black cellphone from his pocket and poked it a few times. He turned the screen in Johnny's direction with a massive grin. "Check that shit out." Johnny looked at the screen and his face turned white as rice when he saw the wide, tall black metal safe, open, and packed from top to bottom with hundred-dollar bills. Johnny's pale face drooped as if he could cry. "Pretty cool, huh?" Julian snickered. "I know you told me not to forget you when I made my first million, but like you said, you make as much money as I do, so you don't need it," he said, shivering with excitement and taking pride in his arrogance.

"Get the hell out of here, you crazy son of a bitch!" Johnny growled.

Julian laughed to mask his pain as he put his phone away and turned back towards the door. "Crazy, huh?" he asked, placing his hand on the knob. "I'd rather be crazy by your standards than whatever the hell you're supposed to be by mine."

"I said get out of here, and don't you ever come back if you're gonna talk to me that way, you hear me?!" Johnny snarled, losing his breath and clenching his chest.

Julian said nothing as he opened the door and stepped outside with inevitable tears in his eyes. He wiped them away and began his walk back up the steep hill, knowing he'd brought it all on himself. Not even God could convince the great Johnny Clemmons he was terrible. *Fuck it*, Julian thought. *This would make a good chapter in my book.*

Chapter Twenty-Five

*A*s long as I live, I will never forget the events that brought my mother and me to Virginia. In the winter of 1990, there was no snow on the ground, but it was cold. Inside my mother and father's house, the heat was cozy. I wore a pair of camouflage shorts and a t-shirt, watching cartoons while my mother folded laundry.

Julian took a drink from a pint of whiskey and returned to the keyboard. *There came a knock at the door. When my mother answered, she was bombarded by several men in swat gear, toting big black machine guns. The police immediately tackled her to the ground, a 5'4" woman who weighed 110 pounds soaking wet. They held their guns to her head, shouting, "Where is he?!" Where is Arthur Frost?!"*

"He's at work," my mother screamed. *With a little research, they could have figured that out, but why do that, when scaring the life out of a mother and her child was more convenient?* Julian rolled his eyes and took another drink. *"I was just doing laundry!"* she cried as I looked on, an eight-year-old boy traumatized and frozen in fear.

Before hauling her off to jail, the police tried to escort me outside to a waiting social worker. "Blow my brains out if you want, but I'll be damned if I'm letting you take my baby out in the cold, just wearing shorts and a t-shirt," my mother sobbed. Surprisingly, one of the cops took me upstairs to my room and let me put on a pair of gray sweatpants and a jacket.

A few nights earlier, my parents were out partying, and I was left with my babysitter, Melissa. She was a skinny little fourteen-year-old girl who only lived three houses away, in our Saint Louis subdivision. She was sweet, innocent, and never hurt anybody. After my parents came home, my mother must have passed out, and my father took it upon himself to pay Melissa for her services another way.

Julian cringed before emptying the bottle and breaking the seal on another, taking a big drink, and wiping a tear from his cheek before continuing. *When the police raided our house, they found my father's stash of cocaine and God knows what else. Needless to say, my mother's parents hired her a divorce lawyer, and after a month in a foster home, I took my father's karma for the first time. There was a shortage of beds, and I had to share one with my older foster brother, Jeremy. "It'll feel good, I promise," he said before forcing himself inside me.*

I told my foster mother, but why would a woman who busted my ass for sleeping above the covers one night believe the son of a rapist? For all I know, she thought I deserved it. Luckily I talked my caseworker into placing me in another foster home, while the previous one remained open for business with no questions asked.

In foster home number two, all was well until the time I had the flu and spent all day in bed. That foster mother, a fat, disgusting pig, beat me for practically the same thing the first one did, but this one used a belt. Thanks to the bruises, she was arrested, and my mother was finally awarded custody.

By then, everybody knew what my father was, and despite once being a popular kid in the neighborhood, no parent dared let their child near me. At such a young age, I had no clue why. It wasn't until our house was broken into, vandalized, and looted, that my mother and I moved into a small apartment in the heart of the city.

She worked at a department store to support us, and after I got off the school bus in the afternoons, I was left alone for a few hours. I made friends with a boy named Kurt, who was a year older than me. At first, I liked him, until God or some other karmic piper came for me again. This time, I was pulled into my closet and taken hard from behind. It hurt; even more than the first time. I was young, but I knew what was happening. I knew it was wrong. Like before, I did not consent, but I didn't say no either. After that, even though I knew I liked girls, I spent much of my teenage years confused. I tried to have sexual experiences before I met Faith, but I was always too scared to perform. Women laughed and made fun of my intimacy issues. "You must be a faggot," they'd say.

Julian took another gulp and shut his eyes, drawing a long, deep breath. *My grandparents came from Virginia and got me shortly after the incident with Kurt. "You shouldn't be here for this* court crap," *my mother told me. Even after everything my father did to us, I still don't know the circumstances of his death. It happened the day his and my mother's divorce was final, when she was preparing to move back to Virginia.*

According to her, my father called that night, saying he was coming to kill her. After that, he was arrested on the highway for drunk driving. My mother thought his guilt took its toll. Although she wasn't there, and her theory was just that, she told me he hung himself in his cell with a bedsheet.

Julian paused again and took a drink. *His parents, who thought their golden boy could do no wrong, claimed he was wrongfully pulled over and arrested by the dirty, drug-dealer cops he'd supposedly ratted on for a lighter sentence. According to the Frosts, my mother was a liar. They said my father was murdered and the suicide was staged. "When you die, you evacuate your bowels, and his underwear was clean. So, they stripped him down before they hung him, cleaned him afterwards, and took the time to redress him in the jail cell before anyone noticed," they told me.* Julian sighed and took another drink.

Nobody wants to believe their child is a monster, but their story breaks the barriers of logic. It's been twenty-eight years, and I will probably never know what really happened. Murder, suicide; either way, he's exactly where he belongs.

"Wha—what if hell doesn't e—even 'xist?!" Julian slurred. He returned to the keyboard and typed: *I will never forget the morning I answered the phone. "Let me talk to Grandpa" was all my mother's crying, desperate voice managed. I gave my grandfather the phone and watched his face turn grim.*

"What? Did somebody die?" I asked sarcastically, with no clue just how dark my joke truly was.

When my grandfather hung up, he turned to me and said, "Your father had an accident."

"Is he dead?" I asked.

"Yeah." Even after everything I saw the man do with my own two eyes, my then nine-year-old mind couldn't comprehend how sick and evil he actually was. Now I am ashamed to admit I cried for weeks, let alone at all.

Julian set the laptop down and wiped the sweat from his forehead before finishing off the second pint of whiskey. With his vision and overall balance impaired, he staggered to the kitchen and a row of cabinets mounted above the orange countertop. Inside the cabinet were more bottles. Whiskey, tequila, and Southern Comfort lined the shelf, but it was a sealed half-liter bottle of imported German absinthe he retrieved. The green glass bottle was shaped like a skull and had a small white sticker on the side, with *89.9%* printed on it in black. He unscrewed the lid and returned to the sofa, sipping the green fairy slowly, as if it were local moonshine. His glazed eyes turned towards the grandfather clock, reading *10:58*. He took a bigger sip before turning the TV to channel five. As the clock chimed at eleven, the late-night talk show he had recently started watching came on.

"Ladies and gentlemen … it is Saturday, April twentieth, two-thousand-nineteen," the presenter began. "Tonight, on The Nathan Oliver Show, we have comedians Paula Gilmore and Billy Tampa, and a very special guest: ex-Navy Seal Christopher Cauldwell!"

Julian nearly choked on the bitter alcohol when he heard the name. He coughed and gagged as the studio audience applauded while the host, Nathan Oliver, walked across the stage wearing a blue plaid sports coat and an obvious, combed-over shiny black wig.

Nathan Oliver took a seat at his desk and said, "Thank you, everyone! We have a great show for you tonight. Comedians Paula Gilmore and Billy Tampa are here to talk about their new movie, Frances Goes to France. But first …" Julian's ears perked like a curious puppy's. "We have a special guest here with us. Former Navy Seal, Christopher Cauldwell, was stripped of his rank and dishonorably discharged back in January, when another former Navy Seal, Christopher's brother Kevin Cauldwell, opened fire in the New York City nightclub Leviticus. The Cauldwell brothers, along with fellow ex-Seal Rick Smith, entered the club to confront the owner. Christopher Cauldwell believes the owner to not only be responsible for murdering his daughter in a long string of unsolved homicides, but to also be a real-life vampire."

"For fuck sake," Julian groaned, taking another drink from the skull bottle. A few members of the audience laughed off camera and even the host bit his lip.

"Well, let's see if we can get some things straightened up," Nathan said, flashing a fake grin to the camera. "Ladies and gentlemen, please welcome former United States Navy Seal Christopher Cauldwell!"

The same audience that had just laughed at him applauded on command as the man Julian had grown to loathe and pity walked across the stage, wearing the same big brown overcoat he'd worn in the club. Cauldwell sat in a black chair next to the desk where Nathan Oliver sat. His curly gold hair was neatly brushed, and he appeared better rested and perhaps more sound-minded than the last time Julian had seen him on television.

"Welcome to the show, Christopher," Nathan said.

"Thank you," Cauldwell replied. "I'd say I'm a fan, but I am not a liar."

Nathan nervously smiled, saying, "I—I was telling my producer backstage, we normally don't feature this sort of segment on the show. However, we think it's awful, just awful, what happened to you and your family, not just since the shooting, but everything before. I want to say that you are a hero to us, and we thank you for your service." The host spoke like he was reading from a teleprompter and the audience cheered accordingly.

Cauldwell smirked and said, "Well, I just did what my superiors told me to do, when I was out in the [censored] overseas, fighting in Afghanistan, but that's not really why I'm here, Nathan. I—"

"Yeah, you're right," Nathan interrupted. "You're here because you wanted to make a public statement, is that right?"

"Yeah, I do," Cauldwell said, glaring at the host. "We have a serial killer at large, here in the city right now, but it isn't just one person. You see, I already knew about Xavier Van Abarrow, but there's even more of them."

Julian grew anxious hearing the soldier speak Xavier's name. His heart fluttered slowly at first, then harder, and gradually so loudly the beat rang in his ears. "Violet Troúton, that's his so-called daughter," Cauldwell announced, and Julian gasped.

"You s—s—on of a bitch! You touch 'er and I'll murder you!" Julian slurred.

"He's no father. I am a father!" Cauldwell jolted forward and snarled.

"Okay, sir, please calm down," Nathan said. Cauldwell sat back and momentarily shut his eyes while maintaining a careless smirk. "I understand you're upset, but do you honestly believe that these two people are vampires?" Nathan asked. Again, a few audience members laughed.

"There's more than just two of them," said Cauldwell.

Julian's stomach churned as an unsettling thought dawned. *Could he know who I am?*

"There are hundreds of vampires roaming the world, but to answer your question, Nathan, yes. I came across the names of four more recently, including a married couple," the militant chuckled. "If you can believe that."

"Look," Nathan said, raising a hand. "I—"

"Their names are Bernard and Annabel Gaunt," Cauldwell interrupted.

"Goddamnit!" Julian shouted, violently stomping his foot. He turned the absinthe bottle up in anger, tipping his head back and taking three large gulps before pulling it away from his quivering, booze-stained lips. His innards burned as the drink poured through him.

"Along with Xavier Van Abarrow, Violet Troúton, and the Gaunts, I urge everyone to also keep an eye out for the others, Eric Grant and Tony Bishop. If you find them—"

"Hey. Listen!" Nathan cut him off. "We're not going to let you give out people's names on the air and encourage the public to go on a witch hunt!" Nathan spoke more forcefully than before, deepening his voice to sound more masculine. The audience applauded him, and Julian took another swig, wondering, *why the hell would he say Eric's name? He's dead.* After swallowing the drink, he slurred, "Yeah! You tell that gold-haired m—military cunt who—who—who the fucking bo—boss is!"

Cauldwell stared into the audience and growled, "You can laugh and clap all you want, but I know the truth! That's only six of them, but there are more, and I am going to find them!" Cauldwell seethed as he slammed his fist in his lap.

"I'm sorry, Christopher, but you do understand how absurd that all sounds, right?" Nathan asked. "You're talking about fictional creatures. Vampires do not exist."

"I know how crazy it sounds, Nathan," Cauldwell began. "But let's just say, when you're as high-level as I was, and you go as deep into the [censored] as I have, you learn secrets: things you were never taught growing up. What typical human being could understand something like that? You'd be surprised what's out there, going bump in the night."

"I get what you're saying, Christopher, I truly do," Nathan sympathized. "I also lost a child once, but look at what this did to your career, and the careers of two others. You were all three considered the 'cream of the crop' when it came to protecting this nation. I mean, your brother, Kevin, is still in jail, isn't he?"

"No," Cauldwell faced the camera and laughed. "No, he's out. My brother was released last week."

"That is good to hear, but what I want to know is, why are you still pursuing these people? Why not let the police conduct their investigation and bring your daughter's killer to justice, morally and by the book? Surely, being a soldier, you believe in law and order," Nathan said.

Cauldwell shrugged his nose, asking, "What law? What order? Those [censored] damn greasy mother[censored]ers—"

"Hey! Let's watch the language, please," Nathan interrupted.

"I'm sorry, Nathan, but the police won't do anything. Nobody does anything anymore unless it's to benefit themselves. That's what I am doing, benefiting myself, and I dare anybody to try and stop me." He panned across the giggling audience and said, "None of you even take me seriously!"

"It's not that people don't take you seriously. You're a grieving father, we understand. Everybody mourns differently, but going into nightclubs and shooting at people isn't ethical."

"Ethical?!" Cauldwell shouted. "You mean the way my daughter was ethically murdered and beheaded?!"

"No, that's not what I—"

"No! You're saying it's okay for some abomination, created by the devil himself, to kill my daughter—the light of my life—but it's not okay for a father to seek vengeance! That's what you, in your stupid little suit and cheap hairpiece are saying!" Cauldwell stood and kicked his seat on its back. "You brought me on here to mock me for ratings!" He turned to the audience and pointed at them, shouting, "All you brainless sheep only know how to do what that stupid overhead screen tells you to do!" The crowd started booing him. "You're all a bunch of cogs in a machine!" Cauldwell brooded like an angry gorilla, his neck veins visibly popping to the surface.

"Go to commercial! Go to commercial!" Nathan commanded and the live feed was cut from the air.

"Holy shit!" Julian blurted. His heart still roared below his ribcage as he thought only of Violet and her safety. With his vision so impaired, everything became a blur. He took another drink and struggled to stand. With the bottle in his hand, he staggered to the front living room door. Barefoot, he walked out onto the cool driveway. The dark night sky was clear, and the pale full moon illuminated the trees. All was silent except a dog barking somewhere in the woods behind the house.

"Violet?! … Violet?!" Julian screamed so loud it became a high-pitched squeal. "Violet! Come back! Come back to me!" Tears slowly dripped down his cheeks.

"Violet?! … Xavier?!" He sobbed and screamed, dropping to his knees, still holding the bottle of absinthe. He turned it up again, taking his biggest drink yet. "Faith? … Anybody! Just come ba—a—ack!" he sobbed.

"Arghh!" Julian growled, throwing the empty bottle over the side of the hill. "Violet! I love you! … I love you, Violet! I. …" Julian lost his breath howling at the sky, and he began to cough and gag before stopping and lowering his head. "I just want to die," he softly whimpered. "Just let me die," he repeated, again and again until falling on his side. He sprawled across the driveway, chanting his desolate request, "Just let me die."

Not even three minutes later, Julian saw blurry blue lights growing from his dark surroundings. Then came the headlights from the distance. Even inebriated, he knew who it was. The blue and gray cruiser stopped just short of the carport and the driver's door opened as Julian slowly staggered to his feet.

"Evenin'," said the officer as he placed his deputy's hat atop his generic clipper-shaved head and waddled forward, appearing wider than he was tall.

"H—hello," Julian replied, placing the cop's morbidly obese silhouette, response time, and pompous tone together in his head. It was Officer Tyler Hicks, who only lived three driveways further uphill from his own, but still too far away to have heard his cries.

"I got a call that you were up here hootin' and a-hollerin'," he said. "Is everything alright, partner?"

"Honestly, Officer Hicks, I had quite a bit to drink tonight," Julian said.

"Oh yeah?!" he sarcastically replied.

"Y—yeah, I—I was watching TV and started thinking about my girlfriend that left me recently. I just came outside to scream it out," Julian explained.

"Well, we can't have you doing that, now."

"Yeah, I—I know, and I apologize, sir. C—could I just go back inside and sleep it off? I'm the only one here, and—"

"Nah, I came over here for a noise complaint, and we can't have you outside, yelling about whatever happened with you and your girlfriend."

Julian nearly teared up again, saying, "Please, sir. I'm not hurting anyone. I've had a really bad night and I'd just like to go to sleep."

"You can sleep down at lockup," he said. As Julian's vision focused, he saw the shit-eating grin plastered across Officer Hicks' canned ham of a face, so fat and swollen a sharp object could pop it.

I'd love to see you split open and roasted on an open fire, like the fat piece of pig shit you are, Julian thought and snickered. Despite the situation, he found a little comfort in the graphic imagery running through his head: Officer Hicks, squealing and bleeding from hundreds of little cuts, lying naked on an ice-cold slab. Thirsty vampires surrounded him, licking their lips like hungry five-year-olds huddled around a birthday cake, ready to shit themselves on command for a slice.

"What's your name, sir?" Officer Hicks asked, snapping Julian back to reality.

"Julian Frost," he said. "We went to high school together."

The proud cop squinted his eyes and stared at Julian for a moment. "Nah, I remember everyone I went to school with, but I don't know you or remember anyone named Frost."

Julian rolled his eyes, thinking, *and that's why you're a cop. Even sucking cock in Vegas would be too complex for a simple twit like you.*

"You got an ID, Mr. Frost?" the officer asked. Julian slowly reached inside his back pocket, removing his baby blue wallet, and handing over his Virginia state ID. Hicks shined a flashlight on the card while reading it. "Alright, Mr. Frost," he began. "At this time, I'm placing you under arrest for disorderly conduct and I—"

"Disorderly c—conduct?!" Julian protested. "Sir, I've been cooperative with you. I know I made a mistake, but please cut me some slack. I'm legally blind and disabled. I'm going through a hard time, and—"

"I understand that, sir, but you can't be out here yelling," Hicks interrupted. "So, right now I am—"

"But I've already done it and now I'd just go back inside and pass out for the night. Then, you could go back home, too. I—I'm not hurting anyone. I don't even know who would've called you."

"I'm not at liberty to say, but if you don't stop interrupting me and just let me read you your rights, I can also tack on a charge of resisting arrest." Officer Hicks said, so eager to make the arrest he might as well have started squeezing his nipples to enhance the thrill.

"Wait," Julian said. "Can I at least put on my sh—shoes?"

"Well, I'd hate to give you the chance to run off on me, now," the cop snickered. "Besides, you didn't mind walking outside barefoot, so you can go to jail barefoot."

There was nothing he could do. Julian sighed and his shoulders sank. He obeyed. Once the cuffs came out, Julian voluntarily extended his wrists. Hicks forcefully pulled Julian's hands behind his back and cuffed him tightly. "Is that too tight?" he asked, as if he gave a damn.

"Is this really necessary?" Julian asked. "I am legally blind and disab—"

"You're blind, huh? You appear to see fine to me," he said. "It's not wise to lie to a police officer, you know."

"Sir, I'm legally blind, not completely blind. I can still see, but I have an eye disease called Retin—"

"Well, you're not blind, so stop complaining," he interrupted, leading Julian to the back of his cruiser. Memories from the video of Cauldwell getting the same treatment on the night of the shooting flashed before Julian's eyes while he imagined Faith and Travis laughing and pointing at him, if they only knew. After he was placed in the backseat, Hicks shut the door and wobbled to the driver's side, struggling to squeeze in behind the wheel and wrestling with the seatbelt.

On the way down the hill, Julian saw the one window in his grandfather's house that faced that side of the street. The den light was on and the curtains were pulled back. Thinking the worst, his heart sank and he shut his eyes before blacking out and falling asleep.

Chapter Twenty-Six

"Grab you a beer, bub," Daryl said, motioning towards a square white cooler at the back of the boat as he steered across Lake Flanigan. "Hell, grab me one too, while you're at it," he added. "Just take it easy today, alright?"

"Yeah," Tara interjected. "You know I don't mind taking you to get your groceries and things when you need me to, but I'm not driving all the way across the mountain again to pick you up from jail, whether if you're my husband's friend or not," she teased.

As Julian reached inside the cooler for two cans, he said, "To be fair, Hicks didn't have to do anything. I wasn't hurting anyone."

"Are you kidding me?!" Daryl scoffed. "That fat fuck loves busting people so much, he probably went home and jerked off afterwards." Everyone on the pontoon laughed.

"Eww! … Dad!" Kayla protested from her seat in the front, next to Lily and their boyfriends, Jamie and Ryan, all four dressed in swimwear.

"Well, what the hell you want me to say?" Daryl asked. "The damn music you kids listen to sounds a lot worse than anything I say."

"You know you sound like our parents, right? 'That garbage you kids listen to isn't even music,'" Julian laughed, imitating the older generation. "At least it's over with, the arrest crap. I paid the fine, and that's that." He started to close the cooler but paused and turned to Tara, asking, "You want a beer, too?"

"Eh, what the hell—gimme one," she said. Julian nodded and gave her the other can in his hand before grabbing another for himself.

"Lily's only nineteen, but her boyfriend, Jamie, is twenty-two, and the only one of them old enough to drink," Daryl stated. "So, if I catch you giving one of them to the girls or Ryan, I'll toss your ass overboard." He laughed and looked at Jamie, widening his eyes in a "same goes for you" glare. Jamie nervously giggled. He wore sunglasses and had a thin dark mustache stretching the length of his lips.

"Don't worry, Daryl," Ryan, with short dark hair and a face cratered in acne, began. "I'll keep my big cousin in line." Daryl pleasantly nodded in approval.

As the bright sun blazed and the wind blew against Julian's clean-shaved face and through the long hair he'd been letting grow out, Daryl tapped the side of his arm. "Julian, you remember that little island Daddy and them used to take us out to, with all the rocks to jump off of?"

"Yeah, why?" he asked, sipping his cold beer.

"Look over there." Daryl pointed ahead of the boat. Julian adjusted his new round glasses, like the pair he'd lost in New York. He followed Daryl's finger off into the distance. A small, blurry island came into focus, growing larger as they approached. "That's where we're going, bub." The boat slowed as Daryl steered toward the shore. He leaped overboard with the loose end of a yellow nylon rope. After wading through the murky water to a tree at the edge of the embankment, he tied the rope around it, anchoring the pontoon.

The island was barely an acre in diameter. In areas along the beach, scorched earth and old ashes remained behind from makeshift firepits. Beyond the shore, the island was full of trees, bushes, and rocks. The land slanted uphill from their starting point towards a thirty-foot cliff. A series of large and small boulders were at the bottom of the cliff. "You think you got the balls to jump off the big one again, Daryl?" Julian asked.

"Hell no! I jumped off that son of a bitch when I was twelve, but I ain't doin' that shit ever again!"

"Pussy," Julian teased.

"Let's see you jump off it then, big boy!"

"Oh, kiss my ass!" Julian shared a laugh with his old friend as he slid out of the boat. Tara handed him two fishing rods and Jamie lowered the cooler to Daryl. The others gathered on the beach, and Julian slowly followed them to the rocky end of the island. Once he found a log to sit on, he sipped his beer and watched the kids jumping from various rocks into the lake.

"Mom! Come swim with us!" Kayla shouted from the water.

"I don't wanna get wet!" Tara yelled back.

"Ah hell, honey … go swim with them," Daryl said. "Julian and I are gonna do some fishing."

"Are you trying to get rid of me or something?" she chuckled. "I'll go sit with them and leave you two men alone, but I ain't swimming." She took another beer from the cooler and headed towards the rocks.

Daryl turned his attention to the fishing rods and a little white container of nightcrawlers. "So, are you doing alright now, bub?" he asked, having not talked to Julian much since his arrest.

"All things considering, I guess I'm doing as good as I can."

"I know you're still hurt. You fell in love again and got your heart broke. After what you tried to do to yourself over Faith, I worry about you." Daryl baited one of the hooks and handed the rod to Julian.

"With Faith, we were together eleven years." Julian sighed. "I don't think it was just her cheating that drove me to try, but several things, like losing my mom, grandma, and the rest of the family. When I found out she was pregnant, I feel like whatever piece of my soul I still had was reduced to a speck of dust."

"I understand, but you and this Violet girl were only together a month, and she left you five months ago. You got to move on," Daryl said, baiting his hook.

Julian's shoulders sank. "What if I can't? What if I am still holding onto hope, and besides that, what if I got myself involved in something deep and dangerous? I have so many disturbing thoughts that are torturing me to death." He shuddered, trying to shake it off as he cast his line into the water, about five feet below the rocky edge.

"What do you mean? I don't understand," Daryl said before casting his line and sipping his beer.

"You would just laugh and call me crazy."

"Bub," he smiled and patted Julian's back. "I knew you were crazy a long time ago." He cackled, and Julian forced a smile.

"You know what I mean." Julian took another drink from his can. "My life hasn't been the same since I met Violet. It was fate, the way we ended up together."

"I thought you said you met in one of your college classes."

"We did, officially, but we first saw each other earlier that morning in a little diner next to my apartment. I mean, I lived on the same road that the college is on, but it was seven miles away, on the other side of the city."

"That's strange, but I don't know if—"

"I'm not finished. After class, I fell down the stairs on my way outside and she caught me. I could've broken my neck or something, but she saved me."

"Well, that's—"

"And." Julian grinned, taking a quick sip. "At the bus stop, I lost my balance on the sidewalk and fell in the road. I landed in front of her car as she was driving by. She almost hit me. It's obvious we were destined to meet."

"Okay, yeah, that's pretty weird, but what do you mean by your relationship being dangerous?"

Julian took a deep breath as his heart started rumbling in his gut like any other time he'd been scared to get something off his chest. "Do you remember Christopher Cauldwell?"

"Who?" Daryl asked, turning up his can and finishing his beer.

"Christopher Cauldwell, that Navy Seal whose daughter got killed. He was in the news, saying 'vampires did it.'"

"Oh yeah," Daryl chuckled. "I remember him." He covered his mouth and regained a straight face. "I don't mean to laugh. It sucks, the guy lost his child, but he was nuts! Didn't he also shoot up a nightclub?"

"Not him, but it was his fault it happened."

"Still …" Daryl rolled his eyes. "What the hell is wrong with people?"

Julian took another deep breath as he watched Daryl take another beer from the cooler. "What if he wasn't nuts?"

"What the hell'r'ya talking about?!" Daryl's eyes locked with Julian's.

"This will sound insane, but I was there, the night of the shooting. I saw the first shot fired."

Daryl nearly choked on his drink. "What?! You were there, in New York?!" Julian nodded. "How? I thought you were in Las Vegas when that happened."

"I—I was … I mean, I went there with Violet. Her father owns the club and we—"

"Wait! You were actually there when that guy and his friends were?" Daryl still appeared lost.

Julian sighed again. "Yeah," he barely whispered before raising the nearly empty can to his lips, finishing it off.

"What happened?!"

"Cauldwell was there the night before, causing a scene, but they kicked him out. Then he and his men came back. There were three of them. Kevin Cauldwell, Christopher's brother, came in with a shotgun and was stopped at the door." Julian's heart pounded faster, knowing he was working towards dangerous territory, but the burden was too heavy to not confide in the only person he could.

"Xavier and Eric …" Julian said before pausing, remembering Violet, and how Eric's death devastated her. "They tried talking to Cauldwell, but he wouldn't let them speak."

"What did they want?" Daryl asked.

"Justice. Cauldwell thought Xavier killed his daughter."

"What?!" Daryl gasped. "You were friends with a murderer?!"

"No! Someone's viciously killing people in New York, and the first time Cauldwell came in the club, right after I …" Julian paused again, remembering he never told Daryl about the song or the women that followed.

"After what?"

"I got to go on stage and sing a song."

"Well, that's awesome, bub! Look at you, a rock star!"

"And then," he giggled. "And then, I was approached by these two hot goth chicks."

"Oh, really?" Daryl laughed. "I bet you fucked the hell out of them, didn't you?"

Julian blushed, "Wouldn't you like to know?"

"I know I ain't stupid, and neither are you. So, how did Faith or Violet stack up to two women at once?"

"It's been so long, I can't even remember what Faith was like. As for Violet, we never even kissed."

"What?!" Daryl's eyes bugged. "You never kissed, had sex, or anything?!"

"No," he mumbled.

"Jesus Christ, Julian! You're letting these damn women run over top of you, and you ain't even getting any? You got to man up, son!"

"Daryl, I love you, but shut the fuck up. Just because everyone fucks each other out of boredom and habit doesn't mean everything has to be about sex!"

"Whoa, calm down, bub! That's not what I—"

"No, that is what you meant! With Faith, she didn't want to fuck me. I still loved her. Even though she refused intimacy, I stayed with her because love isn't all about sex. It's nice, but it isn't everything. Violet was different. She was going through a hard time and I didn't want to pressure her. I love her, and I wanted our first time to be special and happen naturally."

"I just hope you didn't let her use you for your money when she was living up there."

"I already told you, Violet had her own money. She never took a cent from me. Her father was the one who gave me all that money to begin with. He only disguised it as winning a bet in Vegas because he wanted me to look out for her and keep her safe, but it's not the point. She needed more than I could offer. Who am I, a blind cripple, compared to a powerful ..."

"A powerful what?" Daryl asked.

Julian closed his eyes and cringed, knowing he had to come clean for the sake of his sanity. "You know how there's all these miracles and occurrences in the bible, considered beyond belief, things that would never happen in modern times?"

"Yeah? ..."

"How would you feel if you saw someone fly without any assistance, like wings or anything like that?"

"I'd probably think I went crazy, or somebody slipped me some acid or something without me knowing it," he chuckled. "Why?"

A thunderous pounding in Julian's heart nearly drowned out any other sound as he said, "Violet can fly."

"You're joking, right?" Daryl slowly grinned, trying not to laugh. "I mean, come on, bub. You know that's crazy, right?"

"Honestly, I thought so too, but she proved me wrong. I actually flew on her back. She can also read my mind."

"Julian ... I love you," Daryl began while Julian rolled his eyes, knowing what's to come. "I'm seriously worried about your mental health, though, and—"

"You shouldn't—"

"Let me finish," he interrupted. "I think when you drank that *Ayahuasca* crap, something happened. I'm worried that you might be seeing things or have psychosis or something."

Julian sighed. "It's depressing, but I understand why you don't believe me."

"It's not that I don't believe what you feel, but there's got to be more to it than whatever the hell it is you think she can do. I mean, you're telling me they really are vampires?"

"But they are! I know, it sounds unrealistic, but how can you say you believe in magical stories of the bible and be so quick to assume something like vampirism cannot exist?"

"Because those miracles are in the bible, and all those 'magical acts,' as you call them, were acts of God."

"Yeah, but just because it is written in a book by people no different than you or I, it doesn't mean it happened or didn't. We weren't alive when the bible was written or when any of those things happened. So, whether if God had anything to do with it or not, it's just hearsay, and we have no real way of knowing. Do you understand what I am saying?"

Daryl rolled his eyes and said, "I guess, but I really don't want to talk about it. We ain't supposed to question God's word like that."

"You're missing the point. I have seen things. I flew on both Violet and Xavier's backs, so fast, it only took thirty minutes to get from Vegas to New York, and—"

"What the hell did that shit do to you?! It—it's not possible!"

"That's what you are told to believe. If you can say the miracles of the bible were true, basing your faith on words printed by other human beings, it's very closed-minded to immediately write off the possibility that such magic and miracles can exist today. I assure you, the *Ayahuasca* has not made me crazy. My eyes are open, and you don't have to believe me, but. ..." He paused and took a breath. "Vampires do exist, and they could've killed me any time they wanted, but instead, they made me feel loved and accepted in a way my own family never did."

Daryl took a drink of his beer and sighed. "I honestly ... I—I don't know what to say. I know there're some weirdos out there that drink blood and live like vampires, but—"

"That's not even what I'm talking about," Julian said, regretting his confessions. "I should've just trusted my gut and stayed home like I wanted and watched the fireworks from my balcony tonight."

"You needed to get out of that house, bub. I told you I would take you out on the lake with us this summer. I mean, it's the fourth of July. The fireworks at the park will be much better than the ones over on the hill."

"Maybe, but that's not the point."

The mood grew silent and awkward for a few minutes as Julian took another beer from the cooler and focused on fishing.

"So, have you talked to your grandpa any more?"

"No," Julian sighed. "I've kept my distance. The night I got arrested is mostly a blur and I don't remember much before I blacked out, but I'm sure he's the one who called that cop on me. I have nothing else to say to him."

"Why would he do that?"

"I don't know. Maybe he's jealous now that I have money. It's funny. For so long, I looked up to him like he was my father, thinking he would never do anything to hurt me, but after the *Ayahuasca*, I see him in a whole new light. I've been writing about it lately, in my book."

"Speaking of your book, how's that goin'?"

"I have written so much, and lately, I've considered writing about Violet, but I don't know how she would feel about that."

"Who cares? Didn't you say her letter told you to write y'alls story, anyway?"

"Yeah, but I don't know how much of it I should tell, or if I should write it as fictional, or what. Our story was short, and nobody would believe it to be true."

"Only you know what's right, bub."

Julian nodded before refocusing his attention by gazing the serene landscape. On the nearby cluster of boulders, Tara watched her daughters and their boyfriends having fun, happy and without a care in the world. "You know," Julian began. "I hope you don't take offense to this, but I kind of envy you."

"What?! You envy me?! … Pfft! You got what, five million and something left … and you envy me?"

"It's just money. I mean, it's nice to not worry about having financial burdens, but all that extra shit I've bought lately is just eye candy. It doesn't make me any less lonely. You've got it all, though. You're a hard-working man with a wife who loves you, and you love her. You've got two beautiful girls who are practically old enough to have kids." Daryl flashed a pointed glare. "I mean, almost old enough to have kids," he corrected himself and they both laughed.

"Shit … Lily's old enough, but she better not be having any damn youngins' for a long time."

"My point is, you're happy." Julian placed his hand on Daryl's shoulder. "You are a good man. You deserve what you have. You were always there for me when I needed you, and even though nobody's life is perfect, I couldn't imagine life being much better than yours. When you have love, you have everything that matters."

"You know, it wasn't just you who needed me back then, but I needed you too. You know how my parents argued, and I also needed to get away sometimes." Daryl started to take a drink but paused and shook the can. It was empty. "Say, you got your phone on you?"

"Yeah, why?"

"What time is it?" Julian reached inside his jean shorts pocket and pulled out his phone as Daryl rummaged through the cooler for another beer. Julian fixated on the clock, doing a double take when he saw a number he hadn't seen in months.

"It—It's six-forty-four."

"Well, the fish sure as hell ain't biting. So, we'll head back to the boat in a little bit and take it down to the park, over by the dam. When it gets dark later, we'll watch them fireworks from the water." Daryl opened his fresh beer, and Julian put his phone away.

"It's funny," he giggled. "In her letter, Violet said if I don't—"

"Are you okay?!" From the nearby boulders, Tara's loud, concerned shout echoed across the island, drawing Julian and Daryl's attention.

"What the hell?!" Daryl mumbled and hopped to his feet, sprinting in her direction. Julian was slower, but he followed, and watched Daryl practically leap down the rock cluster from stone to stone, disappearing from view.

"What happened?! Is he alright?!" Daryl's voice echoed as Julian reached the edge of the cluster and looked down towards the water.

"I think he broke his foot, Dad!" Kayla yelled as she swam with Ryan towards the shore. Julian squinted and saw the boy's eyes were open, but he appeared dazed.

"You alright, Ryan?!" Daryl shouted from one of the rocks.

"Erm … my foot, it hurts! I felt it snap." He grunted and scowled as his girlfriend helped him to the rocks.

"What happened?" Daryl asked.

"I—I tripped on a vine or something. When I jumped. I—I must've twisted my foot." Ryan groaned as the excruciating pain in his voice spoke for itself. He remained calm but visibly writhed in agony.

"Damn!" Daryl grunted. "Alright, let me get the boat and bring it around to you. We got to get you to the hospital." He looked up the rocky cluster towards Julian, asking, "If I grab the cooler, you think you can get the fishing poles?"

"Yeah," Julian replied. Once they gathered the cooler and rods, Julian and Daryl hurried towards the pontoon. Julian repeatedly looked from his feet to the narrow dirt path ahead, trying not to meet the same fate as Ryan. After making it back to the pontoon, Daryl untied the rope and they climbed aboard.

Daryl started the boat and maneuvered to the rocks on the other side of the island, carefully aligning with the rock where Ryan lay. Jamie and Tara stepped aboard first. With Kayla and Lily on either side of him, they all helped Ryan to a comfortable space in the front. "Does everybody have everything?" Daryl asked, but no one protested. He hit the gas, heading back towards the boat ramp as fast as the pontoon would move.

Chapter Twenty-Seven

While Kayla and Jamie helped Ryan into the front passenger seat of Daryl's green truck, Julian stood aside, watching Daryl work quickly to get his boat back on its trailer. "Hey! … Julian?!" A shout came from a male voice near the parking lot. He turned and looked over his shoulder but saw nothing, until his eyes adjusted. Three men stood by an old wooden picnic table in the grass. He squinted and focused on a short man with dark hair, bald spot, sunburnt face, and a round gut hanging out beneath a plain white tee.

"Mason?" Julian called, taking a few steps forward. "Holy shit! What are you doing out here, cous'?" Forgetting all about Ryan for a moment, Julian approached the men.

"I came out here to meet a friend. We're supposed to meet him over here in about thirty minutes," Mason said, smiling and appearing happy to see his cousin. "How the hell are you? I heard you won big in Las Vegas."

"I did," Julian said. "After that, I decided to come back home, for now at least."

"That's awesome, buddy! I also heard you bought Scarlet and George's old place. You must've won really big, huh?" Mason chuckled as the other two men stepped forward. After scanning their faces, Julian recognized them both.

"Hey, Julian," said the stocky man on Mason's right. He wore a blue and green flannel shirt and a camouflage trucker cap with a silver fishhook piercing the bill. The dark tail of a mullet hung out from the back. The man had a mustache, like a seventies porn star, and the left side of his bottom lip puffed out. He nodded and spit tobacco juice in the grass, but his facial expression never changed.

"Hey, Ross, how've you been?" Julian asked.

"I'm alright," he mumbled. "Just been working." Julian looked at the tall, skinny man to Mason's left, with a five o'clock shadow and a shaved head. He was wearing black pants and a black t-shirt. A silver captive bead ring dangled from his left eyebrow.

"Well … Aaron Taylor." Julian grinned. "I haven't seen you since high school." He extended his hand, but Aaron stuck out his fist instead.

"I don't shake hands, but fist-bump me, bro," Aaron said, moving his hand in such a way that Julian's eyes could not keep up.

"Hold still. I can't see good," Julian said. Finally, his eyes focused, and the two bumped fists.

"Right. I forgot about your bad eyesight." Aaron smirked. "So, how you been? How's the rich life treatin' ya?"

"It's been pretty good, I suppose. I was out here with Dar—"

"Julian!" Daryl called. He turned back towards the parking lot where Daryl waved for his attention. "Come on, bub. We gotta take Ryan to the ER."

Julian turned back to his cousin and said, "Yeah, we were gonna watch the fireworks, but we gotta go."

"Well, hey …" Mason began. "If you want, you can get a ride back with us. I can drop you off at home since we live on the same hill anyway. That way you don't have to spend the fourth in a damn emergency room."

Julian thought fast as Mason had a point. *What could I even do besides sit there, bored to tears? At least at home, I can still watch the fireworks, if nothing else.* He took a few steps towards Daryl and asked, "Do you mind if I just catch a ride back home with my cousin Mason?"

Daryl scanned over Mason and the other two before saying, "If ya want to, bub. We'll be stuck at the hospital for hours, probably."

"Do you mind?"

Daryl shrugged his shoulders, saying, "Nah, bub. I don't mind. Just be careful, alright?" Julian smiled, thinking about the synchronicity of running into his cousin and the offer he presented as he watched the green truck pull away, carrying the boat on its trailer, and the kids in the back, before it all disappeared.

"We shouldn't be here too much longer," Mason said. "Once we meet our friend, we'll get out of here."

"Sounds good." Julian took a seat at the picnic table. "So," he began, attempting small talk. "You guys aren't going to go to the park and watch the fireworks later?"

"Nah, we were just over there, and it's already crowded," Mason said. "Besides, the fireworks on the hill are usually good, especially when old Harold and Benny try to outdo each other," he chuckled. "A year or so ago, two or three others also started doing it. So ours are probably going to be better, anyway."

"Nice," Julian said. "So, how've you been, cous'? I haven't seen you in so long."

"I've been alright," Mason said, impatiently pacing around the table.

Over the next hour, Julian waited as the sun began setting over the lake and mountains. Finally, two headlights approached and stopped near the picnic table. Mason and Ross walked to the dark car. Ross got in behind the driver, and Mason next to him.

As Julian waited and tried to piece together what Mason and Ross were doing in the car, an unsettling feeling washed over him. He kept an eye on Aaron, who kept staring. He'd once had a reputation for stealing from people. In high school, he'd been the butt of a lot of jokes after claiming to be a member of the infamous Los Angeles street gang, the Crips' "local Gunnar chapter." The only people who believed him were thick-headed, naïve girls he could easily manipulate. *And people think I'm crazy.* Julian bit his lip to keep from laughing at the memory before he had another. '*People change,*' *Violet would probably tell me.*

Nearly fifteen minutes passed before Mason and Ross emerged. "Alright guys, you ready?!" Mason shouted with animation, seemingly reinvigorated as he walked towards his red, four-door sedan. Julian stood from the table, and though the sun was mostly set, he saw well enough to make his way to the pavement and Mason's car. Ross sat shotgun, while Julian and Aaron sat in the back.

Mason backed out of the parking space and drove off towards the main road, leading across Haybale Mountain, Gunnar bound. "So, Mason," Julian said, breaking the silence. "Even before

I moved to Staley with Faith, I hadn't talked to you since your grandpa's funeral. How's your wife and kids?"

"Everyone's alright," he said. "You know, speaking of funerals, I'm sorry about your grandma and your mom. They were both sweet, and Gin did a lot for my grandpa when he was sick. It meant a lot to us, and I never got to thank her or your mom."

"Well, your grandpa was my grandma's brother. He would have done the same for her," said Julian.

"Yeah," Mason mumbled. "So, what brought you back here? I figured you'd be living it up somewhere else after winning all that money. I mean, you never really liked it here much anyway, did you?"

"I always loved Scarlet and George's house, and I had the perfect opportunity to buy it, so I did."

"But why buy that big ol' house when it's just you up there?"

"I—I don't know, I guess I just got excited and caught up in the moment, but even before I won the money, I still dreamt of owning it."

Ross, who had remained silent aside from periodically sniffing noisily and spitting in a plastic soda bottle, spoke up. "How much did you win?"

"It was a lot," Julian said.

"Yeah, but how much?"

Julian rolled his eyes. "I ... I don't really—"

"I bet it was at least a few million, huh?" Mason interrupted.

Julian sighed, reluctant to answer, but he did. "It was seven million."

"Seven million dollars?!" Mason shouted. "Holy fucking shit, man!"

"Oh my God, dude!" Aaron gasped like he'd had the wind knocked out of him.

After sniffing again and clearing his throat, Ross looked over his shoulder at Julian. "So, you live in that big ol' house by yourself?"

Julian's heartrate quickened in his chest. Something in Ross's demeanor did not feel right. Between the sniffs and personal questions about his money and living situation, Julian's intuition screamed: *Shut up and stop telling them things!* "For now," Julian replied. "My—my girlfriend and her father are about to move in soon." He shut his eyes, wishing his words rang true. *Stop being so paranoid—Mason is your cousin, and he won't do anything to you,* he assured himself enough to relax.

By the time they made it across the mountain and back to town, the sky was black. Mason pulled off the main road onto his and Julian's street, passing Julian's mother's double-wide with the new owner's shadowy car in the dark driveway. Across the street from that bad memory was another road, breaking away and leading to Mason's house, which was just on the other side of Heiti's old house. But he continued up the main hollow road, past Johnny's house, and to Julian's long driveway on the left. Mason passed the closed brick garage and parked under the carport, in front of the kitchen door, the porchlight illuminating the surroundings.

On the other, more populated side of the hill, neighbors were already celebrating Independence Day, shooting off fireworks and lighting up the night in multiple colors. The loud pops and crackles were so constant that if it were any other night, one would assume the hill was under attack.

Mason chuckled. "I wonder how much they all spend on that shit every year."

"I don't know, but I've got a great view and I'm gonna go watch them," Julian said. "I appreciate the ride, guys. I—"

"Hell, ain't you going to give us a tour?" Ross interrupted.

Julian's heart tremored. He wanted to say no but didn't want to be rude. "I—I …" Before he answered, Julian caught a glimpse of Mason's car stereo. The blue digital clock read *8:44*. "Yeah, I suppose," he finally said. After exiting the backseat, he unlocked the kitchen door, walked inside, and flipped on the light switch as the others followed.

Julian turned to them, proudly extending his hand to the room. "Well, this is the kitchen."

"Hey! I like that table." Aaron pointed towards the dining room.

Julian entered the living room and turned on the light, immediately catching everyone's attention. "Holy shit!" Mason gasped. Above the fireplace, two fat black speakers were symmetrically arranged on either side of the ninety-six-inch television. On each end of the hearth stood a three-foot-tall matching speaker. Several other smaller black speakers lined the walls in various locations around the room, along with an array of colorful psychedelic-inspired paintings of spirals, fractals, and mandalas. The old brown furniture was gone, replaced by a massive C-shaped black leather sofa surrounding a large, round, glass coffee table. To the left of the staircase sat a classic jukebox, red and yellow with an arched top, like one would find in a fifties malt shop.

Mason gasped again, and Julian looked over his shoulder to see him slowly approach a clear glass case mounted on the wall above the jukebox. Enclosed within was a purple Stratocaster with black ink scribbled across a white pickguard. "Is—is that what I think it is?" Mason asked, staring at the writing before reading aloud, "Stay groovy, Jimi Hendrix." He turned to Julian, wide-eyed, his jaw practically dragging the hard stone floor. "Are you fucking serious, dude?! Is that really his signature?!"

"For the price I paid and all the paperwork that came with it, it sure as hell better be."

"This place is so cool," Aaron said, joining Mason at the guitar.

"Yeah, I like it," Julian agreed.

"I really like your fireplace," Ross said, sniffing again as he followed along the mantle, admiring the few trinkets decorating it.

"I love everything about this place," Julian said, taking a few steps towards Mason and Aaron, "You know," he began. "One thing I think I'd like to do—" … *CRACK!* All went black and Julian hit the floor.

Chapter Twenty-Eight

" 'Dear Julian … I am sorry, but I can't do this to you or myself.'" Aaron's muffled voice snaked into Julian's eardrums as he slowly regained consciousness.

"What the hell is that?" Mason asked.

"It's some kind of letter," Aaron said. "It was on the mantle, next to the eight-ball Ross laid him out with."

"Fuck that shit!" Mason snapped. "One of you, come help me take this big guitar display down. This thing has to be worth a fortune!"

"Hey Aaron, keep an eye on him while we grab some of this shit, in case he wakes up," Ross ordered. Julian was weak, and the back of his head throbbed, but he heard everything. Afraid of what they might do if they discovered him awake, he kept his eyes shut and remained still as a corpse.

"Alright," Aaron said. He cleared his throat and continued reading. "'Dear Julian' …"

"Hey!" Mason shouted. "What the fuck are you doing?!"

"Don't worry. I'm watching him," Aaron whined. "But I think this is a breakup letter, and it should be good." He chuckled. "Anyway. 'Dear Julian, I am sorry, but I can't do this to you or myself anymore. You have been so good to me over this past month, and I could never dream of a man that makes me feel as loved as you have.'"

"Wow, what a stupid bitch," Ross chuckled.

"'I know I never said it back, but if you want the honest-to-God truth, yes, I do love you. You are the man of my dreams. In my one hundred years in this world, I've never felt that kind of love, the love I feel for you, and from you.'"

"Oh, never mind," Ross mumbled. "It's just some gross old hag who was probably so desperate she'd say anything to get a man, especially considering he has so much money." All three laughed. "I guess not even being a millionaire can get him a decent woman his own age."

"'The problem is not you, but me,'" Aaron read on. "'I cannot be good for you if I cannot be good for myself. When Eric died, I was crushed. Then, after hearing about William, I got scared. Now that Christopher Cauldwell is out of jail, he's looking for not just my father but for me, and the others as well. Despite all the love I have for you, I refuse to gamble with your life.' ..."

"Christopher Cauldwell?!" Mason interrupted as his and Ross's grunting and struggling to remove the guitar case went silent. "Where've I heard that name before?"

"'I am so sorry to walk away from you like this, but I had to do the right thing, and leaving this way would be the easiest for us both. While I try to deal with our problems, I want you to enjoy yourself and do what makes you happy. You deserve it. My father saw something special in you, just like I do, and he would not have given you all that money if he didn't trust you.'"

"What the hell?" Mason interrupted again. "She's a hundred years old, and her father's still alive?! Pfft ... yeah, right!"

"'Use it however you would like, but never give up on yourself,'" Aaron continued. "'In time, things will change because now is not forever, I promise. As a sign of good faith, I'm leaving my car in the garage, and Dad's ten million dollars in the safe.' ..."

"Ten million dollars?!" Mason screamed so loud he could have raised the dead.

Fuck! ... The safe! Julian thought, as his heart sank lower than ever and he was flooded by a fear he never knew existed.

"Fuck the guitar!" Mason exclaimed. "Where the hell's the safe at?!"

"I don't know," Ross said. "But let's wake his ass up and find out."

"Wait a minute!" Mason barked. "He knows who we are, and if this money really is here, someone will come looking for it. We're gonna have to ..." He hesitated as if something human lurked beneath the mire.

"Fuck it," Ross said. "For ten million dollars, I'll cut a baby's heart out and feed it to 'em. Besides, everybody knows he's blind and was always a pussy who can't defend himself. No one will care or even know it was us."

"I—I don't know, man," Aaron said with panic in his voice. "The guitar's one thing, but I don't want to kill—"

"Then get the fuck out of here and let us handle it! You ain't getting shit if you do, though!" Ross snarled.

"First, we need to see if it's even here," said Mason. "Keep an eye on him, Aaron, we're gonna go look for it."

"What the fuck am I supposed to do if he wakes up?" Aaron asked.

"You're supposed to be some Billy Badass gang-banger, who used to tell all them goddamn pill-whores you've killed people before. So you figure it out!" Mason berated.

Feeling a panic attack coming, Julian struggled to breathe while keeping himself still. He heard the stammering of footsteps as Mason and Ross frantically ran up the stairs. "'In the meantime,'"— Aaron resumed reading aloud—"'keep writing your book. Tell your story and ours. One day everyone will know the pain and suffering you endured and survived. It will help with your healing, and eventually, help others with theirs.' …"

Aaron was interrupted by Mason and Ross running back down the stairs. "It's not up there," Mason fumed. "This place has a basement, though. Let's check there!" Julian heard the squeak of a door opening and two sets of footsteps rapidly descending.

Aaron cleared his throat and continued. "'A day will come when everything falls into place, and'—"

"Found it!" Mason's voice echoed from below. Seconds later, his and Ross's footsteps could be heard back up the stairs to the living room. "It's a digital combination safe," Mason said. "I'm gonna get a knife from the kitchen. Then we'll wake Julian up and make him tell us the combination." There was no need to play dead anymore. Julian was so frightened his body was trembling, anyway. He opened his eyes and saw the dark eight-ball on the floor beside him.

"Hey!" Ross shouted as Julian saw his white tennis shoes and the bottoms of his blue jeans approach. "Wake up!"

"Wha—what's going on?" Julian stuttered, playing dumb but unable to hide his fear. He sat up, noticing his glasses were missing.

He lightly brushed the back of his head and saw the blood on his fingertips. "Why—why are you doing this?" he asked.

"We found the safe," said Ross.

"Wha—what safe?" Without warning, Ross hauled off and kicked Julian in the nose, knocking him back to the floor. Blood spattered and quickly trickled from his nostrils.

Ross knelt to Julian's level. "Let's try this again, dumb shit!" Mason returned from the kitchen with a large carving knife. "Gimme' that," Ross demanded, taking it from Mason's hand and waving it in Julian's eye.

Well … I guess this is it. This is how I really die. Julian thought about everything he could have done differently in the past year and how following his heart had failed him again. He imagined Violet's face, focusing on her brown almond eyes before laughing ironically. "I don't know the combination," he said, but Ross ignored him. In a quick motion, he sliced across Julian's forehead. "Arrrggghhh! … Fuck!"

"If you lie to me again, your throat will be next," Ross said. "Is that money worth dying for?"

Even in pain, fear, and bearing a crimson mask, Julian still snickered. "Do you think I'm stupid, you fucking backwoods inbred piece of shit? At this point, I'm dead already, whether I tell you or not."

Ross and Mason laughed. "The fucking balls on this guy," Ross said.

"He's got a bigger pair than he used to, that's for sure," Mason added. "Why don't you cut them off? Then, he'll talk, I bet."

Ross's laughter continued. "You're a sick fuck. You know that, Mason?"

"I just want to get this shit over with, but if we kill him first, it's for nothing," Mason said. "If we're gonna be murderers, it damn well better count."

Ross shoved the knife back in Julian's face, asking, "Wha'd'ya say, Julian? Are you gonna make us cut your nuts off?" Julian stared with a blank expression before spitting a wad of blood and saliva in Ross's face. "You mother fucker!" Ross shouted. He wiped his face with the back of his hand and grinned psychotically.

With the tip of the knife, he dug through Julian's red t-shirt, into his chest, and slowly carved from left to right.

"Ahh! … Goddamnit!" Julian howled, wincing as his warm blood oozed to the surface.

"Aaron, come over here. Help Mason pick him up," Ross commanded. Julian looked at Aaron, still holding the framed letter. He set it down on the sofa and joined them. He and Mason each took an arm and lifted Julian to his feet. Ross reached out with his free hand and yanked down Julian's blue denim shorts to his knees. Then, his green boxers. "Last chance, Julian," Ross said, staring him in the eyes, but he said nothing.

Ross forcefully gripped Julian's testicles and gritted his yellow teeth before lowering the knife out of view. "Wait!" Julian croaked, finally giving in. "Fucking hell … just wait!"

Ross released his grip and said, "If you say anything other than the combination, I swear to God I will fucking murder you right here, right now, with or without the money. Do you understand me?" His eyes widened, and he spat in Julian's face as he spoke.

Julian shook his head up and down. He said, "Forty-four … twenty-two … forty-six. …" He closed his eyes and gasped. "And two."

"Alright, come with me, Mason," said Ross. He gave the knife to Aaron and said. "If he tries anything, finish him."

Julian swallowed his pride and asked, "May I sit on the sofa?"

"Go ahead," Ross said. Julian pulled up his shorts and slowly walked over and sat down, noticing a shape that had to be his glasses nearby on the floor. "Remember, you try anything, you die," said Ross. He turned to Mason and nodded. They walked back towards the basement door and descended again.

Aaron sat next to Julian and picked up the letter. "Not that it matters, but I'm gonna finish reading this. I think it's funny."

"Go right ahead," Julian smirked.

"'A day will come when everything falls into place. I will come back to you, and we will spend the rest of time and space together, I swear. Love, now and always, Violet.'"

… Ding! … Dong! … Ding! … Dong! … The old grandfather clock began to chime, announcing the top of the ninth hour.

"Motherfucker!" Ross roared from the basement.

… Ding! … Dong! … Ding! … Ding! As the melody concluded, Julian laughed.

… Dong!

"What the fuck's so funny?" Aaron asked.

… Dong!

"Keep reading," Julian snickered.

… Dong!

"P.S. If you don't see me beforehand, I swear, by the stroke of nine, I will come watch those fireworks with you on …"

"On the fourth of July," Julian said along with Aaron, laughing his ass off as he did.

… Dong!

Angry stomping erupted from the stairs, and Ross burst through the doorway with fire in his eyes.

… Dong!

"You're dead, cocksucker!" He roared, marching towards Julian and taking the blade from Aaron.

… Dong!

Ross raised the shiny blade above his head, ready to kill.

… Dong!

… SMASH! From upstairs, a glass-shattering boom vibrated the entire house.

… Dong!

Ross stopped dead in his tracks, and Mason quickly entered from the basement. "What the fuck was that?!" Aaron shrieked, jumping from the sofa. The men stood side by side, on high alert, looking in all directions.

… Dong!

As the grandfather clock finished, Julian tightly squeezed his eyes shut and made a wish.

… Stomp … Stomp … Sto …

Aaron pointed up the staircase and shouted, "It came from up th—" He instantly shot across the room with the force of a cannonball, as if launched from thin air. The back of his head violently cracked like an egg against the rough stonework at the fireplace. The impact left behind a greasy red spot, and his limp body fell to the floor.

"What the fuck?!" Ross cried in terror. He and Mason stood back to back, panning the room in search of something they could not see, something fierce. "What the fuck just happened?!" Ross shouted again.

As if he could fly, Ross forcefully shot to the twenty-foot-high ceiling before falling back to the granite floor. Mason tried to run, but he met the same fate and was also blasted against the ceiling, just to fall back down. Ross wiggled and tried to crawl away, but he was tossed up high again. Then, Mason. Back and forth. Over and over. Julian laughed so hard he nearly pissed himself in joyous disbelief.

The extraordinary force moved too fast for anyone to see, but Julian knew what was happening. "What the fuck are you doing?!" Mason wheezed with the little strength he still had. After hitting the floor again, he looked into Julian's eyes and begged, "Please, make it stop. I—I—I'm sorry!"

Finally, it stopped. Neither Mason nor Ross could move. With all their open wounds, their blood was giving Julian's living room a new paint job. Exposed innards and bones protruded from both their legs and arms. Ross's collar bone pierced from his neck, and Mason's left foot dangled unnaturally below the calf. Julian took the shape from the floor—indeed his glasses—and regained his focus, looking back and forth between the wounded fawns amongst a ravenous dragon, and Aaron, lying dead beside the fireplace. Despite the real-life horror movie, playing out in 4D, Julian admired the glorious justice while scanning the room, searching for his long-lost love. She was nowhere, yet everywhere.

"Why—why—why are you doing this?" Mason whimpered a deathly rattle.

"Why am I doing this?" Violet's sweet, southern voice filled the room and Julian's ears like cheerful birds after an overdue rainstorm, but it was darker, and more macabre than he remembered. He shivered in cold chills as the slow, steady sound of her footsteps descended the elegant staircase. "Why are you attempting to rob and murder your cousin?"

"Wh—wh—wh—why did you do this to us?" Mason murmured as Ross slowly stirred and gargled.

"Why did I do that?" Violet sarcastically chuckled. "So you couldn't run from the fun part." Julian finally saw the bottom of a white skirt and her thin legs from just below her knees, standing in the stairwell while the rest of her remained blocked from his view.

"Run fr—from wh—what?" Mason whimpered.

Violet giggled and said, "From this!" She disappeared from Julian's view, as did Mason and Ross. Loud bangs and thuds led up the stairs, and Julian heard more glass break, followed by his cousin's frantic screams from outside the house. Julian was injured, but he wobbled out to the driveway as each crackle and pop of the nearby fireworks loudly echoed through the hollow.

From at least a hundred feet up the mountainside, somewhere in the woods behind the house, came more screams. He followed the driveway to the bare side of the house near the garage, where the tall streetlight dimly lit the open yard. He peered towards the woods, watching for movement during the short glimpses of extra light from the bright and colorful fireworks.

At first, he only heard the booms from above and occasional movement through the foliage until Ross horrifically cried, "Please help me! … Please! … Somebody!" Eventually, his ineffective pleas fell silent.

Seconds later, more leaves convulsed, and Mason wailed, "Oh my God! … What are you?! I just wanna go ho—o—ome!" He cried and squealed like a cockroach in a flame, but no one else could hear him over the repetitive whistling of bottle rockets. Before a window of silence opened in the hot, summer night, Mason's karmic agony extinguished once and for all.

With fireworks once again lighting the night, over a minute passed before Julian heard footsteps crunching through the weeds, growing louder as she came closer. He watched the woods light up a few seconds at a time, catching snippets of her movement before everything went dark again. Julian's eyes burned from the blood drying around his eyelids and he could not see far, but he saw what he needed. He saw her, wearing white, now tie-dyed red. As she exited the woods and stepped into the yard, the dull orange streetlight illuminated his goddess of gore. As Julian's eyes remained locked on her shadowy face, she stopped only feet away, saying nothing. Her tiny frame glowed, outlined by light, and the wet blood against her flesh glistened and sparkled as her chest moved with every breath.

As Julian scanned her shadowy face, the first thing he noticed was her eyes; those guiltless brown almonds, locked on his ever-dying blues. Finally she took one step closer, and Julian saw the rest of her spattered face and red-caked mouth. Both her hands were gloved to the wrists with her dinner. There was a time Julian would have cowered and soiled himself in fear, but despite the corpse in his living room and dead cousin in the woods, he knew he was safe. He wanted to say so much, yet in the heat of the moment, all he could manage was, "Hi."

Violet smiled. Julian cleared his throat and awkwardly rubbed the back of his bludgeoned head, knowing he'd waited his entire life for a specific moment, and finally, that moment had been reached. It was the moment he stared at the love of his life, not caring that she just murdered three people. He forgot all about the previous months of hell he endured without her. They no longer existed. In that moment, the perfect moment, only Violet, his twin flame, did.

He swallowed a lump and said, "I … I bought you a guitar."

In an instant, Violet flew into his arms and wrapped her own around his unsteady body. He closed his eyes, and after all the times he'd tried, their lips collided like worlds. Julian tasted blood, and he was sure Violet tasted his. The taste of the dead did not matter. All he ever wanted was her. The synchronized trance in the motion was surreal. Their tongues slowly met, each approaching carelessly. He was in a whole other dimension without time or space, and the only thing in it, within thought or reason, was her.

Julian encountered bliss. It was like he'd leveled up in a video game, bombarded with all the bonuses and fabulous prizes at once, lasting until reality became tangible again. All along, the fireworks continued blowing up the sky in the backdrop, just for them, in their perfect, fateful moment.

Chapter Twenty-Nine

T he house was quiet when Julian awoke the next morning. He was sore, but his cuts were mostly shallow. His chest and head were both neatly bandaged. Violet had been kind and gentle, cleaning his wounds and keeping him awake a few hours in case of a concussion.

He yawned and stretched before putting on his glasses and slowly dragging his feet down the hallway and through the game room. As he passed, he fixated on the broken window where Violet had made her dramatic entrance. The surrounding carpet was already clear of glass, and a black trash bag covered the empty frame. He staggered down the stairs and scanned the living room upon reaching the bottom. Aaron's body, along with any traces of blood on the floor, walls, and ceiling, was long gone. Rather than the scent of cleaning supplies, a pleasant aroma of cherries filled the air. Even the eight-ball and framed letter were put back in their proper places atop the mantle. he smiled, thinking, *wow!* After he opened the front door and saw that Mason's car was also gone, Julian had breakfast and spent the day resting on the sofa, watching television, and waiting for the sun to set.

After dark, the basement door creaked open. The sound caught Julian's attention, and he turned in her direction. Violet stood in the doorway, wearing a blue spaghetti-strap top and a white pair of pajama pants she'd left behind. Her long auburn hair was a scattered mess, and her flawless brown almonds drooped like she was still half asleep. She yawned and smiled on her way to the sofa, taking a seat on the opposite end from Julian, whispering, "Hi."

Julian cleared his throat, also saying "Hi." For a moment, they only stared at each other. Even the night before, they'd had little to say. Finally, Violet stood. Following the inside trail between the curved sofa and round glass table to Julian's end, she sat beside him.

"I am sorry," she said, wrapping her thin, pale arms around his back and gently pulling him closer. "I am so sorry that I left you. I just … I had to give you space, for your protection, because ..."

"Because what?" Julian asked.

"Because I love you."

Julian used the back of his hand to caress her cheek and brush the hair from her face, saying, "I love you too."

"I thought I was protecting you, but it was my leaving that almost got you killed, and I—"

"And you saved me. You're my warrior woman and a goddess in my eyes." Violet smiled at his declaration. "At times, I wanted to give up on myself and accept my insanity, but I never gave up on you or us."

She softly pecked his thin lips with hers. "I missed you, Jul."

"I missed you too, my flower." He closed his eyes and kissed her lips properly, experiencing the same magic in her embrace as the night before. After pulling away, they shared an innocent giggle before releasing their grip on one another. "So, what are we going to do if anyone asks about Mason or the others?" he asked.

"Who else might've known they were here?"

"I was over at the lake with Daryl, his family, and their daughters' boyfriends. After jumping off a rock, one of the boys broke his foot or something. We were out at a little island, and when we got back to the boat ramp, I ran into Mason and the others. I knew it all happened for a reason, so I caught a ride home with them while everyone else went to the hospital."

"So, Daryl and his family know, but that's it?"

"Yeah, but Mason lives in his grandpa's old house, down the hill with his wife and kids."

"Hmm … well, not anymore, he doesn't," she snickered, and so did Julian. "I got rid of the bodies and took their car about an hour and a half west, across the Kentucky border. I left it at the end of an old dirt road on top of a mountain. I could go back tonight and take it further, but everyone knows you can't drive. I couldn't see it coming back to you. Besides, those guys were junkies. Even their blood gave me a headache. I doubt anyone will make much of a fuss about them. Even if they do, you'll be fine, I promise. As for Mason's family, they're better off without him."

"It's funny," Julian chuckled. "A person's family are the ones who are supposed to have your back, but mine only stick knives in it."

Violet placed her hand on his shoulder and said, "It's hard to accept, but deceit doesn't know blood from water. Don't worry about them. I will be your family, and so will my father. In our family, you are loved and appreciated."

Julian shut his eyes and slowly inhaled through his sore nostrils, savoring Violet's words. "I'd like that," he said before exhaling through his mouth and opening his eyes again. "Speaking of Xavier, did you ever find him?"

"No," she sighed. "He's alive and safe, though, maybe overseas somewhere, but I don't know where."

"Did you look for him?"

"I did, but I only went so far because I've always feared flying over the ocean alone."

"Why?"

"I never learned to swim. Even if I can fly, I'm terrified of deep water, and if I ever had to land, I didn't want it to be somewhere in the middle of the ocean."

"Where did you go, and how do you know he's safe?"

"Last month, I got a little desperate and flew down to Peru. Even though I am not Taltosian, I was still welcomed by Dajhri."

"What did she say?"

"She said Dad was there near the end of February, and he stayed until the end of April."

Julian tipped his head, asking, "Why would he stay there for so long? I mean, Cauldwell killed Father Grant before that, and—"

"It wasn't Cauldwell. Apparently, William's spine was severed, and he was drained of his blood, just like all the others. Dajhri said they even cut his head off." Her shoulders slumped and she cupped her hands over her face as the memory seemed to upset her.

"If she's down in Peru, how does Dajhri know that?" Julian asked.

"Dajhri is a prophet, and one of the most powerful vampires alive, but even more than that, she's the queen. Even in the vampire world, royalty has its advantages. She has eyes and ears everywhere."

"If it wasn't Cauldwell who killed Father Grant, who was it?"

"It was someone from Raz Ahrim, the Egyptian kingdom," she said. "That's how they do it. When they hunt, they often cut their victims' spines to paralyze them. As for the beheading, they just do that for fun."

"Why would they come all the way to New York to feed? And why kill an old priest?"

"It was never about feeding. When my father first opened Leviticus, it rubbed a lot of vamps the wrong way. He knew he was playing with fire, but if you knew him the way the rest of us do, you'd know how stubborn he can be. He was determined to blend in with human society. He loves humans, and sadly, his love is his weakness."

"If he pissed off so many vampires, how come none of them tried to stop him before?"

"The truce. Since the dark ages, the three kingdoms have agreed to not interfere with the others' affairs."

"But wasn't Xavier banished from his kingdom?"

"Yes, but just the kingdom itself. Even though that was centuries ago, the other kingdoms and covens know my father's story well. They see him as a legend, and still consider him a child of L'abisme, as well as Anna, his sister and the king's daughter. Whether Caanis cares to admit it or not, he has a soft spot for my rebellious father. All vampires who know of Caanis fear him. They would never act out against the king in a way that would endanger themselves their coven, or their kingdom."

"Well, if someone from Raz Ahrim is coming to Xavier's territory to kill, it doesn't sound like they are taking this truce very seriously."

"You're right. According to Dajhri, Raz Ahrim is trying to provoke a war. Targeting William confirmed it, considering it wouldn't take much for a vampire to uncover his connection to my father and Eric."

"But why now?"

"The Ahrims always considered themselves the only vamps who should exist. They are the most ancient and powerful, but it certainly does not give them the right to do this. Many centuries ago, Dajhri said a war between the remaining three kingdoms would happen, and it looks like her prophecy is coming true. After Dad opened the club, the Ahrims were furious, and while I think they know better than to attack him or any of us directly, they've started killing people in the city to gain attention."

"Then why would Xavier run away like that, with the murders, and Cauldwell on his crusade?"

"My father is a great man, with a heart of gold as you know, but he's proud. Dajhri said he fell into a horrible depression over what happened to Eric and William. He stayed there until the end of April, when Cauldwell said all our names on television."

"That night was a blur, but I remember," Julian said, recalling snippets of his arrest and feeling strongly about his grandfather's role in it.

"Everyone at that meeting wanted to kill Cauldwell and his men, but my father did not, thinking it would bring even more attention to us. After he was kicked out of L'abisme, he swore he would only ever kill again when it was absolutely necessary. As a vampire, it made him weak, and because he wouldn't let us take action, he blames himself for Eric. It was a huge blow to his ego."

"You're making it sound like he is a coward."

"Don't say that!" Violet puffed her cheeks and glared.

"Well, what do you want me to say? Now that everything's out in the open, why doesn't he go after Cauldwell?"

"From what I heard, he did. Vamps from L'abisme and Taltosia have also been looking, but after that public appearance, nobody can find him or his men."

"How did Cauldwell find out who everyone was in the first place?"

"That part we don't know," Violet said with a shiver. "The only theory Dajhri or I have is that someone betrayed us. I don't want to believe that, but I can't help it. We've lived in secret this whole time. Since he first came to America, long before I was given the gift, my father, and any other vampire in his company, lived safely." Violet placed both her hands over her face again and sighed once more. "I honestly don't know what we're going to do now."

Julian wrapped his arms around her shoulders, embracing his flame. "We'll figure it out, together," he said. Violet snorted and pulled her hands away from her somber face, forcing a smile.

"We will," she mumbled. "But for now, I just want my daddy back."

"I know you said he's looking for Cauldwell, but do you know where he could've gone after he left Peru?"

"Unless he went back to Paris, I don't know."

"They won't let him in L'abisme, though, will they?"

"They probably would, but I'm not so sure he'd want to go back after how things ended. My father was born and raised in Paris. He had friends and other safe spots in that city, long before the catacombs were created. If he is in Paris, he will be safe."

"What about us?" Julian asked. "Cauldwell knows your name, and although most people assume he's a raving lunatic, all this is out in the public eye now."

"I have faith that my father is taking care of it. He's wise and intuitive, like you," she said, lightly stroking Julian's cheek with her fingers. "He won't let anything happen to us, I promise, my love."

Julian's lips curled upward. "What about the others? Did you find Anna and Bernard, or Bishop?"

"I don't know where any of them are. After what happened at the club, everyone scattered, and I assume they all went to L'abisme."

"What should you and I do—stay here, go to Peru … or?"

"I've never been to L'abisme, but if I took you there or to Peru, they would kill you since you're a human."

"So, change that," he said, staring as dead as a heart attack into Violet's eyes.

She momentarily smiled, as if the thought crossed her mind, before ignoring the request. "Right now, we need to wait."

"So, where did you go before Peru?"

"Alaska."

"Why Alaska?"

"Not long after I became a vampire, I ran away for a while. I needed my space after I went and saw my parents for the last time. Dad had told me there was a vampire coven there. I always wanted to see the Aurora Borealis, so he took me and I stayed there for a while, during one of their long stints of darkness. While I was there, I made friends. It's peaceful there, and the perfect spot for the largest coven in North America. One day, I will take you."

"So, what happened with your parents?" he asked, feeling intrigued.

"I don't want to talk about it," she groaned. "I buried that memory long ago, and with everything else going on right now, I'd prefer to leave it that way." Julian nodded while drawing his own conclusions in his head.

"So, what's going to happen with Raz Ahrim?" he asked.

"None of us want a war, but if they keep coming over here and leaving bodies behind, the other two kingdoms will have no choice but to intervene. No one wants to break the truce either, but when it comes to our survival, I fear it will happen."

"If it does, what am I supposed to do? I can't defend myself against vampires or Navy Seals."

"What do you want to do?" Violet smiled, slowly running her fingers through Julian's hair, giving him chills while keeping eye contact. Both grew silent for a moment as each already knew the answer. Julian opened his mouth, prepared to say it aloud, but Violet spoke first. "Your hair's getting long," she said, attempting to redirect the conversation. "I like it. You could probably pull it back in a ponytail if you wanted."

As her fingers persisted, massaging Julian's scalp, he shut his eyes and slowly laid his head in her lap, stretching his legs along the cool leather sofa. "That feels so good," he whispered. His forehead was still sore, but Violet's tender touch offered relief. He took a deep, relaxing breath as she softly began humming a sweet lullaby in his ear. Eventually he fell asleep, feeling happy, safe, and complete, not just with Violet, but also himself.

Chapter Thirty

Since her return, Violet regularly disappeared, for hours sometimes, returning with enough bags of blood to last her several nights. Then she'd disappear again. Through his insecurities, Julian often lay awake at night, repeating the same thought. *What if she does not come back this time?* She always did, but his doubts were justified. He was in love, with something to lose.

On one particular evening, the sweet aroma of something burnt led Julian into the kitchen, where he found Violet sucking on an IV tube. A lingering curiosity finally got the better of him. Forgetting about the smell, he asked, "Do you think I could try a sip?" He'd tasted his own blood many times, but aside from the night Violet returned, he'd never tasted anyone else's, not like a vampire would.

Her eyes twinkled and fixated on his. She let the makeshift straw fall from between her pillowy red lips and asked, "Really?"

"Yeah, I've been curious."

"Sure, see what you think," she said, handing over the nearly empty pint-sized pouch. He placed the narrow tube to his lips and gently sucked. The intense metallic flavor instantly conquered his taste buds, and he pulled the tube away, nearly gagging on the foul taste.

"Jesus Christ! That's awful!" He handed the bag back, scowling and regretting his decision.

"It takes a while to get used to, but I am impressed." Violet smiled and even appeared turned on by his bold move. She finished her dinner and tossed the empty bag in the trash. After washing it down with a drink of water, she retrieved her little black purse from the countertop and removed something, out of Julian's view.

"I tried to make you a German chocolate cake, since you said it was your favorite, but I am not used to cooking anymore. I accidentally burnt it," she said, blushing, but Julian smiled anyway.

"It's okay," he said. "It's the thought that counts."

"I do have something for you, though," she said. Her hands were tucked behind her back and she batted her eyes. "As you know, I don't normally give gifts, but it's your birthday and I wanted you to have something special that has meant a lot to me." She pulled her hands forward and revealed a square, royal blue jewelry box.

Julian grinned. "What is it?" he asked.

"Open it."

He opened the box and took a few seconds to fixate on the object before his eyes bugged out. "Oh my God!" He pulled a silver ankh pendant from the box. The ancient Egyptian symbol was roughly two and a half inches long and clasped to a thin, silver chain. "Wow … I … I love it."

"You told me you liked it when I wore it at the club."

"Wait!" Julian gasped. "This is yours?"

"It is, but I want you to have it. It's pure silver." After Violet hooked it behind his neck, she scrunched her lips and kissed the ankh for luck. "This necklace was given to me the same day you were born, September 24th, nineteen-eighty-one. It was a gift from Eric, but I don't think he would mind me giving it to you." She wrapped her arms around Julian's shoulders and kissed his lips, whispering, "Happy birthday, Jul. I love you."

"I love you too. I also love the necklace," he said, intrigued by the story behind it. "I will never take it off." He returned a kiss of his own, then another. Caught in the moment, his wandering lips moved to Violet's fair neck, kissing and teasing it with the tip of his tongue.

"Julian," she softly moaned while his lips moved about her flesh. "Julian, please."

He pulled away, asking, "What is it?"

"I … I can't," she sighed. Her shoulders sank and she lowered her head.

"Why not?"

"Vampires don't usually have sex with humans. We get a little wild and intense sometimes, and humans can't handle it." An awkward smile formed across her face as she giggled and blushed. "I don't mean to laugh, but it's embarrassing—quite heartbreaking, actually," she confessed, placing her palm against Julian's cheek. "I want to, believe me I do, but we can't, at least not yet anyway." She shut her eyes, sighing again. "I made the mistake of trying once. It didn't work out the way I hoped it would."

"What happened?".

She blushed even brighter, saying, "Disastrous. I ruined his life," before cupping her hand over her mouth.

"What'd you do, rip his dick off or something?"

She removed her hand, erupting in laughter. "Something like that," she said before calming herself in a way that seemed like she was ashamed to laugh at such a remark.

Julian's face also straightened, thinking of such a brutal way to die. He swallowed a lump and scratched the back of his neck. "That's ... umm. …. I—I don't know," he stuttered. "So, those girls at the club, they weren't vampires?"

"No, they were just two random barflies. The only vampires there were all at that meeting." She kissed his forehead and asked, "Are you disappointed?"

"No."

"If you knew I wouldn't be able to have sex with you as a human, would you have gone through with it? … Would you have fucked them?"

"No," he said. "At first, I thought I wanted to, but that was the alcohol talking. After I went upstairs with them, they ripped my shirt off me and even took my pants off, but it didn't feel right. They were fake and had no interest in the real me. I told them I couldn't because I loved someone else. I told them I loved you." Violet smiled, still blushing. "They were all over each other after that, but I got bored and passed out."

Violet moved in slowly. Her lips connected with his again. Her warm, vibrant energy flowed throughout his body, and the sensation was electrifying. "Come on," she said, taking his hand and leading him towards the living room. "I wanna dance!" She approached the jukebox and pushed a few buttons, making her selection. As a steady rain wept from the dark clouds outside, the soothing patter was abruptly drowned out by a classic love song hitting the speakers surrounding the room.

Julian stood a few feet behind her, grinning over the choice, "Nights in White Satin," by The Moody Blues. Violet turned around and slowly danced towards him, bearing a smile of her own and extending her hands. "I don't really know how to dance," he said.

"Neither do I, but just go with it," she replied, taking his right hand while resting her left below the back of his neck. Julian softly placed his free hand on the small of Violet's back, just below her hair. They moved in unison, letting the romantic tune be their guide. Shortly after they began, Julian stumbled, but Violet caught him and whispered, "Put your feet on mine," in his ear.

"Why?"

She winked and smiled, asking, "Do you trust me?"

"Yes."

"Then put your feet on mine, and don't let go." She gripped Julian a little tighter as he took a deep breath and did what she asked, placing his white socked feet atop her purple-polished tootsies. She slowly ascended into the air until they floated nearly ten feet above the stone floor. "And don't look down," she added.

"I—I'll try." Julian gulped, pressing firmly against Violet's back while the tips of her hair tickled his knuckles. Their right hands were locked, their fingers intertwined. Julian's feet rested squarely over Violet's, and she took control: moving to the beat and passionately staring into his eyes. He relaxed, knowing she would not let him fall. Finding safety and comfort in her embrace, he eventually laid his head on her shoulder and shut his eyes. Violet hovered about the room, with the music creating such a perfect moment for them both. As the song and Violet's beautiful declaration came to an end, Julian opened his eyes. With the sofa below them, Violet slowly descended, and gently placed Julian on the end at which he usually sat.

"Wow," he exhaled. "That … that was amazing."

Violet landed beside him and said, "I've always wanted to do that." She leaned forward and pecked the tip of his nose with her pillowy lips.

The lovers spent the remainder of their evening laughing and listening to music. Julian was so happy, he never wanted the evening to end, but eventually he struggled to keep his eyes open. It was close to two in the morning when he went upstairs to his bedroom. Whenever Julian turned in, Violet usually retired to her bedroom in the basement with a book from the upstairs library, spending the rest of her night lounging in a hammock while she read it.

Although Julian thought he was sleepy, he lay awake for at least an hour, restless, and with his thoughts on a potential future beyond his mortal coil. He was experiencing true love for the first time in his life, and nothing else mattered; not Mason, whom he hadn't heard a word about since his disappearance, not his grandfather, nor the dark memories time had yet to erase.

Occasionally, Julian heard Violet turning a page through the vent on the floor. After an hour of the sound repeating every so often, it was replaced by sudden footsteps echoing from below. Julian froze in fear, thinking, *what the fuck is that?*

"Violet?" A young man's voice called from the vent.

"Daddy?!" Violet shrieked with excitement. Julian heard movement and he imagined her leaping to her feet. "Daddy! Oh, thank God!" she cried in joy.

"I've missed you so much, my sweet," Xavier said. Julian sighed in relief, but his heart still raced as the vampire's deep, silky voice raised the hairs on the back of his neck.

"I've missed you too," Violet said.

"Where's Julian, asleep?"

"Yeah, upstairs, but where the fuck have you been?!" she asked in an angry tone. "Do you have any idea all the hell I had to go through trying to find you, or at the very least, find out what was happening?!"

"Calm down, dear. It's okay," he said. "I am back now, and I know I should not have left, but I too sought answers."

"But you hid in Peru until April!" she chided.

"How did you know I was in Peru?"

"Because I grew desperate and flew down there! I had no clue where you were, and all I did here was cry and mope around, while Julian didn't know what to do for me. So, I felt like I had to do something."

"So that is where you went," he said. "I saw your letter, upstairs. You should not have left him here alone, especially with all that money. If Cauldwell had found him, it is hard to say what he would have done. What if something happened to him while you were gone? Then what?" Violet said nothing. "Did something happen?"

"Yes," Violet shamefully mumbled. "But I came back just in time."

"What?! Cauldwell was here?!"

"No, no, it wasn't Cauldwell!" she frantically stressed. "It was one of Julian's cousins. He and two others were going to kill him and take your money, but I stopped them. … You're welcome, by the way."

Xavier loudly sighed. "Did you kill them?"

"I did. I covered it up, though."

"Goddamnit, Violet!"

"It's fine, I promise. Nobody's come around asking questions or anything."

"I'm not worried about you getting caught. You killed three people. That's four now, and just this year!"

"Chloe was going to tell on us. If I didn't do it, you know Bern would have, and he would have made her suffer. He hated her. As for the others, they were going to kill Julian. They even cut him before I got here. I will be damned if those fucks didn't get what they deserved! I will always support your cause, Dad, but I won't let anyone expose us or hurt someone I love."

"So, you really do love him?"

"You already know I do," she said. As Julian lay silent in the dark, a heartfelt, helpless grin formed on his face at hearing Violet's words. "And he loves me," she continued. "Julian loves me with all his heart, and I could never let anyone hurt a hair on his precious head. Besides, he wants to be one of us."

"Is that so?" Xavier asked.

"Julian is the most intelligent, empathic, and resilient human I've ever known. He's seen how truly awful humanity can be, but he can also appreciate beauty. He's just lost like I was, but fate brought us together."

"I like Julian, but he has underlying rage inside of him."

"Can you blame him? He was a defenseless child, raised and conditioned to feel like he had no one to depend on. That's why now, as an adult, he's lost all hope in humanity. He doesn't even feel like his best friend takes him seriously."

"The way he was mistreated is what frightens me," said Xavier. "You remember the night I took you to see your parents, and what you did when your father said that one word to you."

What the hell?! Julian thought, feeling his suspicions were confirmed.

"What about it?" Violet asked.

"All your repressed anger and emotions over what he did to you when you were a little girl came out, all at once. Your anger, rage, and pain did that. Think of everything Julian has within him. Since he took *Ayahuasca*, all those repressed memories and feelings came full circle. They linger on the surface with nowhere to go. Who is to say he will not murder his family or his former lover and her brother with that kind of power? Does that not scare you?"

Violet sighed. "Honestly, I haven't really thought about it, but if you want my opinion, maybe he should."

"Violet!" Xavier chided.

"I love you, Daddy, but we are vampires, and while I don't like hurting anybody, there needs to be some justice in this world. I think they deserve to pay for what they did to him, just like Cauldwell, his men, and the goddamn Ahrims deserve to pay for what they did to Eric and William," she said as Xavier sighed again. "Besides, Julian is a Libra, and justice is in his nature. In fact, today … or yesterday, I should say, was his birthday."

"Really?" Xavier brightened. "September twenty-fourth was also my baby sister's birthday. In fact, I flew straight here after leaving flowers at her grave in Paris." Another moment of silence passed, allowing the tension to ease. "Do you think turning him into a vampire would be a good idea?" he asked.

"I do," she said. "And I want to be the one who does it."

"I can't let you do that, dear."

"Why not?" she demanded.

"Because we both know the links created when a vampire makes another or shares their blood with other vampires. If you two truly do love each other, and something happened to either of you, it would torture the other to madness until the day you die."

"Whether we like it or not, we are all eventually going to die," she said.

"But for our kind, death is a little more complicated. I refuse to allow you to feel that kind of pain if something should happen to him. If anything ever happened to you, it would destroy me, and Julian as well. Is that something you're willing to risk?"

Violet sighed, saying, "That's just it. I want that connection with him, to share our souls for all eternity. I want to be with him in our dreams when we sleep, and I want to pass my powers on to him."

"No, you don't, my sweet. You never made a vampire before. You are much younger than I, but in many ways, far more powerful."

What?! Julian nearly lost his breath, never guessing it was possible.

"You know I made many vampires in my years, and my soul wears thin. Every time a vampire makes another, they give away a piece of themselves they can never get back. Your soul is entirely intact. With all the skeletons Julian keeps in his closet, passing on your full power to him would be dangerous, not just to those who hurt him, but the world itself. Besides, you could not possibly know how it feels to have the dead souls, of those you transcended, torturing you from beyond with questions you don't know how to answer. Every time I sleep, I am haunted by the ghosts of my past. It is hell, and I cannot allow you to experience that if something should ever happen to him. Can you not respect that, my child?"

"I understand," she mumbled. "I also respect your decision, but I still wish it was me."

"I know you do, and if what Dajhri told me is true, you will make a vampire one day—but not Julian."

"She told you that?"

"Dajhri told me a lot of things when I was in Peru."

"Me too," she said.

"So, she told you about the Ahrims?"

"She said they killed William."

"And Eric," Xavier added.

"What?!" Violet was outraged. "They killed Eric, too?!"

Oh my God! Julian gasped, quickly cupping his hand over his mouth.

"I take it she did not tell you everything," Xavier said. "After you and Julian left, I moved Eric's body so I could bury him. Like William and all the other murder victims, his spine was severed."

"My God!"

"There's something else."

"What?" Violet asked but he said nothing. "What?!" she repeated, louder than before.

"The Ahrims were not acting alone."

"What do you mean, Dad?" A hint of dread showed in her voice.

"Julian is not the only one who was left a letter." Julian now heard the distinct uncrumpling of paper. "This was left for me in Peru."

"Let me see." Violet cleared her throat and read aloud: "'Dear Xavier, what can I say that could make up for the damage I caused, the innocent lives I took, or the unwanted attention I brought upon the coven? Nothing. What I can say is it was never my intention for any of this to happen. I was manipulated and forced to act against my will. The truth is, I killed everyone: Eric, Father Grant, and all the others. I started a chain reaction, on the command of the Raja Kahíjí, to lead a trail back to you. The Ahrims' king ensnared my mind. He told me what to do, how to do it, and I had no control over my own thoughts or actions. I know the horrible mistake I made, and though I do not deserve it, I beg for your forgiveness. I returned home to Taltosia, but upon arrival, I was banished by Dajhri for my crimes against you and for disturbing the truce. She said you would come to her, and as I am a child of Taltosia, she spared my life and allowed me to leave you this letter as a confession in hopes that if our paths ever cross again, you will show me the same mercy Caanis once showed you. Until that day comes, please accept my apology. Forever or never, Bishop.'"

"Holy shit," Julian whispered beneath his breath.

"Are you fucking kidding me?!" Violet seethed. "Bishop did this?!"

"I am afraid so, my sweet."

"Are you sure he wrote this?"

"It's his handwriting, but it was not his fault,"

"How the hell did they get to him?"

"You know how powerful the Ahrims are. Bishop is strong, but not like them."

"And Dajhri gave you this letter? She told me the Ahrims were responsible, but she never told me it was Bishop."

"She gave it to me when I arrived. You know how the queen is. Likely she did not want to alarm you or prompt you to do something foolish, given your spontaneous and hellacious nature."

"So after she gave you the letter, you just stayed in Taltosia for two months, knowing what they did? … Why?!"

"I was in mourning. Dajhri demanded I stayed until I was of sound mind. I have already angered the two kings in my lifetime, and I did not want to do the same with the queen. She is our greatest ally."

"Then why did you leave after Cauldwell went on television?"

"Because until then, nobody knew where he was. He came out of hiding, and with Dajhri's blessing, I went looking for him, but I failed. No one has seen him or his men since. Once I gave up my search, I went to Paris, looking for Bishop."

"Did you find him?"

"I did not," he said. "I visited the catacombs, hoping Caanis would make an exception and grant me audience, but he refused."

"Now that we know who's behind all this, what are we going to do?"

"For now, nothing."

"Nothing?!" Violet scoffed. "The Ahrims are provoking war! Before this gets any worse, we need to bring the other kingdoms and covens together and get rid of the Ahrims once and for all!"

"But the truce—"

"Fuck the truce!" she fumed. "They broke the truce when they attacked us! I know you don't want to kill, but your loved ones need you."

"I am treading lightly. Though I did not kill Eric, William, or any of the others, I did open the club. I brought all this upon myself, and their deaths are my fault. Even Dajhri holds some resentment towards me. I want to protect my family and coven, but Raz Ahrim is strong, and attacking them would be suicide, especially without the support from the other kingdoms. Until Dajhri and Caanis give their permission, nobody can make a move against Raz Ahrim. As for Cauldwell and his men, they need to be dealt with, I agree, but they have disappeared."

The basement grew quiet. Julian remained silent, wondering if they knew he'd been listening. "I am tired and need rest," Xavier said, yawning as he did.

"Take one of these other bedrooms," said Violet. "Sunlight doesn't reach the basement, and you will be safe in any of them. Just make sure not to open the door at the top of the stairs during daylight hours."

"We will talk more tomorrow, my sweet," he said. "I just …"

"You just what?" Violet asked.

"I just wanted to tell you that I love you and I am so sorry. I never meant to drag you or Julian into this," he lightly sobbed.

"I know, Dad, but if we are going to survive, we are going to have to fight back," she said. "And I love you too, but I also love Julian, and you have no idea what I would do to hold on to that love."

Aww! Julian instantly smiled.

"Goodnight, Violet."

"Goodnight, Daddy, and welcome home."

As Julian listened to Violet's bedroom door close, his smile remained until he fell asleep, thinking, *she called this place "home."*

Chapter Thirty-One

Shortly after dark, the basement door squeaked open. "Hello, Julian," Xavier announced upon entering the living room. Julian scanned the vampire's matching black slacks and untucked, half-buttoned shirt with the sleeves rolled to his elbows. His long blond strands lay loose atop his shoulders.

"Holy shit! Xavier?!" Julian croaked, pretending his presence was a mystery. He stood from the sofa, asking, "When did you get here?"

"Earlier this morning, before dawn," he said, approaching the sofa while Violet followed close behind. Julian locked eyes with her, wondering if she knew he'd been awake and listening. She winked and offered the slightest nod. Xavier extended his hand, and after the mutual greeting, Julian could not help but hug the immortal.

"I heard you were good to my daughter. Thank you, son," Xavier said before patting Julian's cheek in praise.

"You're welcome, but it's more like she has been good to me."

"I heard." Xavier took a seat on the opposite end of the sofa, where Violet usually sat. She inched past her father's knees to sit in the middle. "What have you been doing to stay busy? Are you still writing?"

"Yes, I am," said Julian, surprised Xavier remembered. "I've been writing a book about my life. I'm not far from finishing it, and I'd love to get it published if I can."

"Really? That is wonderful," he said, sinking into the sofa. "I feel like I could write a book about my own experiences as of late. They have been stressful but necessary."

"How so?" Julian asked.

"I have been many places and spoken with many other vampires about the murders in New York, those responsible, and the situation with Christopher Cauldwell."

"What are you going to do?"

"About Cauldwell, there is nothing I can do right now. Nobody knows where he is. As for the Ahrims, they have no more use for Bishop. The murders stopped after William, but the damage has been done. They intended to draw us out, and they did. Until the other kingdoms choose to act, my hands are tied." Xavier shut his eyes and lowered his head in regret. "It is my fault. My dream became a nightmare."

"You did what you thought was best," said Julian.

"Obviously, my best was not good enough." Xavier cleared his throat and opened his eyes, staring directly at Julian. "Look, I am going to get this out in the open. I know you were listening last night." Julian's gut immediately turned sour, and the deep bass rhythm of his heart filled his ears. He held his breath, fearing the worst. "Violet and I heard your thoughts reacting to what we said. I want you to know it is okay." Julian exhaled in relief as Xavier added, "You need to know these things if you are going to become a vampire."

Julian's heart still beat fast as he panned between the two. Their eyes remained locked on his, but Violet smiled and said, "It's okay, Jul. You don't have to be scared of my father."

"I—I—I honestly don't know what to say," Julian began. "I mean, I have thought so much lately about it. I know the price of my mortality. I know I can no longer walk in the light. I know I can only consume blood and water, but I know I love you, Violet. If this war is coming, I want to be by your side, and as a human with my disability, my chances of survival are slim."

"I know, Jul," Violet said, scooting closer. "I don't want to put you through this, but I know I want you. War is inevitable. Dajhri always said it was."

"Did she say how it would start?"

"She did not. She said there would be a sign marking the beginning, and we would know," Xavier said.

"So, we're supposed to just sit back and let Raz Ahrim or Cauldwell make the next move?" Julian asked.

"Cauldwell is small potatoes," Xavier said. "He and his men are strong, but they are still human, and nothing compared to the Ahrims. They do need to be taken care of before they cause us any more grief, however. The truce has nothing to do with them. We must kill them all." Xavier took a slow breath between his thin pink lips and said, "I swore I would not kill for food or out of anger again. Alas, it appears I have no choice. I know I have always been stubborn and headstrong, but I will no longer let my people and loved ones be exposed. I'd rather die a martyr than live a hypocrite, but defending my family is the exception. Bernard and Anna are still out there. I will do anything to protect them … and you," he said, looking at his daughter, then Julian again, adding, "You, too."

"What do you suggest we do for now?" Julian asked.

"How do you feel about receiving the gift?"

Julian swallowed a lump as the ripple in his gut returned. "I … I have searched for any trace of reason why I would want to remain a part of the human race, but I come up short. Humans have only ever hurt me. There is only one I still feel a bond with: my best friend, Daryl. He is great, and he was there for me when nobody else was. He's the kind of man who would give you the shirt off his back, but sadly …" He paused, thinking about all the years he and his friend lost. "We grew apart in a lot of ways. The bond is still there, and I will always love him like a brother, but he thinks I'm crazy, and he doesn't understand what I am going through, not like you do."

"Who would, though?" Xavier asked. "Only you know you, and you cannot expect someone who has not seen what we can do—with their own eyes—to believe in us. I see how he reacted when you confided in him on Independence Day."

Julian felt a sudden blast of cold chills. "You saw that?"

"I did, just now. It's okay, Julian. You carried such a heavy burden, and even though he did not believe you, your confession will be safe with him. I can see he is a good, honest man, but like everyone else, lost and easily persuaded by the authoritarians that spent a lifetime convincing him beings like us are only works of fiction."

"You're right. He is a great man, and the only human left that I trust. I don't want to lose that with him."

"There's nothing wrong with maintaining friendships with humans. Look at William. He never wanted the gift and so he grew old, yet remained a loyal friend to the coven. But as I am sure you know, eventually your friend will also grow old and die while you remain young. Throughout my long life I have experienced it many times and it's never easy to watch someone you love enter your life just to be ripped away. That's why most vampires avoid humans, but it still happens."

"There's something I've wanted to ask you," Julian said, and Xavier tipped his head. "Violet once told me since my eyes are still attached to me, and I can still see, there's a chance becoming a vampire could permanently cure them, but she wasn't sure."

"She was right," he said. "Your eyes are still a part of you and connected accordingly. Thus, your Retinitis Pigmentosa would be cured, and you will see unlike you ever have before."

Newfound adrenaline shot throughout Julian's body, and he was bathed in a soothing, warm light. He was not a vampire yet, but he had the sensation he could burst through the roof and fly through the night sky, as if he were. "I've always wanted to see like others do," he said as a salty tear rolled down his cheek. It was truly emotional to hear a cure existed, despite the extreme side effects.

Violet put her arm around him, saying, "You would be so happy. Think of all the fun we could have, and all the places we could go together once you learn how to fly."

"If he can fly," Xavier added. "You likely can, but not all vampires have the ability."

"Fine, party pooper." Violet flicked her tongue. "If you can fly, we will go everywhere together, and even if you can't, riding piggyback won't be as intense as it is for you now."

"I want to," Julian said. "But I am scared."

"I will be honest with you, Julian," Xavier began. "The transition itself will be the most terrifying experience of your life. There are no words or actions that can hone that point enough. The horror you encountered on the second night of your *Ayahuasca* ceremony will be orgasmic bliss in comparison. The fear will be worse than any form of abuse you have ever endured. You will likely kick and scream. You might even evacuate your bowels, but it's normal." Xavier's warning made Julian shudder. "Are you sure this is what you want? You cannot take it back. Even though you experienced a form of death with the *Ayahuasca*, this time you will actually die before you are reborn as a vampire. Do you understand, Julian? You must die as one to become the other."

Julian's breathing grew heavier and his hands visibly shook, but he remained composed. "I—I do," he murmured.

"We'll both be with you the whole time. I promise, my love." Violet pulled Julian's quivering hand to her lips and kissed the back of it.

"Yes, we will. We will not let anything happen that is not supposed to," Xavier reassured.

"You've got this, Jul," Violet whispered in his ear before kissing his cheek.

"If you choose to do this, there is something I want you to do first," Xavier added. "I want you to confront your family and get everything you have been holding back off your chest once and for all." Julian nodded. "I apologize for prying into your thoughts, but I believe your aunt and uncle, Bobbi-Jo and Clint, still gather at your grandfather's house on Christmas Eve, do they not?"

"Yeah, they do, but why?"

"Because it is best to cross over with a clear conscience. Last night, you heard us talk about Violet's parents. When she became a vampire, she had unresolved grievances. When faced with painful emotions, she reacted in a blind rage."

"I killed them," Violet interjected. "I don't know how it happened, and there's no other way of saying it, but I killed my parents in some sort of freak occurrence."

"It was not a freak occurrence, my sweet," Xavier assured. "The fury you tapped into was always there. As a vampire, you released it." He looked at Julian and said, "I cannot allow you to do the same."

"What happened?" Julian asked.

"To a normal human, it would appear as an act of God, but …" Xavier paused, glancing at Violet. "Why don't I let you explain it, dear? I can see you have wanted to tell him for a while." He sat up straight and scanned the room. "Besides, I would like to have a look around the house. I saw little of it when I got here last night." He stood and yawned, stretching his skinny, pale arms high above his head. The tail of his shirt raised, revealing the bottom of his thin, toned abdomen.

"There's a library and a bunch of board games upstairs, Dad," Violet said.

"Oh?" A grin slowly stretched across Xavier's narrow face as he headed towards the stairs. "Is there a chessboard?"

"Yes, Dad, there's a chessboard up there," she said, rolling her eyes and giggling.

"Excellent!" He climbed the first few steps and disappeared.

Violet took both Julian's hands in hers. "You know, I never meant to hurt either of them. I held in something dark from my childhood, and it all came out so suddenly."

"What happened?"

"As I told you before, my parents owned a peach and orange plantation. One year, when I was seven, it was harvest day. My biological father celebrated a little too hard." Julian kissed the back of her hand as he watched the sadness slowly grow in her brown almonds.

"They produced a large crop, and it was our best year. My father hired so many hands to help pick the fruit. Even my brothers, and I, were supposed to help, but we just goofed off all day." Violet shut her eyes and the corners of her lips rose and fell. "Both of my brothers were obsessed with baseball. My oldest brother, Mark, could have gone pro if he hadn't dislocated his shoulder in college."

"I remember it so clearly. Me, in my grass-stained church dress, with skinned knees and braided pigtails, running around, causing trouble … 'Gimme back my baseball, shorty!' Mark screamed at me when I ran off through the field with it. I was so fast he never caught me." She smiled slightly and opened her eyes.

"My father was so drunk that day, and my mother avoided him. I don't blame her. He was a mean drunk. He never laid a hand on her in front of us, but behind closed doors was another story. My mother was a good, proud woman, and she never showed any signs of weakness. She just took it all in stride."

Julian watched a couple of tears roll down Violet's cheeks before she sniffed and wiped them away. "Later that night, after my mother went to bed, and my brothers were out somewhere with their friends, I was alone in my room, scribbling in my diary. My father staggered in, blackout drunk and reeking of cheap whiskey. He had no idea what he was doing." A few more tears fell, and she wiped them away like the others.

"I will never forget this," she continued. "In the middle of it all, he called me 'sweet pea.' He never called me that before then. 'Shh! … You will wake your mother, sweet pea.' He slobbered all over me and I only screamed in shock and pain. He pinned me down and forced himself inside me as I tried telling him to stop, but he wouldn't listen. After it was over, he zipped his pants and staggered out, leaving me face down, against my pillow." Violet sobbed and lost her breath. Julian embraced her in his arms as she laid her wet cheeks against his shoulder and wept.

"It's okay," Julian softly whispered. "You're safe now. He cannot hurt you any more." He gently patted the back of her head. A few moments passed before her tears ended and she pulled away, wiping her eyes with the back of her hand.

"I was so traumatized, and I couldn't deal with it. Eventually, I blocked it out until I met Xavier, and he pulled it out of me the night I was alone with him at the café where I worked. I mean, I knew it happened, but the emotions were dormant for two decades. Then, when I visited my parents, it happened."

"What happened?"

"My father thought Xavier was my lover. 'You went all the way to New York to fuck some kid?!'" Amidst her sorrow, Violet laughed quietly. "The irony, right?" She straightened her face and cleared her throat before continuing. "He was so mad at me. Then, he said it: 'Your mother and I raised you better than that, sweet pea,' and I instantly lost control. A fiery rage burned deep inside of me, so hot the inferno left my body and took physical form. First the white curtains on the windows caught fire, then the walls themselves. My father screamed as he also burst into flames. His high-pitched squeals reminded me of a slaughtered pig, so excruciating and chilling. And my mother. …" Violet cried again. "My mother never knew what he did to me. She tried to get away, but a beam from the ceiling fell on her head. It killed her instantly!" She loudly sobbed.

"Come here," Julian soothed, pulling her against his chest and wrapping his arms around her again. "Shh … it's okay. It's okay …" He gently whispered the only comforting words he could manage, slowly rocking her like a distraught infant.

A few moments passed in silence and Violet pulled back, wiping away the tears and clearing her throat again. "You must think I'm a monster."

"No more than I am, Hell Belle." He smiled, finally understanding the nickname. She giggled, as if using the remark to refocus her horrible memories elsewhere. "We've all got scars," Julian said before kissing her forehead.

"Why are you so good to me?" she asked.

"Because I love you, and we are a perfect fit."

"We are, aren't we?" she snorted, wiping her eyes again. "And I love you, too." She closed her eyes and their lips met with tender grace.

"Wow! ... That librar—" Xavier's newfound enthusiasm halted from the bottom of the stairway as quick as it began. "I ... umm ... sorry." He stammered for words as Violet's and Julian's lips separated. Their attention turned to the blushing vampire, and all three shared a laugh. The trio quickly changed the mood and spent the rest of the night catching up, listening to music, and playing various board games: having fun and enjoying themselves like they were all kids again.

Chapter Thirty-Two

"In Mexico, they call it *Dia de los Muertos*, or Day of the Dead," Xavier said as he and Julian stood at the opening of a chain-link fence, waiting for Violet to join them. "Think of it as a cross between Halloween and Mardi Gras. They decorate everything with colorful flowers and skulls, holding parades and other festivities to celebrate and honor their deceased loved ones."

"Long before I knew such a holiday existed, I often did something similar, visiting and leaving flowers at the gravesite of my baby sister, Sibilla, to honor her memory. She was only five years old and loved climbing trees. 'You're going to fall and break your neck one of these days, Sibby,' I told her many times." Xavier briefly smirked as a tear formed and glistened beneath an overhead streetlight.

"She would dramatically grip her waist and puff out her chubby little cheeks at me, while her long blond hair blew in the wind. It always made me laugh. She also laughed, smiling at me with her mouth half-full of baby teeth. 'I'll be okay, Xavvy,' she would say, mocking me with her squeaky young voice."

Julian extended his hand and patted Xavier's shoulder, saying, "I am so sorry." Violet emerged from the driver's side of her purple Firebird, holding a small blue flashlight in one hand and a bouquet of a dozen fluffy orange marigolds, wrapped in white tissue paper, in the other. She handed the flowers to Julian, and their free hands met, intertwining at the fingers.

"Of all the times I was there with her, the one day that mattered the most, I was not," Xavier continued. "She accused me of stealing one of her toys, a carved wooden knight. I was angry, and when I yelled at her, Sibby ran away to our special spot overlooking the Seine River. She was alone, and she fell from her favorite tree, an oak with narrow branches stretching over the cliffside."

"It wasn't your fault," Julian said as Violet led him through the open gate into a small graveyard.

"That is not the point. I loved my sweet Sibby with all my heart. Our parents trusted me with her. I was only ten but more than capable of protecting her. I was not there when the branch broke, when she needed me the most."

Violet sighed. "It's okay, Dad. Come on." The trio advanced, making their way through the tall, damp grass, passing row after row of headstones in various shapes and sizes.

"When a fisherman finally found her about a mile downstream, and brought her to my mother, Sibby was blue. Her big, beautiful eyes were closed forever, and she never smiled again." Xavier took a moment to clear his throat and take a breath. "A week later, I found her toy knight in the dirt, behind our hut. She must have forgot she left it there," he said, clearing his throat again and dropping the subject.

"Where's your uncle's grave, Jul?" Violet asked, aiming the bright flashlight at multiple headstones.

"He's in the back, towards the left," he said. "We need to be careful. There's a lot of small grave markers hiding in the grass that I used to trip over all the time when I was little."

"Don't worry. I got you. Just hold my hand and take your time." The cemetery was only an acre, and they reached the last row of graves quickly. At the end, they followed a rusty chain-link fence. Beyond the mangled old fence, trees and brush stood atop a short cliffside, leading down to the double-wide once belonging to Julian's mother, Marcie.

"What's your uncle's name?" Violet asked, examining each headstone as they passed.

"James Randall Clemmons," he said as the nostalgia of all the time spent in the graveyard as a scared little boy resurfaced.

"Ah! Here it is," Xavier announced. Violet shined the light on the headstone, and Xavier knelt to brush the dead leaves from the base. "James R. Clemmons," he read as Violet led Julian closer. Xavier stood and backed away, saying, "That is so tragic."

"What is?" Violet asked. She aimed the flashlight on the chiseled writing and read aloud, "James R. Clemmons … January sixteenth, nineteen sixty-four to January sixteenth, nineteen sixty …

oh!" She paused and let go of Julian's hand to cup her mouth. "I … tha—that's awful," she gasped.

"He was my mother's baby brother," said Julian.

"And he was stillborn?" Violet asked, with her hand still covering her lips and nose.

"My mother never went into detail. Nobody did. I would've never known he was here unless she told me."

Violet lowered the flashlight and held Julian's hand again, stuttering, "I—I don't know what to say, Jul."

"There's really nothing to say. My grandparents never talked about him. I imagine we're the first visitors he's had since I last came here over twenty-five years ago. Before that, I don't think anyone was here since he was buried."

"How could anyone do that to their child?!"

"They were probably traumatized. It might have been too painful for them to actively remember him," Xavier said.

"I don't care!" she railed. "He was their child. His mother carried him and gave birth to him. How could they just pretend he never existed?!"

"The same way they pretended like my mother's pain nor mine existed." Julian slowly approached the headstone and placed the bouquet on the base. "They were never strong enough to face anything real." He backed away and took Violet's hand again. "They were too empty and dead inside to face any problem, whether it be losing their newborn child or protecting their oldest and her son."

As the memories of all the times Julian needed his grandfather's support flooded his emotions, he turned to his right, looking through the naked, autumn trees. In the distance, he faintly spotted the den light glowing from a window in Johnny's house. "You never cared! … Coward!" he screamed at the top of his lungs.

"Shh!" Violet cupped her hand over Julian's mouth. "You don't want anyone to call the cops again," she said.

"And you should not do this here," Xavier added. "I know you hurt, son, but this is about your baby uncle James, not your grandfather. Save it for Christmas."

Julian sighed and nodded as Violet pulled her hand away from his mouth. "Why don't we give him a few minutes alone,

Dad?" She handed Julian the flashlight, and along with Xavier, backed away and disappeared into the darkness, leaving him alone.

He bent down and shined the light on the gray stone, silently reading his uncle's name and lifeline again. The headstone was about a foot wide and a foot and a half tall, with an arched top and a bowtie etched above his uncle's name. A thick ribbon circled all the writing. Four flowers and two leaves were engraved below the text. *In heaven* was chiseled at the bottom of the stone.

Julian cleared his throat and said, "Hi, baby uncle. It's been a long time." He crouched and sat on the cool ground, crossing his legs and exhaling softly. "I should have come and seen you more over the years, especially when I lived only yards away. For that, I am sorry."

"So much has happened since I was last here. Your sister and your mother have both passed on, but I am sure you already know that. Remember how I used to tell you about Mom's boyfriend, Bill? He went to prison for stabbing her in Myrtle Beach. He got out of jail about fifteen years ago and went back again for beating some other woman half to death. So, his life is ruined, and why nobody ever shanked him yet is beyond me, but at least he left us alone after he got out the first time. It's not really my concern anymore. He'll get his karma in due time."

"With me, it was tough, but I made it out of high school, despite the relentless torture my classmates put me through after Daryl moved and wasn't there to back me up." He took in a slow deep breath through his nose, remembering another time he wanted to forget. "You know, it's funny … even when I came up here to hide from Bill, I kept telling myself, 'If only Grandpa knew what he was doing to us, he would beat that man to death with his bare hands.' Boy, was I wrong. He knew … he always knew. Mom told me he and your brother, Clint Senior, would show their true colors after my grandma died, but I never believed her until it happened."

"In two-thousand-five, I met someone I thought was my everything. Ironically, her name was Faith." Julian chuckled, saying the contradiction aloud. "Long story short, it lasted eleven years. After it ended horribly, I tried to do something stupid, but luckily, I failed. If you asked me a year ago, I would have said I was disappointed about that, but now …" Julian grinned, looking over his shoulder towards the sound of Violet and Xavier talking from across the cemetery. "I am glad I failed," he said, turning his attention back to his uncle's grave.

"I don't know what my future holds, but after I survived my suicide attempt, I knew I was spared for a reason. I have a purpose. I am learning to trust again, and I am moving forward. I am going to do what makes me happy."

After Julian said his piece, he sat in silence, reflecting on the moment. "I missed you, James," he finally said. "You died long before I was born and we never officially met, but you were there for me when I needed you. It's funny: since nobody else talked about you, I always wondered why Mom told me you were here. Now I know it was so I could have somewhere to feel safe, whether if she knew it or not. The universe might not always give us what we want, but it will always give us what we need. In one of my favorite movies growing up, the main character says a graveyard is the safest place to be. He was right." Julian slowly stood, shining the light on the headstone one last time, and saying, "Thank you for everything, baby uncle. I love you, and I promise I won't stay away this long ever again."

He turned, making his way towards Violet and Xavier, who were near the front gate observing a tall memorial. "Hey guys! … You ready to g—" After only a few steps, Julian tripped over a small footstone hiding in the grass. He fell flat on his face, sarcastically remarking "Ow!"

"Are you alright?!" Violet called, quickly approaching while trying not to laugh, but given the circumstances, they all did.

"Yeah, I'm alright, but that fucking hurt," Julian grumbled.

"Aww … poor baby." Violet playfully pouted, then took his hand and led him back towards the gate where Xavier waited. "Let's go home, Jul. I'll make you something nice for dinner, and since it's Halloween, I am sure there's a good scary movie on TV."

As he passed through the gate, Julian turned back towards the direction of his uncle's grave, whispering "Goodbye."

Chapter Thirty-Three

"Don't be scared, Jul, just let it all out and speak your truth," Violet said, leading Julian through the silent darkness while Xavier followed. The air was freezing, and though the roads and driveways were clear, nearly six inches of snow blanketed everything else.

"Yes, and don't worry about them stopping you. We won't let them," Xavier added.

"Thanks," Julian mumbled. He opened the passenger's door of Violet's car and started to get in the backseat before Xavier stopped him.

"I'll sit back there," he said. "It will be easier on you."

"Thanks," Julian said, sitting shotgun. His heart raced beneath the expensive all white suit and tie he'd bought for the occasion. He swallowed a lump and muttered, "I am so nervous."

Violet patted his thigh, saying, "We'll be right there, and we won't let them harm you, I swear, my love." She put the key in the ignition and fired up the bird. The engine roared, and the trio drifted down the hill to Johnny's driveway. On the right was Johnny's red pickup truck. To the left sat Clint Senior's car, also red.

Violet parked in the middle and Julian got out, with Xavier following. Julian watched him straighten his black jacket and tie as they met Violet near the den door, where the light shone through the window. Not feeling as brave and confident as he thought, Julian took a deep, self-assuring breath, telling himself: *you can do this*.

Violet's long, elegant, purple party dress glistened as she reached for Julian's hand, softly whispering, "Yes, you can. Hold nothing back, and don't be afraid."

"She's right, son. You are strong and brave. Just let go, and do not let them stop you," Xavier added.

Julian had waited years to say his piece. He cleared his throat and stepped up to the door, peering inside the windows. Johnny sat out of view, but Clint Senior and Bobbi-Jo sat side by side on a white loveseat. Their faces were blank, staring off into space and awkwardly looking away as if they already knew who was at the door. Julian took another deep breath before twisting the knob and pushing the door open.

"Merry Christmas!" he announced, looking around the room, stretching his mouth from one cheek to the other, presenting a grin and vocal tone as plastic as his family.

Johnny, wearing an old green t-shirt and a pair of blue jeans, glared at his well-dressed grandson. To the right of the TV sat Clint Senior, wearing a faded pair of blue jeans and a gray t-shirt with a picture of a brown horse head on it. His dopey-eyed expression fixated on the wall, across the room, above his father's head, refusing to move or acknowledge his nephew. Clint had a thin head of short, bleached hair. He was thin and sickly looking, with a sagging face, lightly scarred from healed welts. Sitting to his left was Bobbi-Jo, wearing an ugly red Christmas sweater with a snowman on it. Her brown, ear-length hair was wiry. A large pair of square glasses covered a third of her pointy rat face, and her mouth hung open as if she were a glitched-out computer program.

"How's everyone doing?" Julian asked, smug and sarcastic. He felt the confidence coming back, knowing he had his real family by his side.

"Hey, Julian," Johnny grunted, attempting to sound interested. "How are you?" He sat with an unwrapped box in his lap. A crumpled mess of blue and white wrapping paper lay beneath a small white gift box.

"I hope you don't mind, but I brought a few friends with me," Julian said, taking a few steps farther, allowing Violet and Xavier room to enter behind him. "This is Violet, my girlfriend," he said, indicating his beautiful flower.

"Hello, everyone." Violet curtsied and smiled politely. Bobbi-Jo barely smiled back, without moving her head or looking. Her husband did nothing.

"Hello, Violet. I am Johnny, his grandpa."

"It's nice to meet you," she replied, still smiling.

"And this is Xavier, Violet's fa—" Julian hesitated, but Xavier nodded in approval. "Violet's father."

Clint's eyes wandered in their direction, and he grunted. "That kid ain't old enough to be her dad! Maybe her brother, but there ain't no way he's her dad."

"Well, he's my adoptive father, actually," Violet said.

"I look young for my age," Xavier added.

"May we sit, Grandpa?" Julian asked.

"Go ahead," Johnny mumbled. "Just as long as you didn't come down here to start any of that crap like before, alright?" Julian smirked, and they sat on the white sofa along the wall to Johnny's left. From that angle, Julian caught the time and snickered. *7:44* was displayed in yellow digital numbers on the cable box below Johnny's flatscreen, which sat on a short brown TV stand.

"So, where's Miranda and Clint Junior?" Julian asked.

"They came earlier," Johnny said.

"Eh, just came long enough to get their presents, huh?" Julian laughed.

"No, they've just got other places to go!" Bobbi-Jo snapped defensively in her strong hillbilly accent.

"You're right—it's called getting drunk with high schoolers to maintain their childhood popularity," Julian said. Clint grunted again. His cheeks expanded and his eyes shifted to Julian, but he said nothing.

"That's not true!" Bobbi-Jo retorted.

"Damnit, Julian!" Johnny barked. "If you just came down here to start a buncha' shit, you and your friends can leave, you hear me?!"

"I hear you just fine," Julian said. "Anyway … as I was saying," he turned his head towards Violet and Xavier. "My cousins are idiots, and though they don't even live in Virginia now, they still get drunk with the popular kids when they are here so they can stay relevant."

Bobbi-Jo sat forward, sticking out her index finger, opening her mouth in slow motion. "That is not—"

"Before my grandma died," Julian carelessly interrupted, "Miranda and Clint Junior would stick around here for a while on Christmas Eve, when it was expected of my mom to show up drunk and provide everyone with entertainment to laugh at."

"Is that your mom and grandma, up there?" Violet asked, pointing to a framed picture hanging on the wall near the television.

Julian never noticed the picture before. He took a moment to focus on the details. The angle was from their shoulders up, and they stood next to one another. Marcie's wide grin was genuine. Her brown hair was turning gray, and she wore thick, clear framed glasses. A visible horizontal scar stood out on the left side of her top lip from one of the many times Bill beat her. To her left was Gin. Her curly salt and pepper hair was only a few inches long, and the smile on her thin, frail face appeared forced. "Yeah," Julian said. "That's them. That must've been taken not long before they died."

"Are you finished, now?!" Bobbi-Jo demanded. "Can we get back to havin' a peaceful Christmas? … Because none of that is true! The kids don't even drink!"

Julian laughed. "Bullshit! Back when Clint Junior failed the sixth grade, you were up here that Christmas, laughing about getting him liquored up, so he'd have the balls to ride a baby bull across a rodeo rink, back when his dad thought he was some badass rodeo rider—or whatever the fuck you call it—but we saw how long that lasted." Clint's face scrunched in anger, but still he said nothing.

"That's it, Julian!" Johnny barked. "Get the hell out of here!"

"No, I think I will go when I feel like it. There's a lot I have wanted to say for so long, and you're all going to sit right there and take it, just like you made my mom and me take it! I dare any of you to stop me."

"We don't wanna hear it," Bobbi-Jo said.

"Oh, believe me, I know you don't." Julian smirked. "The truth hurts, but none of you gave a damn about each other's redneck bullshit, but you held everything my mom and I ever did against us! You are all batshit crazy hypocrites! Every Christmas, you made us feel like shit! Any time I tried to defend myself or my mom, Grandma always shook her head, 'No,' and gave me that stern look, with her lips firmly pressed together, grimacing, while implying, 'How dare you even think you're allowed to defend yourself here against the great golden side of the family.'"

Bobbi-Jo stuck her palm up, saying, "We never—"

"Shut up!" Julian growled. "Anytime my mom was drunk, everyone ganged up on her. 'You ruined Christmas for us all,' you'd say. I know she made several mistakes, like staying with Bill and abandoning me, but she was damaged, and needed the love and

272

support of her family! Maybe if you actually loved her, she could have gotten help. God forbid some dumber-than-dogshit redneck stereotypes were smart enough to show compassion for their own family, right!"

Julian paused to take a breath and clear his throat. "As if that wasn't enough, you punished me, a traumatized and disabled child, for my mom's mistakes!"

"Damnit, Julian, just leave!" Johnny demanded.

"Why don't one of you get up off your crusty old asses and make me?!" Julian fumed. "I dare you!"

Violet burst into laughter, saying, "They don't have the balls."

"They never did," Julian said, panning between the three. "You're all cowards who never wanted to face reality. You'd rather live in whatever brash fantasy world you build for yourselves and turn your backs on anything resembling truth. I mean, nobody cared when Miranda or Clint Junior turned their backs on me in high school because I wasn't 'cool enough,' but everyone lost their shit when I wasn't at Grandma's funeral. All any of you care about is an image!"

"What the hell are you talkin' about, Julian?" Johnny grunted.

"I'm talking about all the lies and bullshit! I needed you, but you ignored me!" Julian felt the corners of his eyes getting heavy as he continued. "We got beat to a pulp every night! I was too scared to go to sleep because I'd usually be woken up while getting dragged out of bed and kicked to shit while you sat on your ass and did fuck all to help us!"

"I lay awake every night, hearing my mom getting knocked into things and thrown all over the house for hours while she screamed! Then, when Bill got tired of beating her, I'd hear, 'Julian! You little faggot!' Then, he'd come stomping down the hallway towards my room. My door would fly open, and the light came on. He'd drag me to the floor and stomp me, over and over again! Where the fuck were you? … Huh?! Where the fuck were you when that sick son of a bitch made me take showers in front of all his friends?!"

"None of that is true, Julian!" Johnny yelled. "You're just trying to make me look bad in front of your friends, and—"

"Tell me, sir," Xavier interrupted. "Were your very first words also a lie, or did it take time to develop your craft to a point where even you believed your nonsense?" He looked upon Johnny with sheer disgust, a look Julian never seen from him before.

"What the hell are you talking about, kid? I ain't no liar," Johnny said.

"More lies!" Julian shouted. "You couldn't even tell the truth on my mom's obituary! You said she died at the fucking hospital. She died on her couch, and while you obviously wouldn't have said that, why say where she died at all? Why was it so important to lie on your own daughter's obituary? Was getting the last laugh that important to you?!"

"Yes, Jul, that's exactly why he did it," said Violet. "People like him only serve themselves."

"Alright, Julian!" Johnny growled again. "Get out!"

"Why, because you can't handle the truth?" Julian asked. "You just want to sweep it all under the rug and pretend like it didn't happen because it's what's most convenient for you! We were always a joke to you."

Julian pointed at Clint and said, "When we have a meth head in the family, where are all the cliché junkie truck driver jokes at Christmas, like when everyone pointed out our flaws?" Clint's eyes widened, making him look like an angry pussycat who wanted to pounce.

"You need help, Julian. You need God!" Bobbi-Jo croaked.

"I need God?" Julian laughed. "You think you're so fucking special? Why are you even here? Isn't it obvious this God you speak of doesn't want you here anymore? Your filthy, polluted blood dies with you," he jeered. "How does it feel to know God himself came down from heaven to take that fucking junkie, Earl, from you? It wasn't enough that God gave him prostate cancer, making sure he couldn't even get it up to fuck his wife and leave you with a grandchild. Because Earl couldn't bother driving to work sober, God saw fit to impose his will." Julian laughed, knowing he'd gone too far, but taking pleasure in watching Bobbi-Jo cry.

"Before your son died in that wreck, he stole Clint's truck and horse trailer to sell for meth, because like stepfather, like stepson, he needed his fix."

Johnny pointed at the door, repeatedly shouting, "Get out! Get out! Get out!"

"No, wait," Bobbi-Jo mumbled as she wiped away her tears. "You can sit there and say all this about my son, but at least his wife didn't fuck her brother, like your girlfriend did, Julian. What kind of freak are you to drive someone into the arms of their brother?"

"Yeah!" Clint added, finally breaking his silence. "You act like you're so high and mighty. At least Earl made his wife happy."

Julian laughed incredulously, asking, "So, you think it's my fault Faith chose to commit incest? You're not even going to blame mental illness or it having anything to do with her own choices? That's convenient." He rolled his eyes. "You guys always loved to blame me for everything. I am nowhere near perfect, but the difference between us is I can admit my mistakes while none of you are even worth pissing on if you were on fire." Julian looked at Bobbi-Jo and said, "You called me after my grandma died to tell me she loved and forgave me, but you didn't even tell me she was dead! Why call me at all?!" He waited for a response, but she said nothing.

Julian looked at Johnny and said, "You told her to do it. You had no right! Because of your heartless act, the last thing my mom said to me was, 'If I ever see you again, I will kill you.'"

Julian shoved his finger back in Bobbi-Jo's face, saying, "You could've told me. I could've been here for the funeral, but no! You took advantage of the situation and excluded me!" He turned to Johnny and said, "It was all spearheaded by you! You could've told Mom the truth about what happened. You could have eased some of her pain in her last six months, but why do that? Why offer your dying daughter a little comfort when there was so much pain you could inflict instead? … You sadistic fuck!!" Julian's voice turned dark, almost a death growl. He wanted to strike Johnny, but somehow, his soft heart still beat.

"You all knew my mother was dying, and my grandma's death was just going to speed up her drinking and kill her faster, but she didn't have to take all that extra heartache with her. Because of you, despite everything my mother did to me, she died hating me!" As Julian began to sob, he shoved his finger in Bobbi-Jo's face once more, roaring, "Just fucking kill yourself!"

Violet sighed and leaned her cheek against Julian's, saying, "Maybe we should go, Jul. They will never get it because they will never care."

Clint snickered. "Yeah, 'Jul,'" he said, mocking Violet while making air quotes with his fingers. "Listen to your hired escort and get the hell out of here!"

"Excuse me?!" Violet snarled. She sat up straight, flashing Clint an evil eye, asking, "Did you just call me a whore?" Clint looked away, saying nothing else. "That's what I thought, you tall drink of pussy juice. You're just jealous that your nephew has this hot piece of ass while all you have is that braindead lump of shit."

Clint smirked. He mocked Violet again, saying, "Excuse me?! Did you just call me a pussy?"

"She sure as shit didn't call you a man," Julian said. "You are a pussy. I mean, your wife's name has more masculinity in it than you've ever had in your entire body." Clint stood and took a step forward. Julian chuckled, asking, "What're you gonna do, dig up my mom and have her take up for you, like you always did when you two were in school, and she'd fight all your battles for you, pussy?" Julian and Xavier only laughed, but Violet was nearly rolling on the floor, unable to contain herself. "I remember when I was in second grade, I went to some kind of after school event with you and Clint Junior. An older girl beat me up and you laughed so hard at me. You made fun of me for it, and even told some of your friends—right in front of me—that your nephew got beat up by a girl. Did you ever tell them a girl used to fight your battles for you, pussy? All those times my mom fought for you, but when she needed you to fight for her, you just sat at your old trailer up on the hill and did nothing. What's the matter? Were you scared of taking a punch, and getting that delicate pink pussy meat of yours bruised?"

Clint scowled, and his face squeezed inward. "You son of a bitch!" he shouted, taking another step forward and drawing his fist back. Before he could swing, Xavier appeared behind him and held Clint's arm back.

"It is not polite to hit people," Xavier said. "Especially in your father's house, and when it's your deceased sister's disabled son." As Clint struggled, he elbowed Xavier's chest before he was spun around and restrained while everyone else looked on.

"Let me go!" Clint whined in a high pitch. With one hand, Xavier lifted Clint high above his head. "What the! … Put me down!" Clint screamed, kicking his legs and trying to wiggle free. Xavier chuckled and lifted Clint even higher, gripping his throat with one hand and his ankle with the other. He hovered nearly a foot off the floor, squishing Clint's petrified body against the white tiled ceiling. Julian laughed, but in the back of his mind, he feared them calling the cops. "What the fuck?!" Clint squealed in a way Julian never heard before.

"My God!" Bobbi-Jo wailed in horror.

"Don't leave any physical marks," Julian said while laughing his ass off. "They'll call the cops if you do."

As Clint kicked and screamed, the crotch of his blue jeans darkened and spread outward. "Oh my God," Violet continued laughing. "He's pissing himself!" she said, hysterically clapping her hands and laughing so hard it was a wonder she didn't do the same. "He's pissing his pants, Daddy!"

Xavier let Clint go, and Julian watched him fall to the old brown carpet, desperately attempting to scoot or crawl, whichever got him to safety faster. He quickly backed up against his wife, wrapping his arms around her legs, and quivering like a scared child. "Y—you fu—fu—fucking freak!" Bobbi-Jo stammered in terror. "You're all freaks, and we've always hated you, Julian!" She embraced her nearly catatonic husband, offering him comfort. "You—you look just like your father, Julian. None of us could ever stand the sight of you!" she snarled. "If it wasn't for you and your eyes, your father would have never snapped and beat your mom. It's all your fault!"

"Finally, the truth," Julian muttered, always knowing they blamed him, but wanting to hear them say it.

"Get the fuck out of here, Julian!" Johnny growled. "And don't you ever come back!"

"And take your fucked up friends with you!" Bobbi-Jo screeched.

Violet stood and asked, "What are you going to do about it, you ugly piece of trailer trash?!" Bobbi-Jo said nothing else. Violet smirked and said, "If not for endangering Julian or going against my father's wishes, I would murder all three of you be—"

"Violet!" Xavier shouted.

"No, seriously," she continued, ignoring him. "If I didn't love him the way I do, I would take all three of you, one by one, high in the sky and drop you. I would watch you fall to your deaths and not even feel bad about getting moist off your screams before you went splat. That's the difference between love and hate."

"Come children, we made our point," Xavier said, stepping between Bobbi-Jo and his daughter.

Julian wiped his eyes with his sleeve before he took Violet's hand and walked towards the door. As he passed, he looked Johnny dead in the eye. "I didn't expect this to go well, but I needed to let it all out. Now that I have, you can die, too." Julian extended his middle finger before ripping an obnoxiously long, loud fart. The childish gesture instantly stunk up the room, gaining more laughter from Violet and Xavier. Julian smirked, knowing such a deliberate act was beneath him, but that was the point. "Merry Krampus, assholes!" he joyfully concluded.

As he opened the den door and started to step through, he turned his attention back to the others. Xavier was standing over Johnny, sternly gazing at the old man with cold, unforgiving eyes. "The irony," he muttered. "Our war was always inevitable." He glanced at Julian and back at Johnny, adding "His could've been prevented with empathy."

"Get out!" Johnny yelled, carrying demonic anger in his voice.

"Very well, sir." Xavier nodded. "Happy New Year." He winked at the old man before following Violet and Julian through the doorway. Julian's tears were at ease for the moment, but he sensed the incoming geyser waiting to explode. *Not here*, he desperately thought. *Not yet.*

After getting home, he climbed out of the car and slowly waddled through the snowy yard. The overhead streetlight between the house and garage lit his way. Unable to hold his tears back any longer, he came to a stop just beneath the light and collapsed to his knees. Having released a lifetime of pent emotions, Julian finally broke.

Tears rushed from his eyes like the wrath of Poseidon. Intense physical pain shook him to the core as if millions of needles were violently jabbing his entire body. Never feeling such a thing before, he lost his breath and fell on his side, tensing his muscles as if expecting a grisly impact. All the horrific memories of what his mother, father, and everyone else did, and did not do, replayed themselves like a grotesque snuff film he was forced to watch. The moment of unadulterated torture lasted what seemed like an eternity until he finally regained control of his senses. Once he caught his breath, he wailed, "I am a sheep! … I am a fucking sheep, and I am just like them!"

Julian's misery was relentless until Violet approached with her soft, feminine voice, placing her hand on his shoulder and melodically whispering, "Shh … it's okay, Jul. You are loved," in his ear. "I've got you. I am here. … I am here, and I love you. You are loved. Do you hear me? I love you. Xavier loves you. You are not a sheep. You are a real man, and nothing like them. They could have never survived what you did." Her calm tone soothed Julian's withering grasp on reality. "You are loved," she repeated. "Do you hear me? You are loved. You will live forever, with me, and everyone will know how brave and strong you are."

Julian sniffled as his body relaxed in his love's arms and his tears subsided. He drew a series of deep breaths as Violet wiped his face and kissed his forehead. "I love you, Violet," he said, only catching her distorted silhouette through his tearstained round glasses. She kissed his lips and he muttered, "I thought I was better than them. I thought I was the better man."

"You are," she said.

"No, I am not. I lost control of myself, and I reached deep down into the bowels of hell and became just as hateful as they are. We are all a disease. The human race is evil and ugly. I hate it. I truly hate it."

Violet kissed him again. "They did this to you, and if your emotions hadn't come out like that, it would have been much worse later. I am so proud of you."

Julian removed his glasses and looked up at Violet's hazy face. He cleared his throat and said, "I am ready now. ... I am ready to become a vampire, tomorrow night."

Violet helped Julian to his feet and dusted away some of the snow on his side. She placed her hands upon his cheeks and kissed his lips. "I love you, Julian ... and I ... I want you to marry me. I want you to marry me on New Year's Eve, after you've healed from your transition. I want you to be mine, and I yours, forever." She kissed his lips again. "I want to start this new decade with you and with us. Twenty-twenty will be the year of perfect vision for us both."

Julian knew what he wanted to say, but the shock froze him in place until he took a breath and broke his silence. "I will," he said. "I will marry you."

Chapter Thirty-Four

At the end of a bittersweet evening, the newly engaged couple entered the kitchen to break the news to Xavier, who was drinking from an IV bag. Bursting at the seams, Violet announced, "He said 'yes,' Dad! We want you to marry us on New Year's Eve."

"Aww … young love," Xavier marveled. "How grand." He embraced Julian and asked, "Are you ready for tomorrow night?" He nodded, saying nothing. Knowing he should be terrified, he actually felt refreshed after his breakdown in the snow and the proposal that had followed.

"It's settled, then," Xavier said. "Tomorrow night will be your transition. However, in the morning, I ask that you watch the sunrise, as it will be your last chance to see it. The sun is a glorious delight, and you will not know how much you will miss it until you can never gaze upon it again."

"I will," Julian gulped.

Xavier nodded, and Violet took an IV bag from the freezer. "While this bag thaws, I'm going downstairs to take a shower," she said before brushing Julian's long hair from his face. She kissed his forehead and said, "I'll be back shortly." He watched her turn towards the living room, unzipping her purple dress from the back as she disappeared from his view.

"So," Xavier began, drawing Julian's attention. "I bet you are scared to death, are you not?"

"I … I guess you could say that."

"You realize what this has all been about, yes?" Xavier asked. Julian shrugged his shoulders in confusion. "You are on a deep, spiritual journey. You have worked so hard to let go of your past, and after tonight, you are nearly there. Do you feel better now, having gotten everything off your chest?"

"Yes and no," he said. "I honestly didn't know I had all that in me, but I was right. I was always right. They blame me for what my father did. When I was four, I was diagnosed with RP. My father went nuts, and that's when all the abuse started. Before that, he was good to my mom."

Xavier took the last drink from the IV bag before tossing it in the trash. "Your aunt and uncle feel that way. Your grandfather does not," he said. "Tell me, have you ever heard anyone say, 'If only Adolf Hitler had been accepted into art school?' or 'If only Charles Manson got his record deal?'"

"Yeah, why?"

"Some people carry evil inside them their whole life. When something traumatic happens, it triggers that evil. If it were not your diagnosis that unleashed your father's evil, it would have been something else. His actions were never your fault or your mother's. They had no right to hold that against you. As for your grandfather, do you remember the night we first met, and I asked you what your dream is?"

"Yes."

"Have you figured it out yet?"

"To find happiness within myself."

"Are you happy?"

Julian scratched the back of his head, thinking about the question. "I'm working on it."

"I looked deep into your grandfather's thoughts tonight. Did you know he had a dream once?"

Julian tipped his head. "What was it?"

"His dream was to join the Marines, but he was unable to enlist and achieve that dream when your grandmother became pregnant. After that, he felt obligated to give up his life and future to support a family he was not ready to have. Did you know your mother was conceived out of wedlock?"

"No," he gasped. "Is that why he hates me?"

"Your grandfather does not hate you, Julian. He is a cold, cowardly, and distant man who carries self-resentment and a grudge, but he does not hate you. He has demons, but he also has a heart, along with difficulty showing it."

"If he doesn't hate me, why did he call that cop on me?"

"I wondered that myself, but after more insight, I realized it was not him."

"What?!" Julian gasped again. "Who did it, then?"

"I could not say. Perhaps another neighbor, maybe the couple who live next door, in your other aunt and uncle's house."

"I don't know what to say."

"You need not say a word. I am proud of you. Your grandfather needed to face what he did to you. It is true—for your mother's mistakes, he favors Clint's family, but he does love you in his own twisted way."

Julian lowered his head and sighed. "Both of Clint's kids were also born out of wedlock. He never married their mothers until they became pregnant. Every narcissistic family has the golden child and the scapegoat. I suppose it makes sense the legitimate son of a bastard daughter could never compare to the bastard half siblings of a legitimate son."

"Don't think of it that way. Johnny loves you, just not the way he should have. Unfortunately, he was raised to believe kind-hearted, sensitive men are to be looked down upon as weak and inferior specimens. His father likely never showed him the same compassion he should have shown you." Xavier placed his pale hand on Julian's shoulder, patting it softly. "As for Bobbi-Jo, she acted alone. When your grandmother passed away, Johnny gave her your former lover's contact information, but he had nothing to do with her refusal to tell you."

Julian said nothing. He shed a few remaining tears before accepting the truth and settling in for the evening. After Violet's shower, she returned upstairs to kiss Julian goodnight. He knew he would be too nervous to sleep, so he rested on the sofa with the television on and a head full of mixed emotions.

After he dozed in and out of consciousness for several hours, the sky began to brighten over the Appalachian Mountains. Taking Xavier's advice, he watched the sunrise from the frigid balcony, observing the white Christmas morning unfolding before him. He carefully examined every snow-covered tree he could see. He counted all the rooftops below, and squinted to see some of the visible headstones near James's grave on the cliff behind his mother's old house. Taking a mental note, he burned the images in his mind, knowing he would never get the opportunity to see such a phenomenon again. He drew a long, deep breath and exhaled as he lightly glanced at the bright sun approaching from the east.

After closing his eyes, Julian mumbled a prayer. "Dear God, Spirit Guides, Guardian Angels, Universe, and anybody listening … please, be by my side tonight and guide me." He opened his eyes and gave the landscape one last look before going back inside and downstairs. He tried to sleep, but when he shut his eyes, thoughts of his childhood raced through his head at high volume. He saw himself young again, he and Daryl, spending every quarter they had on arcade games at the local bowling alley, enjoying their youth. Even in his darkest times, Julian always found something to smile about.

Once he gave up on trying to sleep, he took to his laptop and wrote about the night before. *I've never cried like that in my life. After I let it out, my sweet Violet, my heart, soul, and purpose, asked me to marry her. It was so unexpected.*

Julian focused his thoughts on the unforgettable moment, the most romantic gesture he ever experienced. *Who says a man can't get swept off his feet?* he wrote, as if he were in an old romance novel with the traditional roles reversed. *I was always far too sensitive for my own good. In the past, I let my soft nature hurt me, but without pain, there is no discipline, and without discipline, we learn nothing. I let go, and now I am in love, and less than a week away from my wedding. This decade was hell, and I lost everything, but we must fall to stand again. 2020 will bring perfect vision.*

Julian closed his laptop and yawned. Feeling comfortable enough to fall asleep, he stretched out on the sofa and shut his eyes, but then he heard a vehicle approaching outside. Seconds later, a knock came at the kitchen door. *Who the hell is that?* He headed for the door, yawning and rolling his eyes. With his vision blurred, he opened the door.

"Hey bub, Merry Christmas!"

Julian smiled. "Merry Christmas, brother. What are you doing here?"

"I just wanted to ride over and see you, since it's Christmas, and I haven't been over here since July. How've you been?"

"I'm alright," Julian said. "What about you?"

"I can't complain, bub." Daryl looked over his shoulder at Violet's Firebird. "I see your old lady came back. Is she here? I'd like to meet her."

"She is, her and her father, but they're both sleeping."

"That's right, I forgot, they're vampires, right?" Daryl chuckled.

Julian grunted under his breath, ignoring the smartass remark. "Speaking of Violet, I have some good news."

"What is it?"

"We got engaged last night. We're getting married."

"Really? That's great, bub! I'm happy for you."

"We're getting married on New Year's Eve."

"This New Year's Eve? … Next week?!"

"Yeah, and I'd like you to be my best man."

"Really?!" Daryl smiled, appearing surprised.

"Remember when we were kids and told each other we'd be one another's best man? Well, I might not have gotten to be yours, when you and Tara got married, but I'd really like you to be mine."

"I'd be honored, bub," Daryl said, patting Julian on the shoulder. "I just hope she's good to you. I hate that I ain't even got to meet her yet, but since she sleeps during the day, I can't ever catch her while she's up."

"Violet does her own thing, and I don't get in her way, but she's the greatest thing that's ever happened to me—her and her father, Xavier."

"So, her daddy's good to you?"

"If it wasn't for Xavier, I wouldn't have this house."

"Well, I trust your judgment, bub."

Julian stepped aside, asking, "You wanna come in for a bit?"

"I can't stay. I'm getting ready to go with my girls and the old lady to her mother's house in West Virginia for supper and to open presents. I just wanted to come by and drop off your present first."

"You got me a present?" Julian focused on a small box in Daryl's hand, wrapped in shiny green paper.

He smiled and handed it to him. "Go ahead and open it, bub."

Julian's heart warmed. "You've always been the greatest," he said as he tore away the paper. The box underneath was slim, brown cardboard. He opened the flaps and retrieved a small photograph, bordered in a wooden frame.

"I found that a few weeks ago, when I was cleaning out some old things," Daryl said.

Julian adjusted his eyes and stared at the photo. Two young boys stood side by side, one noticeably taller than the other. Each wore similar buttoned white shirts with black neckties. The shirts were tucked into black slacks. Spiked brown hair poked 3/4s an inch above the shorter boy's head. A crooked pair of rectangular glasses rested along two happily raised cheeks. The taller boy on the right, much thinner than the large frame he grew into with age, bore a closed mouth smile. His hair, also short and brown, lay flat atop his head. As Julian took a moment to observe every detail, he smiled. "Seventh grade prom. ... I can't believe you still have this."

"Your grandma took that picture of us."

Julian wiped the moisture from the corner of an eye. "Thank you so much. I used to have a lot of pictures from back then, but Faith and her brother threw them all away."

"Well, now you have a new one. You can set it above your fireplace, next to that eight-ball and love letter from your sweetheart." Daryl giggled.

Julian shut his eyes, smiling and remembering the best school year he had. "Remember the seventh grade trip to the Carowinds?" he asked.

"Hell yeah, I do! That was one of the best days of my life, bub."

"Remember that picture on the bus, coming back home? We were passed out from exhaustion. Your head was on my shoulder, and my head was against the top of yours." Julian opened his eyes and laughed.

"Yeah," Daryl said, also laughing. "I can't remember who took it, but I remember how all the girls in Mrs. Fuller's class thought that was the cutest thing ever."

"I miss those days," said Julian. "There's no going back, though, is there?"

"No, there sure ain't, bub."

"Do you still have that picture?"

"Hell no," Daryl said. "I never had it to begin with. One of them girls kept it."

"That's too bad. I'd love to have that one, too."

"Yep," Daryl sighed. "Well, bub, I better get going, but I'll talk to the old lady and tell her about your wedding. Do you know what time it'll be?"

"Probably around midnight. You know, all special and shit," Julian chuckled.

"That's what I figured," said Daryl as he took a step back. "Well, I'll holler back at you, bub."

Julian nodded and said, "Thanks again for this picture, Daryl. It means a lot." He nervously inhaled, thinking about what was to come. "And Daryl. I love you," he said as a tear formed in his eye. "Thank you for always being there for me." He wanted to tell him everything but knew it would be useless.

Daryl reached out and hugged him, saying, "I love you, too, bub. Merry Christmas."

"Merry Christmas, Daryl. The next time we meet, I'll be a whole other person."

"Yeah, you'll be somebody's bitch, and she'll make an honest man out of you." Daryl cackled, and it instantly brought a teary grin to Julian's face. "You alright, bub?" he asked while his smile faded.

"I'm okay, just been a little emotional the past few days, but I'll be alright."

"Okay then, bub. I'll holler back at you," he said. Julian nodded and watched him head back to his truck. After starting it, he backed up, turned around, and drove away.

Julian went back inside and checked the clock on his phone, which read *11:55*. He took the framed photo into the living room and placed it atop the fireplace mantle, with the eight-ball and letter on the opposite end. He tried shutting his eyes again, but he was far too scared to sleep. Instead, Julian spent the remaining daylight hours working on the final chapter of his book and mulling his choices.

Life will always be uncertain and scary, but it's still life, nonetheless. Make every moment count like it is your last! Tell that person, you love them. If someone hurt you, tell them how you feel. Yesterday is over and tomorrow is not certain. This moment is all we have. If you were to die right now, would you be satisfied with all you have and have not done or said? If not, you are the only one who can change that. So, change it while you still can! Leave no stone unturned and no regrets behind.

Chapter Thirty-Five

"How do you feel?" Violet asked, sitting beside Julian on the black leather sofa.

"I don't know; scared, overwhelmed, maybe." He cleared his throat and took a drink of water from a clear glass on the coffee table.

"You're very brave about this," Violet said before pecking his lips. "I hope you know that," she added.

"That night when I got in your car, and you took me out on the strip, did you know, then?"

"Did I know what?"

"That you wanted me to be a vampire."

"Yes," she said, batting her eyes. "That's why I had to test you."

"Test me how?"

"Jul," she grinned. "I've been a vampire for seventy-five years. If there's anybody that can keep track of time, it's me."

"You mean, when you hid in my bathroom, it was intentional?" He chuckled, feeling like he should be angry, though he was not.

"Yeah," she confessed, flashing a guilty smile as if caught with her hand in the cookie jar.

"You would do something like that, wouldn't you?"

"I told you I'm an Aries, and a bitch by default," she said, and they both laughed.

Julian kissed her lips. "I love you, future Mrs. Frost."

"I love you too, future husband," she replied, stroking the side of his head. "Your hair's gotten so long," she said, moving her thin, black-polished fingertips through his brown locks. "It looks good like this." She pulled away and took his hands in hers, while making eye contact. "Listen, Jul, I know you're scared. You have every right to be, but I will be by your side the whole time, and I will take care of you while you heal."

"I believe you, but what if something goes wrong, and I—"

Violet placed the tip of her index finger over his lips. "What're you avoiding?"

He kissed her finger and said, "I don't know, but I'll finally have to face it."

"We'll help you through it, and I will hold your hand."

As Julian nodded, Xavier appeared in the doorway leading to the basement, catching their attention. "It's time, Julian," he said.

Violet stood first, extending her hand and softly saying, "Come on, sweetie." His heart raced, and his mind was flooded by second thoughts, but Julian's intuition nudged him onward. He drew a deep breath and took Violet's hand, letting her lead him down to her bedroom.

He took a good look at his bed from upstairs, which had been placed next to Violet's hammock. It was a queen, with a wooden headboard; the mattress covered in a clear sheet of plastic. On the floor next to it were five white buckets. Three were empty and two were full of ice. Next to the buckets lay a few folded red washcloths.

"Okay, so this is what will happen," Xavier began. "First, you will place your hands, up to your wrists, into the ice to numb yourself. Afterwards, I will make a horizontal cut down each." Julian shivered at the thought, growing nauseous and minding the fear chipping away at his remaining ego.

"As your blood drains, you will quickly feel dizzy and cold before your consciousness fades. After I drain you to the point of death, I will cut my own wrist and place the open wound over your mouth. Acting on sheer instinct, you will try to fight it, but you must drink my blood."

"Wha—what will I experience when I black out?" Julian asked.

"Death," he said. "It will be intense, and you will face your remaining fears, but do not fret, son. Once my blood enters your body, you will be reborn."

Julian took a few deep breaths, repeating aloud, "I can do this … I can do this …"

Violet placed her hand on his shoulder and said, "Yes, you can, Jul. We love you, and we'll both be right here for you, I promise." She kissed his forehead and smiled.

Xavier took a step forward. "After you drink, you will eventually purge anything that might be in your stomach. We have a pail for you to use and rags to wipe your face or mouth." As Julian began to sit on the side of the bed, Xavier added, "You should probably disrobe. There will be a lot of blood, and you might soil yourself. We have buckets to hold your wrists over, and I put down plastic, but I would not want you to ruin your clothes." Quivering in fear, Julian nodded, and removed his shirt, jeans, socks, and finally, his boxers. Aside from his silver ankh necklace and glasses, he stood fully nude.

"You can take those off too," Xavier added. "You're not going to need them anymore." Julian's adrenaline shot skyward, as he'd forgotten about the effect his transition would have on his eyes. Focusing on this silver lining, he handed his glasses to Violet. Then he sat his bare bottom on the plastic-covered mattress.

Julian's breaths grew heavy, and his teeth chattered as he stuck his hands into the ice, all the way to his forearms. "I—I don't know if I can d—do this," he managed.

"Do you want to stop?" Xavier asked, placing his hand on Julian's shoulder. "If so, I understand."

Violet sat on the bed next to Julian, saying, "You can do this, and when you do, we can be together forever, and we can see everything, just us."

Julian cleared his throat and muttered, "Okay, I'm ready." After a few moments, he removed his numbed limbs from the buckets and lay flat on his back, stretching out his legs. Violet turned off the lights and returned to Julian's side. Her long hair dangled, tickling his naked flesh as she kissed his lips. "I believe in you, Jul. Remember, twenty-twenty is perfect vision, and the year of the Frosts."

"I love you," Julian said.

"I love you too," Violet replied.

She backed away and Xavier moved in. "When you are ready for me to make the first cut, just say so. After that, I will make the second. You will get scared and try to fight it, but you must not resist. Let death take you, and we will bring you back."

"How long will the process t—take?"

"From the first cut until you come back to us? Fifteen to twenty minutes," Xavier said.

Julian nodded before shutting his eyes and focusing on his breathing: in through his nose and out his mouth. "Okay," he mumbled. Xavier took his left hand while Violet stood on the other side, holding his right.

"Just relax," Xavier said, stretching Julian's arm off the side of the bed and making the first cut. Julian barely felt it. Xavier rushed to the other side of the bed and made the second cut.

Violet rubbed Julian's head, whispering, "I love you," in his ear.

Knowing there was no turning back, he felt panic set in fast. His cheeks rapidly puffed in and out as his body tingled and his life force faded. He listened to his blood trickling into the bucket until the point of no return. "Wait! … Wait! I can't breathe! I can't breathe!"

"Just relax, Jul," Violet calmly whispered. "Clear your mind and don't fight it. Let it take you." Julian turned his head side to side as the room spun, spiraling inward like a whirlpool. Desperation swept in the moment he accepted he was about to die. Knowing his life was ending with a triumphant return or not, he gave up and submitted to death, preparing to greet it as an old friend.

"I'm c—c—cold. Why am I so cold?" he lightly whispered as his surroundings and senses began fading to black. Along with any physical sense of self, reality compressed to a single molecule, and all that remained of himself.

"You're doing great," an indistinguishable, muffled voice echoed from the dark.

As Julian drew one of his final breaths, a last stand of panic struck what remained of him. "Oh my God! I can't! … I can't! … Please … Plea—"

Life as Julian knew it ended. In his final thought, he accepted peace. No sound, sight, or reason existed, only the infinite void and absolute balance of all and nothing. It was then, a microscopic white light came to be, followed by a faint, foul taste, expanding and producing colorful shades of red and yellow. As the colors surrounded, faces formed, and a peal of frightening laughter joined the infinite pattern of sacred geometry that made up the universe.

Electronically vibrant yellow creatures stood side by side, growing larger and drawing nearer. Long, thick tentacles waved out of their heads like court jester caps while they bobbed their heads in unison. With glowing red eyes and jagged white teeth exposed, they all raised their middle fingers, taunting something that should be there but was not. The demonic sounds coming from their snarling mouths intensified, and a genderless voice sang, "Here we go!"

"Aaagghh!"

Julian sprung up, covered in sweat and screaming bloody murder. With his heart beating out his chest, he quickly looked side to side, but Violet and Xavier were not there. He was in another location altogether. He lay on a blue sofa with a black coffee table in front of him, littered with empty green beer bottles and an orange prescription pill bottle, lying on its side and empty as well. *Oh God!* Julian thought, looking to his right, fearing the worst. *No Love* was written on the wall in black magic marker. "What the fuck?!" Julian immediately remembered everything. He'd written the short suicide note before swallowing the pills.

"Oh my God!" a shrill female voice rang out. Julian shifted his attention to the open front door next to their bedroom doorway. A thin woman with shoulder-length strawberry blond hair, thick lips, rosy cheeks, and a green four leaf clover tattooed between each ear and eye stood, horrifically staring at him. "What the hell did you do, Muffin?!"

"I … but … what?" Julian was at a loss for words.

"What did you do to yourself? Where did all these beer bottles come from, and why did you write on the wall?"

"Oh my God!" Julian wailed, placing his hands over his face and breaking into tears. "No! … No! … Why?! … Why did it have to be a fucking dream?!" he cried.

"What the hell are you talking about? Did you try to kill yourself?" The woman walked to the sofa and sat next to him.

"Faith … I … I just had a dream that was so real. It—it felt like four years passed and—"

"And what?!"

"I … wh—why are you here? After you came over yesterday to tell me you were pregnant, I—I thought you never wanted to see me again."

"Yeah, about that … I made a mistake, Muffin. Last night, I barely slept. I knew what I did to you was cruel, and when I woke up this morning, I asked my grandma to watch Michael so I could come and talk to you."

"About what?" Julian asked, trembling and unable to understand how a dream could be so real and feel like it lasted so long.

"You were always good to me. I treated you like shit, and I … I wanted to say I am sorry." Faith looked at all the empty bottles, asking, "Why would you do this? Why would you try to kill yourself?"

"Because you broke my heart. There was a time you were the one good thing I thought I had. It took me twenty-two years to find you, and I loved you with all my heart. For the last five years, you wouldn't touch me, and as soon as Travis came back into your life, you fucked him! That's why! I gave up everything for you!"

Faith stepped forward, saying, "Come lie down with me, and let's cuddle." She took Julian's hand and led him into their bedroom. They both lay down on a full-sized bed, with Faith spooning him from behind. "I made a mistake," she said.

"I don't know what to do anymore," Julian cried. "I mean, that dream was so real, and I learned so much from it. I don't know how I am here. I—"

"Shh," Faith whispered. "You are safe now."

Julian sobbed, not just for Faith but for Violet and all he'd lost. As he took deep breaths, Faith lightly stroked the back of his head. Julian closed his eyes, trying to relax. He drew a long, deep breath and felt a quick, sharp slice across his throat. He opened his eyes, struggling for another breath, but his effort was useless.

As panic set in, Faith whispered. "It's okay." Julian saw his blood flowing onto the bed and he heard the gurgling from his gaping wound. He tried to speak, struggle, and get away, but he was too weak to do anything but die.

"Just let go. Just let it happen. I will be so much happier without you," Faith continued as the pain became too much to bear.

"We will be so much happier without you … me, my brother, and our baby growing inside me. You mean nothing to me. You don't matter, and when you are dead, I can finally be happy."

Julian lay motionless in shock and terror as his body grew cold and his consciousness faded. All that existed was the taste of blood and the darkness that followed.

"Drink, Julian! … I need you to drink!" A muffled man's voice faded in from nothing. "Yeah, that's it! Keep swallowing! We got you, son." The voice became clear. It was Xavier's voice, and it echoed inside Julian's micro-verse. The flavor and taste intensified as darkness gave way to light again.

"I love you, Jul. Come back to me."

Julian saw Violet, surrounded by light and waiting for him ahead. He clawed and gouged his way towards her, leaving the darkness behind. As a twisting sensation squeezed out the last remaining breath of his human life, his eyes burst open, and he savagely gasped for air as something else entirely. A new life emerged, seeing not just his smiling bride to be standing over him, but a whole new world and endless possibilities through new eyes: a vampire's eyes.

Chapter Thirty-Six

Over the next few hours, Julian vomited until his digestive system was empty. After his transformation was complete, Violet cleaned and clothed him, telling him, "You did great."

"Yes, and we are very proud of you, son," Xavier added. Too weak to move or respond, Julian slept through the rest of the night and the next day. When he woke, Violet and Xavier were still by his side. He slowly opened his eyes, panning from one to the other. The overhead light was bright and more intense than he remembered. His peripherals stretched further than before, and every color popped in brilliant vibrance. He saw everything as if for the first time; even 3D patterns on the rough ceiling above stood out like Rorschach designs he never would have known were there.

"How long was I out?" he groaned.

"It's Monday the twenty-sixth, and almost midnight," Xavier said. "How do you feel?"

"I … I don't know yet. Am I … am I a vampire?"

"You are, but you are weak. You must build your strength, and you cannot do that without blood." Xavier moved to the left side of the bed and gently helped Julian sit up. Violet stacked two pillows behind him and helped lean him in an upright position.

"Are you comfortable?" she asked.

"Yeah," he groaned, scanning the room, so astonished by his new sight, it brought tears to his eyes.

"Are you alright?" Violet asked, sitting next to him on the side of the bed.

"I'm cured. I am fucking cured!" Even with little strength, Julian managed to cheer.

"I told you that would happen. Your entire perception is changing," Xavier said.

Violet brought an IV bag of blood into view, saying, "You need to drink this slowly. Do you wanna try to do it, or do you want me to hold it for you?"

"He might drop it," Xavier remarked. He placed his hand atop Julian's and said, "You will feel weak for another day or two, but by the wedding, you should be moving with ease. It takes a little time to heal."

Violet held the narrow tube to Julian's dry lips and said, "Take small sips." He opened his mouth, allowing the tube entry, and he sucked, getting a mouthful of the metallic substance. Violet pulled the bag away, saying, "Easy … swallow it slowly." Julian gagged. The taste was like a combination of rusty metal and citric acid. Violet could not help but giggle at his reaction. "As I said before, it takes getting used to."

"After all these centuries, I still hate it," Xavier chuckled. After three small swallows, Julian cleared his mouth.

"Oh my God," he gagged. "That was awful!"

"You need to take one more little drink if you can," Xavier said. Violet placed the tube back to Julian's mouth and he sipped, swallowing slowly and scrunching his lips as he did.

After finishing, Julian stretched out. Despite his weakness, he gained an instant flow of energy he'd never felt as a human. The sensation blanketed him like a soothing hot bath. "Will I be able to get up and move around tomorrow?" he asked.

"Maybe," Xavier said. "We will have to wait and see." There was a twinkle in the vampire's eyes that Julian never noticed. "For now, you need more sleep."

Violet leaned in, whispering, "You're doing great, and soon it'll be our wedding night. I'm gonna tear your ass up," she giggled before kissing his bloody lips and playfully licking away the red remnants. "Until then—sweet dreams, jellybean." She kissed his lips once more and ran the back of her fingers down the side of his face. "I love you."

"I love you, too." He shut his eyes and slept the rest of the night.

It was not until Julian's nearby phone pinged with a text message that he awoke. Feeling energized, he took the phone from the end table next to the bed and saw the text clearer than ever. *Hey bub, I talked to Tara. Her mom is having a New Year's party, and they want me to watch the ball drop on TV with them. If you have the wedding earlier, I can come.* Julian rolled his eyes, figuring

Violet would rather get married at midnight. Too tired to care, he dropped the phone and shut his eyes again.

Later that night, when Violet and Xavier awoke, so did Julian. He lay in bed, looking at the ceiling and wiggling his toes before randomly bursting in laughter. "What's so funny?" Violet asked.

"Everything. I mean, I'm a fucking vampire!" It's so trippy!"

She giggled and said, "You're adorable, like a kid on Christmas. You don't know how happy that makes me. It's smooth sailing from here. After we are married, our future begins."

"About the wedding," Julian began. "Daryl texted me and said his wife's mother is having a New Year's Eve party, and he wanted to watch the ball drop on TV at midnight. He said he could come if we have the wedding early."

"You wanted him to be your best man, did you not?" Xavier asked.

"I did."

Xavier turned his gaze to Violet, saying, "We can do it early, maybe six-thirty or seven, perhaps?"

"But I wanted to get married at midnight!" she pouted. "Although, you won't have anyone here for you if we do." She rolled her eyes and sighed. "I guess we can have it early."

"What about you?" Julian asked. "I'll have a best man, but you won't have a maid of honor."

"I know," she sighed again. "At least I will have my father here."

"Actually," Xavier interjected. "I have a few gifts I wanted to collect for the two of you before the wedding."

"Really?!" Violet smiled. "What are they?"

"Surprises," he chuckled. "Your wedding will not be conventional, but a special occasion nonetheless, and my family deserves the best. It will take a few nights to gather everything I need, but I will return before the wedding."

"So, you're just going to disappear again?" Violet placed her hands on her hips while glaring.

"For only a few nights, my sweet."

"A few nights or not, I worry about you out there."

Xavier rested his hand on Violet's shoulder and said, "I understand. I am so sorry to put such stress on you, but I will be fine."

"Are you sure?" she asked, tucking her bottom lip over the top.

"Trust me," he said, letting his hand fall to his side. "However, before I make my foray, I want to make sure Julian can walk."

Although he'd mostly just moved his arms so far, Julian was feeling better than the previous night. He placed both palms down on the mattress, supporting his weight while sitting up straight.

"Wonderful!" Xavier cheered. "Try to move your legs off the side of the bed." Julian inched to the edge, allowing his legs to dangle and his feet to touch the floor.

"Good job, Jul!" Violet praised. "Let's see if you can stand." With both hands, she gripped Julian's right arm while Xavier took his left.

"On three," she instructed. "One … two … three." Together, they lifted Julian slowly.

At first, he wobbled, but caught his balance. He took a step, then another. Violet and Xavier held him, but he walked with ease. "Let me see if I can do it on my own," he said. They let go, and he walked straight as an arrow. "This is amazing!" Julian was so ecstatic he nearly cried as he walked out of the bedroom and caught a glimpse of the staircase. "Can I go upstairs?"

"If you think you can," Xavier replied. "Hold on to the rail."

Julian approached the steps and took hold of the wooden banister. One by one, he ascended to the top and opened the basement door. Violet followed close behind as Xavier turned on the light. Julian's bare feet against the rock floor were neither cold nor warm, but something else entirely, and a vibration welcomed each step he took. "Why do my feet feel this way?" he asked.

"What way?" Xavier replied.

"I feel something funny coming from the floor and moving up my legs."

"Ah, that's just your body adapting to environmental energies. You will notice it from time to time. It's to heighten the senses, and it is one of your many new gifts," he explained.

Julian walked steadily, feeling no pain or discomfort. "So, does this mean I'm healed? I seem to be feeling better, and I can move around okay." He continued forward, locking his eyes on everything in sight.

"Not entirely, but your progress is astonishing," Xavier said. "You should still take it easy for the next few days."

"Keep an eye on him, Dad," said Violet as she turned towards the kitchen. "I'm hungry and need to feed."

Xavier stepped up to Julian's side, putting his arm around him, saying, "Before I go, I want you to promise me something."

"Anything."

"Be good to her. She loves you, and she will need someone to be there for her when I am not."

"I promise," he said. "I will always treat Violet as my queen. I love her too, and she is my everything." Xavier nodded and patted Julian's cheek. "But what do you mean by—"

"If I am not back until the wedding, do not fret," Xavier interrupted. He leaned closer and whispered, "I want to surprise her with something special."

"Alright," Julian whispered back. "Just please be careful."

"I will be fine, I promise."

After walking around the house, upstairs, and back down, Julian grew tired. He took a few drinks of blood and went back to bed. Over the next couple of nights, Violet kept an eye on him as his senses, mood, and optimism flourished. Then, on the night before the wedding, he barely slept. His ego cracked. He'd never known such feelings of peace, love, and bliss could exist, but they did, and they'd finally found him. For the first time in his life, Julian Frost realized his dream. He was on top of the world, in love, and truly happy with no regrets.

Chapter Thirty-Seven

" … and that is why I tried to kill myself. It was not just Faith's infidelity. She was only the catalyst. A lifetime of anguish took its toll and became more than I could bear. I tried, my God, I tried, but after losing the only pieces of my heart that mattered, I lost my will. It wasn't until I woke up the morning after that I knew my purpose had yet to be fulfilled."

"Four years have passed, and I can proudly attest: I am a new man, with everything I always wanted, the woman of my dreams, substantial wealth, and perfect vision. I have a new family now, one who loves and accepts me, while the old one withered away and collapsed beneath the weight of an unstable foundation."

"Tonight, the most difficult decade of my life comes to an end, giving way to humble new beginnings of a bright future ahead. Tonight, I start anew with Violet, my love, light, and reason to exist at this moment in time. She is my sweet flower, my flame, through sickness and in health until death do us part. To her, I present my heart on a silver platter, as we begin a life together forever."

Julian stood in the doorway separating the kitchen from the living room, watching and listening as Violet finished reading the completed manuscript on his laptop. She sat facing away, seemingly unaware of his presence. "That was so beautiful," she muttered, softly weeping. Julian's heart warmed as he took slow steps forward, catching her attention. When she turned to face him, her cheeks glowed beet red. "Did you see and hear all that?" she asked.

"I did. Do you think it's ready to be sent out? Surely out of the forty-four agents and publishers in that mass email, one will reply."

"You're a silver-tongued teddy bear, Jul,"

Also blushing, Julian approached the sofa and sat beside her, with the laptop in front of them on the coffee table. He opened the email he'd already prepared, with the manuscript, appropriately dubbed *Through Dead Eyes*, attached. He took a deep breath and asked, "You dare me to push send?"

Violet quickly extended her left index finger and tapped the button for him. "Oops … sorry," she snickered. He grinned and flicked his tongue at her, admiring her passion.

"I love you, Mrs. Frost."

"I like the sound of that: Mrs. Violet Frost. … And I love you too, Mr. Frost," she said. "And I'm certain your book will touch a lot of people's lives, people looking for stories of hope and inspiration. It has certainly touched mine."

"I can't wait to marry you," he said, looking into her beautiful brown almonds, seeing them in a way he never could as a human.

"If Dad doesn't get back in the next hour, though, I don't know what we're supposed to do. You told Daryl to be here at seven, right?" Julian nodded. "It's after six now!" Beginning to stress out, Violet turned on the television and flipped through the channels to the news. Her mood grew tense, and she cupped her hands over her face. "I'm sorry, Jul," she sighed. "I'm just worried, and I want to make sure nothing's happened."

"It's okay, sweetie. I understand, but Xavier told me not to worry if he shows up at the last minute. I think he's going to do something nice for you. Everything will work out, I promise."

"You're right," she sighed. "I just—"

"And everything worked out, did it not?" A familiar voice sounded from out of nowhere. Both Julian and Violet turned towards the kitchen and saw Xavier standing in the doorway.

"Daddy!" Violet cheered. Wearing an all black suit, as usual, Xavier took a few steps forward to reveal two others behind him: on the left, a bald man with a goatee and mustache, wearing a blue suit and tie, and on the right, a pasty, slender, redheaded lady in a simple burgundy dress.

"Oh my God! Anna?! … Bern?!" Violet instantly dropped the television remote and leaped from the sofa, dashing across the living room into Anna's arms.

"How're you, love?" Anna asked as she and Violet embraced like two long lost sisters reuniting, both grinning and adoring one another.

"Doing much better now that I know you two are safe," Violet said, glancing between them.

"Xavier came and found us. He said you're getting married, so we told him we'd come, and here we are," Bernard said. He looked past Violet towards Julian. "Well, you certainly look a little livelier than the last time we met," he said.

"Life altering experiences have that effect on me," Julian chuckled. "How've you two been since shit hit the fan?" he asked, looking from one to the other.

"Eh, it was tough at times, but we managed," Bernard said. "We had to move around a lot, but when you're a flying vampire, moving is the easy part."

Julian noticed Xavier holding two large black shopping bags, one in each hand. "What are those?" he asked.

"I told you, I wanted to get some things," he said. "Now, I believe the two of you have a wedding to get ready for." Xavier turned to Violet, asking, "Why don't you and Anna take this bag upstairs and get dressed?" He handed her the bag in his left hand.

Grinning ear to ear, Violet asked, "What is this, a dress?"

"Maybe, maybe more," he winked. "But as they say, 'time's a-wasting,' so, go get ready." Violet fell into Xavier's chest, hugging him tightly.

"Thank you, Daddy," she said and kissed his cheek. "I love you."

"I love you too, my sweet Violet." He kissed the top of her head. "Now, go get ready."

Like excited children, the ladies rushed upstairs with the bag. Julian, Xavier, and Bernard went down to the basement with the other. Inside Julian's bag was an all-white tuxedo. "Wow! This is really nice, Xavier. Thank you," Julian said. He put on the matching pants, shirt, jacket, and shoes. Finally, he clipped on the white bowtie and pulled his silver ankh pendant from beneath his collar, letting it dangle in the open. After brushing his long hair back, Julian was ready.

"You look quite handsome, Julian," Xavier said.

"Thanks."

Xavier sighed, saying, "If only Eric were still here to see this. He and Violet were like brother and sister and losing him was like losing a son."

"I still can't believe what you told me," Bernard said. "Manipulated or not, Bishop better hope we never cross paths again."

"It wasn't his fault," Xavier said.

"I don't care!" he fumed.

"We shall deal with it when the time comes." Xavier patted Bernard's shoulder. "Now, it is time for a wedding. Come!" The men all headed towards the stairs until Xavier halted. He placed a finger in the air. "Oh, wait! I almost forgot." He reached inside his pants pocket and retrieved a little black jewelry box. "Neither of you had a chance to go looking for wedding rings, so until you can make it more official by choosing what you want. ..." He opened the box and showed it to Julian. "I thought she might like this one." A shiny, yellow gold band, wedged upright in its velvet slot, featured narrow Celtic etchings.

"Oh, wow! That's beautiful," Julian admired. "I am sure she will love it." He took the ring in his hand and observed it closer. "I know I do," he added before placing the ring inside his jacket pocket. After making it back to the living room, Julian checked the clock: 6:44 it read, as he heard a vehicle approaching from outside. "Daryl's here!" he announced.

"Who's Daryl?" Bernard asked.

"My best friend, brother, and best man. He's human, and he doesn't know about vampires, so don't say anything."

"Yeah, yeah. ..." Bernard countered. Seconds later, a knock came from the kitchen door. Daryl stood on the other side, wearing a brown pair of khakis with a black belt, and a tucked-in, buttoned, blue-striped shirt.

"I'll go upstairs and see if they're ready yet." Bernard turned towards the staircase.

Julian opened the door. "Damn, bub! You're looking sharp!" Daryl said.

"Thanks," Julian replied. He moved aside, saying, "Come on in for a minute. Violet is upstairs getting ready."

As Daryl followed Julian inside, he asked, "Where're your glasses?"

"You wouldn't believe me if I told you, but I can see everything now. Twenty-twenty, perfect vision, baby!"

Xavier cleared his throat and took a step forward, smiling politely and extending his hand towards Daryl. "Hello, I am Xavier Van Abarrow," he said.

"Van Abarrow?!" Daryl raised an eyebrow. His deep Appalachian twang struck laughter in both Xavier and Julian. "Is that a European name or something?"

"Anglo-Saxon," Xavier said. "My family is quite old."

Daryl nodded and shrugged in confusion before shaking Xavier's hand. "Well, it's nice to meet you, Xavier. I'm Daryl Stillwater."

"Stillwater. ..." Xavier stroked his chin. "Hmm ... very nice."

"Julian told me you're Violet's father," Daryl said, tipping his head in confusion at the youthful vampire.

"That is correct, sir," Xavier replied, looking over his shoulder towards the living room. "She should be ready by now, unless she is doing something with her hair. That is my girl, though—always a taste for theatrics." Xavier walked to the foot of the stairs. "Hey! Are you ready yet, ladies?!"

"'Ladies?' Who else is up there?" Daryl mumbled in Julian's ear.

"Violet's friends, Anna and her husband, Bernard."

"Hey!" Xavier called again.

"What?!" Anna yelled back.

"Is she ready yet?!"

"Almost, love. We'll be right down. Go on outside, and we'll be out in five minutes. ... Bern's comin' down now."

Footsteps descended, and Bernard appeared. With a glare of displeasure, he took one look at Daryl and asked, "Who the hell are you?"

"I'm Daryl. Who the hell're you?"

"I'm Bernard, the maid of honor's husband."

"Alright, gentleman, let's go outside," Xavier said, motioning towards the door. "Violet and Anna will be right out."

"Hey, wait, Dad!" Violet shouted from the top of the stairs.

"Yes?!" Xavier replied.

"I know you're marrying us, but I also want you to give me away," she said.

"Very well, then." He turned to the others and said, "Okay, then … you gentlemen go outside, and we shall join you shortly."

"Come," Julian said to the men, leading the way towards the door. "Humble new beginnings await!"

Chapter Thirty-Eight

A winter breeze swept across the yard as the streetlight illuminated the sparkling sheet of snow, with footstep trails leading from the driveway. Julian waited with the others for the bride, her father, and the maid of honor to arrive. As Bernard paced, Daryl stood behind Julian. "You know, there's something different about you, bub. You look happier than I've ever seen, but you don't look quite like yourself. I guess what I'm trying to say is, you look more confident."

Julian swiveled, turning to face his best man, saying, "I appreciate that, brother, and I love you. Thank you so much for coming."

"I love you too, bub, and I'm proud of you, but why ain't your grandpa here?"

"It's over with him. I doubt I will ever see him again. My real family is here with me now."

A moment later, Anna joined the men, and everyone faced the lit carport. First Xavier appeared, stopping just past the door, and turning towards the others.

Julian shivered with anticipation as Violet's shape appeared, covered in white, her head draped in a translucent crystalline veil. Then, her slender bare legs stepped towards her father. The back of her ruffled, lacy skirt was long, nearly dragging the ground as she walked. *My God*. Julian gasped, and his jaw dropped, admiring such beauty. Violet's right arm locked with Xavier's left, and her eyes met Julian's. They both smiled. Her flower-pattern blouse was short-sleeved and low-cut, revealing the top of her cleavage and curving over her shoulders. Even from thirty feet away, Julian observed every minor detail in a way he never could have before.

From below the veil, her long, auburn hair hung in multiple thin braids. "How in the hell?" Julian muttered under his breath.

"What?" Daryl asked.

"Oh, nothing," he said, taken aback by how quickly her hair had been styled. *She's gorgeous!*

"Pretty neat, eh?" Anna smiled proudly.

"Way to go, bub," Daryl whispered. "She's beautiful."

"Thanks, brother. She sure is."

"Huh?!" Daryl gasped.

"I said, 'thanks. She sure is.'"

"Sure is what?"

"Beautiful … you said, 'She's beautiful.' I was agreeing with you."

"I never said that. I—I thought it, but I never said it. … Wait, did I?"

"Oi!" Anna yelped. "Would you two pipe down?" She winked at Julian before turning her attention back to the bride.

When they reached the others, Xavier presented his daughter to the groom, taking his place between them. The lovers gazed madly at each other, meeting their foreheads while sharing heartfelt smiles and giggling like children. Once they separated, Violet offered a polite smile and nod to Daryl.

Julian mouthed the words, "I love you."

"I love you, too," Violet said aloud.

Xavier cleared his throat and began. "Friends … both, new …"—he smiled at Daryl—"And old." He panned from Anna, standing behind Violet, to Bernard, standing off to the side. "And family." Xavier smiled at his daughter and new son. "We are gathered here tonight, on New Year's Eve, at the end of another decade." He shut his eyes, smiling and taking a deep breath of cold air.

"Tonight, we bear witness to the coming together of two vibrantly blessed souls in love, uniting as one." He looked from person to person again, maintaining eye contact as he spoke. "Love is a diverse word. However, with twin flames, love is pure, unconditional, and grows beyond life, death, and creation itself. It takes two extraordinarily destined souls to connect in such a way."

"As two become one, my daughter, Violet Cordelia Troúton, and Julian Malcolm Frost, have chosen to write their vows from the heart." Xavier nodded for Violet to begin.

As she stared into Julian's eyes, Violet smiled, took his hands in hers, and said, "Julian, I've experienced much in my long life. I have loved and lost the same. When we met, I was in a vulnerable, fragile, and some might even say a reckless mindset."

Anna giggled from behind her. "But they say you have to lose everything to find it again. You were so close to giving up, but you did not. You trusted me because you trusted yourself and followed your heart. I too followed my heart. It was my dreams where we first met. Then, when the universe brought us together, everything changed. I knew from the first time I saw you we were destined. From that first glance, I fell in love with you. Since then, we descended the rabbit hole and built this foundation from the ground up, and it is together that we will transcend all time and space. You are my immortal beloved and the king I deserve."

Shedding a few tears of glee, Violet looked over her shoulder. Anna relinquished a gold band, engraved like the other. Violet held Julian's right hand and gently placed the symbol on his extended finger. She kissed the ring and said, "I love you."

Xavier smiled and turned his gaze to Julian. It was his turn to speak, but he stammered, unable to remember the vows he'd written and rehearsed so many times while bedridden with little else to do. "I … umm …"

"You got this, bub," Daryl whispered from behind.

He cleared his throat, took a breath, and winged it from the heart. "Violet … my love, my light, my everything. … You said I am a silver-tongued teddy bear, but at moments like this, it's hard to express myself properly. But if I had to sum the year up in one word, it would be per—" A sharp sting bit Julian's neck. "I … I …" He reached for the spot but staggered off balance. "What the fu—" He immediately lost all mobility, crashing to the snow.

"Julian?!" Violet squealed. He tried to speak, but neither his lips, tongue, nor a muscle moved. Panic set in as Violet knelt to his aid, with a look of dread in her brown almonds. "Julian?! … Jul—" She also fell silent and collapsed atop his lifeless body, and her veil slid off her head.

Julian's eyes remained open as she stared directly into them. Neither could move, only face the other. *What the fuck is happening?!* he screamed in silence, feeling trapped and witnessing the fear blooming in Violet's wide-open eyes.

"What the fuck?!" Daryl shouted.

"Xav—" Bernard began before his voice was silenced.

"Bern!!!" Anna shrieked in terror. "Aghh! … What the fuck?! … Someone's shooting at us!"

"Ahh! My foot!" Xavier growled. Julian could only listen as his visuals were entirely that of the desperation in his soon-to-be wife's eyes. "Go!" Xavier grunted just before Julian heard another thud against the ground.

"What?! … No!" Anna cried.

"Anna! You cannot help us!" Xavier implored. "Take Bernard and go!" The ginger howled, and Julian felt a light breeze sweep across his feet.

"What the fuck?!" Daryl wailed as he tried to move Violet and help his friend. Even after she was moved aside, Julian still saw both of her eyes with one of his own.

"Vi—Violet?!" Xavier's weak voice gurgled as Julian caught a glimpse of something falling from the darkness above, closing in fast.

Oh my God! *Can anybody hear me?! Please!* Daryl's horrified face entered Julian's peripherals as he looked up just in time to see six shadowy figures strapped to parachutes, bracing for impact.

Before Daryl could say or do anything, the men landed and surrounded him. "Hey!" he snarled. "Just what the fuck are you doin'?! This is my brother's we—"

A loud, hammering shotgun blast rang, blowing out Julian's eardrums and silencing Daryl. Gunsmoke blew overhead, accompanying a red mist, followed by another loud thud.

Daryl! No!

"Well, now … how the tables have turned." Julian could not see faces, but he knew the man's voice. "I am truly going to savor this! You don't have some nightclub full of witnesses or anyone to protect you now, do you?" The man chuckled. "It looks like your coward friends took off and left your ass high and dry, huh?" Cauldwell and all his men laughed.

"Some friends," one of the other men said.

"Some friends, indeed," Cauldwell repeated. "And then, we had the hero make his stand, but he's going to lie over there and bleed out while he thinks about what happens to heroes."

Footsteps crunched through the snow towards Julian while he stared into Violet's eyes, staring back at his. A warm, wet sensation oozed against the tips of his fingers on the right. It was then that Christopher Cauldwell leaned into view, and Julian came face to face with the man himself. His curly golden-brown hair blew in the wind, and he bore a smug grin while holding what appeared to be a large mallet or hammer, but Julian could not get a good look at it.

"Well, hello there." With a free hand, Cauldwell dangled the round pair of eyeglasses Julian lost at Leviticus. "I think you dropped these," he said before tossing them aside. "I would say that I am sorry for disturbing your wedding, but I'm not a liar." His men laughed again.

"You know," he continued. "It's thanks to your pussy-whipped friend here that all this was possible. You see, when he sent you that text the other day about having the wedding early so he could go watch the ball drop …" he paused and chuckled. "Well, it gave us an idea." Cauldwell turned his attention away and stepped out of view. "I bet you're all wondering how we caught you, huh?" Julian's heart pounded, and though he was still able to breathe, his lungs grew noticeably heavier by the moment. "Kevin, pull up that video on your phone, brother," Cauldwell directed as he approached Julian again.

Kevin Cauldwell also entered Julian's field of vision. Sadistically grinning, he held his sawed-off shotgun in one hand and a black cellphone in the other. He gave the phone to his brother. "Here, look at this!" Christopher said, shoving the device in Julian's face. A video began playing, and there he was, standing on the stage at Leviticus, singing his song with the band playing behind him.

"Mystic woman … do your dance. …" Julian's own words played back to him. Cauldwell smirked and pulled the phone away. The music silenced and the only sound was the militia's laughter and mockery.

"We're Navy Seals, and you can't hide from us," one of them said.

"Why won't you leave us alone, Christopher?" Xavier's voice dragged like that of a dying old man.

"Oh, wow! Look at you, Xavier! It looks like one of our darts wasn't enough. You're a tough one, huh?"

"Why are you doing this to us?" Xavier asked.

"You know why!" Cauldwell snarled.

"It was not me, or any of us," he gasped. "It was—"

"Tony Bishop, I know." Cauldwell chuckled. "But it was still your kind."

"But how do you—"

"How do I know?" Cauldwell laughed. "Funny you should ask. The truth is, we've been watching you for a while, long before my brother ever called that fat cop up the road and got Julian arrested. Speaking of which, Kevin, you paid him to stay home tonight, no matter what he heard, right?"

"I sure did, Chris," Kevin said.

"That night when I was on TV, Julian got triggered. My brother was already hiding in the backyard here. He took advantage of the situation, and after Julian got hauled off to jail, this house was bugged and wired for sound. Ever since then, we've heard everything, and we were only waiting for the right moment when you would all be here at the same time," Cauldwell explained. During his next pass by, Julian watched him turn towards Xavier, asking, "Do you know what this is, demon?"

"It looks like a war hammer," Xavier mumbled.

"A war hammer?" Cauldwell laughed, and so did his men. "It's a little more than that."

"Christopher, please, just allow me to talk to you about all this, and—"

"Talk?!" Cauldwell snarled. "What the hell is there to talk about?!"

"My people … we are peaceful, and we do not kill."

"Your people? … People?! … I'm sorry, did you just refer to you and these two other demons as people?"

"We are not savages!" Xavier snapped. Again, everyone erupted in laughter.

"You're not savages?" Cauldwell mocked. "Well, that's too bad because we are."

"That's right, baby!" one of the men howled, and the others cheered on.

My God … Julian thought, still only able to move enough to breathe and pump blood from his petrified heart. With Violet's lifeless body draped over his, all they could do was look in one another's eyes, frozen in fear, until Julian experienced a second rhythmic pulse. Violet's left breast lay atop his, and their hearts beat only inches apart.

I don't know if you can hear me, Violet, but I love you, and I am so scared. Her heart immediately beat faster, catching up to his, and the two wept in sync, together as one.

"Now, if we are through playing make believe," Cauldwell went on. "As I was saying, this isn't just any ordinary war hammer. This piece of medieval craftsmanship has been a staple in the Cauldwell family for over nine hundred years, and it's even older than you are, Xavier. This weapon has slain many demons in its time." Julian heard more crunching through the snow. "Take a look at it, Xavier. … I said, look at it! Do you see that big spike there? Do you know how many vampire hearts it's pierced? … Answer me!"

"I do not," Xavier lifelessly muttered.

"Well, technically, I don't either, but once my ancestors took it, they swore to use it to rid the world of its blackness and terror." Cauldwell came back to Julian and hovered. "Wha'd'ya think? That's pretty badass, huh?"

He shoved the hammerhead in Julian's face. It was nearly as wide as the end of a cinderblock on the thicker end, with a shiny, flat metal head. Cauldwell smirked as he flipped the hammer around, exposing a pointed end. The tip was the width of a pencil, tapering up to the size of the bigger end. "Let's make sure your whore also sees it."

You motherfucker! If you touch her, I will kill you!

Cauldwell violently kicked Violet on her side, and she fell from Julian's view. "Look at that shit, bitch," he said as his men laughed. "I bet when you woke up earlier, you thought your pathetic little man over there was the only thing you'd fuck tonight, huh? Well, that's just tough titty, said the kitty."

"Please, Christopher …" Xavier begged. "How can we settle this?"

Cauldwell grinned and turned his head away from Julian, asking, "What do you think we are doing right now, blondie?"

"If you're not going to be satisfied until you take one of our lives, take mine and leave them out of it," Xavier pleaded. "They are both so sweet and would never hurt anyone unless they had to." He broke down and sobbed.

"I am a fair man," Cauldwell snickered. "I took an oath, when I joined the military, to protect this wonderful nation from all threats, and vampires are a threat to not just America, but the human race at large. Given our family history, my brother and I have known about vampires our entire lives. And as New Yorkers, we've known about you and your coven for years, but there was a time we wanted no part in the family tradition. After joining the military, I was happy with just being a Marine, and then later training to become a Seal. But after my sweet daughter was murdered by one of you, I could no longer deny my birthright. It was then that my brother and I both took the holy vow to seek vengeance and protect the world from the demonic forces that still exist."

"Christopher, please!" Xavier cried.

"I made one crucial mistake, though," Cauldwell said, ignoring Xavier's plea. "I went on television, and everyone laughed. Tonight I will correct that mistake, and no one will ever laugh at me again. After tonight, the whole world will know vampires are real, and none of you will ever be safe again." Julian's gut turned toxic with nausea as he listened, unable to do anything else. "In addition to being an honorable man, willing to die for God and country, I am also a fair man, as I said. So, you will not die tonight, Xavier. Justice always comes first, and everyone, humans and demons alike, must pay for their sins. Do you understand?"

Xavier said nothing, and all grew silent except the whispering wind. "No?!" Cauldwell snarled. "It doesn't matter. We all must pay an eye for an eye." A hefty smash echoed through the air. Xavier loudly shrieked, and the sound immediately sent sharp chills throughout Julian's stone frame. An accompanying crunch filled his ears, followed by a slimy crackle.

Cauldwell grunted like he was putting his back into it. Another hard gasp was followed by a trail of red viscera, and a small white ball flying across Julian's field of vision. *Xavier?! Violet?! Daryl?! Somebody, please help us!*

Xavier gasped and groaned as the others laughed. "And a tooth for a tooth," Cauldwell continued. Again the militant grunted as Julian heard the hammer crashing down a second time. The smash was loud, and this time Xavier screamed in agony before Julian heard sounds of gurgling, spitting, and gasping for air.

As Cauldwell and his men's laughter carried on, footsteps approached Julian once more. Through his left eye, he saw the waving gold hair illuminated by the streetlight. "And finally," Cauldwell said, leaning out of view. He returned holding Violet by her hair, dangling her head only inches from Julian's eyes. "A daughter for a daughter."

What?! No! No! Please, God! ... No! With Violet's doomed, enlarged pupils locked with her husband's again, a single tear dripped from the corner of her left eye, splashing against Julian's cheek. *Violet! I love you!*

"God! ... Please, don't!" Xavier squealed and sobbed, struggling to utter the plea.

With his free hand, Cauldwell presented a long shiny bowie knife. He grinned, first at Violet, then at Julian. "I'm going to fuck your wife with this knife, right in front of you, and there's nothing you can do about it," he said.

"Violet!" Xavier cried. "I love you! ... I am so sorry I failed you—ou—ou!" His heartbroken cries echoed across the mountain.

Julian wept on the inside, as the twin flames could only stare. Cauldwell raised the shiny blade to Violet's fair throat and viciously dug in: sawing back and forth, laughing with the others. "Violet!" Xavier howled while Julian watched it all. Violet's blood sprayed everywhere, especially in Julian's face, filling his open mouth and running down his throat.

God! ... Please, just make it stop! Julian watched Violet's life drain away. Her eyes rolled back in her head and the color faded from her cheeks and lips.

"Violet!" Xavier screamed again, but it was too late. Julian witnessed the final slide of the blade before Cauldwell ripped her auburn-tailed head from her narrow shoulders. Blood gushed in globs from the gaping stump as her dead body fell and landed atop Julian.

Cauldwell smirked, dangling Violet's severed head by her hair, asking, "Was it as good for you as it was for me?" He cackled and walked out of Julian's view. "Now, as I said earlier, Mister Stillwater gave us an idea," he said as if nothing had happened. "What time is it, brother?"

"Umm … it's seven-forty-four, Chris," said Kevin.

"Shit! We gotta get outta here and haul ass if we're going to make it back home by midnight. Just toss those two in a pile, over there, boys. Stillwater will be dead long before dawn, and the headless whore will turn to ash. We can come back in the morning and get rid of the evidence before the dead one's wife comes looking for him."

"You got it, boss!" one of his men said.

Julian saw movement from his right, coming towards Daryl, who hadn't made a sound since he was shot. His blood had turned cold and began clotting against Julian's hand. On his left, Violet's corpse was pulled away. "Yeah, just stack them over there," Cauldwell instructed.

As Julian stared at the sky, with Violet's sweet, metallic blood still running down his throat, he only wished to trade places with her and Daryl. "Before we put another dart in the two of you, you got any last words for your failed creation over there, Xavier?" Cauldwell asked.

"I am so sorry, my son. Please forgive me." Xavier's heartbroken words ripped through Julian's soul. If he could speak, he would vow to drag all the men to hell.

"Touching," Cauldwell snickered. "Jonesy, put another dart in Xavier." He returned to Julian, retrieving a small walkie-talkie from a pocket on his brown overcoat. "Alright, Ben, lower down the ropes. We're ready," he said as Julian heard the tranquilizer gun discharge. Xavier's panicked breaths ceased. "Is he out?" Cauldwell asked.

"Yes, sir!"

"Alright, gimme' the gun and I'll take care of this one." After Cauldwell was handed a large black pistol, he pointed it at

Julian's blood-soaked face. Without another word, he smiled sadistically before squeezing the trigger, and all went black.

Chapter Thirty-Nine

Peaceful birds chirped from above, and a warm breeze tickled Julian's nose. His eyelids cracked open in the blistering sunlight and instinct took priority. He quickly covered his face and curled in a ball, trying to shield himself from certain death. When nothing happened, he gently pulled his hands away, observing the thick, surrounding forest. The warmth and vibrant foliage suggested a summer atmosphere, with winter nowhere in sight.

His right hand was caked with Daryl's dried blood, his face and tuxedo with Violet's', her taste on his breath. Remembering what happened, Julian fought off the tears as he slowly stood, scanning the woods, detecting a shadowy figure in the distance. The shape was framed in sunlight, dressed in black, and leaning against a tall oak tree on the edge of a cliff. Their back turned, a blond ponytail whisked in the wind. "Xavier?!" Julian cried, approaching through the tall weeds and brush.

"I … I could not save her," Xavier shuddered, lowering his head and standing straight while his unsteady right hand pressed firmly against the tree trunk.

Julian halted in an open patch of grass nearly ten feet away. "Where are we? What is this place?"

"It was supposed to be me," Xavier said, ignoring the questions. He looked up, fully extending both hands towards the heavens. "It was supposed to be me!" He lowered his hands and took a step closer to the edge. "Not her. Not them."

"Xavier?" Julian called, slowly advancing with caution. "Are we … are we dead?"

"No."

"Where are we, then? How are we—"

"The Seine River, in Paris," he mumbled. "This is where my sister died and where I should have joined her."

"But it's daytime. How is this possible?"

"This is a dream," he said. "Vampires have a special bond with their children and others we share our blood with. We can often interact through dreams."

"If that's true, bring her here!"

"No," Xavier sighed.

"I said, bring her here!" Julian cried.

"And I said no!" Xavier turned around, facing Julian and revealing his mangled face. The flesh surrounding his empty left eye socket was ripped and gouged. The barren pit exposed red, meaty tissue. Most of his teeth were either missing or broken. Julian looked on as the damage was already healing itself.

"Why?!" He dropped to his knees in tears. As he wept, Xavier approached, placing a hand upon his wet cheek, extending his long fingers, and brushing Julian's hair aside.

"Because she is dead, son," he said, fighting tears of his own. "Only she can come to me now."

"Why did this happen?" Julian sobbed.

"I …" Xavier paused and sniffled. "Cauldwell was supposed to kill me, not her."

Julian looked into Xavier's one eye, asking, "What do you mean?"

"I knew something would happen, but I thought it would be me who died. Dajhri said I would have to give my life to save others. I thought he was supposed to kill me tonight, not her or Daryl. Dajhri's prophecies are never wrong."

"It's my fault they are dead, not yours," Julian said. "I sang that fucking song, and one of Cauldwell's men recorded me." His head remained hung while the tears continued.

Xavier moved his hand atop Julian's head and gently patted him. "It was not your fault. Nobody can stop fate, and the only one who is truly to blame is Cauldwell. He knew Violet and I were innocent in his daughter's death, but he killed her and your friend anyway."

Julian cleared his throat and asked, "What are they going to do to us?"

Xavier sighed, pulling his hand away and turning back towards the cliff. "Cauldwell said the ball drop in Times Square gave him an idea. He said he wanted to get home by midnight, and nobody else would laugh at him again." He took a deep breath. "I think they are taking us to New York. It's New Year's Eve, and the whole world is watching." He turned back towards Julian and said,

"I believe they are going to drop us on the crowd at midnight. If they do, it is all over." Xavier balled his fist and slammed it against the tree.

"What about Anna and Bernard? Where did they go?"

"I sent them away because Violet, Bernard, and you were all down, and even if they hadn't shot him, Daryl was powerless. I was able to speak but not move. Anna is strong and fast, but she could not have saved us all on her own in a situation like that."

Julian's heart sank as the unfathomable memories and horrors repeated. The gunshot that took Daryl's life blew his eardrums out again while Violet's helpless brown almonds looked on as she was beheaded once more. He shut his eyes and covered his ears, but the exhibition remained, incinerating his thoughts. "I … I can't believe they're both gone," he sobbed, wiping his eyes, trying to stop the tears. "Daryl was innocent! He had nothing to do with this, and now. …" His shoulders slumped. "He's dead!"

"We can't do anything about that now, but there is something I need to tell you." Xavier dropped to his knees, meeting Julian's level, taking his hands and making eye contact. "Your body is still weak, and you have not fully healed. I fear if they drop us, and you fall far. …" He hesitated and looked away in guilt.

"I'll what?"

"You will die."

Julian cackled unnaturally. "Let it kill me, then! Just let it fucking kill me. I already lost everything tonight, and I don't care anymore. I want to die, so I can be with her and find the peace in death that was stolen in life."

"You do not mean that."

"You wanna bet?!" Julian seethed. "And if I have anything to say about it, I'll take that motherfucker straight to hell with me! Then I would gladly give my life to be with her again. So how do we get out of here?"

"This is a dream. You just have to wake up, but I do not want anything to happen to you. Not only did you lose a friend and your wife tonight, but I also lost a daughter, and while you might not see it the same as me, you are my son, and all I have left. If I have anything to say about it, I will be the one who drags myself to hell before I willingly let anything happen to you."

"What can we do?"

"If I regain control of my body before you, I will try to protect you." He extended his hand, saying, "Now, come here." Julian inhaled deeply, still only able to see the grisly image of his dead bride as he stood and joined Xavier on the cliffside. He peeked over the edge. Nearly a hundred feet below, the water sparkled in the sunlight.

"By the time I was fifteen years old, my mother had died from pneumonia, and my father, a knight, and smith, was killed in battle," Xavier said. "I was left alone, and just like my sweet Sibby, I fell from this cliff after throwing myself off. I wanted to join her in death, but it was Caanis who saved me and gave my life a new meaning." With his right hand, Xavier took hold of Julian's left. "The quickest way to wake from a dream is a sudden shock," he said before looking over the edge and quivering. "I have made this jump so many times now, and it is never easy."

"I'm scared," Julian confessed. "It's not death that frightens me anymore, just the act of it. I thought becoming a vampire would cure that, but I guess I was wrong."

"I am so sorry, my son. Whether it be in this life or the next, I hope you can forgive me."

"I already have," Julian replied, squeezing Xavier's hand. "I wish it could have lasted, but I guess nothing does. I love you, Dad."

Xavier smiled and squeezed Julian's hand in return, saying, "I love you too. Are you ready?" Julian nodded. "On three," Xavier instructed. "One … two … three!" Together, they leaped from the edge. Their grip broke as shades of blue, between the water and sky, rapidly twirled through Julian's vision until a hard blow ended it all.

Julian! A shrill and alarming echo burst his lids wide open. He lay on his back against a cold, hard surface while the roaring thunder of an engine filled the airwaves. His eyes roamed but he saw nothing in the darkness, though his shallow breaths were growing fuller.

At times, he caught distorted voices, unable to understand anything they said. *Violet?! Can you hear me?* He waited, hearing nothing, but he sensed Xavier's warm, unresponsive touch. His hand lay atop his own, and a blunt pulse oscillated directly into his heart. *Can you hear me, Xavier?*

A clanking of footsteps on metal approached. "Yeah, two minutes!" a man shouted from out of view. Again, Julian attempted to move. First he tried his left hand, then the right, but nothing. Then he tried his right pinky beneath Xavier's hand, concentrating hard. Finally, there came a single tremor.

A dull overhead light flicked on, illuminating the dark ceiling as a figure passed Julian's view. "Alright, we're crossing the Hudson now. By the time we get ready to toss them, we'll be right over the crowd," said another voice. It was incoherent, but Julian knew it was Cauldwell's. "What time you got, brother?" he asked.

"Eleven-fifty-eight, Chris!"

"Right on time! Get ready to open the cargo door!" Julian was overcome by a cold chill as he felt a movement from beneath him.

I am so scared, was all he thought. The pain, anger, and building rage took a backseat once the final seconds of his life began counting down. He remembered the night Violet swept in, saving him at the last minute, and how truly lucky he was. *But she's dead*, he told himself. *She is dead, and now, I am too. I will see you soon, my flower.*

"We're approaching the crowd!" one of the other men shouted.

Cauldwell entered Julian's viewpoint and knelt between him and Xavier. First, with a cocky sneer, he hovered over Julian and shouted, "You are going to die!" As he snickered, Cauldwell turned towards Xavier. "And you … you will live for now. When you hit the ground and survive, everyone will know just how wrong they were about me! Soon enough, your day will come, and your kind will rot in hell where you all belong!" He stood, the same psychotic look on his face, and backed away.

For the first time since he was shot, Julian blinked his eyelids and moved his tongue, but it was too late. From beneath, the cargo door emitted a loud click and high pitch squeal before swinging open. Just as the long way down began, Xavier's hand suddenly came alive, taking hold of Julian's and gripping it tightly. Amidst the freefall, a cold wind baptized Julian's bod; flashes of light and darkness swirled along with his relentless tumble down to Earth. His heart raced and he lost his breath. The spinning never seemed to end as they sunk towards a waiting crowd whose screams grew louder as they drew closer. Xavier held on tight and managed to pull Julian against his chest, wrapping his arms and legs around him as a shield.

Finally, it ended. Julian was struck by catastrophic injury like he'd never felt before. His body ached beyond belief, and every molecule sang their agonizing swansong before going numb. He could not move. He could not breathe. His heartbeat faded. The surrounding crowd either ran away, screaming in horror, or hovered over him, staring and doing nothing to help. Lying on his back, Julian focused his fleeing vision past the petrified faces to the flashing white light of the helicopter, hundreds of feet above. *No one's going to save me*, he thought before his vision faded entirely and the void opened, swallowing him whole and delivering him to death's door once again.

***

Open your eyes, Jul." Violet's calm whisper became his entire universe. Julian had a sudden urge to persist, although he still could not move. "You must push on, my love."

How? I can't … Just let me stay dead so I can be with you.

"My blood is with your blood now. We will be together forever, one day, but now, they need you."

They? … Who? I … I can't! I—

"What're you avoiding?" Her soft touch caressed his cheek as Julian tried with all his might to open his eyes. When he finally could, he saw himself in the clouds. A bright orange sun and a beautiful blue sky filled the backdrop. Violet held him, appearing as a white robed angel; her auburn hair flowing without end. Julian tried to speak, but nothing came out. "Now is not forever. Time is an illusion, and one day you will see," she sang. "I love you, Jul." Her angelic lips kissed his. "Now, go be a Libra."

The heavenly atmosphere instantly dissolved, and Julian's eyes burst open like ravenous barbarians breaking through a gate. He drew a deep, scratchy breath and coughed hard as the cold air probed his dry throat. He panned the surrounding crowd when an abrupt and horrendous fire ignited from the depths of his soul, searing bright and blue. On the outside he regained feeling, and a cold sweat trickled. Inside, he had one thing on his mind—justice—as he stared at the passing chopper above.

"Julian, I am here to help you!" a deep, masculine voice announced. Feeling a firm grip against his hand, Julian instantly regained control of his body, strength, and senses. As the hand lifted him to his feet, the first thing he saw was the abundance of tattoos covering the hand's accompanying arm. "Come on, Xavier." With his other free hand, the man reached for Xavier, still lying on the street.

"Bishop?!" Xavier moaned. "What the hell are you—"

"Listen," Bishop interrupted. "I know I fucked up and disobeyed you. I don't deserve your forgiveness, but I am here to make things right. So let me make things right!"

"Where are they?" Xavier asked.

"Up there," Bishop said, pointing to the sky. Julian looked high above the tall buildings at the massive helicopter, hovering in the New York skyline. "Can you fly?" Bishop asked.

"I … I am not sure," Xavier groaned. "I can move, but I am weak."

"Alright, I've got you both," he said before turning to Julian. "Jump on my back. Let's go bite them where it hurts!" With new energy pumping through his veins, Julian nodded and wrapped his arms around Bishop's shoulders, watching him take Xavier in his hands. All three shot to the sky, leaving the fading screams of the crowd in their wake.

Within seconds, Julian found himself dangling from the black chopper's skids as if they were monkey bars. To his left, Xavier also held on. Bishop shimmied towards the cockpit. With agility he'd never thought possible, Julian flipped himself up towards the open doorway on the side of the chopper as the silhouettes from within quickly approached. Bishop ripped the pilot's door from the hinges, and a loud squeal of twisted metal overshadowed the roar of the engine. As Julian and Xavier climbed inside, Bishop tossed the pilot, like balled paper, to his death.

As everyone else inside rushed towards Xavier and Julian with their weapons drawn, the helicopter spun out of control and flipped on its side. Along with three of the soldiers, Julian and Xavier fell straight back and out the door they'd just entered. Julian swung his arms wildly, trying to grab anything he could to keep from falling again.

Xavier caught him just in time with one hand, while hanging from the landing skid with the other. He helped Julian get his grip. Bishop took the pilot's seat, trying to stabilize the aircraft before it crashed into the crowd below. "Hold on! I don't know how to fly this fucking thing!" he shouted.

The other men inside the chopper rushed to the door and began shooting at Julian and Xavier. They hung on tight and avoided the bullets, but the helicopter nicked against the rooftop of one of the tall buildings. As the aircraft caught fire, the side opposite of Julian and Xavier skipped along the edge of the rooftop like a flat rock on a pond, leaving a trail of smoke and flames until coming to a stop and teetering over the edge. The propeller detached from the top, and as Julian hung on for dear life, he watched it somersault away and down the side of the building before smacking into the crowd below. A trail of corpses and spattered red was left in its wake as the sharp object pinwheeled from one end of Times Square to the other.

Two gunshots rang from the cockpit. "For my daughter, mother fucker!" Cauldwell roared. Bishop's lifeless body fell from the open doorway with the top half of his head missing.

"No!" Xavier shrieked. From inside the demobilized death trap, the remaining men base jumped from various openings, towards the crowd, as the chopper slowly veered closer to its dropping point. Despite the fiery carnage, Julian and Xavier still held on to the skids with nothing beneath them but a long drop. As Julian looked down, the tail edge of Cauldwell's big brown overcoat, flapping from beneath the white orb of a parachute, caught his attention. He followed him with his eyes until the militant landed and disappeared into the cache of frozen onlookers.

"We have to jump!" Xavier shouted as the flames overtook the rooftop and quickly approached them.

"Again?!" Julian shrieked. "But what if it kills us?"

"Come on," Xavier said, ignoring Julian's concern. "I got—" A gunshot from above connected with Xavier's hand. He lost his grip on the skid and fell.

"Xavier!" Julian screamed. He looked up at the shooter's face. It was Rick Smith, the man in camouflage from the club. From inside the chopper, he aimed a revolver directly at Julian's head. An impulse took charge and he lunged upward, tackling Smith against the helicopter's sloping floor as the aircraft finally slid the rest the way off the edge of the roof. Both struggled to hold on as the chopper plummeted towards the oncoming street, but Julian violently stomped Smith in the teeth and watched him fall straight back, out the door, to the street below. Smith landed and his blood splashed. Seconds later, the helicopter, with Julian still inside, crashed atop the dead soldier and exploded.

The mangled heap lay atop the only visible exit, trapping Julian in the smoke and fire. As the flames closed in, he felt the intensity, but not the heat. He quickly removed his tuxedo jacket and wrapped it around his hand, relying on old instincts to move and search for another way out. Within seconds, the white jacket was in flames. When Julian dropped it, he noticed the fire had never burned him. *What the hell?*

He desperately turned side to side, unable to see where to go as the flames won, engulfing his entire body. "Fuck! I am on fire!" he shouted as a natural reaction before noticing there was no pain, only energy. The foul stench of his clothes, shoes, and hair burning filled his nostrils as he finally charged through the flames and eventually found his way to the cockpit. There, he discovered the shattered windshield and managed to crawl through it, out to the street.

Before Julian could stand, four of Cauldwell's men emerged from a newly surrounding crowd, with the barrels of M-16s pointed directly at him. One of the men shouted, "Game over, demon!" and Julian braced himself. But instead of the blast he anticipated, in an instant, all four men sustained invisible slashes to their throats before dropping dead, blood spraying from their wounds. As Julian looked on, a bald man wielding a blood-soaked knife appeared overtop them. He licked the blade, laughing at his handy work while the surrounding witnesses screamed and tried to run, but the crowd was too thick to move.

"Bernard?!" Julian gasped while jumping to his feet.

"Where's Xavier?" he asked.

"Freeze!" A police officer screamed, rushing forward with two others following behind. He aimed his handgun, shouting, "Get down on your knees!" The hand holding the gun was instantly severed and the officer cried out in pain as blood shot everywhere. From behind, he and the other two cops were all quickly impaled by a long, thin blade. They fell dead while the trapped crowd could only react accordingly.

Anna emerged, wielding a long knife of her own. "Come on! We gotta get outta here!" she squawked. It was then Julian took a breath and noticed the horrified look on Bernard's face as he stared back at him. Julian's clothes and hair had all burnt away in the fire, but his naked skin, silver ankh, and gold wedding band were unscathed. Growing impatient, Anna took his and Bernard's hands, repeating, "Come on!"

They made their way through the crowd of screaming and petrified spectators as Julian observed the path of dismembered bodies and blood scattered as far as he could see. Then he caught a glimpse of the fire overhead, which had engulfed nearly the entire building closest the destroyed helicopter and was spreading to others. Most of the onlookers had thinned the street, either escaping the area or backing away as far as they could. Even the remaining police were afraid to approach. "Xavier! ... Where are you?!" Anna shouted as she, Julian, and Bernard searched.

"I'm here!" Xavier faintly called with all his strength. Nearby, Bernard spotted him, broken down on the sidewalk, propped against the building on fire from above. Anna followed her husband to Xavier's side. Waiting for them to return, Julian only looked on until a blunt force from behind knocked him to the ground.

He rolled over and stared down the barrel of a sawed-off shotgun. Julian clenched his teeth and snarled, but before Kevin could pull the trigger, an unknown animal instinct took over. Like the speed of light, Julian surged forward at Kevin without touching the ground. He gripped the other Cauldwell in his clutches, and seconds later they landed atop a parked yellow taxicab, hundreds of feet away.

… *What the fuck?!* Julian was unsure what had just happened. He stood on the cab's hood, and once he recovered himself, smirked down at Kevin. The man's crimson head was lodged through the broken windshield, and every little movement he made sliced at his own throat. Instantly overcome by fury, Julian burned red with vengeance. He gripped Daryl's killer by his blood-soaked black jacket and violently pulled him forward. As more glass ripped away at Kevin's throat even further with the action, Julian balled his fist and lost control. Releasing a lifetime of rage, he swung repeatedly, snarling like a rabid animal. With each violent blow, he saw another tormenter's battered face laughing back: his father, grandfather, Bill, Travis, Christopher Cauldwell, and everyone else who took something from him. For so long he waited to unleash the wrath Xavier warned him about. In the moment, he could rip the universe in half just to spit in God's face and say, "Here I am. Do something about it!" The ruthless assault lasted until Julian finally caught his breath and regained his senses. First, he saw the blood on his hands, then, the raw lump of meat and bone fragments that were once a man's head. As more blood poured from the deceased's openings, Julian licked his lips like a starving dog. His belly growled, and he asked himself, *dare I?*

"Julian!" From afar, Anna screamed his name and drew his attention away. Unsure how he'd flown the first time, he tried again but fell to the ground. He got back to his feet and ran naked down the street towards the flames, passing several people watching him and keeping their distance.

"Anna!" Julian shouted, looking in all directions. "Where are you?!" As he grew closer, the vile smelling black smoke became thicker, and he barely saw anything. "Anna?! … Bernard?!" He called their names but heard nothing aside from occasional screams from the people trying to escape the area, and the spreading fires above. "Xavier?!" The further into the smoke he went, the less he saw and the harder it became to breathe. He barely even heard anything until a stomping set of footsteps echoed in his direction against the sidewalk.

An angry voice growled, "Julian! … Where is he?! Where the fuck is my brother?!" Not far ahead, Julian made out a faint dark figure standing alone. "What did you do with him?!" Cauldwell's voice showed desperation.

"A brother for a brother, bitch!" Julian shouted back. He could not help but laugh as the ironic words prompted a furious howl from the militant. Unsure if Cauldwell could see him, Julian cautiously advanced, his eyes locked on the silhouette.

"Julian," Bernard whispered, approaching his side. "Come on, I don't think he can see us."

Julian followed Bernard through the darkness as Cauldwell roared, "Where the fuck are you?! Fight me, you coward!"

"He killed my wife. Let's finish him," Julian muttered.

"No," Xavier said at a normal volume as he and Anna joined their side.

"There you are!" Cauldwell snapped. His rushing footsteps were loud as he came charging.

"He killed my daughter," Xavier protested. He lightly pushed the others aside and headed in Cauldwell's direction. "And now I am going to kill—" The tall, burning building overhead, where the helicopter had first crashed, finally gave way, collapsing and falling straight towards everyone. Before Julian could react, Anna took him in her clutches and swooped away into the clear as the building hit the ground.

Dust and more smoke further polluted the air, and all Julian could hear was near and distant screams. "Xavier!" he shrieked, looking in all directions, but he only saw burning rubble while he hovered in midair with the others.

"We have to get out of here!" Bernard insisted.

"Wait! What about Xavier?!" Julian asked.

"He's dead!" Anna cried. "And if we don't go now, we will be too." Julian had no choice but to comply. Naked, hairless, and smeared in dried blood and ash, he clung tightly to Anna's back. As they began their flight south, Julian looked over his shoulder, watching the once happy occasion light the sky in hellscape orange before distantly fading to desolate black.

Chapter Forty

B
y the time the three vampires landed in Virginia, Julian's hair had all grown back the way it was before. Despite the icy weather and snow, his nude body was neither cold nor warm but numb and callous. After touching down at the end of his long driveway, he and the others rushed towards the streetlight where his world had ended. "What the fuck are we going to do now?!" Bernard asked as they drew closer. Julian ignored the question, fixating on the red snow and stacked bodies ahead.

He tried to avoid looking but could not. The sight of Violet's headless corpse, draped atop Daryl, was a horrific punch to the gut. Anna carefully moved Violet's body away. "My God!" she shrieked. All three of them were floored by what they saw: Daryl's chest slowly rising and falling with his breaths.

"Daryl?!" Julian rushed to his side. "He—he's alive?! … How?!' He observed Daryl's bloody, torn shirt without a wound beneath it. "But they shot him! I … I don't understand."

"But he's healed now," Anna said. "He—he's …"

"He's what?"

"A vampire," she said. "It's … it's unheard of, though!"

"What do you mean?"

"Violet's blood must have seeped into his wound. It healed and turned him! I've never heard of that before."

Bernard turned towards Julian, saying, "And I've never heard of a fireproof vampire before."

"We need to get your friend inside, and Violet needs a proper burial," Anna said. "Bern, could you find a shovel and dig a hole for her?"

"I think there's one in the garage," Julian sadly mumbled.

Bernard nodded. "I will go look for it."

As he headed towards the garage, Anna picked Daryl up and said, "Come with me, Julian. I need you to show me where I can put him, and you need to put some clothes on."

Julian led the way, inside the house and through the living room, ignoring the television nobody turned off, showing live coverage of the apocalyptic aftermath they'd left behind. Once they reached the basement, he showed Anna to his and Violet's bedroom. She gently placed Daryl on the bed, and Julian got dressed. With so many thoughts running amuck at once, he asked, "Will Daryl survive this?"

"He'll be fine," she said. "He just needs to rest and heal, but your friend will never be the same again. He must live as one of us if he is to survive."

"What are we going to do?"

"I don't know," she said. "Nothing will ever be the same again. For the time being, we should be okay here while Daryl heals, but eventually someone'll figure out who we are. We cannot stay here long."

"What did Bernard mean when he said he's never heard of a fireproof vampire before?" Julian asked. "Is that not common for vampires?"

"No, it's not. I don't even think any of the Ahrims have that gift."

Julian paused, finding difficulty in thinking about it. "When Violet's head was getting cut off, a lot of her blood poured into my mouth, and I swallowed it. Could that be why?"

"I don't know. Violet wasn't fireproof, but as far as I know, she never shared her blood with anyone until tonight, which means her blood was quite powerful. Perhaps that's why you survived the fire and that long fall."

"Speaking of the fall, why was Bishop there? How did he know?" Julian gasped, remembering he saw it happen in his *Ayahuasca* vision the year before.

"Wait! Bishop was there?!" she asked incredulously, and Julian nodded. "I didn't even see him. What happened?"

"After we fell, he saved us and took us back up to the helicopter, but Cauldwell shot him."

Anna sighed, saying, "For as long as I've known him, Bishop always celebrated New Year's Eve in Times Square. I honestly never thought he'd show his face in New York again after what happened, but I guess some habits never die."

After watching Daryl breathe and lightly hum in his unconscious state, Julian looked over his shoulder at Violet's empty, white netted hammock. "I can't believe she's gone," he cried. "We were supposed to spend eternity together."

"Since you drank her blood, Hell Belle'll always be with you now, in life and death." Anna took Julian's hand as tears continued falling from his eyes. She said, "I am so sorry." They shared a moment of silence before he wiped his face. "Come on. Let's go outside and tell her goodbye."

With his head hung, Julian followed Anna back outside and behind the house where Bernard was finishing the grave he'd dug into the frozen ground. After he finished, Bernard leaped from the hole and stuck the shovel into the nearby pile of dirt. Julian followed him to collect Violet's body. Close by, he spotted her veil lying on the ground. He picked it up and returned to the grave. Anna assisted her husband with gently placing Violet's precious corpse inside, along with her severed head.

Julian wiped away the tears as he stepped up to the hole. He cleared his throat and softly spoke. "I ... I don't know what to say, my love. This was supposed to be our wedding night, not your funeral. We were going to be together forever, across all time and space." He took a breath and snorted. "I love you, Violet, and I want you to know you did not die in vain. We got them. We got them all!" Julian tried to force a smile, but he only wept harder. "And look what you did. ... You brought Daryl back and made him a vampire. Now, you live vicariously through us both, you and your father."

Julian paused for a moment, remembering the last time he'd seen them both, Violet's final tear, and Xavier walking away from him. He cleared his throat and forced himself back to the present. "I love you, my flower. Thank you for the best year of my life." Julian held her crystalline veil to his nose, inhaling her sweet vanilla scent before he let it go and watched it fall atop her body.

He blew her a final kiss and said, "May we meet again in dreams and the eternal afterlife." As he stepped away, the build-up of tears became unbearable. Anna came to his side and wrapped her arms around him. He laid his head on her shoulder and loudly sobbed.

"It's okay, love. We understand," Anna muttered, holding him tight and patting his back while slowly rocking him side to side.

"Let it out. It's okay to cry." Julian's shoulders rose and fell as he wept, enduring a calamitous sorrow he never experienced. His entire world crashed and burned while the only people who could possibly understand were strangers for the most part. Soon enough, Anna's tender care temporarily eased his external grief. He pulled away and cleared his throat again while wiping his eyes.

After everyone said their goodbyes, Bernard took the shovel from the pile of dirt and began filling the hole. As he did, Julian and Anna headed back inside. "It'll be dawn in a few hours," Julian said.

"You're right," Anna replied. "I'll clean up outside and move Daryl's truck out of view, in case someone comes looking for it." They entered the kitchen, and she said, "After all that shit, I know you are weak, and you need to feed, then sleep. I saw a few other bedrooms downstairs, so once Bern and I are finished up here, we'll come down."

Julian mumbled, "Thank you," as he took a bag of blood from the freezer. Along his way towards the basement, he noticed the television, still showing a live feed from the wild blaze in New York. When he turned away and opened the basement door, the cruel reality of what lay ahead overcame his fragile psyche. Despite the mood, he broke into a burst of mad, ironic laughter, thinking about the old saying "Be careful what you wish for."

Julian's inappropriate laughter continued as he headed down the steps. "Joke's on me!" he howled. Once he took a moment to settle down and collect himself, he entered the bedroom, watching Daryl sleep on what was supposed to be his and Violet's marital bed.

He took to Violet's hammock next to the bed. The hammock smelled like her, filling his head with pleasant memories of a happier time. As he drank from the IV bag, Julian smiled, remembering when they had first locked eyes at the little diner in Las Vegas. Every smile, giggle, and flick of her tongue crossed his mind. When he finished the blood, he threw away the bag before turning off the light.

In wake of the forlorn tragedy burrowing its gritty hooks deep into his brain, Julian's depleted body could no longer stand to be awake. After one final thought of his butchered bride and her enchanting brown almonds, the forsaken widower gave in. With nothing left to gain or lose, he drew a breath and shut his eyes, listening to the television upstairs and accepting the unforgiving night and the reality of things to come.

"… the President has just declared a 'State of Emergency' after boarding Airforce One, heading back to Washington after cutting his visit to Geneva short. He has ordered both the nation's borders closed until further notice, as well as all U.S. interstate highways. All commercial and private aircraft have also been canceled or grounded."

"Again, the current number of deaths and injuries are unclear, but believed to be in the hundreds. Firefighters are working relentlessly to put out the blaze as search and rescue teams are looking for and assisting survivors who were inside or below the collapsed building."

"As investigators continue searching for answers as to what caused this tragedy, our video footage is unclear. Sources say two men were thrown from a Black Hawk helicopter onto the crowd in Times Square, just as the ball was being dropped at midnight. Then, the helicopter reportedly spun out of control and collided with the rooftop of the residential building that collapsed soon after. Once the helicopter crashed, the propeller detached and fell onto the crowd below. Next, the helicopter fell from the building onto the crowd and burst into flames."

"One survivor on the scene reported, and I cannot believe I am saying this, 'The two men who were thrown out flew back up to the helicopter with a third man, as if they had super powers. That is when it crashed.' … Obviously, that is unheard of, but after the men initially fell, all live coverage was taken off the air. All we know at this time is the incident is being referred to as an 'act of God.' Several cell phone videos capturing the incident have hit the internet over the past hour, but they are being removed immediately."

"As we reach the bottom of the hour, we will continue with round-the-clock coverage. Coming up next, Ray Spencer will be reporting until noon. My shift is over, and I am going to go home and tell my family I love them. On behalf of everyone here at JVFE Worldwide News, I am Duncan Beaumont, saying good morning, good luck, and may Jesus Christ have mercy on our souls as we begin two-thousand-twenty."

About The Author

Darren Frey is an American dark fantasy / horror writer, adventurer, and seeker of knowledge. As a survivor and legally blind man, he has faced and overcome several obstacles and learned many valuable life lessons that he incorporates into his writing. It is his philosophy; difficult experiences teach us how to be better people and connect with others in ways that are relatable and easy to understand. It is his hope that through his words, others can find their way out of the darkness, embrace love and light, and create something positive with it.

If you enjoyed *Psychonautic*, and you would like to know where the story of Julian Frost goes from here, check out *In Dreams*, now available on Amazon Kindle and Paperback!

For more information on Darren Frey, look for him online!

Facebook: @darrenfreyauthor
Instagram: @darrenfreyauthor
YouTube: @darrenfreyauthor

Printed in Great Britain
by Amazon